A HARD TRUTH

A Gin Reilly FBI Thriller Book 1

C.R. Chandler

Thank you for buying A Hard Truth! There is no greater compliment to an author than knowing someone is reading your book.
∼ CR Chandler

If you'd like notifications for new releases, and a free e-book, you can subscribe to the author's newsletter here:
SUBSCRIBE TO NEWSLETTER HERE

Other ways to contact the author:
Author Contact Form
Facebook:
CR Chandler Facebook Page

17 Years Earlier

Why didn't they come? She stood inches inside the huge door, pressed against the splintering wood of the framed opening. Her green-eyed gaze darted past the deserted space between the barn and the old farmhouse thirty yards away, to stare down the rutted dirt lane leading to the paved county road. But the lane was empty, just like the road beyond it, and she couldn't hear any sirens. Not even one. If they were coming, she was sure she'd hear sirens.

It had been four days since her visit to the police station. She'd ditched school, pleading bad menstrual cramps because no one ever questioned those, and walked the four blocks to the run-down house with a detached garage. Old Mr. Crawley had lived there for as long as she could remember.

She'd carefully picked that day because the elderly man's sister always took him into Des Moines for his weekly visit to the VA hospital there. Even though she was barely a week past her fourteenth birthday, she knew how to drive. Thanks to all the chores needing to be done on the farm.

C.R. Chandler

The twenty-minute trip to the city of Nevada, where the Story County Sheriff's office was located, had gone off without a hitch. She'd dressed in faded jeans and a plain, dark colored shirt that wouldn't draw any notice, then had pulled her long, wavy mass of copper colored hair into a low ponytail, secured by a brown rubber band at the nape of her neck. And she'd made sure that no one had seen her leave the package on the front desk.

She'd simply waited until the desk sergeant had gotten up from his seat, carrying a thick coffee mug as he headed for the heavily stained pot sitting on a table against the back wall. She'd been careful to leave the large manila envelope in plain sight before sidling back out the front door of the station. The envelope had "To Captain Frank Wilkins" printed in block letters on the front. She'd found out his name by calling the station and asking to speak to the person in charge of the detectives, and he had answered the phone. She hadn't actually said anything to him. All she'd wanted was his name.

The sound of a distant engine drew her attention. Her nerves jumped as she strained her neck, trying to see down the road. Her hopes picked up as the engine's rumble grew louder, but it was only a beat-up pickup truck. Her top teeth bit into her lower lip as she watched the white truck with the extended cab flash by on the road before slumping against the door frame and letting her chin drop to her chest.

She couldn't hide in the barn pretending to do chores forever. Dinner would be ready soon, and she'd have to sit at the table with her parents pretending everything was normal, all the while acutely aware of her father's constant stare and the empty seat across from her. It was usually occupied by her older brother, Devin. But he was away at a football camp and wouldn't be home for another week. She'd planned it that way,

A HARD TRUTH

thinking it would be all over and done before the camp was finished.

Of course she had never been sure what would happen after that. Didn't know what her mom would do. The only certain thing in her life at that moment was that she could never live in the same house as her father again. And if things didn't go the way she'd planned — and right now it wasn't looking too good — then she'd take the cash she'd squirreled away, along with the family car, and drive until both the money and the gas ran out. Then she'd walk off and keep walking for as long as it took to completely disappear.

The last thing she wanted was for *him* to catch up with her. If he did, she'd end up in an unmarked grave where no one would ever find her. Just like all the others had. And something that belonged to her would take its place on that shelf in his secret room, along with all the other odd bits and pieces of other lives he stole. Except for the three she had put into that envelope as proof of what she'd said in the letter to Captain Wilkins.

"Dinner's ready," her mother's voice called from the back door of the house. "Your father is ready for us to sit down at the table. Come inside and eat. You can finish those chores later."

She wet her lips and sucked in a deep breath. "Okay. I'll be there in a minute," she yelled back even as she closed her eyes, fighting the tears.

She couldn't last another night pretending everything was fine. He was going to take one look at her face and know what she'd done. He'd just know. If she got through the meal, she'd plead exhaustion and go right to bed. Then tonight, she'd steal the car keys off the hook, sneak out, and be gone before anyone could stop her. There wasn't any other choice. She had to go now.

With her mind made up, she pushed away from the door

and started across the tired-looking yard of tightly packed dirt with a few lone weeds poking through the hard crust. She'd covered half the distance when she spotted a dozen cars driving almost bumper to bumper down the highway. Some were dark sedans, but most were white cars with the gold lettering of the county sheriff's department. She froze in her tracks when the lead car turned into their small lane and raced toward her with lights flashing, but no sirens.

As the first car skidded to a halt in a cloud of dust, her father stepped out of the house. A tall, burly man with bushy eyebrows and an unruly mop of hair, exited the lead car and stalked across the yard. His hard gaze lasered in on the man who was watching him with narrowed eyes.

"Byron Reilly?" The tall man flashed a badge right in front of her father's face. "I'm Captain Wilkins, with the homicide investigation unit of the Story County Sheriff's Department. We have a warrant to search your house and premises, and to take you in for questioning regarding multiple homicides."

Her father remained silent, not making a sound or moving a muscle as several officers streamed past him and the captain. Somewhere in the background she heard her mother's shrill protest mingled with the growing hum of conversation between the groups of deputies.

Even with all the noise and movement of bodies and activity flowing around her, she remained rooted to one spot, her eyes on her father. When he suddenly twisted his head around and looked straight at her, she felt all the color drain out of her face, making the freckles stand out in stark contrast against her pale skin. Eyes the identical shade of green met hers, and in that moment she saw understanding flash across his sharp features before his gaze turned to granite in an unblinking stare. Like a giant snake marking its prey.

A HARD TRUTH

Sheer panic exploded in her stomach and raced up her spine. Captain Wilkins followed Byron's gaze, and spotting her, his shaggy brows first lifted in surprise before he deliberately stepped between them. With the contact broken, she shook her head once to clear it, then swiveled on her heels and ran deep into the barn, not stopping until she reached the back wall. As far away from her father as she could get. Leaning over, she braced her arms against her knees and dropped her head down as she sucked in a lungful of life-giving air, then made gagging sounds as her stomach churned, threatening to empty itself right at her feet.

"They came, they came," she whispered over and over, wrapping the words around herself like a protective cloak despite her heaving stomach. Several long minutes passed before she could safely straighten up again. She was barely aware of her mother's screams, or doors opening and banging shut. Then everything seemed to calm down until there was a shout and the chaos of lights and sound started up again. She huddled against the rough wood of the wall, her eyes glued to the opening into the barn, half expecting her father to stride through it and come right at her.

When a large figure appeared in the doorway, she cringed, trying to make herself smaller. But the voice that called out wasn't her father's.

"Gillian?" He didn't shout, but simply said her name in a quiet, almost conversational tone as he took one step into the barn and stopped. "I was told that your name is Gillian. I'm Captain Frank Wilkins, and I believe you left an envelope for me at the police station?" He slowly moved forward, the narrow beam of his flashlight tracing a circle on the floor in front of her. "Byron Reilly's your father, isn't he? We found his room in the basement, right where you said it was, and he's on his way to the county jail. He won't be coming back here for a long while, and you don't have to be here either. I can take you to a place you'll feel safe."

She blinked twice then slowly pushed away from the wall. Her whole body trembled as she fought to keep her balance, and her breathing was wild and erratic, making her chest hurt, and the hands she was clasping together felt cold and clammy. But the man had said clear as day that the monster was on his way to jail. She wouldn't have to run after all. At least not tonight.

The Black Cross Killer had finally been caught.

Chapter 1
Six Weeks Earlier

Spring in Colorado was his favorite time of year. There was no doubt about that. Even with the threat of rain overhead, there was something about spring that always promised magic. Or it seemed that way to him. If you closed your eyes, you could almost smell it in the air. It was the only time he felt as if the world was in a good place.

Of course you'd have to give up reading the papers or listening to the news in order to maintain that fantasy for any longer than a minute or two. The latest headlines rarely varied much from the standard reporting of destruction and impending financial doom that was the reporter's bread and butter for selling the news. Most of which he usually had no trouble ignoring.

However the latest reports about the disappearance of one Benjamin Stampler, CEO of a large pharmaceutical company, had his own society wife and all her friends gossiping in shocked voices. Gang murders never had them lifting an eyebrow in concern, but one of the rich and powerful disappearing right off his own yacht? Now that was something that demanded their full attention. Then there was the legal paperwork that would have to be done to keep everything running while the rest of the men in power, from both the political, legal, and business arenas, decided if one of their own should be treated as dead or alive.

He shook his head while his pragmatic and more-than-slightly-cynical side quickly kicked his whimsical thoughts on the magic of spring to the curb as he considered what he would have done if one of his high-profile clients suddenly disappeared.

It would depend on who it was, he thought with a soft chuckle.

It was that same, practical side that had allowed him to thrive as one of the top personal and corporate attorneys in California, with a fair number of his clients coming from beyond the state's borders.

Unlike many of the wealthy men and women who had a prominent place in his electronic contact file, Andrew Darquin hadn't inherited his wealth but had worked hard for it, and he enjoyed the power and influence that came with his position as head of his own law firm. He had several other partners in the firm, of course, but the practice was his, and no one at Darquin, Connors & Smith would dispute that.

Still, even high-powered lawyers needed some decompression time, and whenever he found himself on one of his regular business trips to Colorado, he always took one evening and went to the same place.

Stanley Marketplace was an eclectic collection of shops, restaurants, and bars housed in the old, cavernous building that had once been home to Stanley Aviation. A pleasant ten-mile drive from his plush hotel room in downtown Denver, the marketplace had kept the building's original industrial look, which was a far cry from his office in a high-rise near the

A HARD TRUTH

famous Fisherman's Wharf in San Francisco. And certainly bore no resemblance to his pricey home in the wealthy subdivision of Pacific Heights near the bay. Not that he'd grown up in any neighborhood like the one where he was raising his own family.

He came to Stanley Marketplace because it reminded him of a simpler time in his life, when his folks had owned a small house near the old airport and his dad had gone to work every day at Stanley Aviation. In the very same building that now housed the marketplace.

He pulled his rented Mercedes sedan into an empty parking space in the big lot surrounding what was really a retail mall in a unique setting and checked his watch. His time was short. In fact, he probably should have skipped the ritual of stopping in at the marketplace on this trip. He had a meeting back at the hotel's rooftop bar in two hours with one of those high-maintenance clients, and he'd wanted some quiet time before what was undoubtedly going to be a one-sided rant.

So he'd made the thirty-minute drive to the marketplace and had set an alarm on his watch to give him enough time to drive back. Picking up his briefcase, since he never left important papers in his hotel room or car, he exited the vehicle and strolled across the parking lot, ignoring the unusual bite of cold in the crisp night air.

He hated late-night meetings. Although he'd attended hundreds of them over his thirty-year career, he still felt that twinge of resentment whenever one of his clients demanded one. Most of their bank accounts were far bigger than his, though, and it was those bank accounts that kept him, his wife, and their two college-age children in a comfortable lifestyle. So after hours business meetings had become a fact of life.

However, he usually avoided them on Wednesdays. It was the one night a week he took for himself and did whatever he

C.R. Chandler

was in the mood for— a drink, a quiet dinner, or even a walk in the crip night air or the fog that San Francisco was so famous for. He needed that stretch of quiet, so he guarded that bit of time like a junkyard dog down to its last bone.

Unless it was one of his handful of premier clients who called.

Fortunately, they didn't call often, leaving him free to enjoy his favorite bar in peace. Unfortunately, this wasn't one of those times. At least he'd managed to carve out enough time to be able to drive out to his childhood neighborhood and enjoy one drink.

With a sigh, his sharp blue gaze did a quick scan of the room, settling on the bouncy server with a long ponytail hanging halfway down her back. Catching her eye, he raised one hand, keeping it flat as he tapped a finger of his opposite hand into the center of its palm in the age-old gesture to call for his check. She beamed back a smile and bobbed her head up and down. Satisfied, he reached for his glass and drained the last of its beer before reaching into the inner pocket of his suit jacket to draw out a slim billfold.

The blonde waitress appeared on the other side of the compact round table and laid a small tray with his check down on its rough wooden surface. "Just the one beer tonight, Mr. Darquin? It seems a shame to drive all the way out here from downtown for just one beer."

"I'm afraid so." He laid a twenty-dollar bill on top of his check, then stood and gathered up his raincoat, returning her smile while he shrugged into it. She reminded him of his daughter who had the same expressive eyes and cheeky grin. "I'll have to take a rain check on my usual burger until I get back here next month."

"Then it's a good thing you brought your raincoat, because rain is exactly what's going on outside. Everyone is coming in

A HARD TRUTH

soaked. I guess it's pouring down really hard." She scooped up the money along with a questioning look.

He chuckled and shook his head. "No change."

Her mouth widened until it stretched from ear to ear. "Thanks." Adding a wink, she reached over and plucked a brown leather briefcase from the empty chair next to him. "You're my best tipper and I so appreciate that." She held the briefcase out in front of her. "Don't forget this."

There was no chance in hell that would ever happen, but he just nodded his thanks as he took it in a firm grip. "I'll see you next time." Switching the briefcase to his other hand, he headed for the nearest exit. He held the door open for a young woman, automatically returning her smile before he flipped up the collar of his coat and stepped out into the rain.

He didn't notice the two figures who slipped out from the shadow of the building. Both wore long black overcoats with the hood pulled over their heads. Halfway across the parking lot, the larger of the two moved out in front and quickened his pace while the smaller one shed the overcoat and pulled the hood of the sweatshirt underneath down and over a face that was already half-covered with a red bandanna.

A small noise behind him had the attorney glancing over his shoulder. His mouth immediately pulled down into a frown as he turned to face the man, who was rapidly closing the distance between them.

"What are *you* doing here?" he demanded. His gaze was fixed on the man's face, not his hands, and too late he saw the flash of a knife, arcing upward as it sliced through the jacket of his three-thousand-dollar suit and easily slid into his midsection. His gaze dropped down, an astonished look in his eyes, before the knife was given a vicious twist then ripped back out of him. Without a sound, Andrew Darquin slid to the ground, his eyes already fixed and unseeing when the knife was swiped across his throat.

His attacker silently lifted the briefcase from where it had fallen onto the ground and turned to hand it to the figure standing behind him.

"Hurry up," his companion hissed into his ear in a high, feminine voice. She reached into the front pocket of her sweatshirt and pulled out a thick, round object. Water dripped off its smooth surface as she held it out. "Put this into his pocket before you take his watch and his wallet, and then we have to get him into the trunk of his car. It's parked in the next aisle."

The big man tossed a set of keys into the air, forcing his accomplice to make a wild lunge for them. "I'm not carrying this much dead weight that far. You go get the rental and bring it here. Once he's in the trunk, you can take off. I'll see to the rest of it."

"Gladly," the woman muttered before disappearing into the dark night.

Chapter 2
Present Day

"Just have it all hauled off."

Gin rolled her eyes. Even through her phone's speaker she could hear the thick layer of impatience coating Devin's voice. Her older brother had been very outspoken about not wanting to have anything to do with their grandparents' house. She didn't either, but someone had to deal with all the large decisions and mountains of details that were part of a death.

Her mouth pulled into a reluctant smile despite the grim circumstances that had her standing on the very old-fashioned front porch, absently staring at a worn set of matching rocking chairs as she listened to her only sibling continue his list of complaints. She'd bet a month of her FBI pay she knew what Devin was going to say next.

"Look. You've hired an estate agent."

"We," Gin mildly corrected. "The estate, such as it is, will be split fifty-fifty, with you being the other half of that equation. So 'we' have hired an estate agent. I just happen to be the one standing here taking care of the pesky details."

"Fine," her brother groused. "Tell that person *we* hired to go through the place and do a D or D, and that we don't care which. If she wants, I can text that to her, so she has it in writing."

His sister's grin widened. And there it was. Just as she'd predicted. D or D was her brother's shorthand for "donate or dump" everything. It was the same tune he'd been playing since the minute they'd been informed of the single-vehicle accident that had killed both their grandparents.

According to the officer who had drawn the short straw in notifying the next of kin, their grandfather had misjudged a turn in the dark and run the car into a ditch, pitching both himself and his wife of sixty years headfirst into the windshield. Apparently neither John nor Meredith Dillon had bothered with seat belts, any more than they'd troubled themselves to contact either of their grandchildren in the last seventeen years.

"It's literally been decades since we've heard from them," Devin went on. "Not even a postcard when Mom died. Hell, it took them a month before they had a lawyer contact us about her death, since it was obviously too much for either of them to pick up a phone. At least that's what the pissant attorney said." The sarcasm in his voice was followed by a loud snort of impatience. "So why should we give a flying shit about any of their stuff?"

A flush of guilt crept up Gin's cheeks. Devin was right. There hadn't been a postcard. But unknown to her big brother, there had been a letter. It had arrived at her tiny apartment the day after the attorney had called. There was no return address, but she'd recognized the handwriting from the birthday cards her grandmother used to send. That was before her son-in-law had gone to prison and her only daughter had melted into a complete breakdown.

At the time, Gin had actually welcomed the sight of that

A HARD TRUTH

letter. She'd sat on the small couch, the single piece of furniture in her living room, and had eagerly opened what she'd assumed would be a note expressing sympathy over their shared loss. Maybe even a request that they get together again. But the single handwritten sheet hadn't contained even one word of comfort, much less a request to see her only granddaughter.

Gin could still feel the venom behind her grandmother's nasty tirade, accusing her of being the real reason for her mother choosing to end her own life.

Meredith Dillon claimed her only child had told her all about Gin walking away from her father and offering no support to her mother during what her grandmother had called "their difficulties." That Gin's cold behavior is what had driven Kathleen to take her own life, leaving nothing for her grieving parents but a few carboard boxes packed with her personal things. The letter had closed with Meredith wishing her granddaughter a very time on this earth, and every minute of it filled with the grief and misery that was deserved by a spawn of the devil.

It still made Gin's stomach tighten into a knot whenever she thought about that letter. Without a second of hesitation, she'd walked into her kitchen and rummaged through her cabinet, pulling out a stainless- steel bowl. Dropping the letter into it, she'd lifted the box of matches she kept by the stove, lit one, and calmly tossed it into the bowl. She'd watched the letter go up in flames, and when it was nothing but ashes, had carried the bowl to the sink, ran cold water over the blackened contents, and tossed the whole mess down the drain, turning on the garbage disposal for good measure.

And had never breathed a word about it to anyone, much less to Devin. Mostly because she hadn't wanted to give the old witch even a sliver of influence in her life. But also because Devin would ask why their grandmother would say such a thing to her and not a word to him. She'd never been able to manufacture and explanation for that question, so avoiding it all together seemed like the best thing to do. Besides, she'd never had been any good at lying to him.

He'd always been able to see right through her, and the last thing she'd wanted to do was tell him the truth. He would have gone ballistic, and then she'd have spent the rest of her life listening to him demand to know why she hadn't come to her big brother about their father, instead of going it alone. Probably a valid complaint if she was being honest, but a moot one at this point.

Their father had been securely locked away in the supermax prison in Colorado for the last fourteen years. That was after the three years it had taken to get through the trials so that his cell door could be permanently slammed shut. But it was done, and now there was zero chance he would ever be getting out of there.

The rest of the disaster he'd made of their lives had taken care of itself once the world moved on from the sensational headlines he'd commanded. The Black Cross Killer was no longer part of the news and might as well be dead. Now their mother and grandparents were gone, too. She had destroyed that damning letter, and as soon as she took care of things here, the last of any connection between her and Devin to the horrors of their family's past would be sold or discarded.

And good riddance to all of it.

Determined to see the task through and put a final period on that entire chapter in her life, she took an envelope out of her pocket. Removing the single key inside, she walked to the front door and inserted it into the lock. A hard push got the slightly warped door open, allowing her to step inside that house for the first time since she was ten years old.

Taking a deep breath, she put her back to the room and

carefully closed the door behind her before slowly turning around. The front entrance opened directly into the living room, with a redbrick fireplace dominating one wall, and a small two-cushioned couch pushed up against another. An old recliner and several overstuffed chairs were placed in a circle, all facing a narrow wooden table with a flat-screen TV on top.

There were several paintings adorning the walls, mostly of Niagara Falls, which dominated the landscape about an hour and a half west of the small town where her grandparents had lived all their lives. Over the fireplace was a large, ornately framed photograph of a younger version of her mom. Kathleen Dillon, cursed to become Kathleen Reilly, wore a graduation cap and gown in sea-blue, along with a forced smile on her face.

Gin walked over, stopping in front of the fireplace, her hands on her hips as she carefully studied the picture. Somehow she'd forgotten just how much Devin looked like their mother. The same golden blond hair and vivid blue eyes, along with even features and a generous mouth. Except when Devin smiled, he exuded warmth and friendliness. Her mother's smile had always been a different story.

The only times Gin could remember her mother genuinely happy was in the presence of the husband she'd worshiped. The man who killed total strangers simply because he enjoyed the slaughter and had gotten away with it for twenty-five years before he'd been caught. Kathleen had devoted every waking moment to Byron Reilly — abandoning her children to attend his succession of trials, and then holding a constant vigil for five years outside the prison where he had finally been incarcerated for good.

It had taken that five years for her to accept she would never see her husband again, which had driven her to make that last trek from Colorado back to her hometown in Henrietta, New York. She hadn't bothered to collect her children on the way but had driven her old Ford straight home, only to hang herself in her parent's basement.

Gin hadn't shed a tear over the news about her mother, or ever felt even a twinge of guilt about her father rotting away in prison. The Black Cross Killer spending twenty hours a day in solitary confinement seemed fair enough to her. As for the rest of it? She lifted her shoulders into a quick shrug.

"It is what it is," she said in a soft voice.

Deliberately turning her back on her mother's picture, Gin crossed her arms over her chest. Devin hadn't understood why she wanted to do a walkthrough of the house. He thought it was a waste of her time. And she sure as hell wouldn't be here if it wasn't for that damn letter from long ago.

Her grandmother had mentioned the boxes of her daughter's personal things. She was betting that nothing belonging to her daughter would have ever been discarded, and that Kathleen would never have tossed away even a scrap of paper from her husband. If there was a stack of personal letters from the Black Cross Killer to his wife, Gin wanted to make sure there weren't any new admissions or victims' names in them. Then she was going to personally burn them and anything else that had once belonged to Byron Reilly. She could only imagine the price they would bring at an auction, not to mention the uproar they'd cause in the press. Which was exactly the last thing she needed.

Locate, go through them, and then destroy. That was her assignment here. Focused on that, Gin arrowed her green eyes as she considered the options. If there were any such boxes, as her grandmother had claimed there were, they'd either be in the bedroom her mother had occupied or stored in the basement. They might be in the personal space of her mother's bedroom, but none of the rooms on the top floor were very big, so she was betting they'd been tucked away in the basement

A HARD TRUTH

when Kathleen first arrived back at her parents' house. Which meant they were likely still down there.

She gave a speculative look toward the opening leading into the small dining room and the kitchen just beyond it. The stairs leading down into the basement were off the kitchen.

It only took her a moment to reach the swinging door that separated the kitchen from the dining room. Gently pushing against it, she hesitated in the narrow opening, a guarded look on her face as she glanced around the room.

A mint-green stove dominated one wall, with white linoleum counters stretching out on either side of it. A plain wooden table with two hard-backed chairs tucked neatly underneath it took up the opposite wall. She could almost see her younger self, sitting in one of those chairs, her legs dangling over the side and her feet swinging back and forth as she watched her grandmother move around the kitchen. Cooking, Gin remembered.

They'd only visited the house two, maybe three times with their mother while their father had stayed behind on their small farm in Iowa. But on those rare occasions, her grandmother had always been standing in that kitchen. The woman never stopped cooking or baking something. Shaking her head at the random memory, Gin crossed the old linoleum floor with its large pattern of black and white squares, straight to the wooden door at the far edge of the room.

She looked at it for a long moment, her shoulders rigid and her back stiff. Her mother had died in that basement. And although she'd come to resent Kathleen Reilly and the choices she'd made in life, she still wasn't too eager to tramp around the space where her mother had chosen to die. Drawing in a big breath, she placed her hand on the old-fashioned brass knob of the door separating the kitchen and the wooden steps leading into the dark space beneath the house.

Her mouth flattened into a thin line as the memory of sitting at the kitchen winked out, replaced in an instant by the image of a slender body hanging by the neck from one of the thick pipes crisscrossing the ceiling. She'd seen a lynched body before and knew exactly what her mother would have looked like.

Unable to control the sudden shiver that raced down her spine like a runaway freight train, Gin's breathing quickly ramped up, sounding like a piston beating in her lungs and chest. Fortunately, years of practice had taught her when panic wrapped around her like a swaddling cloth, to take a deep breath and hold it before letting it out slowly. And keep doing that, repeating it over and over until the blanket of fear dissolved away and she could think straight again.

As she held her breath and counted to ten, her lips slowly formed into a snarl. She didn't want to be in this house, or go down to the basement where she and Devin had spent hours playing whenever they'd come on one of their infrequent visits. Mostly because the adults upstairs had no interest in being with them. She didn't want to have anything to do with this place and had made that emphatically clear by never responding to her grandmother's devastating letter, or ever setting foot her house again.

But now it couldn't be helped. She had to find those boxes and make sure they held nothing the rest of the world shouldn't see. And get rid of it, if they did. Once that was accomplished, the estate agent could do Devin's D or D and mail her any other paperwork that needed to be done to sell the place and get it out of their lives once and for all.

Gritting her teeth, she took another deep breath and slowly let it out.

"Get a grip, Gin. You've done worse things," she muttered under her breath. With a firm twist of the knob, she pulled the

A HARD TRUTH

door open, only for her shoulders to stiffen again. She didn't believe in ghosts, but the truth was, she half expected something, or more to the point someone, to jump out at her.

But when no solid body or shadowy apparition appeared, she silently scolded herself for having an overactive imagination and flipped the light switch next to the door jamb. Thankfully, her grandmother never had liked dark and spooky places, so the whole area lit up like it had its own personal sun.

She tentatively set a foot on the first step, testing it with her weight. It creaked but didn't feel the least bit rickety, which had her starting down the rest of the stairs, treading as lightly as she could until she reached the bottom and stepped onto the cement floor. Aside from the old monster of a furnace in the corner, all that was left in the basement was a small mountain of boxes, liberally covered in cobwebs. and stacked neatly into the corner opposite the furnace.

Gin's eyebrows lifted in surprise as she silently measured the height of the pile. There had to be at least fourteen, maybe fifteen boxes there. Frowning, she walked over and laid a hand on the first one she came to. They couldn't all belong to her mother simply because they'd never owned that much. She didn't remember them being present when she and Devin had built their forts and haunted houses down here. But then, they'd been kids. Like kids everywhere, they'd been too busy with their own games to notice much around themselves.

Gin set the huge roll of garbage bags she'd brought with her on the ground. Once she'd filled them up, she had a felt pen tucked inside her shirt pocket to mark them for the recycle bin or the dump.

She leaned in and read the writing on every carton she could see, then deliberately pulled several boxes off the stack simply labeled "to be saved" in her mother's handwriting. She shoved them to the side before taking her cell phone and an elastic hair band from her jacket pocket. Setting the phone down on top of the closest box, she laid her jacket on the cold, unforgiving cement floor and sat on it. Using the elastic band, she gathered up her thick, wavy hair into a high ponytail, letting the light-brown mass with hints of copper running through it hang down and brush against the collar of her shirt.

Now that she was as comfortable as she was going to get, she reached for the first of Kathleen's boxes and opened it. There were stacks of notebooks with plastic covers, and each one had a label taped to the front, with a year and a span of months written on it. She remembered them. Her mom was always making notes, mostly of household stuff.

The first one she grabbed was the same year and month her father had been arrested. Taking a deep, steadying breath, she opened it up. Despite her best efforts, her eyesight blurred with a quick well of tears at the pages covered in her mother's handwriting. Telling herself she was a fool, she rubbed a hand across her eyes, blinking rapidly until the tears receded and no longer threatened to spill down her cheeks.

Focusing on the words, she wrinkled her nose. Kathleen Reilly had jotted down short sentences, and lists of expenses, and anything else that had to do with running a household. Weekly grocery receipt totals, routine purchases, and even the yield from the vegetable garden were dutifully recorded on the pages, along with the date of the entry.

Gin picked up a handful of loose pages and flipped through them, not spotting anything of interest. Grabbing a garbage bag, she dumped all the papers into it, then tossed the now-empty plastic notebooks into another bag. That one could go to the dump, and the papers to the recycle bin.

The only reason she was skimming through the papers at all was to be sure there wasn't anything tucked in there from her father. Like a list of all his victims, including the ones yet to be found. She heaved a sigh. And unless she did, by some miracle, find something from Byron Reilly among the last possessions of his wife, the total extent of the Black Cross Killer's murderous rampage would never be known.

She tackled the second box and at the bottom found what she'd been looking for. Tucked inside several shoe boxes were letters from her father to her mother. Dozens of them. She'd have to go through them, just in case he'd started documenting all his kills to her, or even mentioning just one or two. But that wasn't going to happen today.

Not by a long shot.

She'd need some mental preparations and several large glasses of wine for that task. Tucking the shoe boxes away into their separate garbage bag, she sighed at the stack of remaining boxes. They all looked to be labeled by her grandmother, but she still needed to go through them. Just in case.

Two hours later, a massive headache was brewing behind her eyes, the pain pulsing in tandem with the backache from sitting on a cement floor. She'd rummaged through most of the jumble of boxes, and there was now only one left. It was tucked in with the rest of her grandmother's boxes and was marked "old linens". She might have unceremoniously emptied it into a dumpster garbage bag except the label was in her mother's handwriting, and she had no idea why her mother would have held on to some old tablecloths or bed sheets. Pulling the box closer, she settled on her protesting backside and opened it up. Sure enough, the top layer looked like neatly folded bedsheets, and so did the layer beneath it.

Thinking her mother had probably been helping her grandmother pack stuff away, Gin was sorely tempted to simply dump the whole thing into one of the many bulging trash bags strewn across the floor. Then she'd be free to head for her car with the one garbage bag containing the letters from her father to her mother, and more importantly get to her backpack, to search for some aspirin. Instead, she sighed and rubbed two fingers against her throbbing temple as she stared down at the pastel-colored sheets. Having come this far, she might as well tough it out and finish the job.

She was halfway through the box when she pulled up a heavy folder. Three thin, braided cords held two leather covers together using three holes punched along one side. There was a good six inches of paper sandwiched between them, with the entire folder bound by a red ribbon tied around it. Lifting it with both hands, she frowned. It felt and looked very different from her mother's household accounts. Older, and more fragile, and made of a stiff leather.

She shifted it to one hand and tested the weight. It was also a lot heavier, and the leather on the outside was not only cracked and dried out, but elaborate tooling across the front. And it wasn't the only one. She could see more stacked on top of each other in the box. When she carefully lifted the two other ones out, it was clear they looked alike and appeared to be part of a matched set of three.

Frowning, she slowly set the bottom two on the floor and picked up the first leather bound portfolio. She untied the ribbon holding the edges of the volume together and ran her fingers over the raised tooling on the front.

"Legacy Book," she murmured softly. Now what the hell did that mean? She carefully opened the cover, startled when she heard an odd crackle, as if the pages might crumble all together. Frowning, she sat cross-legged and carefully set the book down in front of her. With her head cocked to one side, she stared at a blank piece of paper that was thicker than normal and the color of dark cream. Gently turning it over, her hand froze over the next sheet. It was the same type of paper in that odd color, and was yellowed with age. Instead of the abbre-

A HARD TRUTH

viated notes and lists her mother always jotted down, this page was written in a more flourishing style, with ink that bled slightly at the edges. And there were only two words. "Legacy Book," she read out loud. The same words tooled onto the leather cover. She turned the page and drew in a harsh breath. This sheet was not bound into the book with the braided cords, like most of the others were. It was thinner and a pure white. But she barely noticed that difference as she stared at the words covering the page. She knew *that* handwriting. Having seen it often enough throughout her childhood, it was easy to recognize now. And it still made her skin crawl. It belonged to her father.

There was a date in the upper left-hand corner and the page was filled with his words, but it might as well have been written in an alien language because her brain couldn't process any of them. Picking up a handful of loose sheets, she slowly turned over each page. On the third one, Byron Reilly's signature was at the bottom.

She stared at it for a long moment, her tongue wandering over her mouth to wet her suddenly dry lips. Also turning that page over, she set it on top of the other sheets, then glanced down at the new page that had been exposed. This one was bound into the journal, and looked as old and fragile as the sheet that had held the words "Legacy Book". But this one had a date in the corner. 15 June 1753. And it was in that same, flowery handwriting that had each word ending in a flourish.

She stared at the date, her mind completely blank before her gaze automatically shifted over to the first words elaborately scrawled on the page.

To kill without mercy is a glorious feeling.

Gin blinked, shook her head, and then blinked again.

Gingerly picking up the journal, she carefully went to the last page. The writing was different. Not as many flourishes as the first few pages. These last entries were definitely written in another hand. Her gaze slid to the bottom of the page where there was a signature, Francis Tomaine, followed by a date. Her eyes widened as she stared at it. 11 August 1851—almost a hundred years after the date of the first entry. What the hells was she looking at? And who was Francis Tomaine?

The jarring ring of her cell phone echoed between the cement walls of the stark and mostly empty basement. Her mind still blank, Gin automatically reached for the phone and held it to her ear. "Special Agent Gin Reilly."

"Are you still at your grandmother's place up near Rochester?" her boss's voice barked out. Todd Moore was a senior agent in the FBI and headed up the newly formed Critical Crimes Unit. Todd, Gin, and her long-time partner, Stephen, along with two other agents who hadn't been assigned to their little group yet, made up Team Two, that was based out of Denver.

The sound of her boss's voice had Gin shaking her head to clear it. "Yeah," she confirmed, her gaze still on the date that was almost one hundred and seventy-five years earlier.

"Okay. That's good. It puts you about an hour away."

Gin frowned. The clear urgency in his voice had her mind snapping back to the present. "Away from what?"

"A celebrity dead body. Remember Benjamin Stampler, whose disappearance graced all the headlines four or five weeks ago?"

Gin frowned, still struggling to concentrate so she could place the name. Luckily her brain finally kicked in. "The big-shot pharmacy CEO who went missing in Miami?"

"Yeah. Him and one of his regular crew members. Well, there's still no sign of the crew member, but Stampler's body has been found halfway between Rochester and Buffalo. I'll send you the details, but you need to get your butt on scene. Another agent will meet you there."

"Stephen is back in Denver." Stephen was not only her partner in the Critical Crimes Unit, but came with the added benefit of being part of what little extended family she had left. He was married to her cousin, Callie, who was busy moving their family to Colorado. Or maybe she was already in Colorado and trying to sell their house back in Iowa? She could never keep everyone's whereabouts straight. But she did know Stephen was currently nowhere near upstate New York.

"Yeah. He can't get there in time so I'm assigning someone else. I've sent you both a file on what we know about the case. The other agent will meet you on scene. The locals are only going to keep the body there until nightfall, so like I said. Get your butt into gear. Pronto."

When he hung up, Gin held her phone out and stared at it, then shifted her gaze to the three journals stacked on the basement floor. Weird journals from hundreds of years ago, check. Get your butt in gear, also check. And that second check paid her salary.

With a sigh, she pushed herself to her feet, then leaned down and picked up the three journals. "Butt in gear," she said out loud, heading for the stairs as the echo of her words died down.

Chapter Three

It only took an hour to reach the point where the Erie County deputies were waiting for her. A dark SUV sat on the side of the two-lane highway, along with a large, white utility vehicle sporting National Grid written on the doors in blue letters. Two patrol cars were parked at an angle, nose to nose, blocking the entrance to a dirt road. The three men who were standing in front of the cruisers turned in unison when Gin pulled her rental car onto the shoulder and came to a stop. As she exited the car, one officer detached himself from the group and walked over to check her out.

She used one hand to flip back her jacket so the badge attached to her belt was clearly visible while holding her credential case up with the other. Even though she'd taken vacation days, she'd brought her badge with her out of habit. And on the off chance something would hopefully come up to given her an excuse to abandon the project of going through her grandparents' house and put her back on the clock.

She barely resisted the urge to roll her shoulders, missing the familiar weight of her holster and service weapon. Leaving them behind had saved her the hassle of getting carry permits for the plane ride, even if she hadn't felt completely dressed without it. Now she wished she'd sucked it up and filled out all the forms.

"I guess you'd be the FBI?" the officer asked, studying her badge when he stopped in front of her.

Gin smiled. "Not all of it, just one agent." She tucked her credentials into her pocket and held out a hand. "I'm Special Agent Gin Reilly from the Critical Crimes Unit."

The officer's brows winged upward over a pair of dark brown eyes as he shook her hand. "Deputy Bob Hurley." He stroked a hand under his chin. "Critical Crimes Unit, huh? I don't think I've ever heard of that one."

"The captain mentioned it a while back." A second deputy had come up behind him and nodded at Gin. Much shorter than Hurley, he barely topped Gin's five feet, five inches and looked like he was barely out of high school. "I'm Deputy Jim Martin." He tilted his head to the side. "As I recall, the captain said the FBI's bulletin made it sound like you guys would be handling all the really nasty stuff." He didn't wait for an answer before poking a finger into Hurley's arm. "Critical Crimes caught the guy who kidnapped that family out in New Mexico and then proceeded to leave a body in four different states. Remember that one?" Before Hurley could say anything, Martin shifted his finger to point at Gin. "Did you have anything to do with that?"

The Watson family's kidnapping and murders had been her and Stephen's case, along with a support teams from multiple law enforcement agencies, but she wasn't about to get into it on a back road in upstate New York. Actually, hell would freeze over before she stood around and casually discussed what had happened to the Watson's. She hoped she never had to deal with another case like it.

"A lot of agents were involved in that one," she said with a shrug. When Martin opened his mouth again, she pointedly looked at Hurley. "I understand someone found a body." She glanced over at the empty utility truck and then toward the cruisers. All the windows were rolled down and each backseat was occupied by a single man. She gave both men a quick look as they stared back at her from their separate windows. "Are the utility guys the ones who called it in?"

"Yeah." Hurley turned his head and looked at the white truck before his gaze shifted back to Gin. "Keith Turnball and Adam Burns. They called it in. The body is near a pylon about a mile in."

Gin glanced up at the huge power lines running overhead, crossing the pavement and following the dirt road blocked by the cruisers. "They were both out here working?"

"That's what they said, and their ID checked out." Hurley lifted broad shoulders into a careless shrug. "They're a little spooked about the whole thing. We've kept them separate, but they had plenty of time before we got here to sync up their stories if they needed to."

"Yeah, that's what usually happens," Gin agreed.

Hurley dipped his head in an acknowledging nod. "That's been my experience, too. Do you want to talk to them now, or take a ride up to see the body first before the forensics team gets here? Last report I got was they're about twenty minutes out."

"Body first," Gin decided. "And who's the other guy with you?"

"He's from the Fish and Wildlife Service," Martin cut in. "There's a big wildlife refuge nearby, and they manage it. The body was found just a mile up the access road, so it was close enough they sent someone out to take a look."

Gin's gaze narrowed on the deputy's face. "Interesting.

A HARD TRUTH

How did the Fish and Wildlife Service happen to hear about a body that wasn't actually found on the refuge?"

Martin blinked. "I don't know," he stuttered. "News travels fast, I guess. Or maybe our lieutenant called them as a courtesy?"

Amused that the deputy had asked her the question at all and then expected her to have an answer to it, Gin turned and openly stared at the middle-aged man leaning against the hood of the cruiser, a disposable coffee cup in his hand. She lifted her arm and waved him over, nodding a greeting as he strolled a bit too casually for it to be natural, across the short distance between them and joined their little group.

"I'm Special Agent Gin Reilly, with the FBI."

"Of the Critical Crimes Unit," the man said with a smile. "Yes. I know. I'm Colin Merced, the manager of the wildlife refuge."

Gin automatically stiffened at the manager recognizing her, but a long-standing habit had her quickly relaxing her shoulders and holding out her hand. Over the years, she'd learned that acting as if she didn't know or care when someone recognized her was the best line of defense. "Mr. Merced. I hope we haven't wasted your time since I've been told the body isn't on any federal land."

"Call me Colin," he said with a wide smile. "I was told that about the dead body, but the Tonawanda Wildlife Preserve is right across the road, and the tribe's reservation lands are just south of the preserve. I'll need to give them a report of what happened so close to their holdings, and my boss is also waiting to hear about it. Those two combined are the second reason I'm here."

Gin swiped a hand across her forehead, shoving stray wisps of hair out of her eyes. "And what's the first reason?"

Colin's mouth formed into a crooked grin. "Plain nosiness."

Well, she certainly couldn't fault his honesty, but she didn't need any extra bodies, or ears open for gossip, hanging around her crime scene. On the other hand, she needed a ride up there. The compact two-door sedan she'd rented wasn't built for dirt roads. Barely able to tamp down a sound of annoyance, she jerked her head toward the dark SUV parked in front of the National Grid truck. "Is that 4Runner back there yours?" When he nodded, she turned to face Deputy Hurley. "Are you okay holding the two utility guys here until I get back?"

Hurley nodded. "Yep. That's the plan."

"There's another agent on the way." She reached into the back pocket of her jeans and drew out a card. "Here's my cell number. I'd appreciate it if you would call me when the agent shows up."

The deputy took the card and held it between two fingers. "I can do that. Got a name for me?"

She shook her head. "Nope. Sorry."

"Okay." He frowned as he eyed the card in his hand. "Any particular reason the FBI sent someone from the Critical Crimes Unit? I heard who the victim is, but even being a big-shot corporate executive doesn't make it a critical crime."

"I think it was more a matter of the nearest available agent."

The deputy made a scoffing noise deep in his throat. "There's an FBI office in Buffalo which is barely half an hour to the west of us. I guess all those guys are out of the office or on vacation?"

Gin couldn't blame him for being skeptical, but all she could do was shrug. "The boss calls, he says go, and I go. He gave me the victim's name, and that was about it. For all I know, the other agent might be from the Buffalo office."

Hurley stared at her for several long moments before he tucked her card into his shirt pocket. "Yeah. I hear that. If anyone else shows up, I'll send them your way."

A HARD TRUTH

Gin nodded her thanks and took several steps toward the SUV before looking back over her shoulder at Colin. "Are you coming?"

The Fish and Wildlife manager hurried after her, scrambling behind the wheel as Gin fastened her seat belt and rolled down her window.

Deputy Martin pulled his cruiser forward just enough to let the SUV squeak through before returning it to its blocking position. Gin stuck her hand out the window in a wave of thanks before settling into her seat.

"Any idea where we're going?" Colin said into the silence.

"They found the body about a mile up the road, near one of the electrical pylons. We'll know it when we see it."

Colin took a firmer grip on the wheel as the SUV bounced along the dirt track. "Why? Did the workers hang a sign on one of those huge towers saying 'dead body here'?"

Gin shot him a sideways glance. Judging from the eager look on his face, it seemed the manager was looking forward to walking in on a murder scene, complete with a dead victim. "No. But I think all the parked cruisers might give the location away. The county sheriff's deputies arrived on scene first."

"I was told the dead. . ." Colin stopped and cleared his throat. "I mean the victim is Benjamin Stampler. That pharmacy bigwig who went missing from Miami a couple of months ago."

"Did Deputy Martin tell you that?" Gin guessed, and knew she was right when Colin shot her a guilty look.

"I asked," he said in defense of the talkative deputy. "And I do work for the federal government. I guess he felt I had a need to know, so to speak."

"It would seem so." Gin looked out her side window so he wouldn't see her roll her eyes. She was pretty sure the Fish and Wildlife Service wasn't on any of the FBI's need-to-know lists.

Especially for a crime that didn't happen on land they were managing. "Did Deputy Martin have anything else to say?"

"No. Hurley gave him a 'keep your mouth shut' look, and that was that."

Good for Hurley, Gin thought.

"Do you know how he got way up here? We're a far piece from South Florida."

Ignoring his question, Gin deliberately let the conversation lapse into silence as she focused her attention out the front windshield, keeping an eye peeled for her crime scene. It didn't take long to come up on it, and just as she'd predicted to Colin, half a dozen cruisers were parked along the dirt track. Most belonged to the county sheriff's department, with one sporting the black and orange colors of the Akron police.

"It's a small town about fifteen minutes from here at the most," Colin said in answer to Gin's question about the Akron cruiser. "The county must have called them out."

Thinking the local police had probably been first on scene, Gin made a mental note to be sure to talk to them as she unbuckled her seatbelt and stepped out of the car. A dozen cops were spread out in a line, their heads down, doing a slow walk across the open field. She flashed her badge and credentials at the deputy who peeled off and came to meet them. He barely glanced at the black case she held out before directing Gin and the wildlife manager to a tall man, with stripes on his sleeve, standing in the center of a smaller group of deputies on the far side of the massive pylon.

She had crossed half the distance to them when the captain broke out of the group and strode toward her. He held out a hand and shook hers as white teeth flashed in stark contrast to his smooth, dark skin.

"I'm Captain Wade Moreau, with the Erie County Sheriff's Department."

A HARD TRUTH

Gin smiled at the rich tone of his voice that held a cadence straight out of the Deep South. "Special Agent Gin Reilly," she said as she took his outstretched hand. "You're a long way from home, Captain Moreau."

His friendly smile remained as he shook his head. "This has been my home for the last twenty years. Shoveling a mountain of snow every winter and all. But you aren't wrong, Special Agent Reilly. I grew up right outside of Jackson, Mississippi. Left when I went to college and never looked back."

"It's Mississippi's loss." Gin nodded at Colin as he came up and stood beside her. "This is Colin Merced. He's with the National Fish and Wildlife Service."

When Moreau gave her a puzzled frown, Gin stuck her tongue in her cheek and struggled to swallow her amusement. "It's my understanding that his boss, as well as the council on the Tonawanda Reservation, would like a report on what's going on over here."

Moreau turned a hard stare on Colin that had a streak of red crawling up from beneath the collar of the manager's shirt. "I manage the wildlife preserve across the road," he said, as if that explained why he was at the crime scene.

"Which is not where our victim was found," Moreau replied in a clipped voice. "And besides verifying that there was *not* a body found on federal property, is there anything else we can do for you?"

"Um." Colin glanced at Gin, who had no intention of helping him out. "No. That verification should be sufficient. But I will need to give Agent Reilly a lift back to her car when she's done here."

"We'll see to that," Moreau stated flatly. "See that you don't make a U-turn, and back your SUV down the road at least fifty yards. I don't want you driving over any potential evidence on the side of the road."

Colin reluctantly nodded, then stuck his hands into the pockets of his pants. "Fine. No problem." He sent a last pleading look toward Gin. "Are you sure you don't want me to wait?"

"I'm sure," Gin said politely. "Thanks for the lift." She turned her back on the manager, who huffed out a breath then did an abrupt turn on his heel and stalked back to his SUV. Once he was out of earshot, she nodded toward the group of deputies still gathered together and now openly watching her and their captain. "Is the body over that way?"

Moreau dismissed the wildlife manager as easily as she had. He turned and slowly started toward the waiting group. "A short walk beyond them. Behind that row of bushes just outside the tree line."

Gin frowned as she studied the distance between the trees and the pylon. "I assumed the utility guys were out here working on the tower. What were they doing over there?"

"Taking a leak and checking on a couple of trail cameras. At least that's what Turnball said when I asked him the same question." He shifted his gaze back to her. "And of course Adams corroborated that."

"Trail cameras?" Now that was something new. "They set up cameras out here? When did they do that?"

"Two cameras, according to Turnball. He positioned them here, along with several other sites along his regular route, about a year ago," Moreau said. "They usually work the same section of towers, and they check the cameras whenever they're out on this end of their assigned territory. He stated that happens every couple of months."

Gin did a quick, visual scan of the area, taking in the cleared swath of land that the long row of huge electrical grid pylons occupied. There were a lot of trees and open country all around the huge steel structures supporting the heavy electrical lines one hundred feet overhead. What she didn't see were any cellular towers mixed in with them, or randomly popping up along the tree line.

"So I'm guessing internet service is spotty enough out here that their camera has an SD card in it rather than sending everything to the cloud?" she asked.

"That's about the size of it," Moreau agreed. "Which is why they have to check on it and manually switch out the SD cards."

"When's the last time they switched it out?"

Moreau smiled and nodded his approval. "Good question."

"Which I'm sure you asked them," Gin prompted.

The captain's smile widened. "Of course I did. The cards were switched out just over two months ago." He stopped several feet away from a taped-off area where two deputies stood guard at the edge. They straightened up as the captain and Gin approached. "Which would put it at about two weeks before the victim disappeared."

Gin's nerves began to hum. It would be a phenomenal stroke of luck if they caught the killer on camera. "Have you seen what's on the cards?"

Moreau ran a big hand over the back of his neck. "Not yet." At Gin's startled look, he shrugged. "The truth is, we don't know exactly where this camera is, so it might not be near enough to the body to have caught much of anything."

Her eyes narrowed. Now why wouldn't Turnball have told the captain where this trail camera was? If he had something to hide, then why had the man mentioned the camera at all? "Did Turnball give you a reason for not disclosing the location of the camera?"

"No." Moreau held up a hand to stop Gin's next question. "He didn't tell me where it was because I didn't ask him." He nodded at his men before introducing them to a silent Gin.

Not satisfied with Moreau's answer about the location of the game camera, Gin let it go for the moment and followed him as he stepped over the crime scene tape. When he moved aside, she walked over to the body and did a slow circle around it. Whoever had killed the Miami executive hadn't bothered to conceal his body inside the stand of trees but had left it lying near a thick cluster of tall bushes. Tucking that bit of information away, Gin gave her forehead a quick scratch before she knelt down and studied the decaying remains of Benjamin Stampler.

He was on his back, with his arms and legs splayed out from beneath the pile of trash heaped high on his chest. From the position of the body, it looked as if he'd been dumped and left in whatever position he'd landed in before a large bag of trash had been poured on top of him. Her nose twitched at an unexpected smell. Leaning in a little closer, she caught the faint whiff of peppermint.

Now that's saying something, she thought as she did a two-legged, crab walk shuffle closer to Stampler's head to get a clear look at his face.

His head was turned to the side, and open, sightless eyes stared at the bushes. Gin leaned over and waved a hand in front of her face as she fended off the army of flies buzzing around the open wound across Stampler's neck. Judging by the deterioration of the body, Gin guessed he'd been dead at least a month, probably more. And the lack of any blood staining the surrounding ground said as plain as day the man had been killed somewhere else and his body dumped here.

Straightening up, Gin stuck her hands in her pockets and studied the ground between the bushes and the start of the tree line a few yards away, but she didn't spot anything that even remotely looked like a trail camera. With a mental shrug, she returned her gaze to what was left of the pharmacy CEO. "He wasn't killed here."

"Nope," Moreau agreed. "There's not enough blood, and judging by that gash in his neck, there should have been plenty." He blew out a deep breath. "Stampler disappeared over six weeks ago, and looking at his body, I'd say that was about the last time he was seen alive. Which means the odds are good he was killed somewhere between New York and Florida, and then dumped here. And until we can establish where he was murdered, it's going to be a toss-up over who has first priority on this case. Which is why I told my men to tape it off and put those two who claimed to have found the body under wraps while the sheriff made a call to the local FBI office in Buffalo." He caught Gin's gaze with his. "I have to say, I'm a little curious about the Bureau sending out someone from that fancy new unit of theirs instead of one of their local guys."

"I was in the area on some personal business," Gin said in answer to his blunt observation. When he only lifted one eyebrow, she sighed. "My grandparents lived in Henrietta. They passed away recently, and I was settling their affairs."

Sympathy crept into Moreau's eyes. "I'm sorry to hear that. And even sorrier you got interrupted and dragged out here for this. But that still doesn't explain why the local agents are sitting on their collective asses in Buffalo."

Gin wasn't exactly sure why that was either, but like she'd told Deputy Hurley, maybe an agent from the Buffalo office was on the way, but when the boss says to get your butt somewhere, you move without asking too many questions. "I don't know," she said, going for the truth rather than a vague lie. "That's above my pay grade."

Moreau let out a snort of laughter. "Mine too."

The steady beat of rotor blades overhead had Gin, the captain, and both deputies looking up. She lifted a hand to shade her eyes as she scanned the skies, looking for the source of the noise that was rapidly growing to a thunderous roar. In less than a minute a helicopter appeared, heading straight for them. It passed close enough overhead she could see the two men sitting in the cockpit. She blinked in surprise when the copter swept in a tight circle, passing overhead once more before slowly dropping toward the ground somewhere near the point where she'd left her rental car.

"Any idea what that's all about?" Moreau demanded.

Gin adamantly shook her head. "Not a clue."

"Captain?" one of the deputies standing guard called out. "Hurley reported the forensics team just arrived and wants to know if he should send them in."

Gin set aside the mystery of the unexpected helicopter and looked over at Moreau. "Could they bring in the two utility workers? I'd like to hear what they have to say, and check out that trail camera."

Moreau nodded. "Consider it done."

Chapter Four

Gin was walking a slow grid search of the area just inside the tree line when an unusual bump on the forest floor caught her eye. There was a black patch among the pine needles, higher than the surrounding ground. It was easy to overlook in the shadows of the trees towering overhead, but if you were searching for something out of place, the dark, bumpy area stood out.

It was something out of place, and exactly what she was looking for.

Watching where she stepped as she covered the distance to the unknown bump, she stopped and stared at the small patch that wasn't dirt after all. A corner of black plastic stuck out from its partial cover of dried pine needles. Reaching into her back pocket, she pulled out a set of latex gloves, snapping them into place over her hands as she crouched next to the partially covered plastic.

Carefully brushing the pine needles aside, she lifted what turned out to be a bag up from the ground. It had some weight to it. Wondering if it was just simply a discard from a long-ago hunter, or if it was part of the puzzle of how Benjamin Stampler had ended up near an electrical tower in upstate New York, she got to her feet.

With her head down, she continued her scan of the area around where she'd spotted the plastic bag, slowly walking in a tight pattern over the crunchy ground cover of pine needles. She only looked up when she heard footsteps coming her way and stopped walking altogether when Moreau appeared through the trees.

"Agent Reilly?"

"Over here," she called out, then watched patiently as he changed direction.

The captain came to a halt a few feet away and looked around. "What are you doing out here?"

"A quick search to make sure there isn't anything we should look at outside the taped-off area." When he frowned, she shrugged. "Filling a square for my report, basically. But I did find this." She held up the bag.

Moreau leaned forward to get a better look. "What's in it?"

She shrugged. "I don't know. I thought I'd let the forensic team process it while I continued looking around."

He nodded his agreement. "I can have a couple of my guys help out with that."

Gin smiled her thanks. "I'd appreciate it. It would free me up to interview the utility guys. Has the forensics team arrived on the scene yet?"

"Yeah. They're here, along with the assistant medical examiner." He crossed his arms over his chest and stared at her. "Are you sure you don't know anything about the helicopter that came in a couple of minutes ago?"

Now it was her turn to frown. "Nope. What about it?"

"Well, the guy who was flying it put that bird down on the highway about the same time the forensic team got to the turnoff for the access road coming in here. And the funny thing is, he claims he's with the FBI's Critical Crimes Unit." Moreau paused and uncrossed his arms to wag a finger at her. "*Your* unit, to be precise. He even said that he's your partner."

Gin shook her head hard enough to loosen the band holding her thick hair into a high ponytail. Several copper-colored strands fell to her shoulders as she leaned to the side to look around the captain, but the trees blocked her view of anything and anyone out in the cleared-off space. "My partner is in Denver."

"Deputy Hurley said that you were expecting another agent, and his credentials looked as real as yours," Moreau stated flatly. "The guy introduced himself as Treynor Robard. Does his name ring a bell?"

It did, but very dimly, and she couldn't quite place it. "Maybe," she admitted. "There are a lot of agents in the Bureau, and I certainly haven't met all of them." She sighed and rolled her shoulders to stretch out her back and neck. "I guess I'd better go introduce myself."

Moreau fell into step beside her. "He said he was from your unit. How many agents are in that?"

"Right at the moment, there are two of us," Gin answered. "And like I said, the other one is in Denver." Remembering the two figures she'd seen in the cockpit, she shot him a questioning look. "Did you say he was *flying* the helicopter?"

"He sure was," Moreau confirmed. "One of my deputies did a stint in the Navy and he recognized him. Said the guy was a hot shot search and rescue pilot, and big deal among the pilots in the service. He also claimed Mister Hotshot could fly just about anything with an engine." He smiled when Gin stopped in her tracks. "So I'm guessing you just heard that ringing bell?"

Oh, yeah, she thought. Treynor Robard. The decorated

pilot, who Ricki, her good friend in the National Park's Investigative Services Bureau, had worked with on a murder in the Great Smoky Mountains National Park. After Ricki closed her case, she'd given Gin an earful about Treynor Robard, who had suddenly quit the active military branch of the Navy and moved to their Criminal Investigation Unit under some very cloudy circumstances. Which basically meant no one but the top brass knew why. He couldn't have done anything too bad, though, because the man apparently got whatever assignment he wanted.

"Yeah, I remember," she finally said. "I thought he was with NCIS. He might have moved over to the FBI." She tried for a careless shrug. "I haven't had a lot of time to follow his career choices."

"Not that much to follow."

Gin did a double take as she automatically reached for the missing Glock in her non-existent shoulder holster while Moreau's hand went to the weapon at his hip.

"I'm friendly," a deep voice called out. "I just came in on that helicopter."

Moreau exchanged an annoyed look with Gin before they turned around in tandem and stared at the man who had silently come up behind them. Given that the captain was clearly armed, the newcomer was wisely standing with his feet braced apart and both arms held out from his sides, keeping his hands in plain sight. He had thick, jet-black hair that barely brushed the top of a blue flannel shirt tucked into a pair of worn jeans.

She judged him to be about six feet tall in his hiking boots, and was nice looking enough, but she silently decided the man was nothing to swoon about. Which was a good thing. She was already irritated enough that he'd taken her by surprise.

"Sorry." He removed his sunglasses to reveal a pair of light brown eyes that displayed deep crinkles at the corners when he smiled. "I didn't mean to startle you."

"Dangerous to come up behind two people like that. Especially when at least one of them is carrying a gun," Moreau stated before walking forward and holding out his hand. "I'm Captain Wade Moreau with the Erie County Sheriff's Department. And you must be the guy Special Agent Reilly here has been waiting for?"

"Special Agent Treynor Robard with the FBI's Critical Crimes Unit." He slid a backpack off his shoulders and held it with one hand before giving the captain's hand a firm shake, then looking past him at Gin. "It's good to meet you, Agent Reilly."

"Yeah, good to meet you too." Gin kept her gaze on him as she jerked a thumb over her shoulder. "The crime scene is over there." She switched her hand to point in the opposite direction. "Why were you coming in that way?"

Robard clasped both hands around the straps of his backpack and drew himself up just short of standing at attention. "I was told you were back here and figured you were doing a grid search. Thought I would circle around so I wouldn't walk somewhere I shouldn't." He cocked his head to the side. "Just in case you'd found something interesting." He gave a pointed look at the plastic bag Gin was holding before his gaze returned to her face. "*Have* you found anything?"

Gin's green eyes narrowed a fraction of an inch. "I don't know yet." She didn't shift her gaze even when Moreau loudly cleared his throat.

"I think I'd better go and check on things. Are you two coming?" the captain asked into the silence.

"We'll be along in a minute," Gin said, her voice flat. "I need to bring Agent Robard up to speed on the case." She held her hand out to the captain. "Would you give this to the forensics team? I'll leave it to their judgement to process anything that looks interesting."

The captain's mouth twitched as he obviously fought to keep from smiling. He reached out for the bag with a nod. "I can do that."

As Moreau made his way back toward the sound of activity on the other side of the trees, the heavy beat of rotor blades sounded overhead. The helicopter skimmed over the treetops, rapidly gaining altitude as it flew west. The noise of its engine faded away as Gin put her hands on her hips. "Well. I guess there goes your ride back to wherever you came from, Agent Robard."

"It's Trey, and I came in from Buffalo," he supplied helpfully. "I would have rented a car, but I was told you had a rental we could use, and the bird would get me here faster."

"And I go by Gin to anyone inside the Bureau." She lifted a skeptical eyebrow. "So you're expecting us both to go back to Buffalo?"

"Since that's where the closest FBI office and forensics lab is, yeah, I do." Trey frowned at her. "I read the briefing on the victim and assumed we'd want the evidence run through our own lab. Why are you acting like you have a stick up your ass?" he added without missing a beat.

"The autopsy will hopefully be done by the county medical examiner, but I haven't been able to verify that yet. And yes, I do want the evidence processed at our own facility, but I haven't had a chance to arrange anything there either. And I'm acting like this because you're standing as if you have a stick up *your* ass, or you're about to salute someone."

A startled look crossed Trey's face before he relaxed his stance. Hefting his backpack up onto one shoulder, he stuck his free hand into the back pocket of his jeans. "Sorry. Force of habit." He studied her face for a moment. "So you're okay with me coming on the team?"

"I'm used to my partner having a lower profile than a hotshot pilot, but whether you're on or off a case isn't my call," Gin said, then returned the favor and studied him, taking in the air of authority that he wore so easily. "You told the deputy that you were not only part of the team assigned to this case, but that you're also in the Critical Crimes Unit." She made it a statement, then paused to wait for his nod. "Are you?"

He nodded again, his smile back. "As of yesterday. My assignment is Team Two." When she kept a silent stare on him, he added a third, confirming nod. "We're on the same team, along with Stephen Jones. And I understand we'll be meeting a fourth member whenever we get back to Denver."

Gin blew out an exasperated breath. It seemed Treynor Robard knew a lot more about what was going on than she did. Which meant that she needed to have a serious talk with their now mutual boss.

"Good to know," she said on a sour note. "Any other developments back at the office I should know about?"

Trey shook his head. "Nope. Technically I wasn't supposed to report for my first day with the team until next week. I've spent most of the time apartment hunting in Denver."

Well, the guy was here, and she could use the help, so she'd just have to get on with the case and shelve that talk with the team's senior agent about popping celebrities on her with no warning. She knew Robard had spent some time with NCIS, so hopefully he knew how to do investigative work.

"If you were apartment hunting in Colorado, how did you get yourself to upstate New York so fast?" she wondered out loud before turning and following Moreau's path back to the crime scene.

Trey quickly fell into step beside her. "I wasn't in

Colorado. I found a place, so I was taking a few days to visit my brother and his family. They live in Buffalo."

She cast him a sideways glance. "Buffalo? No kidding. It's a small world, I guess."

"How about you?"

Used to the curiosity about her past, Gin was careful to keep her shoulders and hands relaxed. "What about me?"

"Like you said, the team is based in Colorado, so I assume you live there too. I was surprised to be told you were already on scene. How did *you* get here so fast?"

Gin blinked. Not quite the question she'd been expecting. "My grandparents lived just south of Rochester. They passed away recently, and I was at their house settling their affairs." An image of the journals she'd found, and were now safely tucked away in her backpack, popped into her mind. She had a feeling settling her grandparents' estate was going to be a lot easier than figuring out what those leather-bound books were all about.

"Huh. Your grandparents lived in upstate New York? It's a small world, I guess."

She had to smile at the humor in his voice as he turned her own words back on her. But that still didn't mean she was happy with the situation. She was used to working with Stephen, who knew all about her past and didn't spend any time covertly staring at her as if she'd leap into a murderous rage at any moment. "My regular partner and I have been working together for five years now and have developed a routine that lets us move very quickly on cases. We came to the Critical Crimes Unit as kind of a package deal."

Trey shrugged. "Then I guess we'll both have to adapt." He pulled a cell phone out of his shirt pocket. "We can start by getting a jump on that autopsy and the forensics team. I can call the office in Buffalo and get that moving along."

A HARD TRUTH

"That would be good." Gin's tone lightened up quite a bit, almost bordering on friendly. She hated that kind of follow-up work, no matter how necessary it was. And was bad enough at it that Stephen always handled all those kinds of details. If Robard was willing to take them on, this temporary partnership might not be so bad. At least there was a sliver of hope for it. To ease her conscience about dumping any and all future busy work and errands on him, she would think of it as his breaking-in period. Satisfied with that justification, she smiled.

"Consider it done," Trey declared. "And Todd emailed our hotel reservations in Buffalo, so we're all set there."

So, it seemed the new guy was already on a first-name basis with their boss. Her smile dimmed as she felt the sliver of hope collapse into an annoyed heap.

Once they broke through the trees, Trey stopped on the edge of the open clearing and turned to face Gin.

She stopped as well and sent him a curious look. "Is something wrong?"

"Nope." He shook his head, sending the ends of his dark hair sliding across the top of his collar. "I was just wondering why you were doing that grid search back there?"

Gin shrugged. "I had a hunch. But I usually do a three-sixty grid search anyway, so that wasn't out of my normal routine."

The newest team member frowned at her. "Okay. But a hunch based on what?"

"Logic." When he lifted an eyebrow, she sighed. "And the usual behavior of human beings." When he continued to stare at her, she stuck her hands in the pockets of her lightweight jacket and rocked back on her heels. "Did you get a look at the body when you first arrived on scene?"

"Yeah. A quick one. He was on his back with his head, shoulders, arms, and legs sticking out from underneath what looked like a pile of garbage dumped on his chest," Trey volunteered without any prompting.

Pleased that she didn't have to drag anything out of him or lead him by the hand to the glaringly obvious, she nodded. "That's right. And I'm pretty sure he was naked under that trash, which means all of his clothes and belongings were removed, and that's pretty telling in itself."

"Yeah?" Trey held a hand up, palm out. "Maybe later you can let me in on why you think that, but what you're saying is you were back in the woods looking for his personal stuff? Again, why? They could have been dumped anywhere between here and Miami."

"It's possible," Gin agreed. "But we have to assume Stampler was either killed on his yacht or taken someplace else and killed. I didn't see any ligature marks on his hands or ankles, although from the looks of it he's been rotting here at least a month. The medical examiner will have to verify that."

"I didn't see any marks either, so for the moment, let's assume he wasn't bound," Trey put in. He glanced over to the body still lying on the ground while the forensics team in their white hazard suits scurried around it. "And if he wasn't bound, then he was probably killed close to the time he encountered his killer." When Gin lifted an eyebrow at him, he blew out a quick breath. "Like you said — normal human behavior. In combat, when prisoners are caught and immediately executed right there on the spot, their hands and legs aren't bound either."

"I would guess not," Gin said quietly. "If Stampler wasn't tortured or even tied up, which again, the ME will have to verify, then he was killed on, or somewhere near, his yacht in Miami, and I'm guessing the body was driven up here in the trunk of a car, or maybe flown up in a box and dumped here." She glanced around. "But I'm leaning toward a car trip. The killer was looking for a spot to dump the body someplace far away from the kill site, again for reasons unknown, and found that access road and simply made the turn."

"Probably wouldn't stop somewhere on the way just to strip a body only to dump it back into the trunk," Trey said, easily following her train of thought. "That would increase the chances of being seen." He nodded, as if he could envision the scene rolling out in front of him. "Strip the body, stage the garbage dump, toss the personal stuff that could identify him into the woods, and he's got it all done in one stop. Get back in the car and drive off." He rubbed his hands together. "Job complete and on to the next one."

Gin choked out a short laugh. "You're assuming it's a male, and that he's going to kill again."

Trey shoved his hands back into his jeans pockets. "I guess it could be some kind of corporate revenge, or even a personal revenge thing. Jilted lover or something along those lines. But I read in the file that Stampler was six-one, one ninety. Hard to see a woman dragging that much dead weight into a car trunk and then out again."

"Hard, but not impossible," Gin pointed out. "She might have had some help. Or maybe the guy who dragged him here was the help."

Trey's eyebrows winged upward. "As in more than one killer? Or a contract kill?"

"Either is possible," Gin repeated. She reached up and tugged on her hairband until it slid off her ponytail. Efficiently gathering up the mass of coppery hair, including the strands that had escaped and were now hanging down past her shoulders, she efficiently secured the hairband around it again, restoring the high ponytail before pointing a finger at the dead body lying on the ground. "And we've got nothing to indicate the killer went on for a repeat performance unless you've seen a bulletin alerting us to another executive gone missing, or someone else disappearing off a yacht in Miami. Until we establish some other link, we don't have any reason to think this was anything but a one-and-done killing. Which would make Stampler a specific target because someone wanted him dead."

"That would lean toward a contract kill."

Gin lifted an eyebrow and tilted her head to the side. "Again, it's possible."

With nothing more to add she got her feet moving again, setting her sights on the man who looked to be in charge of the forensics team. But she smiled when she heard Trey mutter "the guy sure wasn't popular with someone," behind her.

Chapter Five

"Are you two the agents from Critical Crimes?" At Gin's nod, the heavyset man bobbed his head in answer. Only the oval of his face was exposed by the tightly drawn hood of his hazard suit. Deep-set, dark brown eyes crinkled at the corners over a nose that looked as if it had been broken more than once.

He smiled as he held up his gloved hands. "Tony Rossini. FBI, out of the Buffalo office. I'll offer a proper handshake later. Right now I don't want to have to glove up again."

"Understandable, Mr. Rossini," Gin said, smiling at the heavy Brooklyn accent. "I'm Special Agent Gin Reilly, out of the Denver office." She tilted her head toward Trey, who had moved up to stand beside her. "This is Special Agent Treynor Robard." She hesitated briefly, then gave a mental shrug. She wasn't high enough up the food chain to argue with who the top brass assigned to the unit. "Also with Critical Crimes out of Denver."

Trey smiled when the forensic technician's gaze cut over to him. "I go by Trey."

"And I'm Tony." The tech's lips split into a wide grin as his gaze shifted back to Gin. "I come from a big family. You call out Mr. Rossini, and an entire roomful of people might stand up." His smile disappeared as fast as it had come when he turned back to the body. "You can see we've bagged and tagged the trash covering him." He pointed to a neatly lined-up row of bright orange garbage bags. "Most of it is over there. It was mixed in with some rotting food and the wrappers it came in. But not as much as you'd expect to see if this came from a dumpster behind a fast-food joint."

Gin stuck her hands into her pockets and glanced over at her newly acquired fellow agent. "Which is what makes it trash instead of garbage." At his frown, she gave a quick shrug. "A short-hand description so we know what a report is referring to. Trash is mostly non-food. Garbage has a heavy mix of food or other organic matter in it." Her gaze slowly scanned down the length of the naked body on the ground. *Still no signs of torture*, she thought, noting that the unmarked chest, along with everything else, looked intact.

"At least at a thirty percent mix," Tony chimed in, still intent on explaining what he'd found dumped on top of the body. "Which is not what we have here, although you'd expect at least that much discarded food from a dumpster near West Chippewa Street back in Buffalo. Not sure how it got here, but this trash definitely came from there." All business now, Tony bent down and picked up two small evidence bags stacked next to the body. "I kept these out. Thought you'd like to see them." He held up a bag. "Take a look at this one first."

Both Gin and Trey stepped in closer and stared intently at the bag. "Is that an address printed on that wrapper?" Trey asked.

"Uh-huh," Tony confirmed. "From a local hot dog joint. And I recognize some of the other wrappers, even with no address printed on them. Not to mention there were a couple of receipts tucked in here and there. All from places along Chippewa. I'd say someone hit up a dumpster down there and picked out most of the food before dropping the rest all over this guy." He jerked a thumb at the body lying on the ground next to him.

"Why do that?" Trey asked. "Are we looking for a homeless guy?"

Gin almost rolled her eyes. Trey's investigative experience, or lack of it, was going to be on full display if he didn't keep his mouth shut now and ask his questions later. "No, just the opposite. This guy knew what he was doing. Food attracts things that tend to destroy bodies. Like insects and rodents." When Trey opened his mouth again, Gin flashed him a warning glance. The touch of heat in it had him snapping his jaw closed hard enough to click his teeth together. Satisfied that he'd read her correctly, Gin turned back to Tony. "No food covering him, and I thought I smelled a peppermint mixture of some sort."

Tony nodded his approval. "Probably the oil mixed in with some water. That will keep the insects and most other varmints away too. Even the occasional coyote that might wander over from the wildlife preserve." He lowered the arm holding the evidence bag with the food wrapper in it. "Your guy must have a peppermint fetish of some kind." The tech lifted wide shoulders into a shrug. "Or maybe it's his favorite cologne and he wanted something to cover up the odor of a body that had to be getting pretty rank during its trip up here from Miami." At Gin's pained look, his mouth twitched at the corners. "The story hit the papers here too. I recognized the vic as that guy who went missing from his yacht. If his body was hauled this far in somebody's car, I wouldn't be putting anything into that trunk again for a long time."

She'd bet that using the peppermint spray wasn't to cover

up the smell of a decaying corpse. Or at least not the main reason. It was a great insect repellant. A necessary thing if you wanted to keep a body recognizable longer, as opposed to becoming a bug feast. But instead of voicing the thought out loud, she pointed to the evidence bag in Tony's other hand. "What's in that one?"

He looked down in surprise, as if he'd forgotten all about the second bag, then slowly raised it to eye level. "Now this stood out like a flare on a dark road. It's a flower, preserved in some kind of resin, if I had to hazard a guess. Kind of like you see in some jewelry, but it's way too big for a necklace or earrings, or some shit like that."

Gin held out her hand, her fingers closing over the top of the bag when Tony gave it to her. She held it up high enough that Trey could get a good look at the preserved flower as well. "How far into the pile was it?"

"Right on top," Tony said. "It was in one of those flimsy cardboard boxes that hamburgers sometimes come in. The lid was closed, and this was in there along with a rock. Got both of those bagged separately."

"A rock to weigh it down so it wouldn't blow away," Gin muttered as she continued to study the flower forever trapped in the clear resin. She glanced at Tony. "I need to take this with me. If you have a chain of evidence form, I'll be happy to sign it."

The gruff-looking tech let out a loud whistle, then pointed at a member of his team who came trotting over. "We always carry those forms. You sign it, and that flower is yours."

Nodding her thanks, Gin held the bag out to Trey. "Agent Robard can sign for it. What else have you got?"

"Not much," Tony admitted. "The assistant ME only stayed long enough to officially declare the vic dead, and that the probable cause was from the cut across his throat. If there's anything else, he said it would be flagged at autopsy."

Annoyed, Gin looked toward the access road. "Really? Did he have a hot date?"

Tony snorted out a laugh. "Kind of. He came in with us just ahead of that helicopter, and the guy riding shotgun offered the assistant ME a lift back if he didn't take too long."

"Wonderful," Gin said with a sigh. "What else?"

"It's not what we got, but what we don't," Tony stated. He flicked a glance at Trey, who had walked over to join them, having finished the chain of evidence paperwork. "Or rather what we didn't see. No tire tracks leading over from the access road. It could be they were there and got washed away. We've had some rain in the last month or so. But it also could be they were never there at all." He glanced down at the body which was now covered with a black tarp. "Not enough blood for him to have been killed right where he's lying. Even the rain wouldn't have washed all that blood away. Might have happened at some kill site you haven't found yet, but either way, he had to get from that road to here somehow." Tony took several steps away from the body and tugged off his gloves before tugging on his hood until it hung down his back. He ran a beefy hand over the top of a scalp covered with curly black hair. "Don't know how that could have been done unless he was carried over here."

He reached into a hidden pocket and drew out a pack of gum, offering one to Gin, who declined with a slight shake of her head, and then to Trey, who also shook his head. Unwrapping a piece, the tech stuck it in his mouth before returning the rest of the pack to its hiding place. "If someone carried the vic from the road to here, that was one powerful guy. Didn't find any shoe prints, which is no surprise. The body's been here a while, and like I said, we've had our fair share of rain over the last month. So no shoe prints. Which means I can't tell you if there were two of them, but I sure couldn't rule it out either." He cocked his head to one side. "We also have whatever's in that plastic bag Captain Moreau handed me. He said you found it back in the trees."

"About twenty, maybe twenty-five feet in," Gin said. "I'm not sure what's in it, but there's a good chance it's Benjamin Stampler's personal effects."

Tony only grunted at that. "Not bulky enough to include his clothes. Unless you think he was brought up here naked?"

She shrugged. "No idea at this point. That bag might be something some hunter or one of the utility crews left behind. I didn't open it. I thought I'd leave that to you guys."

"Right." The tech rolled his shoulders back and forth, then locked his hands together and twisted his body around at the waist. "This job has a way of bringing out the aches and pains."

"Yeah. I hear that." Gin pulled her hands out of her pockets and rested them on her hips. "How long will it take to process the rest of the evidence?"

Tony's entire face turned down into a scowl. "You'd know that better than me. We were told to collect, log, bag, and tag, and then send it all to Quantico by courier." His brows dropped even lower over a narrow-eyed stare. "I figured your boss back in Virginia didn't trust the local guys to get the job done right, since all the calls were coming from there and not you. I know that because you're here." He half smiled at his own joke, then rocked back on his heels. "So you'll have to ask the lab guys at Quantico that question, since it's all going to be sent to them. At least that's what I was told."

Gin lifted an eyebrow but kept her voice neutral. "Is that so? It would save time to have it immediately processed right here. Who knows what the backlog at Quantico is." She

A HARD TRUTH

smoothly pivoted around on her heels to face Trey. "Think you could make a phone call or two about that?"

She saw the flash of exasperation in his gaze. Clearly he didn't like being treated as the team assistant, but he didn't voice any complaints as he jerked his head into a nod.

"Sure. I'll take care of it."

"Consider it part of a break-in period," she said, trying not to grin.

He frowned. "Break-in period?"

"Yeah." She lifted her shoulders in a careless shrug. "Like a rookie thing."

He gave her a bland look before pulling a cell phone out of his pocket and moving off to make the call. Allowing herself a smile now that his back was safely turned, Gin switched her attention back to the forensic tech. "I wouldn't be too quick to ship the evidence off. Agent Robard might be able to swing something to keep it here."

Tony flashed his big smile once more. "Thanks. I appreciate that." He reached out a long arm and slapped her on the shoulder. "You're okay, Special Agent Reilly. I'll be sure to pass that along to the rest of the team."

She barely kept her knees from buckling underneath the friendly gesture and took a quick step forward in order to stay on her feet. "No problem. It would be a big help to us to cut down on that processing time. I'm not sure how long we'll be in Buffalo."

"Yeah." Tony gave her a knowing look. "You'll need to head down to Miami and take a look at that yacht."

"That's the plan." Gin smiled when Captain Moreau appeared behind Tony.

"Glad to see you two are hitting it off." Moreau smiled at the lab tech then pointed at the pair of men dressed in worn jeans and different colored plaid shirts. They were huddled together and flanked by two deputies. "I've got the utility workers over there. My guys had them retrieve the SD cards while you were talking with Tony."

"No objection from our utility workers about those cards being confiscated?" Gin asked.

"Nope," the captain responded. "It seems Turnball is the one who sets up the cameras. One was inside the tree line, pointing into the woods, and the other was attached to a tree and set to capture any movement out over the open area around the pylon."

"For the last two months," Gin said, then frowned. "That's what they told you, isn't it? The utility guy said that the SD cards were changed out two months ago for a fresh one?"

"That's what they said. Or rather Turnball did, since the whole trail camera thing is his hobby." He glanced over to the far side of the taped off site. "What's going on over there?"

Gin turned her head just in time to see Tony give her new partner a couple of hard slaps on his back. "Quantico wanted to process the evidence, and judging by Tony's reaction, I'd say Agent Robard talked them out of it and agree to leave the job with the Buffalo office." Gin flushed at the nasty bite in her voice.

The former naval captain didn't deserve that. So he had a lot of influence in high places? That didn't bother her. At least not much. But she didn't want to have to break in a new member of the team. Everyone in the Bureau knew about her family, and it had made for some uncomfortable moments in the past. Stephen was very good at deflecting most of the negative attention, but with a new guy, she was feeling very exposed.

Looking surprised at Gin's tone, the captain switched his gaze back to her and hooked his thumbs on his belt. "Is there some kind of bad history between you and Robard?"

A HARD TRUTH

"No. I don't have any history with him at all." She shifted her weight from one foot to the other. She liked Moreau, but not enough to turn him into some kind of buddy you'd exchange secrets with.

"Uh-huh. Then you don't know much about him?" Moreau asked.

She shrugged. "Just what I heard from a friend who worked a case with him." Feeling another twinge of guilt, she added, "And it was all good. He's a solid agent."

The captain shook his head. "Then if you trust your friend, I suggest you take some advice and lighten up on the guy. Polite and nice get you a lot further than the attitude you're displaying."

Gin's shoulders stiffened. He was right, but she didn't appreciate hearing it. "I don't have an attitude," she protested anyway, but when Trey walked in their direction, she made a point of pasting a smile on her face. "Get that all straightened out with Quantico?"

Trey shot her a questioning look, but only said, "Yeah. We're good." He switched his attention to the captain. "I asked Tony to have a team finish that grid search back in the woods, so you don't have to redeploy any of your men. Maybe Tony's guys will find the clothes that are still missing."

"Okay," Gin answered, even though he hadn't been talking to her. She took a deep breath and reminded herself what Moreau had just said. Lighten up. At least unless, or maybe until, Robard got overly curious about her past. "That's a good call about the grid search." She pointed at the men standing wide-eyed between the two deputies. "We need to interview those two. They found the body, and had trail cams set up in the area, with an SD card that fits into our timeline."

"Trail cameras?" Trey's hands went to his hips as his gaze cut across the area. "Where were they set up?"

"That's what we're about to find out," Gin said. "Do you have a laptop in that backpack you've been toting around? We need to get a look at the cards."

White teeth flashed behind Trey's smile. "Sure do. And it's fully charged, so we're all set."

Not the least surprised that a former rescue pilot had come prepared for anything in the field — even needing a charged laptop, Gin nodded, then headed over to where the two utility linemen were waiting.

"I'm Special Agent Reilly with the FBI, and this is my partner, Special Agent Robard," Gin said. "Which of you is Mr. Turnball?"

"That would be me." The shorter of the two men gave Gin a tentative smile as he slowly raised his hand. Keith Turnball sported a thinning cap of brown hair graying at the edges and a short, neatly trimmed beard. "I'm just Keith. Adam and I found the body." He gestured toward his companion, who looked a decade younger and towered over him.

Adam's head bobbed up and down in a vigorous nod. "Yeah. We did." He pointed at the tarp-covered figure surrounded by forensic techs. "We found him right there."

"That's what we were told," Gin said in polite response to the blindingly obvious, since the body hadn't been moved. "And you are Adam Burns?"

"That's right." Adam's head kept on bobbing, as if he couldn't get it to stop. "We both work for the power company."

"That would be National Grid," Keith cut in. "We do vegetation management."

"Yep," Adam went on. "Vegetation management. That means we cut back the bushes, grass, and any other stuff from the pylons." His head bobbing switched to head shaking. "We don't climb the towers or nothing like that."

"I used to," Keith volunteered. "Climb the towers, I mean. I

A HARD TRUTH

used to, but I went over to vegetation management when I hit the big five-oh. Got too old to do all that climbing."

"His balance got bad too," Adam chirped out, still shaking his head. "Keith was in a car accident, and it affected how good he could stay on his feet and stuff. You can get killed climbing towers when your balance is off."

Keith gave his partner a solid poke in the arm. "They don't want to hear about that." He reached into his pocket and held out a baggie containing two SD cards. "I was told you're after these. The cops came with us to get them, so they haven't been messed with or nothing. The fact is, I haven't seen what's on them yet."

Gin took the bag with a smile and immediately passed it over to Trey. "Thanks. We might have to keep these, depending on what we see on them."

"Not sure you're going to see much of anything." Keith's shoulders drooped as he looked from Gin to Trey. "Since the body was there," he pointed to the remains of Benjamin Stampler, then turned ninety degrees to the west. "And the cameras were over there. About twenty feet in that direction. That's how I find them. Go straight back from the pylon toward the trees, then walk twenty feet west, and bam." To emphasize his point, Turnball struck a closed fist against an open palm. "They're right there."

When both agents remained silent, he cleared his throat and stuck his hands into the front pockets of his jeans. "Anyway. One of them is about ten feet inside the trees, pointing into the woods along a small game trail. Probably made by the deer in the area. At least that's what has mostly shown up on it. Along with some mice, and even got a couple of skunks once."

"And where was the other camera?" Gin asked, cutting off his list of animals caught in the act of walking through the trees.

"That one I had mounted on a tree, looking out over the

open space," Keith said. "But it was pointed at the area on the other side of the pylon, and I don't see any reason why someone would drive that far up and then leave the body way over here when you can come straight in from the road. But if there is anything, those are both top-of-the-line cameras, and they date and time stamp any picture they take."

"That's good," Gin responded automatically as she silently gauged the distance. Turnball could be right about not seeing much on the camera pointed toward the far side of the pylon, but they might get lucky with the trail camera. It wouldn't be too far from where she'd found the plastic bag. Provided, of course, the killer had actually discarded the thing. "We'll still need to take a look." She paused for a moment as an effective way to switch topics. "What were you two doing out here?"

"Like Adam said, checking on the plant growth." Keith pointed back toward the giant pylon. "Making sure the grass in the cleared-off area doesn't get too high, so if one of those big wires comes down, the whole place doesn't go up like a torch."

"It's an important job," Adam interjected solemnly. "We all know what a wildfire can do, and there're folks living not too far from here, not to mention the reservation is just over thataway." He waved his hand around, vaguely covering the area behind them.

Going with another polite nod, Gin kept her attention on Keith. "Was this stop part of your planned schedule today?"

"Sure was. First one this morning," Keith confirmed. "And we haven't budged from here since. We've been working our way down this line for the last month, heading toward Rochester."

"I live in Buffalo, and Keith lives just outside the city limits," Adam interrupted again. "We gave all our contact info to the cops."

"Thank you." Gin shot a sideways look at Trey, impressed

despite herself when he got her silent message and immediately stepped in front of Adam.

"Mr. Burns? To help speed things up, why don't you and I go over here and talk?"

Adam's eyes gleamed as his mouth spread wide in a huge grin. "Sure. Did you come in on that helicopter? One of the cops said you did, and that you were even flying it."

"That's right." Trey smiled even as he took Adam's arm in an unshakable grip and tugged him off a short distance.

While her partner was thankfully dealing with the talkative Adam, Gin switched her attention back to Keith Turnball. "We'll get your personal information from the sheriff's office. What I'm interested in knowing, Keith, is how you discovered the body."

Keith lifted a hand and scratched underneath his beard with his index finger. "Well, we got here just after nine this morning. We could see right off that the grass needed some cutting back, so while Adam was getting the equipment out of the van, I went to check on my cameras." He stopped to draw in a deep breath. "Like I explained before, I came straight back from the pylon. When I reached the tree line, I happened to look over this way, and there he was. Maybe about ten feet away, lying right behind those bushes. I'm not sure what happened next. I guess I must have yelled or something, because Adam came at a flat-out run. When he saw that body, he started yelling too. The cell service isn't so good out here, so we both hightailed it back to the truck. Adam got it started up and headed back to the main road, while I used the radio to call for help. We waited for the cops where the access road cuts off the main highway."

He paused and gave his beard another scratch. "I thought we'd be sitting by that road waiting for a while, but it didn't take them long to get here. The locals first, and even the county guys showed up pretty quick." He looked down while he shuffled his feet. "There's not much else to tell. We've either been hanging out in a police cruiser, or standing right here ever since."

Gin nodded her understanding. "How close did you get to the body? Did you walk up to be sure that was what you were seeing?"

Now Keith shook his head just as adamantly as Adam had. "No ma'am. We could see it plain enough. We didn't need to get any closer. The guy was lying there on his back, looking like a garbage dump with just his head, arms, and legs sticking out. But the worst of it was that he was staring right at me." He took in another deep breath. "I'd be happy to live out the rest of my days never seeing anything like that again."

Chapter Six

"Get anything out of Turnball?" Trey asked as he unzipped his backpack and drew out a slim laptop. He easily balanced it in the crook of his arm, watching the screen as it powered up.

Gin also kept her eyes on the screen as her shoulders moved in a light stretching motion. "Not a lot. This stop is part of their routine schedule, and they didn't go anywhere near the body. According to Turnball, he and Burns both took one look, then made a beeline for their truck and went right back to the main road where they called for help." She sent Trey a quick glance. "Do you have the SD cards?"

He responded by taking the baggie out of his shirt pocket and handing it over. "If you'll dig the first one out and pop it into the slot on that side, we'll take a look."

"There probably isn't much to see on the camera that's facing the pylon," Gin said as she pushed one of the cards into an open slot on the side of the laptop. "But the trail cam might have picked up something."

"Well, let's see what we've got." Trey slid his fingers across the mouse pad, opening the SD card.

When the first frame came up, Gin leaned in closer to read the date stamp. "That's about two weeks out from the day Stampler disappeared." She continued to watch as Trey skipped over several photos before pausing on one that had her gesturing for him to stop. "Okay. This is good. It's about five days out." She squinted at the screen. "What is that?"

"Just got a glimpse of a tail, but I'd guess it's a skunk moving through the grass," Trey said.

"Turnball mentioned skunks. Okay. Go ahead and scroll slowly through the pictures." Gin watched the screen, straining to see anything besides grass and the tree line on the other side of the service road.

When they reached the last image, Trey shook his head. "Besides the possible skunk sighting, all the camera caught was the grass movement. Unless our guy crawled through the grass, I'd say this camera was a bust."

"Agreed." Gin pulled the second SD card out of the baggie before dropping the one Trey was holding out to her back into it. "Okay. Fingers crossed we have better luck with the camera facing into the trees."

Once again Trey scrolled through the images until they came to a timestamp just a few days before the pharmacy executive disappeared. He slowly continued, moving past the date Stampler had seemingly vanished into thin air.

The trail cam had recorded enough activity that it was another five minutes before they reached three days past the disappearance date. Gin suddenly shot a hand out and grabbed Trey's arm. "Stop. What was that?"

"I saw it," Trey said. He scrolled backwards, freezing the frame when Gin gave his arm another hard squeeze. His eyes narrowed. "It looks like legs in some pants with old-fashioned cuffs on them, and a pair of shoes."

Gin angled her body so she could lean in and get a closer look. "Uh-huh. And not just any shoes. We'll have to get this blown up, but I'm pretty sure those are loafers. And it looks like there's something on them." She straightened up. "Keep going. But slowly. Very slowly."

They watched the pair of legs and shoes move forward five feet or so and then stop. A few frames later, the legs and shoes were still evident, but a faint blur appeared beyond them, hovering just above the ground.

"I think that's the plastic bag I found. He must have thrown it." Gin nodded in satisfaction. "Oh yeah. We'll get all these enlarged. Let's keep going."

At the next few frames, she frowned. "What's happening here? It looks like he's still walking on the trail."

Trey stared intently at the screen, moving between several frames. "He is. But I think he's walking backwards." He straightened up and looked at Gin. "He walked into the trees, threw the bag, and then backed out the way he came. That's what it looks like to me. The thing someone does when he wants to keep an eye on what's in front of him."

She thought that over, seeing the sense in it. "Yeah. Like he's not comfortable where he's at." She met Trey's gaze with a tight smile. "Sounds like a guy who would wear dress slacks and expensive loafers into the woods."

Trey blinked and then nodded. "But not any farther in than he has to. Just far enough to toss the bag where it isn't likely to be found, at least not right away." He cocked his head to the side as his smile faded into a thoughtful look. "That was a good call. Doing that grid search back in the woods when the guy had to have come in from the road. I'm not sure I would have done that."

Curious, Gin faced him and crossed her arms over her chest. "Why not?"

"I would have searched that open space from the access road to the dump site."

"Which the sheriffs on scene were doing when I arrived," Gin pointed out.

"Yeah. I saw them too," Trey said. "But they weren't back in the woods. The body was already found, and like I said, he had to have been brought in from the road. I can't see anyone carrying or dragging that much weight through the woods from who knows where. That, and it's a long way from Miami to here. Lots of places to get rid of the personal effects, and more logical to do that than wait until you get to the dump site."

Gin considered that for a moment. "True. But he also took the guy's clothes off. Which would be more likely to have happened at the dump site since there were no visible signs of torture." When Trey frowned, she shook her head at him. "Which is a reasonable assumption since we saw nothing to suggest that, and I'm sure the ME will verify." She took a step back. "You might want to add walking a grid for at least one hundred feet from the body to your arsenal of investigative tricks. And in all directions, no matter how unlikely it seems. It's come in handy for me on more than one occasion." She lifted an eyebrow when he continued to stare at her. "What?"

"You went back there because you had a feeling about this guy. You called it a hunch," he stated, his expression neutral and his tone blunt. "I was told that about you."

Well, if he could be direct, so could she. "Who told you that?"

"An agent I met at Quantico during my training. He was teaching a course on interrogation techniques as well as profiling, and your name came up."

Not at all what she'd expected to hear. Gin's mouth

dropped open, and she gaped at him as if he was crazy. "*My name came up?* When the Bureau has the top profiler in the country working for it? You know, the guy who was responsible for starting up the Critical Crimes Unit."

"You're talking about Dr. Blake?" Trey's rigid back relaxed. "I haven't had the pleasure of meeting him."

"I wouldn't exactly call it a pleasure," Gin said. "He's more than a little manipulative, so he leaves something to be desired as a human being. But as a profiler? He's brilliant. He's the guy that instructor should have been talking about. Not me."

"Probably." Trey took the SD card out of the laptop and held it out to Gin. "But Special Agent Fionn Sullivan sounded pretty impressed with your ability to dissect the thinking and the movements of a killer. Especially of the serial variety." He paused, a smile tugging at the corners of his mouth. "And that's a direct quote."

Gin plucked the SD card from Trey's outstretched hand and popped it back into the clear-plastic evidence bag. "Finn likes to exaggerate." She waved a dismissive hand but made a mental note to call the irritating and talkative Finn and give him hell for mentioning her in front of an audience. She got enough sideways looks without him dropping fuel on that particular fire.

"Yeah. I picked up on that. But he was an excellent instructor." He shifted his gaze to the road at the sound of a vehicle coming up the road. "Looks like the transport is here to take the body to the ME's autopsy."

She turned around and held her hand up to shade her eyes from the sun. A white ambulance with red lettering on the side was slowly making its way up the access road. She lifted a hand when Captain Moreau waved at her. "Why don't you put the laptop away and let's head over to see what else Moreau has to tell us?" She didn't wait for a response from Trey before heading toward the captain. It didn't take long for Trey to catch up with her, and they approached Moreau together.

"We're going to load the body up," he said without preamble. "It's being sent to the county ME's office in Buffalo. I've already called him, and he said he'd start on the autopsy at nine tomorrow morning. I also let him know to expect the FBI to be there. Now will that be one or both of you?"

"At this point, it will be both of us unless a hot lead crosses our path and we need to split up," Gin said. "I'll give the ME a call and confirm."

"Okay." Moreau reached out and shook Gin's hand. "Then I guess this is goodbye, Special Agent Reilly. I wish you and your team luck in running this asshole to ground. If you ever get tired of the FBI and want to settle down in one place, give me a call." He added a nod before turning to shake Trey's hand as well. "Same goes for you, Agent Robard. Deputy Hurley took the two witnesses back to their truck, and now he's over there waiting to give you both a ride back to the main road."

"Thanks. I appreciate it," Gin said.

"No problem." With a last friendly salute, the captain turned and headed for a group of deputies gathered near the cruisers parked along the edge of the road.

"Nice guy," Gin commented to herself as much as to Trey. "I like him." She pointed to a deputy leaning against the fender of his cruiser. "That's Hurley. I'm just going to have a word with those two local deputies who arrived on scene first, and then we should get going."

Hearing nothing new from the locals, Gin quickly wrapped up her questioning, and twenty minutes later they were watching the taillights of Deputy Hurley's cruiser disappear around a curve in the two-lane highway. Gin pulled her rental car out onto the road and headed northwest, toward Buffalo. From the corner of her eye, she saw Trey shrug out of his

A HARD TRUTH

jacket. He retrieved an evidence bag from one pocket then tossed the coat into the back seat.

He held the bag up to the light coming in through the windshield and slowly rotated it in a complete circle. "Wanted to get a second look at this," he said, lowering the bag before glancing over at Gin. "Just wanted to confirm it's eggs-and-bacon in there."

"Which means what?" Gin asked without taking her eyes off the road.

"The resin-preserved flower." Trey lifted the two-inch wide rectangle up until it was at Gin's eye level. "It's an eggs-and-bacon." He twirled the baggie in a circle. "That's the common name. See the three yellow flowers? Makes it look like a wide bird's foot. Which is why its formal name is birdsfoot trefoil. Basically, three petals that look like a bird's foot."

Gin gave the baggie a sideways glance. "I've seen those before." She frowned as she pictured the small flowering plant hugging the shoulders of a highway. "Alongside roads, mostly."

Trey nodded and lowered the baggie. "Yeah. They're pretty invasive, and can take over the natural vegetation, so aren't used much. But they work pretty well for erosion control, and that kind of thing. Mostly out West and in the Midwest. Not too much back east."

She drummed one finger against the steering wheel. "Is that right? You seem to be really familiar with flowers. Is gardening a hobby of yours?"

"Search and rescue requires a lot of survival training. It pays to know the environment around you, which includes the plant life."

She'd never given it much thought but had to silently admit that he made sense. "So not a popular plant in Florida? Say the Miami area?"

He shrugged. "I'm no expert, but I wouldn't think there's a

lot in Florida. I know there's plenty of it in California, but other than that, I'd have to look it up."

"Hmm." Gin's fingertips rubbed lightly against the steering wheel. Unless there was a fast-food place in Buffalo that gave out hamburger boxes with flowers preserved in resin instead of a burger in them, then whoever dumped Stampler's body also left that token. Which screamed that the killer had a ritual. Which was the mark of a serial killer, and some contract killers as well. Given the specific target, she was still leaning more toward the latter. "So we've got a preserved flower in a box, weighed down by a rock to be sure it's still there whenever the body is discovered. He might have bought it in Florida. Off a shelf at some gift shop on his way to make the kill."

Trey didn't look convinced but nodded anyway. "I guess that's one theory."

But not likely, she thought. It didn't feel right. What did make sense was the killer bringing it with him. Which was weird.

"Weird," she repeated, this time out loud. "Killers usually take souvenirs from their victims, not leave them."

Trey kept his gaze on the passing view. "It sounds like you're talking about a serial killer. Don't they usually take souvenirs, not leave them?"

"Sometimes they take a physical object, but not always." Gin kept her voice just as neutral as his. "It's even rarer for them to leave something behind. Although I read about a case where the guy used to leave behind a beer can."

Trey let out a disbelieving snort. "A beer can? You're kidding."

"Nope. He was in Mumbai," Gin said absently, still silently turning the weirdly named flower over in her mind. "But leaving a token is unique enough that it makes me think the preserved flower means something to this killer, or his reason to kill someone in particular. Which would mean that Stampler wasn't a random victim of convenience, like a serial killer would pick out, but a targeted one."

Trey turned his head, staring at her for a moment before slowly nodding. "So that flower might be some kind of message? Like the stories about the old-time mafia leaving a fish wrapped in paper?"

Gin responded with a nod of her own. The fish in newspaper thing was as good an analogy as any. That was also done with the intention of being deliberately found, with a specific meaning attached to it. The box was weighed down with a rock, so it was meant to be found. With a message about the victim. "Leaving Stampler naked was a way of humiliating him, which could apply to any victim stripped down like that. But the flower most likely means something specific about Stampler."

Which was what? Gin's eyebrows drew together in concentration. "Can you get out your phone and look up this birdsfoot trefoil? See if it has any particular meaning or symbolism attached to it?"

Trey set the baggie on the dashboard and took his phone out of his shirt pocket. Silence descended as Gin drove on toward Buffalo and Trey tapped commands into his phone. It wasn't long before he let out a long, low whistle. "Well, look at that." His mouth pressed into a thin line. "The common meaning for a birdsfoot trefoil is revenge. Now, isn't that interesting?"

"Revenge," Gin echoed. "A message that was preplanned. Which means that flower wasn't picked up on the way here, or somewhere in the vicinity where Stampler disappeared. Unless we find out it grows all over Florida, there would have been too much of a chance that the killer wouldn't find exactly what he was looking for."

"Then he brought it with him," Trey said.

"Yeah." Gin's eyes narrowed in thought. "A specific message for a specific target. Now I'm wondering if our guy hasn't played out this drama before." She sent Trey a quick glance. "Can you make a call for me?" When he nodded, she rattled off a number. "If Stephen doesn't pick up, you can call him on my phone so he'll recognize the number."

Trey nodded, then put the phone on speaker. The ringing on the other end came through loud and clear and was quickly answered.

"Special Agent Stephen Jones, and if you're a telemarketer, I might have you arrested."

Trey grinned. "I didn't know we could do that. I'm Special Agent Treynor Robard."

"Hey." Stephen's voice was cheerful as he cut Trey off. "You saved me a call. I was going to tag you and tell you welcome to the team."

Gin's expression turned sour as she silently stared out the windshield. It seemed everyone had known about Robard coming on board except her.

"Thanks. I appreciate that," Trey replied smoothly. "I'm on my way to Buffalo with Special Agent Reilly, and…" He paused when Stephen cut him off again.

"Now I wasn't expecting that. How are you two getting along?"

"Just fine, thanks," Gin spoke up. "Why wouldn't we?" She had to grit her teeth when her long-time partner laughed.

"Oh, I can think of half a dozen reasons," Stephen said easily. "But I'm going to let Robard figure that out for himself. So what can I do for you? Or for Treynor?"

Gin gave an inward sigh. No doubt Stephen would call her later to get the whole lowdown on their new teammate. Not that she really knew much about the guy, other than what Ricki had told her along with the usual watercooler gossip that had traveled up and down the agency's grapevine about the former naval aviator. "We need you to do a quick search for us on like crimes."

"Okay. I heard Stampler had been found and you got the call out. Your bad luck you were in the area at the time. Did anything else weird happen, like maybe out at your grandparents' house? I know you weren't looking forward to going there."

"No," Gin said. "The only weird thing happened was between my grandparents' house and Buffalo. Benjamin Stampler's body was found by a couple of utility workers, and like you said, I got the call out and Trey happened to be in visiting his brother in Buffalo at the time, so he got stuck too."

"Oh. It's Trey now, is it?"

She found herself gritting her teeth again at the amusement in Stephen's voice. "Yeah. It's Trey. Because that's what he wants to be called. Now about that like crime?" Rustling noise came through the speaker. She waited until Stephen said a quick, "go ahead."

"We're looking for any crime where the body was sprayed with some kind of solution containing peppermint oil. You can add in if the body was naked and covered in trash, along with something preserved in resin being left at the dump site. It doesn't matter if the dump and kill site are the same or different."

"Sounds weird enough," Stephen said. "What was preserved in resin?"

"A flower," Gin said. "In this case, a birdsfoot trefoil. But that exact flower isn't as important as some kind of flower, or plant, or bug. Just something encased in resin."

"That's still pretty specific," Stephen observed. "I'll put it all through NIBRS," he said, referring to the FBI's national database for reported crimes. "I'll ask for victims with at least two of those points."

The widely used database not only listed crimes, but detailed anything that made them stand out — like a peppermint solution or an odd souvenir left at the scene. It was a powerful tool to link similar crimes, and Gin was sure they were going to need it. Hopefully, Stephen would find something to help them out.

"I'll get on it first thing tomorrow."

Gin's eyebrows shot up. "Hello? High-profile case, here. We need you to get on it tonight."

A loud snort echoed from the phone. "Come on, Gin. I have a wife who's trying to get our new house set up and is threatening to divorce me if I don't start showing up at a reasonable hour to help her out. You remember Callie? She's your cousin. The two of you grew up together."

Gin glanced at her watch. It was close to 5:00 pm. He would have had a good argument for getting off at a reasonable hour if he was in the car with her. But his butt was in Colorado, which was two full hours behind New York. Unless the universe had suddenly done a massive shift and the two states were now in the same time zone. "Okay. Then a compromise. Just do the search for two hours, and then go home."

When he started to complain, she ran the edge of one hand across her throat, indicating to Trey to cut off the call. "Thanks," she said with a nod. "He should be able to dig up something in a couple of hours."

Trey settled back into his seat. "Then you think there's something to dig up?"

"Yeah." Whatever else this was, Benjamin Stampler's murder was not a one-off thing, and his killer was no amateur. He'd done this before. She'd bet her badge on it.

Chapter Seven

Gin pushed open the door to her hotel room, then shoved it closed with the heel of her tennis shoe. She slid her backpack off her shoulder and set it slowly down on the bed. The three journals were in it. Protected inside two pillow cases, they took up most of the space. Everything else, including her laptop, was crammed into her small suitcase. She'd have to figure out how to fit it into her backpack along with the journals, but that was a task for tomorrow.

She lifted her carry-on suitcase onto the small ledge built into the wall and considered the immediate chores of settling into yet another hotel room as done. Taking the three steps back to the bed, she sat down and gave the room a quick once over as she toed off her shoes.

It was on the second of three floors and looked exactly like dozens of other hotel rooms she'd stayed in. The only thing identifying its location was a colored pencil drawing hanging on the wall. It was a decent enough rendition of Niagara Falls with the caption "Buffalo, N.Y." sketched across the bottom.

Since the room didn't require any more notice than that, she stripped off her jacket, retrieving her cell phone from the pocket before tossing the lightweight garment across the end of the bed. Swinging her legs up to rest on the coverlet, she wiggled backwards until she was comfortably propped up against two of the four pillows.

It had been a long day, and a trying one. She was entitled to be tired and more than a little grumpy. And it certainly didn't help her mood any when her stomach emitted a loud growl. *Okay, great. Add hungry to the mix.*

She'd noticed a small grab-and-go area next to the lobby desk, and as tired as she was, that was going to have to suffice for dinner. Besides, the newest team member had asked for the car keys, presumably to go see his brother, so she had transportation to go out in search of food anyway. Which was fine with her. She didn't want to run around town looking for something to eat. It wouldn't be the first time she'd made a meal of a bag of chips and a packet of cookies. She'd survive.

But even that pitiful meal would have to wait until she'd checked in with her boss. Lifting the phone she still held in one hand, she scrolled through her contacts, stopping at the senior agent's name. She tapped on the mobile phone number, waiting for the call to connect as she glanced at her watch. It was getting late, even with the two-hour time difference between New York and Colorado, it was now well past their normal office hours. But she knew Moore would answer his phone no matter what time it was. It went with the territory. But given the late hour, it wasn't going to do much to lighten his mood.

He picked up on the first ring — a bad sign that he'd been sitting around, waiting for her call. "Hey, Reilly. I've been waiting to hear from you." His brusque tone told her she'd been right. He didn't sound the least bit cheerful.

"I just got into the hotel room." She closed her eyes and

quickly organized her thoughts. A habit she'd had for as long as she could remember. Her eyes stayed firmly shut as she delivered her report, keeping it direct and efficient while the senior agent listened without saying a word. "If the forensic team finds Stampler's personal effects in that plastic bag we uncovered in the woods, then the trail cam caught the killer tossing it away," she said before finally taking a breath.

"With our only working description being a guy who possibly wears fancy loafers and pants with cuffs." Moore sounded both annoyed and amused. "That's going to look great on a most-wanted poster. So you figure this guy didn't want the body found right away, but when it was found, it had to be recognizable? And that's what the peppermint oil was for?"

Gin opened her eyes and let out a long sigh. "Yeah. And covering the body in trash made a pretty obvious statement."

"Someone sure didn't like Stampler much," Moore said with a grunt, unknowingly echoing Trey's same opinion at the crime scene. "Are you going to check with the county ME after the autopsy is complete?"

"Right before we head over to the forensics lab at the Bureau office in Buffalo," she confirmed. "Then we'll need to get the case file from the Miami PD. I thought I'd pass that over to Stephen. I already have him looking for like cases."

"Good. We need to know if this crazy has killed anyone else. And don't bother Agent Jones about the Miami case file, I've already got you covered on that. I contacted the local PD today and picked my way through a very painful talk with the assistant chief who heads up their criminal investigations. He's not a fan of the FBI and wasn't too keen on sending his file to us. But after some persuasion, which included me pointing out that his case had gone stone cold and we not only had the body but also some evidence we'd be happy to share, he reluctantly agreed to let us come down there and look it over. He sounded a little surprised when I took him up on that without any protest. But the upshot is that it's all arranged for two days from now. I have you and the rest of the team on a five p.m. plane out of Buffalo tomorrow, so you can make that eight a.m. appointment with Assistant Chief Alvarez the following morning. Once you're done there, an agent from our local office in Miami has arranged for you to meet with Stampler's widow in the afternoon. From there?" He left the question hanging just enough that she could imagine him scrunching his face up in exasperation during the short pause. "You'll have to hope something turns up so you'll know where to sniff around next. Stampler's company is a big donor to the campaigns of several very powerful people in Washington D.C., so our boss wants this one solved. And in a time frame a lot less than I'd like."

"Politics. That's really wonderful," Gin said, her tone bone-dry, even as her eyes narrowed in thought. "We'll have to see what the Miami PD came up with in their investigation before the case went cold. From the writeup that you sent over, the last place Stampler was seen was on his yacht. I'd like to take a look at that."

"Agent Robard should come in pretty handy then, since he spent a dozen years in the navy," Moore said.

"In a helicopter," Gin pointed out. "He might not know anything about boats."

"He couldn't know less than you do," Moore countered, then lightly cleared his throat. "How are you two getting along?"

"Jury's still out."

"Well, he can't be any worse than the last two. Neither of them made it over eight weeks, and you had a lot to do with that, Reilly."

Since he couldn't see her, she silently made a face. "It wasn't my fault that they didn't like all the travel."

A HARD TRUTH

Moore laughed. "Uh huh. I think you having a serial killer for a father made them nervous. Which tagged them as spineless morons in my book, and not suitable candidates for the CCU. I don't think you'll have that problem with Robard. Or with Hedron."

Gin went still. She already had one new team member to deal with, so hoped whoever this Hedron was, she wouldn't have to put up with him too. "Hedron? Who is he?"

"She," Moore corrected. "Americk Hedron. Dr. Americk Hedron to be precise, although she rarely uses the title. She's a lead tech, and I've worked with her on a couple of cases before the CCU was formed."

"A lead tech?" Gin's eyebrows drew together. "I've never heard of that."

"It's a real thing and only one person has that job," Moore stated. "And that would be Americk Hedron, since the title was made up just for her. She didn't want to be a supervisor, insisting it was too much paperwork and not enough field work. So to keep her happy, the powers that be in the Bureau came up with Lead Forensic Technician, which floats somewhere over any other title in forensics that doesn't have the word 'director' in it." He indulged in a soft chuckle. "The woman's a genius at forensics. Blake recruited her into the Critical Crimes Unit, and she'll be at the Buffalo office tomorrow to look over what they've got."

"Here? Tomorrow?" Now wasn't that just great? Gin squeezed her eyes shut and rubbed two fingers across the center of her forehead. The last name hadn't rung a bell with her, but the unusual first name had. Moore had hit that nail squarely on the head when he'd called her a genius. Americk was known all over the Bureau for her forensic skill.

"And I suppose you're going to tell me she's also coming to Miami with us?"

"There's forensic evidence there too," Moore was quick to point out. "You'll like her. If you don't, you can have her and Robard sit together on the plane while you hide out in the bathroom. I'll send you the flight and hotel details," he added without missing a beat. "A word to the wise. Don't call her Dr. Hedron. She hates that. And you make sure to call after you've made the rounds and done the interviews in Miami. And try to make it at a more decent hour," he tossed out just before he ended the call.

"Ha ha," Gin said into the dead phone.

Shaking her head, she leaned over and set the cell on the nightstand, then rolled onto her back. When she shifted her weight on the bed, one knee bumped against her backpack. Right on the large pocket where she'd stowed the journals. Reaching over, she pulled the pack closer, then laid a hand on the zipper. Her eyes narrowed as she considered digging one of them out and taking a closer look.

But her hand stayed where it was.

Even with her eyes wide open, she could still see that first page, filled with *his* handwriting. She'd seen it every day from the time she was five years old until the sheriffs had come and unceremoniously marched him off to jail.

Every day when the noon bell rang at school and she'd opened her lunch box, there was always a note inside lying on top of her peanut butter and jelly sandwich. *Wisdom only comes with age, so be good and mind your elders today.* But more often it was his favorite— a twist on one of the ten commandments: *Honor thy father or you will be sent to hell.*

As she'd grown older she'd stopped reading them, but had never thrown them away. He'd told her not to, and she knew he'd check, so she'd always opened them, crinkled them up a little, then refolded them and left them in her lunch box.

Since her older brother was given money to buy food in the

school cafeteria, he never had to carry a small metal box with brightly colored, smiling animals on the outside and that note always waiting inside. Of course she'd never even mentioned the notes to Devin. She hadn't wanted him to worry, or worse yet, intervene with their father. Even though he was four years her senior, she'd always felt protective of her brother.

Maybe that was because their mother hadn't bothered with that kind of thing, and never had.

Even though she'd never seen her father lay a hand on Devin, usually her brother had gone out of his way to avoid him. And although Devin never said it out loud, she instinctively knew that he was afraid of their father. But then, she had been too.

And still was.

The same could have been said of her mother, except she had seemed to thrive on that fear. Even welcomed it from what Gin saw. And despite what her grandmother thought, Kathleen Dillon had been lost the minute she'd set eyes on the man she would end up marrying, and whose absence had left a huge void that eventually drove her to take her own life.

Gine finally lifted her hand off the backpack and rested it in her lap. She didn't know what secrets Byron Reilly had hidden in that journal, or who else had written in it, or if she'd ever be ready to find out the answer to either of those questions. But it wasn't going to be tonight. She had more immediate problems to think about. Like food.

I should just burn the things and be done with it, she thought as she retrieved her cell phone. Firmly putting the journals out of her mind, she scrolled through her text messages, checking for anything urgent before she headed to the lobby to pick up some chips and cookies.

A loud knock on her door had her lifting her head. She considered ignoring it but hadn't even finished the thought before she swung her legs over the side of the bed and planted her feet on the floor. Pushing herself up, she headed down the short hallway, taking a quick look through the peephole before opening the door.

Trey stood on the other side, holding two large brown bags, one in each hand. When he held them up, the smell of fried food almost had her drooling, and when she recognized the logo on the side of the bag, she broke out into a huge smile. "You've been busy, and in a practical way, too. I like that."

"All part of the breaking-in period. And I'm starving, so I figured you had to be too." When she stepped back, he walked past her and into the main bedroom while she closed and secured the door. He set one of the bags down next to the TV and pointed at it. "That's yours. A burger, large order of fries, and a big cup of ice. I didn't know what you wanted to drink, so I thought water would be fine."

"It is," Gin said. "And I appreciate the thought." She dug out the food and cup, then held up the empty bag. "Isn't this the same logo that was on some of the trash our vic was buried in?"

"Yep. I thought if I had to go out and get us some food, I might as well kill two birds with one stone."

Feeling that twinge of guilt again at barely being civil to the guy, Gin glanced his way as she held up a french fry. "I know you're a full member of the team and not my personal assistant, but I'm not going to apologize for having you go through a breaking-in period. In this unit, you're still the rookie."

He smiled. "And I know you have seniority, and I'm the new guy, so I don't have a problem with taking the jump seat for this op."

Gin took a healthy bite of the fry as she studied him for a long moment. "I think you're better than a trainee pilot, but I'll

A HARD TRUTH

go along with the rest of it if you promise not to use a military reference for everything."

"No promises there," Trey said.

When her phone pinged, she walked over to where she'd left it on the bed, picking it up before gesturing for Trey to sit down on the edge of the mattress. "Go ahead and sit. The only chair in here is that plastic one at the desk, and I sure wouldn't want to spend any time in it." She nodded at his thanks and pulled up the new text.

"What's up?" Trey asked.

When she saw the concern in his gaze, she pressed her lips together into a straight line, effectively erasing her frown. "I'm not sure. Stephen says I'm going to get a call from the five-three-zero area code, and I need to take it." She glanced back down at her phone. "And he says we both need to look at our email, and that he'll check in with us in the morning, but right now he's on his way home." The text ended with a "good night", which was their secret code meaning, "don't call me unless it's a life-or-death matter."

"Okay. I can take a look." Trey held up his phone and then lowered it again when Gin shook her head. "No? I shouldn't take a look?"

"If it were urgent, he'd have called one of us," Gin said. "Let's eat first and check emails later. Then I have to call Moore back and give him an update."

Trey picked up his hamburger. "I can get behind eating." He took a big bite, silently chewing as he carried his cup of ice to the bathroom and filled it with water.

Gin followed right behind him, downing most of the water and filling her cup again before returning to the bedroom. She was halfway through her meal when her cell phone rang. Leaning over it, she saw the caller ID flash a number she didn't recognize, but she knew the area code. Five-three-zero, as promised. Setting her burger down on its empty wrapper, she picked up her phone and hit the connect icon.

"This is Special Agent Reilly."

"Agent Reilly? I'm Sheriff Daniel Prin with the Siskiyou County Sheriff's Department in Northern California. I got your name and number from one of your fellow FBI agents in the Bureau's office out of Denver." There was a brief pause and the sound of papers being shuffled. "A Special Agent Stephen Jones with the Critical Crimes Unit?"

"He's my partner." Gin cast a quick glance over at Trey. "One of them. What can I do for you, Sheriff Prin?"

"Some months back, going on seven to be more exact, we input data into the NIBR's system on a murder victim found in my county. I also had my deputy put in a note that if anyone found a like crime to give me a call. Today I got that call from Agent Jones."

Gin sucked in a quick breath. "Sheriff Prin, I'm going to put you on speaker. Special Agent Robard is also in the room, and I'd like him to be in on this conversation." At the sheriff's "that's fine," Gin switched on the phone's speaker. "Thank you. Can you hear me all right?"

"Loud and clear," Prin said. "Now, I'd like to know something about the case you're working on. That Jones fellow was a little light on the details."

"It needs to stay confidential for the moment, because of the victim's identity," Gin stated.

"No problem. Shoot."

"The vic is Benjamin Stampler." She waited out the low whistle from Prin. "His body was found near a remote utility pylon in upstate New York," Gin supplied. "He was naked and covered in trash. Cause of death is pending verification from the medical examiner in Buffalo, but on scene it appeared that his throat was slit. No other visible injuries."

A HARD TRUTH

When she deliberately paused, the sheriff spoke out. "We've got the same MO. A remote location, slit throat, and a naked body covered in trash. But our vic here doesn't have the name recognition that yours does. I can see why you need to keep this one under your hat for as long as you can."

"Which won't be long," Gin stated flatly. "Two utility workers found the body, and half the Erie County Sheriff's Department was on scene, as well as the fish and game manager for the local reserve. I'm betting it will hit the papers tomorrow morning at the latest."

A chuckle echoed through the speaker. "I wouldn't touch that bet with a ten-foot pole. Anything else?"

"There was also a flower preserved in a block of resin that was found on top of the trash."

"Yeah." Prin's voice dropped several notches. "That would be it. Found the same thing here. How about the peppermint? Our forensic guy swears he found traces of some kind of peppermint oil on an old baseball cap that was buried in the trash pile. He thinks it picked up the peppermint from the body, since it was lying right on top of it."

"Stampler had the same smell. Where exactly was your body found?"

"Down in the southern part of the county, about forty-five minutes south of my office in Yreka. We're up on the northern border, and the county is mostly forest which includes the area surrounding Mt. Shasta. There isn't much else around the spot where the body was found. Just an unpaved access road that's mostly used by hunters, although it's a popular way into the forest for the residents of the county that know about it. That's who found the body, a couple of guys out hunting. They went up that access road and parked their truck near an open field. When they headed for the tree line, they spotted the dead guy behind a heavy row of bushes at the far edge of the field."

Gin's grip on her cell phone tightened, turning her knuckles white as she exchanged a heavy glance with Trey. "Yeah. That's almost a word-for-word account of what happened here. Body behind a row of bushes, on the edge of a forest. How long before your vic was found?"

"ME estimated it at somewhere between eight and nine weeks. It was fairly intact, all things considered. Usually the scavengers get to them before we do."

"That's what the peppermint oil was for," Gin said. "To keep the damage from scavengers at a minimum. They don't like the smell or the taste."

A sigh came through the phone. "Yeah. That's what the forensic guy said. Did your guy have an ID on him?"

"No. Not on him. But we found a plastic bag in the woods behind the dump site. The Buffalo forensic team has it, and I'm pretty sure his ID and personal effects are in that bag." She went on to explain about the trail cam and the images it caught, eliciting another low whistle from the sheriff.

"Now that's almost a piece of luck. I say almost because I don't know what a picture of the perp's legs is going to do for you. Too bad nothing else was caught on it."

Gin didn't bother to disagree with him. "Who was your victim, Sheriff Prin?"

"We didn't find any ID on him, so it took us almost a month to figure out he was a forty-eight-year-old male named Miguel Rivera. Lived in the Fremont area, which is over four hours from where the body was found, and six hours from where the guy was supposed to be working. No wife or kids, but he had a lot of relatives around Fremont. His sister is the one who reported him missing. Gave a detailed description, including the fact he was minus a finger on his right hand. So was our dead guy."

Wondering what the connection was between their two

victims, Gin took a quick stab in the dark. "I don't suppose Mr. Rivera had anything to do with the pharmacy business?"

"Nope. According to his family and his employer, he was a highly skilled electrician who traveled to job sites for Ralfin Construction. That's a fairly big outfit in Northern California. He was one of their master electricians. The manager I talked to from Ralfin was almost as upset as Rivera's family when he called to find out what had happened to him. Insisted Rivera didn't have an enemy in the world. That he just wasn't that kind of guy. Rivera's family said the same thing."

Gin absorbed that for a moment. She'd be surprised if she heard that about Stampler. No one got to his position in the executive suite without seriously stepping on some toes along the way. "Was Mr. Rivera killed where he was found?"

Prin made a negative sound deep in his throat before answering. "Nope. His throat was cut and not nearly enough blood where the body was found to account for that. We figured this county was the dump site but he wasn't murdered here. Never did find the kill site, which is why it remains an open homicide." A chair squeaked, as if Prin had leaned back in it. "Did you find where Stampler was killed? As I recall, they didn't find any evidence of a murder on that big yacht of his. At least nothing they let out to the public."

"No idea," Gin replied. "But just like your vic, he wasn't killed where the body was dumped."

The sheriff snorted. "And because it was obvious the killer came across state lines, I'll bet those Erie County guys didn't have any problem tossing the case over to the Bureau. And believe me, Agent Reilly, if my lead detective on this case agrees that that these are solid links between the two homicides, I'm going to be happy to pick up the phone and have my case punted over to you too."

"I'll keep that in mind," Gin said in a dry tone. "Would you be agreeable to sending me a copy of your case file, with all the notes of any interviews and contact information? I'd appreciate it."

"No problem. We have a digital copy of it and I'll have one of my guys shoot it over to you. Anything else I can do to get this one off my open case list?"

Gin looked at Trey and made a face that had his mouth curving upward at the corners. "Just one last question, and then I'll give you my email to sent that digital copy of your case file to. What kind of flower was encased in that piece of resin you found on top of the trash pile?"

"What flower was it? Hang on a minute." The speaker went dead except for the soft click of a computer mouse. After several moments, Prin's voice came through again. "Report here says it was a red petunia. The tech noted that you won't see any of those growing wild around here, but I doubt if they're hard to come by. Petunia's are easy to find in just about any garden. Why? Did the resin block you found also have a petunia inside it?"

"No. Not a petunia. Did you run across any other cases similar to these two?" When the sheriff answered in the negative, Gin held back a sigh. There were going to be others, so now it was a question of whether none of them were entered into NIBRS so Prin didn't know about them, or if they didn't have enough details for the sheriff to have picked up on them. "Okay," she said, just before rattling off her email address. "Thanks for the info, Sheriff. I appreciate you taking the time to reach out to us."

"No problem." The sheriff's voice took on a hearty, bordering-on-jovial, tone. "You'll keep me apprised of any solid connection between these two cases?"

"Yes, sir. I will." Gin took that as a good time to end the conversation, so she said a quick goodbye and tapped the disconnect button before slowly setting the cell phone back on the nightstand. "I just know he's going to call Senior Agent Moore in the morning and make a pitch for us to take on his case."

"And I'd say you're right." Trey turned the phone in his hand around. "Looked up petunia. It has several meanings, but the one that jumped out at me is resentment and anger, with a dose of trouble."

Gin leaned in closer and squinted at the screen. "Yeah. That would fit." She straightened out again and picked up her burger. It was stone cold, but she was hungry enough not to care. She took a big bite and slowly chewed as she thought over the conversation with Prin.

"What do you think?" Trey asked.

She swallowed her food, then picked up her glass of water and took a long drink. Setting it down again, she nodded. "Oh, yeah. Stampler and Rivera were murdered by the same guy, and he definitely has a pattern. Maybe Stephen has found others that Prin missed, but the big question now is how many more bodies are there, and what's the connection between them?"

Her phone dinged with a new email. She took a quick look, then rolled her eyes. "Just got an email from a deputy in the Siskiyou County Sheriff's Department. With a file attached. Prin doesn't waste much time."

Trey stood and stuffed his empty wrappers into the paper bag. "Well, if you forward it to me, I'll take a look at it tonight as part of those rookie duties." He switched his gaze to Gin as he held up the bag with the familiar logo printed on it. "I took a quick walk up and down the street where this place is located and saw plenty of dumpsters, but no cameras. Our guy picked a good spot to boost a bunch of trash."

Gin shrugged. "It was a long shot." She felt the headache

forming at the base of her neck, undoubtedly brought on by lack of sleep. She stared at the half-eaten hamburger she had lost interest in finishing. *And not enough food.*

"I'm going to let you finish that up in peace," Trey said. "Meet you in the lobby at eight? We can grab some breakfast and then head over to the ME's office."

"And I'm guessing you know where that is?" Gin asked.

"Yep." He turned and headed for the door, calling back over his shoulder. "I'll see you at eight."

Chapter Eight

Gin was stifling a yawn when she walked into the lobby at exactly eight o'clock the next morning. The backpack she was determined to keep close at all times was slung over one shoulder and she dragged her small suitcase behind her. Just as she had expected he would be, Trey was already standing at the front counter, talking to the clerk. From his relaxed body stance, it was obvious nothing serious was being discussed, but she hoped it was entertaining enough to keep him distracted while she scared up a cup of coffee.

A fast glance around the lobby didn't reveal a complimentary pot of the brew anywhere, though. Thinking she was out of luck until they found a place for a quick breakfast, she headed toward the reception desk to drop off her room key.

That was when she spotted the pair of to-go cups with steam rolling off their tops. "Tell me that's coffee."

Trey grinned and slid one over to her. "Yeah." He inclined his head toward the young girl standing behind the counter. "Mandy here was kind enough to share from the pot she has going in the back room."

Gin smiled at the young woman with the long brown hair and bangs that hung down her forehead and covered half her eyes. "Thanks. I appreciate this very much."

"No problem. It's been great to have Special Agent Robard stay with us." Completely oblivious to the subtle insult to Gin, who was standing right in front of her, Mandy's gaze was all innocence and admiration when she stared star-struck back at Trey. "I'll bet you looked great in your uniform."

Despite herself, Gin laughed. "They all look great in their uniforms. But Special Agent Robard? I think he got a medal for that." She returned the annoyed glance from Trey with a blank look that became smug when she was saved by the ringing of her cell phone.

Digging it out of the back pocket of her jeans, she stepped away from the desk and held it to her ear. "Special Agent Reilly."

"Reilly? I'm Doug Kent, one of the agents assigned to the Buffalo office."

"My partner and I will be at your office later this morning, Agent Kent," Gin said. "Is there something I can do for you now?" She listened for a minute, then ended the conversation with an "Okay. We'll head right out." She tucked her phone away and walked back to the desk. "We need to get going," she said to Trey before shooting the young clerk a relaxed smile. "It was nice to meet you, Mandy." She held up the to-go cup. "Thanks for the coffee."

"No problem," Mandy chirped in a cheery voice. "Come back and stay with us anytime," she called after the retreating Trey and Gin.

Biting back a grin, Gin nudged Trey with her elbow. "I think she was talking to you."

"Funny," he muttered.

When he stomped out the door, she grinned at his stiff

back. It seemed the even-keeled former rescue pilot had a temper after all. Good to know she wasn't working the case with a saint.

Still grinning, she opened the back door and gently set the backpack onto the rear seat since it now held her laptop as well as the journals, then slid in behind the wheel before giving her stone-faced partner a sideways glance. "Change of plans this morning. That call was from Special Agent Kent in the Buffalo office."

"Doug, yeah, I've met him." When Gin turned her head and lifted an eyebrow, Trey shrugged. "When I got here, I stopped by the office and introduced myself before heading over to my brother's place."

Of course you did, Gin thought, but she turned her attention back to getting them on the road. "Can you get us there without the GPS?"

Trey folded his arms over his chest and settled back against his seat. "Sure. Go out the front driveway and take a right."

Except for a few terse directions given periodically by Trey, the ride to the FBI office was made in silence. When they pulled up to the front of the building, Gin left the engine running and turned halfway in her seat to face Trey. "Look, I'm sorry. I didn't know you were that sensitive about being teased in front of young desk clerks."

"I'm not sensitive," he snapped, then at Gin's smile he blew out a breath and shrugged. "Not usually. But I've had some bad experiences with women who put too much glamor on the uniform without realizing service in the military isn't all admiring shiny medals and being able to show someone off to your girlfriends. There's a lot of sacrifice that goes into it, and not just from those who serve, but from their families and friends, too."

Gin nodded. "Nicely put. So. What you're trying to say is

that you don't want to deal with any crushes, or jump-your-bones kind of offers?"

He barked out a laugh. "Now that's putting it right out there, but basically, that about says it all. It can get old, and I don't want to hurt someone's feelings." He tilted his head to the side and smiled. "And that's the right order too. No dealing with schoolgirl crushes, or unwanted bedroom offers. The older I get, the faster that gets older too. I prefer to make my own offers."

Now Gin laughed as she turned off the engine and reached over the seat to retrieve her backpack. "Okay. Boundary line about giving you a hard time in front of non-team members of the female variety is dutifully acknowledged. Now let's go meet this forensic tech that your buddy Doug said is waiting for us."

Trey quickly grabbed his pack and exited the car, slamming the door shut before hurrying to catch up with her. "What tech?"

"One Americk Hedron, according to what Moore told me last night," Gin said without breaking her stride. "A genius with forensics, who is a doctor but doesn't like to be called one, and is the only Lead Technician in the entire Bureau according to Moore. Oh, and let's not forget that none other than Dr. Blake himself picked her out for us."

"We get our own forensics tech?" Surprise ran through Trey's voice.

Gin shook her head. "Not us, if you mean Team Two in the unit. My understanding is that she's assigned to the whole CCU and will step in with whatever team needs help." She stopped at the double doors before pushing one open. Heading to a small desk manned by a single clerk, she reached into her jacket pocket and pulled out her credentials while Trey did the same. "I'm Special Agent Gin Reilly, and this is Special Agent

A HARD TRUTH

Trey Robard. We're with the Critical Crimes Unit and are here to see Agent Kent."

The clerk gave Gin's credentials a cursory look before nodding at Trey. "Good to see you again, Trey. How's the visit with your brother going?"

"Fine, until it got interrupted, Stan," Trey said, obviously already on a first-name basis with the man.

"I hear that." Stan switched his gaze to Gin. "I also heard that you're on the Benjamin Stampler case with a scary good agent from that new unit you hooked up with." He glanced away from Trey to smile at Gin. "Which I'm assuming is you, Agent Reilly. Word is that his body was found between here and Rochester, near one of the big power lines."

Ignoring the 'scary good agent comment, Gin frowned. "Where did you hear that?"

"Got around the office. But it was also on the late news last night." Stan looked down and studied the clipboard in front of him. "Agent Kent is expecting you. I'll give him a call and let him know you're out here waiting."

Gin audibly sighed. Apparently she'd been overly optimistic when she'd told the Siskiyou County Sheriff out in California that they'd be lucky to keep the discovery of Stampler's body under wraps until this morning. Turning away from Stan as he made his call, she slowly walked to the far side of the lobby, studying the spacious area boasting tiled floors and stone walls. Barely a minute had passed when she heard her name called out by a familiar voice.

Tony's Brooklyn accent bounced against the walls as he strode across the lobby. His thick lips split into a wide smile as he tried without much success to push Trey along in front of himself like a bulldozer shoving rocks.

Seeing the look on Trey's face, Gin calculated she had about three seconds to close the distance between them before her new partner turned around and clocked the forensics supervisor. Breaking into a sprint, she just made it, grabbing onto Tony's arm and pulling it away from Trey as she skidded by the duo.

"Whoa, whoa," Tony yelped as the unexpected grab spun him around in a circle. "I don't bend that way." He snatched his arm away from Gin and glared at her. "What are you doing?"

Gin planted her feet apart and her hands on her hips. "Keeping you from being arrested for assaulting a federal officer. Why were you shoving Agent Robard around?"

"What?" Tony blinked, then slowly swung his gaze over to Trey. His mouth turned up at the corners in a sheepish grin. "Hey, man. I'm sorry. I shouldn't have done that. Didn't even realize I was doing it."

Since that much was obvious, Gin shook her head. "Which brings me back to my question. Why were you shoving Agent Robard?"

The heavyset supervisor shuffled his feet for a moment before finally breaking out into a wide grin. He lifted a hand to slap Trey on the shoulder, but at the narrow-eyed look from the agent, prudently dropped his arm back to his side. "I wanted to thank both of you, and especially you, Agent Robard." He settled for giving Trey an enthusiastic nod.

"Next time, try a handshake," Trey said. "And whatever I did, you're welcome."

Relieved there wasn't any heat in his voice, Gin frowned at the still-grinning Tony. "Same here. You're welcome. Now what exactly did Robard do that you're so thrilled about?"

Tony's eyes widened as he stared back at Gin. "He sent her here. I mean, she's a legend in forensic science. Maybe even more than that Dr. Garrison out in the Northwest somewhere. But that's no surprise since she's been at it longer than Garrison, and it's not quite apples to apples there. She isn't a medical doctor like Garrison. Just a pure forensic tech who happened to get a doctorate. Which makes her one of us, and the best there is."

"I'm guessing this walking legend you're talking about is Americk Hedron?" Gin said, interrupting Tony's glowing account when he finally took a breath.

"Who else?" Tony demanded. "I know you've heard all about her. Her forensic findings and reports are gospel within the Bureau."

"Of course I've heard of her." Acutely aware of Trey's silence, Gin jerked her head toward the lobby desk. "Tony, would you mind keeping Stan company for a few minutes? I need a brief consult with Agent Robard, and then we can go in and meet Americk, the legend." When Tony walked off, she turned to face Trey. "Are you still pissed off at Tony? Because we don't have time to patch up any personal grievances." She paused to look him straight in the eyes. "Not now, and not on any case. And since he's still processing our evidence, at least as far as I know, we need to keep on his good side."

Trey shook his head. "No. I'm good with Tony. But this is only the second time I've ever heard of this Americk Hedron, and the first was from you just before we walked into this building. If Hedron is such a heavy hitter in the forensic world, why did her unit back in Quantico agree to keep the evidence here in Buffalo instead of sending it back to them?"

Gin pursed her lips, since she was sure that decision was not made by Americk's forensic unit back at Quantico. "Since she'd probably already switched over to the CCU, I'm betting Blake made that call, so you'd have to ask him. Personally, I've given up trying to figure him out. Maybe Americk has, and will be willing to share." She glanced over at Tony, who looked comfortable leaning against the lobby desk as he talked to Stan. "Another thing. We're headed for Miami at five this afternoon.

We have a meet tomorrow morning with the Miami PD to take a look at their case file in person, since they weren't inclined to send it. And Americk will be traveling with us."

"I thought Miami was where we'd be headed next, only without the extra person. Anything else on our itinerary?"

"Yep," Gin said. "The local Miami office is setting up an interview tomorrow afternoon with the victim's widow. And I'm thinking we need to take a close look at that yacht as well. Where we go from there will depend on what we find in Miami." Gin paused when her name echoed across the open lobby.

"Agent Reilly." Tony called out again as he steadily closed the distance between them.

Jogging along next to him was a short, solidly built woman, comfortably into her fifties. Hair the color of aged wood was piled in a messy bun on top of her head, and her long pure white lab coat reached well below her knees. It was unbuttoned so the ends flapped behind her, showing a pair of well-worn jeans topped by a shiny satin blouse in sky-blue.

When she stopped in front of Gin, it was easy to see that her hair was shot through with fine strands of gray. The woman's generous mouth stretched into a big smile beneath deep brown eyes that shone with amusement at Gin's open scrutiny.

"You have to be Special Agent Gin Reilly." A hand shot out and grabbed one of Gin's, pumping it up and down. "I've wanted to meet you for a while now. I'm Amerik Hedron, out of the forensics lab at Quantico. Well," she pushed straight on, switching her attention to Trey. "At least until I move out to join you on Dr. Blake's latest brainchild. I was told the CCU is based in Denver for the moment, so I guess we'll be relocating there."

Startled, Gin exchanged a confused look with Trey before

practically dancing in place in order to catch Americk Hedron's gaze with her own. "You said we're based in Denver for the moment? Is the CCU moving?"

"No idea," Americk responded as she carefully studied Trey. "And of course you would be Special Agent Robard, newly recruited from NCIS, I believe?"

Trey cleared his throat before managing a polite smile. "I asked to be brought into the CCU. But yes, my last assignment was with NCIS."

Americk chuckled as she stuck her hands into the oversized pockets of the lab coat. "I'm surprised to hear that. So it seems even bona fide heroes have someone monitoring their moves." Before Trey could say a word, the lab tech plowed straight ahead in what was clearly a habit of hers. "You *are* a hero. Some of those rescues were the stuff of movie plots." Her face sobered as she stared up at him. "I'm sorry that last one ended so badly."

Trey's back visibly stiffened, but he remained silent, simply returning her stare. After a long moment, she directed her gaze toward Gin. "I've wanted to talk to you for years. I have so many questions."

"Questions?" Gin repeated cautiously, not sure she was willing to be asked one much less many.

Americk blinked in surprise. "Certainly. I'd love to know how you selected those souvenirs you passed along to the police to get them to take you seriously about your father. The choices were brilliant." She looked over at Tony and beamed. "The Black Cross Killer must have had dozens of little mementoes, but most wouldn't have been recognized because they belonged to victims whose bodies had never been found. But only three were picked out, and every one of them was from a victim who the police already knew about and had on record." She nodded, her eyes glowing with satisfaction as she gave Gin an admiring look. "Brilliance. That was pure brilliance. And you had to have still been a child at the time."

"I was old enough, and it was just plain common sense." Feeling heat creep into her cheeks, Gin's tone held a clear layer of frost that had Tony shuffling his feet and fixing his gaze on a distant point. "Maybe we could concentrate on some real brilliance of your own? And hopefully more relevant to our current murder case?"

"We certainly can." Not looking the least bit taken aback by Gin's tone, Americk nudged the uncomfortable-looking Tony in the side with her elbow. "Shall we go to the lab and do our reveal?"

"Yeah. Let's do that." Tony turned on his heel, and with exaggerated enthusiasm, marched straight across the lobby. Americk followed right behind, matching him stride for stride despite the differences in their heights and the length of their legs.

Trey and Gin fell into step together as he leaned down and whispered. "I just put a deposit down on a place in Denver. Have you heard anything about moving?"

"Nope," Gin whispered back. "Are you going to explain that whole thing about your last rescue?"

"Nothing to explain," Trey muttered. "How about that memento thing? What was she talking about?"

"No idea," Gin stated without even a slight pause.

No one, except herself, Captain Wilkins of the Story County Sheriff's office, the lead attorney for the state's prosecuting team, and the trial judge knew that she'd been the source that had finally brought the Black Cross Killer's decades-long killing spree to an abrupt end. Oh. And Her father, of course.

Judging by that last, venomous look he'd sent her across the yard of their rundown farm, Byron Reilly had made it clear without saying a word that he knew who had turned him into

A HARD TRUTH

the police. But that one moment had been the longest and most terrifying one of her life.

Not once during the long trial had Gin's name been mentioned. Captain Wilkins had seen to that. The statement she'd had to give happened behind closed doors, alone in front of the captain and the judge. Both men had attested to the reliability of the source witness, and then the judge had put her name and testimony under a permanent seal.

He had passed away several years ago, but Wilkins, who had stood like an impenetrable wall between herself, the attorneys, and the press, as well as Byron Reilly, was still alive and kicking in retirement. She knew that because she called him every few months to catch up. As far as she was concerned, Frank Wilkins was her oldest and most trusted friend.

"Are you coming in?"

Trey's question had her quickly shoving the past back into its mental hole. She gave a jerky nod to her current partner on this case, who was patiently holding open a door with large green letters spelling out "Forensics Lab" stenciled on the front. Stepping past him, she walked into a room with a double row of long work benches, all crowded with small equipment used to examine and dissect evidence.

Tony and Americk, the only other occupants of the large room, stood together on one side of a gleaming, stainless-steel table that was relatively free of clutter. Americk's mouth was fixed into that same wide smile she'd worn in the lobby, and her eyes fairly glowed as they stared back at Gin.

As Gin and Trey positioned themselves opposite her, the lead forensic tech lightly tapped a finger on the epoxy-coated steel of the work surface. "First, I'd like to express my appreciation to you for finding that garbage bag back in the woods." She glanced over at the tech supervisor, who blushed in return.

"Tony told me you were very thorough in your methods to search for any evidence."

"Thanks," Gin said, cutting off any further compliments over her practices in the field. "What was in it?"

Americk lifted the cloth covering of a tray that took up most of the worktop. She picked up a clear plastic bag on the far end, holding it high enough the contents were easily visible. "Identification for a Benjamin Stampler, along with a wallet, ring, and very expensive Rolex watch with his initials engraved on the back. The personal effects will have to be verified by his family, of course, but the ID is definitely his." She lowered the bag and placed it back on the tray. "No prints. No surprise there." She pointed to another bag that was filled with discarded food wrappers. "That's the trash. Thoroughly picked over to discard any food, although there are some residual grease and pickle-juice stains. Along with leftover ketchup and the usual assortment of condiments that goes along with fast food."

She took a long step to the side until she was facing a computer screen. Tapping on the keyboard, Americk leaned forward, the glow from the screen lighting up her face as she studied its contents. Apparently satisfied, she straightened up and turned the screen around until it faced Gin and Trey. "Now these are test results from swabs Tony took of the victim's skin, as well as from several of the food wrappers. Traces of peppermint oil mixed with water were found on the skin, and especially on the cotton balls."

"Cotton balls?" Trey shifted his gaze from the computer screen to Amerik's face. "What cotton balls?"

"The ones that were sprinkled on top of the body and mixed in with the trash. According to the field techs, who I rousted out of bed to talk to this morning, they were mostly under the top layer of trash and directly on top of the body, which I think was the point."

A HARD TRUTH

Not following the logic, Gin frowned. "I'm a little rusty on all the uses of peppermint oil. What point are you talking about?"

"Cotton balls will retain the smell longer than say, bare skin, so they will give a longer period of time to expel any insect scavengers looking for an easy meal, or a larger predator, too, I would imagine," Americk's tone had easily switched into lecture mode. "Which is why you could still smell the peppermint despite the body having been dumped there for weeks. And I would guess that the trash also served as protection, so both the spray on the skin and on the cotton balls would last as long as possible." She shrugged. "Although I think a cotton blanket of some sort would have been more effective."

"But not in conveying the message that the man was trash," Gin said absently.

"Ah. A double purpose then." Americk's nod threatened to send the hairnet-encased bun perched on top of her head sliding down over her eyes. "That isn't the most significant find, however." She held out her hand, palm up. "But before we get to that, I understand you found a preserved flower at the scene?"

At Gin's slight nod, Trey slid the backpack off his shoulders and unzipped a side pocket. He withdrew the evidence bag holding the small square of resin with its three-petaled, yellow flower forever trapped inside. "Here it is."

The lab tech took it with one hand and held it up to the light. Turning it slowly around, she carefully studied the bag's contents. "Birdsfoot trefoil." She glanced at Gin and smiled. "More commonly known as eggs-and-bacon. In the language of flowers, it's generally thought to mean revenge." She dropped the bag lightly onto the tray.

Reluctantly impressed, Gin lifted an eyebrow at the renown forensics expert. "We had to look that up."

Americk chuckled as she turned the computer screen back to face herself and started tapping on the keyboard. "My wife and I have a well-tended garden in the small space around our townhouse. She spends hours perfecting it every weekend. It's her passion." She looked up and wiggled her eyebrows at Gin. "One of them." She returned her gaze to the computer screen and bent over the keyboard. "We've been together for twenty-six years. And the only reason I know that particular fact is that Gayle has the date we met printed on a sticky note that she keeps right on our dresser mirror." She straightened her back again and swiveled the screen around once more. "Aha. Here it is."

Gin stared at the multiple images of what looked like very weird plants. "And what is this?"

"Seeds mostly. Stuck to those cotton balls. And Tony here did an outstanding job of finding this." She pointed to the image in the center of the screen. "That distorted-looking thing is actually a petal of a tiny flower. Smashed up a bit, of course, but you can take my word for it. That's a flower petal. It took us a while to figure out what had that kind of blue flower and those kind of seeds." She pointed at two other images on the screen. "But we came up with it, and I'm sure further tests will verify our research."

Trey glanced at his watch. "You've only been here an hour or so, Ms. Hedron."

"Dr. Hedron," Tony cut in. "She has her doctorate in toxicology."

"Which has nothing to do with this plant," Americk said calmly before she winked at Trey. "No. *You've* been here in the lab for an hour or so. I got in at six this morning, and Tony picked me up at the airport. We've been at this for several hours." She pointed at the screen again. "Most of it was spent researching this plant."

A HARD TRUTH

After Moore's warning, Gin wasn't surprised Americk Hedron had ignored her doctor title, but wasn't getting the reason for spending so much time on a little blue flower petal. And its seeds. She folded her arms over her chest. "What is that plant?"

"I'm almost certain that this little charmer came from a California lilac. But we'll need to run further tests to absolutely verify. Its most often found both cultivated and growing wild, all over the Northwest and especially Northern California." Americk cocked her head to the side as she kept her gaze on Gin. "It's very odd to find it on this body, considering that I was told it's only been in two places, and a California Lilac would be hard to find in Florida. Unless Mr. Stampler kept one in a pot on his yacht. Which leaves the second place the victim has been, and the California lilac does not grow wild in upstate New York. Like around an electricity pylon. So the question becomes, how, how, how did these little bits and pieces get stuck to our victim's body and in those cotton balls?"

"Any ideas on that?" Trey asked, breaking into the sudden silence.

"Oh sure," Americk tossed out. "Transference would be my first pick. They were transferred from one surface to another. The trunk of a car being a good candidate since Tony also found a couple of carpet fibers."

"What? Were you here working all night?" Gin asked the burly supervisor, who grinned back at her. She didn't really notice, though, because a coherent picture was forming in her mind. California lilac? Now, wasn't that a coincidence? Too bad that no one in law enforcement, and especially not in homicide, was a big believer in coincidences. "Trey? Can you pull up that file we got from Prin?"

Americk's gaze instantly sharpened. "Prin? Who's Prin?"

"The sheriff in Siskiyou County," Gin replied as she watched Trey scroll through the email on his phone.

"Really?" Americk drew in a sharp breath. "Now, isn't that interesting?"

Tony sent Americk and then Gin a perplexed look. "Where is that?"

"Northern California." The forensic expert grinned back at him. "Home of the California lilac."

"Little blue flowers," Trey said slowly, drawing the words out. "Yeah. I remember them. In the background of some of the crime scene photos." He pulled up an image and smiled in satisfaction. "Yeah. Here they are. More like a bush than a single plant." He held the phone out to Gin.

"A bush would be good," Tony chimed in. "They usually grow on a bush."

Gin ignored the impatient tapping of Americk's finger against the countertop as she studied the picture on Trey's cell phone. After a long moment, she pushed Trey's hand around until the phone was facing the impatient Americk. "Do those bushes behind the body look like California lilac?"

Americk all but snatched the phone from Trey's hand and enlarged the image on the small screen. "I would say so. Right color, right shape to the petal, dark green leaves. Looks like it to me." She glanced at Gin. "Where was this body found? In Siskiyou County?"

"Yep," Gin confirmed. "Naked, right next to a line of bushes, with trash dumped all over him, and the cause of death was a slit throat."

Tony let out a long, low whistle. "Wow. That's just shit-ass weird."

Only if you considered tracking down a possible coast-to-coast killer as being weird, Gin thought before turning to face Trey. "I think we'll let Tony continue on here while we check in with the medical examiner. See how the autopsy is going." Her fingers curled around the phone Americk was silently holding out to her. She took another look at the lifeless face of Miguel Rivera before giving the cell phone back to Trey and shifting her gaze to Americk. "We're leaving for Miami on the five o'clock plane. Should we come back and get you, or do you want to meet at the airport?"

"I'll get Dr. Hedron there," Tony eagerly volunteered. At the lead tech's pointed look, he hastily cleared his throat. "Americk. I'll get Americk there.

"I'd like to stay here and spend a little more time examining this evidence. I got your number from Tony's notes," Americk put in. "I'll send you a text so you'll also have mine in case something comes up before we leave."

"Okay." Gin nodded at both the lead tech and Tony. "We'll see you in a few hours."

Chapter Nine

Dr. Irwin Trader was a no-nonsense medical examiner who did not allow non-county personnel into his autopsy room. Which is why Gin and Trey found themselves sitting in a narrow-seated visitor chairs in a small office deep in the basement underneath the Erie County Sheriff's complex. It had only taken a few minutes to make the drive from the FBI's building, and even less than that to be summarily escorted to the medical examiner's compact office.

Gin folded her hands and planted them on top of one thigh as she gave the ME a pleasant smile. Dr. Trader looked to be near retirement, with a head of thinning, white hair, and stern hazel eyes.

"'There's not much the body can tell us apart from what was apparent after a visual examination of the remains." He picked up a pair of glasses lying on his desk and adjusted them on the bridge of his nose. Once he was satisfied with their placement, he leaned over and flipped through several papers attached to the clipboard lying in front of him. "Time of death is estimated at over one month ago, and less than two, and fixed more precisely at five weeks once the victim's identification was verified. The slit across the throat was the cause of death. There was surprisingly little insect activity, probably due to the peppermint oil sprayed on the body. Several swabs were taken from multiple places on the body and sent to the designated lab at the FBI office here in Buffalo, as were samples of the victim's hair and scrapings from beneath his fingernails and toenails." When Trey opened his mouth, the doctor held up an index finger. "I will finish this oral review of my preliminary report and then take your questions." He tilted his head down and looked at Trey over the rim of his glasses. "I assume that is acceptable, Special Agent Robard?"

Trey settled back into his chair. "Of course."

"I was told by my assistant," the doctor went on as if there had been no break in his monologue, "that the officers," he waved a hand in front of him without looking away from the clipboard. "And the federal agents on scene believed the victim to be one Benjamin Stampler, from Miami, Florida, which was verified by the FBI's forensics lab located here in Buffalo. A request was made last night to the Miami police department for any available dental records or information on birthmarks and any scarring from a serious wound or surgical procedure. The dental records were waiting in my email this morning, and comparison to the victim's teeth positively verified that the recovered body is Benjamin Stampler, who disappeared from his yacht five weeks ago." He gave a self-satisfied nod before setting the clipboard aside, then lifted his gaze and stacked his hands on top of his desk. "Now. Are there any questions?"

"Why clippings of the victim's hair?" Trey asked.

"To be thorough, agent. It had an unusual quality. Stiffer and grittier than I would have thought it should be, even after sitting under trash and out in the elements for so long. So I was being cautious. The same with the nail scrapings. Not only to be thorough, but to exercise a prudent caution to be sure everything was appropriately examined and studied." When Trey murmured his thanks, Dr. Trader switched his attention to Gin. "And you, Special Agent Reilly? Do you have any questions for me?"

Thinking she was lucky she had gotten a look at the body before it was turned over to the stiff-necked ME, Gin shook her head then rose to her feet. "Thank you for your time, Dr. Trader. I look forward to reading your final report."

He inclined his head in acknowledgment. "I'll be sure it is included with the report on any forensic results or findings."

Since his smile was pure dismissal, Gin turned and followed Trey out the door, her mind on stiff and gritty hair. As she wove her way back to the lobby, she took out her phone. She scrolled past a text message from Stephen and opened the promised one from Americk. She responded with one of her own about the hair sample coming the lead tech's way, then tucked her phone out of sight again. But not before she'd noted the time.

"How about heading for the airport?" she asked Trey once they were back on the street. "We can grab some lunch, then find a quiet corner to catch up on emails and start reports. I also need to check in with Stephen. Maybe he's dug up anything else."

Trey nodded his agreement. "Sounds good. The airport is about fifteen, maybe twenty minutes from here, depending on the traffic. And I'm starving."

Gin unlocked the car and climbed in behind the wheel. "That seems like a theme of yours. Always being hungry."

Trey shrugged as he reached over to buckle his seat belt. "I burn a lot of calories."

That had her rolling her eyes. Rescuing people was obviously hard work, but she refrained from bringing up that he

A HARD TRUTH

wasn't in that line of business anymore. So far, the extent of their activity today had been to drive around and talk to people. Not exactly the kind of thing to work up a big appetite. Unless you happen to be Treynor Robard, apparently.

The ride to the airport passed without incident, or much conversation. Once they'd checked in at the kiosks and had gone through security, they decided picking up a sandwich and soft drink suited them better than a restaurant. Luckily, the gate area for their plane was deserted, and they sat down at the end of two different rows of chairs that faced each other across a six-foot space. Gin set the paper bag holding her sandwich and some chips on the small table separating her seat from the next one in the row and slid her laptop out of her backpack.

She went straight to her email, scanning down the list of unopened messages as she retrieved her sandwich. Unwrapping it, she took a big bite as she did the politically correct thing and opened the email from the unit's senior agent first. Moore had sent some additional background information on Benjamin Stampler. Deciding to look at the attachment later, she spotted an email that had her smiling from ear-to-ear.

"Special Agent Fionn Sullivan," she read softly to herself. "Now what have you been up to, Finn?"

Assigned to the organized crime investigative unit with the FBI, she'd first crossed paths with Finn when they'd both worked a drug smuggling case in the North Cascades National Park. Technically, it had not been her case. It had belonged to the National Park Service, but the FBI agents had tagged along and Finn had won a special place in her heart. He'd easily slipped into the role of an older brother who didn't approve of her chasing criminals while he did it himself. Which meant she could ignore him whenever it suited her.

The message he'd sent was short and to the point, which was classic Finn. *I'm your contact in Miami. I'll pick you up at the hotel tomorrow for your talk with the PD and the grieving widow.*

Happy to have a rare chance to hang out with the big Irishman again, which almost negated her concern about how he even knew she was headed that way, Gin was still smiling when she opened an email from Stephen. The smile was gone in an instant. She picked up her laptop, lunch, and backpack, then walked across the aisle to sit down next to Trey.

He looked up from his computer with a frown. "Something wrong?"

She balanced her laptop on her knees. "Yeah. It looks like Stephen has found two more possibles connected to ours."

Trey immediately leaned to the side to get a look at her laptop screen. "He says that first one is a closed case."

"I saw that, too." Gin's gaze quickly scanned through the message. "But it fit our scenario, so he sent it along. The body was naked, with a slashed throat, and buried under a pile of dead leaves."

"In his business partner's backyard," Trey pointed out, reading right alongside her. "And dead leaves aren't exactly trash."

"No," she was forced to agree. "Like he said. It's possible. He also stated right here that this is the second case he found and it's less of a match than the first. Which he didn't bother to expand on, which in Stephen code means that first one must have some solid links to Stampler's and Rivera's murders. He's expecting both files sometime tomorrow morning, and he'll send them along then." Gin sighed and stood up, her open laptop in her hands. "Anything interesting in your email?"

Trey shook his head. "Not unless you classify my nephew digging up his mother's favorite flowerbed looking for bodies like his Uncle Trey does, as interesting. Nothing else on the case except for the background info that Moore sent. How about you?"

"I'll forward Stephen's email to you, but aside from that, not much more on the case. Hopefully our luck will get better in Miami." She stretched her back and sat down again, deciding against returning to her seat in the opposite row. "At least we've caught a small break. I know the agent who is our contact in Miami. Fionn Sullivan is a good investigator."

Gin lifted an eyebrow when Trey chuckled. "*The* Fionn Sullivan? I heard a lot about him before I got to the FBI and ended up listening to his lectures. I happened to be assigned to a case where a friend of his was the primary suspect." He raised an eyebrow right back at her. "I assume you know all about that one?"

Since she was good friends with both the suspect as well as most of the people who worked on the case, she nodded. "You're talking about Anchorman, and I think you're the only person on that case who I've never met." Her lips curved into a wry grin. "Aside from Anchorman's attorney, who I understand was a force all by himself."

"He was." Trey laughed then gave her a sober look. "So you knew who I was before we met?"

Gin leaned back in her seat. "Before you decide to be annoyed I didn't cough that up right away, I'd like to point out that you'd also heard about me. From Finn, no less. Your instructor at Quantico."

Trey stared off into the distance for a moment before his expression relaxed. "Okay. That's a fair tit-for-tat."

Willing to follow his lead, she leaned back and shot him a puzzled look. "I didn't think Finn worked on that case where Anchorman was charged with murder."

"He didn't," Trey confirmed. "But I sure heard all about him. He was the agent they wished was there instead of me, even though the almighty Finn was in the wrong agency. That case belonged to NCIS, not the FBI. But I'm glad I'm going to get a chance to spend more time with the man and another legend in the FBI."

"Unlike Americk, Finn is only a legend in his own mind," Gin said dryly. "But I'm not surprised that the two of you took to each other." When Trey frowned, she grinned. "You both have the same. . . well, let's call it self-assurance."

Trey only grunted as he lifted the lid on his laptop. "Okay."

They spent the next two hours going through emails, answering emails, and deleting emails. Whenever she had to go into that mode, Gin considered tracking down whoever had invented email and tying him up in a room where thousands of the damn things flashed perpetually all over the walls. That seemed like a just punishment to her.

It was still over an hour before boarding for their flight got underway when Trey announced he needed another sandwich and went off to hunt one down, leaving Gin to guard his laptop and backpack.

She had her headsets on to drown out the surrounding noise, and was reading through the extensive background information on Benjamin Stampler, when someone sat down in the seat next to her. Expecting to see Trey, she instead found herself staring into Americk Hedron's smiling face.

"Hello, Gin. I made it on time, which is not always a sure thing with me." When Gin frowned, Americk's smile faded a little. "I hope you don't mind me calling you Gin?"

"No." With a silent, inner sigh, Gin closed her laptop and returned it to her backpack. "And what about you? I know you don't like to use the title of 'doctor'."

Americk gave a mock shudder. "Oh, heavens no. The minute I'm called Dr. Hedron, everyone assumes it's the medical variety and immediately launches into a litany of phys-

A HARD TRUTH

ical complaints from A to Z, usually starting with Alzheimer's. Americk will do just fine, thank you."

"Why Alzheimer's?" Gin asked, genuinely curious.

"Because most people think if they've forgotten any damn thing, no matter how trivial, it's a sign of the disease," Americk stated with a pained look. "It's one of those bizarre human things that is impossible to explain." She hesitated for a moment as she chewed on her lower lip. "Kind of like why people choose to kill. We can explain the heat of the moment, or money. Then there's jealousy, of course, but that doesn't come into play very much except in the movies."

In Gin's experience, that was very true. Overall, heat of the moment during an argument usually came in at number one, and those cases were almost always handled by the local law enforcement.

But in her world, greed was usually the number two reason. M for M— murder for money, also ranked high on the list.

Still, the number one reason was simple enough and summed up in a single word. Crazy. The killers were just plain crazy. She should know. She'd lived with that kind of crazy for fourteen years. Shrugging it off, she shot the doctor a sideways glance. "Do you have something on your mind, Americk?"

Americk curled her lips under but kept her gaze steady on Gin. "Yes. I'm glad I caught you alone. I wanted to apologize."

Not bothering to pretend she had no idea what the woman was talking about, Gin looked around the rapidly filling seating area. "We aren't exactly alone so this isn't the time and place to go into any details, but that's okay. You took me by surprise. That's all. But I would appreciate it if we didn't discuss my father unless it has something to do with a case we're actually working on."

"Of course," Americk said with a quick nod, then promptly ignored Gin's statement about the proper time and place. "I understand. But I wanted to give you a warning before we never spoke of it again. Which I was sure you'd insist on. No one told me you were the sheriff's anonymous source. No one had to. That case, and how your father was caught, is the subject of study in every school that teaches forensics in the country. It isn't difficult to figure out who sent those mementos to the police."

"Why isn't it difficult?" Gin demanded in a low voice. "You won't find my name attached to any court document in any of the trials."

"Which in itself is a tell," Americk responded calmly. "Who else would the court go to such great lengths to protect, if not a minor child? Your brother was over eighteen and might have been compelled to testify because he wasn't a minor. Not at the time of the trial, or when your father was arrested. Besides, your brother was away at the time of the arrest, according to all the follow-up publicity, and he would never have left you there to go through all of that alone."

Which was true enough, and the reason she hadn't told Devin, but it was a little weird that Americk knew that about her brother.

"I've met him," the tech said softly.

Gin blinked. "Him? Exactly what him are you talking about?"

"Devin, of course." Americk shrugged at Gin's startled look. "I'd tell you it was a coincidence, but no one in law enforcement believes in those." When Gin's eyes narrowed, the doctor smiled. "And no. I wasn't stalking him either. I happened to be in Seattle on a case. As I usually do, I stopped in at the university. It has a wonderful department that studies environmental forensics, and I know several of the professors there. I saw a flyer inviting anyone to an open lecture being given by Devin Reilly on something to do with computers. I was curious, so I stopped in."

"Learn anything?" Gin asked as she continued to stare at Americk. The jury was still out on whether the woman just happened to be at the university or had been deliberately tracked down her brother.

"Not a thing. All that computer gibberish was far too advanced for me. But he does seem to radiate being a decent guy, so that's where I came to my conclusion he would not have left you alone on that farm, holding the bag, so to speak." She reached over and patted Gin's knee. "So, there. A complete confession about everything."

Maybe. Thinking she'd need to keep an eye on Dr. Americk Hedron, Gin forced her shoulders to relax. "And that warning you mentioned?"

"Simple enough," Americk said. "If I can figure out who the informant was, so can anyone else interested enough to reason it out. And if Byron Reilly has any admirers outside those prison walls, you might want to be on your guard." Her mouth pulled down into a frown. "And his kind of broken mind always seems to have admirers."

Gin snorted. "I spent over a decade living with a serial killer. I'm always on my guard."

"On guard about what?" Trey's voice broke in. He was standing in front of them, a paper bag in one hand as he bent down to pick up his backpack. "What are you on guard about?"

"Ghosts from the past," Gin stated as she grabbed her backpack and stood up along with Americk.

"I hear that," Trey muttered, then cleared his throat. "'They've called our flight. Are you two ready to go?"

Gin made her way onto the plane. After stowing her backpack and buckling into her seat, she put her large headset over her ears. Plugging them into her phone, she brought up a podcast she'd downloaded earlier about traveling across Europe on a budget. She didn't care a single whit about whatever the perky social media "influencer" was saying, but it was noise, and it kept her from having to make conversation with anyone.

Leaning back, she closed her eyes, dropping into sleep the minute the plane took off. It was a great habit she'd perfected after she'd first joined the Bureau and her nomadic life had kicked into full gear.

It wasn't until someone gave her a solid poke in the arm that she opened her eyes. The first thing she saw was Trey's face leaning close to hers.

"Wake up. We're about fifteen minutes out."

Gin nodded, lifting a hand to stifle a yawn. Outside it was pitch black. The only visible thing was the flashing red navigation light on the end of the plane's wing. In the distance she could see the faint glow of lights against the dark night sky. *And that would be Miami,* she thought, wiggling until she was sitting straight up in her seat.

"You sleep really well on planes," Trey remarked.

"Don't you?" Gin asked with a shrug.

He grinned. "Not if I'm flying it."

She looked up toward the ceiling. "Considering the cost of those helicopters you zipped around in, I'm sure the Navy appreciated that."

She stowed her headphones and settled in more comfortably as she tracked the plane's progress on the monitor built into the back of the seat in front of her.

The landing was smooth enough to earn Trey's nod of approval, and the deplaning went the same as usual, with some passengers leaving quickly, while others made a career out of gathering their mountain of carry-ons and making their way down the narrow aisle.

Once in the terminal, Gin waited impatiently for Americk

A HARD TRUTH

to appear since she had been sitting farther back in the plane. When the doctor finally joined them, they made their way toward the exit and baggage claim. Gin dropped her backpack at her feet, resigned to the delay in picking up her suitcase. She didn't normally travel with a checked bag, but she had started this trip as a kind of unwanted vacation, not for business. She'd been hoping to spend a few days in New York City, which was now definitely off the itinerary.

"Glaring won't make them arrive any faster."

Gin bowed her head in silent laughter before turning around and confronting a grinning Finn. "I hadn't expected to see you until tomorrow morning." Her words were cut off as she was engulfed in an enormous bear hug, which she was happy to return.

When he stepped back, Finn's smile was reflected in the green of his eyes — a definite hand-me-down from his Irish ancestors. "You're lucky to see me at all. I'm supposed to be in New Mexico, chasing down some very, very bad guys."

She laughed and gave him a light punch in the arm. "Everyone you chase is a very, very bad guy." She turned her body half-way around and gestured toward Americk. "This is Dr. Americk Hedron." She never got to finish the introduction because she was rudely pushed aside by Americk before the doctor threw her arms around the much taller Finn's waist.

"I know Finn. We've worked quite a few cases together." The older woman stepped back and beamed up at the FBI agent. "How have you been?" She looked around him. "Where's Kate?"

"Kate?" Gin echoed.

"For a later discussion," Finn said in a firm voice. He looked over Americk's head toward Trey. "And how is Robard, the navy hero?"

Stepping forward to shake Finn's outstretched hand, Trey nodded. "Just Robard, the FBI agent."

Finn returned the nod. "I'm good with that. I have a car outside, which I rented for you in case I get suddenly called away, and there's an upgraded hotel in your near future. Let's collect your suitcases and make a beeline for the bar there."

Having no trouble getting behind that, Gin waited impatiently until her suitcase appeared. It didn't take long for Trey's to show up as well, and the group moved off to the parking garage. Within minutes they were on their way through the bright lights of Miami. When Finn turned into the driveway of a name brand hotel which rarely accommodated the FBI budget, Gin leaned forward to get a good look at the grand entrance. "And what did we do to deserve this?"

"Nothing," Finn said as he opened the car door. "I know a guy who knows a guy." He reached into his jacket pocket and produced six electronic card keys. "Two keys apiece, and you're all checked in. Fifth floor. Probably not the best view in the house, but still better than the parking lot and trash bins. Which is usually all we rate."

"Sounds more like an Italian thing than Irish," Gin stated with a philosophical shrug. She wasn't going to look a gift horse in the mouth, but she hoped there wasn't some price she hadn't heard of yet that was attached to all this luxury.

"No strings," Finn said, accurately reading her mind. "I really do know a guy who knows a guy, and from what I've heard, you're headed for two annoying interviews tomorrow, so a little pampering tonight shouldn't hurt."

Gin walked into the hotel with him, handing Trey one of her keys and leaving him to deal with the bags. "So I'm guessing you've talked to the assistant chief, who Agent Moore set us up with?"

A HARD TRUTH

"Alvarez," Finn supplied. "Yeah. We've met several times. Nice enough guy, but pretty set in his view of the FBI."

"Wonderful." Gin entered the lounge area and quickly scanned the room before heading to a quiet corner without a view. Once they were settled, she ordered a glass of wine, then waited for the cocktail waitress to move away before squarely facing Finn. "Is there some kind of illegal drug connection to our case? Is that why you're here?"

"Nope," Finn said with a quick shake of his head. "I'm here to tell you we couldn't find any of those kinds of connections. Benjamin Stampler is clean as a whistle as far as we can tell. But I'm not so sure the same claim can be made about one of his executive vice-presidents."

Gin frowned as she absorbed that. "Which one?"

"Hugh Lamon. He heads up one of their research divisions." Finn reached inside his jacket, pulled out a folded sheet of paper, and laid it on the table in front of her. "He came up through the management ranks and has been with the company for twenty years. He's a Princeton graduate with all kinds of letters after his name. Smart guy," he added. "Smarter than the bad habit he's developed."

Surprised, Gin picked up the paper, then went silent as she skimmed down the page. "Fentanyl? Seriously? You'd think a guy in the drug industry would know better."

"His driver has been spotted making regular buys." Finn paused when the waitress arrived with their drinks, giving her a wink that left her smiling. "At first we figured it was for him, but he let it slip that it was for his boss. Didn't take long to find the heavy cash withdrawals from a bank account Lamon keeps separate from the joint one with his wife." He shrugged. "We don't think she knows about his habit."

"Or pretends not to," Gin stated. "I imagine they've got a very nice lifestyle that would be hard to give up." She frowned at the paper. "And he's got no other drug connection besides his personal habit?"

"None," Finn said. "But he's still a weak link."

"A weak link that could have set up the CEO of his company for some reason. Most likely to keep from being outed as a drug addict." Gin picked up her glass of wine and took a sip. It was good, but it still left a sour taste in her mouth. "If that's true, then it creates a problem."

"Which is?"

She pressed her lips into a flat line. "We've found at least one like crime, and potentially two more." At Finn's startled look, she quickly went over the evidence they'd found in upstate New York, and what had been in the case file for the murder of the electrician in Northern California.

When she finished, Finn's index finger was tapping a steady beat against the table. "Well. A trash pile and a flower preserved in resin. That's way too out there not to be connected somehow."

"I think so," Gin said slowly. "But it also makes it hard to see the executive's drug problem being a factor." She sighed loudly before taking another sip of wine. "But it can't be dismissed until we eliminate it. So the next step is to talk to the Miami police and take a look at their case file."

Finn picked up his drink and drained it. Setting it back onto the table, he pointed to her unfinished glass of wine. "You can take that up to your room. I need to get going." He slid out of his chair and stood up, waiting for Gin to do the same before giving her a wink. "I have a hot date."

Chapter Ten

It was barely eight in the morning when Gin walked through the double doors and into the lobby of the downtown building that housed the headquarters of the Miami Police Department. The all-white facade with its domed entrance was set off by a sprinkling of palm trees and fit right into the image of the town the department served. It was an impressive-looking place, and she silently admitted that she preferred the look of it to the decidedly square and flat stone building of the Bureau's headquarters located one thousand miles to the north.

Finn took the lead, since he'd spent what he'd called "way too much time" visiting the city's police department, all of which he'd been quick to swear had been strictly on the Bureau's business. Given the big Irishman's tendency to attract trouble, she rather doubted that, but kept silent as she trailed after him into the lobby, standing quietly while he navigated the protocols for the pre-arranged meeting.

It didn't take long for an officer to appear, giving the brief explanation that he was their escort while they were in the building. Suppressing a smile at the clear message that FBI agents were not allowed to wander around the place on their own. Nothing new there. Gin politely fixed the visitor's badge to the front of her jacket, then once again fell into step directly behind Finn.

Their escort stopped in front of a door marked as a conference room, politely opening it before stepping aside to let them pass by. The room was a comfortable size, big enough to accommodate a large conference table with a cherrywood top and ten chairs around it. There was one sturdy cardboard storage box sitting on the table, marked with a case file number and the name Benjamin Stampler written on the outside.

Gin took a seat, along with Finn, Trey, and Americk, with the four of them lining up on one side of the table. They'd barely sat down when a well-groomed mustache and a thick head of hair the color of rich coffee stepped through the door.

Brown eyes swept over the room before settling on Finn. "Special Agent Sullivan. It's good to see you again." His gaze moved on to Gin and then Trey. "I'm Assistant Chief Richard Alvarez." Without waiting for Finn to make his own introductions, he turned slightly and nodded at the man who had come in behind him. "This is Captain Michael Crandon. He's head of the detective unit that worked on the disappearance of Benjamin Stampler, which is now a homicide."

"Chief Alvarez." Finn stood up and reached across the table to shake the assistant chief's hand before sending a quick salute and grin toward the captain. "Hey, Mike. It's been a while."

The captain smiled and ran a beefy hand over the top of his completely bald head. "It usually is, Finn. Have you caught any nasty cartel members lately, or are you still running around chasing your tail?" He accompanied the insult with a wide grin of his own which had Finn barking out a laugh.

"About the usual amount," Finn said. "Let me introduce our team assigned to the case."

As Finn quickly went through their names, Gin politely nodded, feeling that familiar tightening in her stomach when the assistant chief pinned his gaze on her.

"Reilly?" Alvarez repeated when Finn had finished his introductions. Clasping his hands behind his back, he drew his dark eyebrows together. "Are you any relation to Byron Reilly?"

From the corner of her eye, Gin saw Finn's shoulders go stiff and his jawline harden. While she appreciated the show of support, she didn't need it, having gotten used to the question after her first few years with the Bureau. "We're related." She stared back at him, unblinking, waiting to hear how the assistant chief would respond to that.

Alvarez cocked his head to the side and smiled. "I was told his daughter was with the FBI and was one hell of an investigator. Glad to have you on this one." He let his arms drop to his sides before pointing at the cardboard box placed on the end of the table. "That's all we have on the case. With your help and insight, we're hoping to add a lot more." He pulled out a chair and sat down, waiting while Finn retook his seat and Captain Crandon pulled out a chair near the box. His gaze moved from Gin to Trey. "I'm assuming all of you have experience with homicides, and not just Agent Reilly?"

"We do," Gin said. "And we can verify that the body found in New York is that of Benjamin Stampler."

"Hmm." Alvarez leaned back in his chair with a loud sigh. "We had hoped for a better outcome but aren't surprised." He glanced at his captain. "Mike has the best homicide staff in the state, and they've been working this case since we were first notified of Mr. Stampler's disappearance."

Gin turned slightly in her chair to face the captain, who nodded back at her. "Did you have any reason from the start to think Stampler had been murdered?"

Alvarez remained silent, clearly deferring to Crandon. "Yes," the captain said. "We found what appeared to be blood spatter on the ceiling of the inside cabin on Stampler's yacht. It didn't test positive as human blood at the scene, but we sent it to the state lab for DNA testing anyway. They have a three-month backlog, so we're still waiting on the results."

"There's no rush for a victim as prominent as Benjamin Stampler?" Finn's tone clearly conveyed his skepticism. Despite his friendly greeting earlier, he gave Crandon a hard stare.

The captain didn't appear to be rattled by the tone or the question. "Not when the on-scene test didn't identify the sample as human, not to mention that we didn't have a body, or even know if there was a victim. And we didn't find any other foreign substance except in that one spot."

"What about the other guy?" Gin asked. "The crew member. The report we have stated there were two people on that boat. Stampler and a crew member. We didn't have much on him except his name."

"Because we didn't give out much," Crandon replied with a shrug. "We didn't even confirm to the public that Gerald Mobley was actually on board at the time Stampler went missing. We thought it might make him complacent enough to come out of hiding, if that was what he was doing."

Gin frowned. "You thought this Gerald Mobley might have abducted Stampler, or maybe killed him and then fled?"

Crandon rubbed a hand across the back of his neck. "We didn't know, but we couldn't rule it out. Still can't. Maybe he's on the run, or maybe that blood on the ceiling of the cabin is Mobley's and he was murdered too. What we do know at this

A HARD TRUTH

point is that both men are gone, and as of today, only one of them has shown up, and that one is dead. We couldn't find any reason for Mobley to turn into a killer. We didn't turn up any side pieces, or gambling debts. And as far as Stampler is concerned, there was nothing unusual in his bank activity, or something wonky going on at that drug company. At least, not that anyone would admit."

"How about drugs? Stampler was surrounded by them and had to have some easy access if he had a taste for them," Gin asked, careful not to smile when Crandon's shoulders hunched in slightly, although she had to give him points for keeping his gaze steadily on hers.

"Nothing like that turned up."

Sure that the Miami PD knew all about Hugh Lamon's drug addiction so likely looked into it for Stampler as well, she switched gears back to the other man on board the yacht. "Can you fill us in on Mobley?" She waited as the captain reached over and opened the box.

Taking his time, Crandon lifted out a file folder and placed it flat on the table in front of him. Opening it, he flipped over several pages before looking back at Gin. "Mobley had a birthday a few weeks ago which would make him thirty-one now, and thirty at the time of his disappearance. He's medium height, about one-hundred and sixty pounds according to his mom and Mrs. Stampler, brown hair, brown eyes, no known birthmarks, tattoos or other distinguishing scars. He grew up in Maine and came down here to college and never left. His bank account was about what you'd expect, and he had no other bad habits as far as we know."

"Was he a full-time crew member on the yacht?" Trey's forehead wrinkled in thought. "Did Stampler spend that much time on the water that he needed a full-time crew member?"

Crandon leaned back in his chair and folded his hands

together, resting them on his stomach. "I'd call it more a retainer kind of thing. Mobley had a small business where he supplied crews on demand to a client list who paid a monthly fee for the service. At least that's what his partner explained to me. The two of them were available twenty-four seven to a select group of clients, and offered the same service with varying degrees of advance notice to others who weren't on the regular client list. The company has two full-time employees, who would be Mobley and his partner, and three part-time employees, plus using a lot of contracted labor when necessary." He shrugged. "At least that was the official spiel from the partner. Who also swore up and down that Mobley would never hurt anyone, much less kill them. But that doesn't mean he didn't do it." He paused. "And we checked out his partner too. Couldn't find anything and he had a solid alibi. He was on a flight to Australia with his wife and got on a cruise ship from there."

"Any lead on a motive from Mobley?" Gin asked. "Why would he kill his employer? Was there any money involved?"

"If there was, no one knows anything about that. The boat wasn't taken and sold in some foreign country. It's still sitting in its berth over at the Miami Beach Marina. And as far as Mrs. Stampler knew, her husband wasn't carrying any large sum of cash, and there weren't any unaccounted-for withdrawals from their bank account." He reached over and laid a hand on top of the cardboard box. "We checked all that out, and did extensive interviews, and except for that small blood spatter, we pretty much struck out on following the money. But that still doesn't rule out Mobley and Stampler getting into an argument that spun out of control and ended up with one of them dead and the other on the run."

"You can look through everything we have while you're

here," Alvarez cut in before Gin could ask anything else. "And maybe we can send you an electronic version of this file, depending on how our discussion goes about who has jurisdiction over this case."

"This case has now come across state lines," Finn quickly pointed out. "That makes the FBI the lead."

"He was killed here," Crandon immediately countered. "Not to mention Stampler was a resident of Miami."

"It hasn't been established where Benjamin Stampler was killed," Gin stated, cutting through what could easily escalate into a nasty argument. "I'm assuming that both our agencies will be investigating this crime." She paused to fix her gaze on Alvarez. "Of course we will freely share any and all information."

Alvarez pursed his lips as he considered the matter before finally nodding. "That seems fair. What about New York?"

"They're happy to turn it over to us," Gin said. "And so is California."

That had both men from the Miami police giving her a stunned look. "California?" Alvarez echoed before shaking his head. "What does California have to do with this?"

Having already decided that a bit of sharing would go a long way to developing a line of trust, Gin's mouth formed into a grim smile. "We found a like crime committed about six months ago in the northern part of the state. A Miguel Rivera was murdered and then dumped up near their border with Oregon."

Crandon let out a low whistle. "You're kidding?"

"It looks like a solid connection." She glanced down the table at Americk, who nodded in return.

"Aside from the marked similarities in evidence found at both crime scenes, in the preliminary forensic results for Mr.

Stampler's body, we discovered evidence of a flowering bush called a California lilac," Americk began, taking up the narrative. "It isn't native to either Florida or upstate New York but grows freely in the wild in Northern California. It's also the same bush that was growing next to the body discovered there in a case that has several other similarities to your victim's murder." She efficiently outlined the two crime scenes, ending by explaining the possible transference of evidence by the killer from one crime scene to the next.

When she settled back in her chair, Crandon had a stunned look on his face. His gaze slowly wandered from Americk back to Gin. "So what you're saying is this all might be the work of a serial killer? Or is there some other connection between this Rivera and Stampler?"

"Not on the surface, but we haven't dug into it yet," Gin replied before glancing over at Trey, wanting to establish the authority of everyone on the team. "What do you think, Agent Robard?"

Trey didn't so much as blink in surprise when Gin tossed the question at him. "Rivera was an electrician, so he wasn't a big company exec of any kind, and had nothing to do with the pharmaceutical industry that we know of. He also wasn't anywhere near a boat or an ocean. However, the similarities between the crime scenes are too strong to ignore, so it seems logical there is something connecting the two victims." He sent a neutral look toward Crandon. "Whatever that connection is, we'll find it."

"Has an autopsy been done on Stampler yet?" the assistant chief asked quietly.

Gin nodded. "Yes. Time of death was four to eight weeks ago, which puts it in the same time frame as Stampler's disappearance. The ME in Buffalo is satisfied with a five-week time of death."

A HARD TRUTH

"And the cause?" Alvarez prompted.

"His throat was slit, and he bled out." Gin waited for the flash of pain in the chief's gaze to pass. "There wasn't any blood at the crime scene. It looked like a dump site."

"Why up there?" Crandon mused out loud. "And we still don't know where ground zero is. Where was Stampler killed? And what the hell happened to Mobley?"

"We don't know," Alvarez stated before turning a stare onto his captain. "But we will continue this joint investigation by sending everything we have to Special Agent Reilly." He turned his head to look at her. "I'm assuming you're willing to do the same?"

"Of course," Gin agreed. "We can start by you telling us why Stampler and Mobley were on that yacht the day they disappeared."

"It's in the interview notes," Crandon said. "We got the same story from Mobley's partner and from Mrs. Stampler. They'd gone there to check out a reported leak. Cameras on the dock confirmed that Mobley went through the security gate about an hour before Stampler. That was around four in the afternoon. They supposedly took the boat out, then came back sometime later that evening. But the cameras didn't pick up either one of them coming back through the gate, and it's the only way in or out."

"Supposedly?" Gin asked, picking up the skepticism in Crandon's voice.

"One witness was sure it went out," Crandon admitted. "But we couldn't find any corroboration of that at first. And that single witness wasn't all that close to the water."

"They thought the boat had a leak and they still took it out?" Trey asked.

"That's what we thought. Guess it wasn't much of a leak," Crandon said. "But this witness claims to have seen the *Traci*

Marie leaving the marina sometime between five thirty and six. None of our canvassing turned up anyone who saw it come back, but it was tied up at its berth the next morning when Mrs. Stampler called in a missing person report. So we went out to take a look."

Finn's eyebrows shot up. "With him missing less than twenty-four hours?"

The captain shrugged. "Big name, so exceptions were made, I guess."

"Not unusual anywhere," Alvarez cut in. He looked at Trey. "We also had a look at the navigation system on board the yacht. It took us a few days to find someone to interpret it for us, but it turned out the boat was taken out, supposed leak and all. They went up the coast for a few miles, just past Key Biscayne, then came back."

"Does your file have a copy of the location and time points recorded by the nav system?" Trey asked.

"No," the captain said, his jaw hardening when Trey frowned at him. "We had a guy go out to the *Traci Marie* and read it on board. I was there. He said there wasn't anything unusual about it. They went out, turned around, and came back in. The guy said it was consistent with doing a trial run to check something out."

"Thanks." Trey added a polite nod, then fell silent again.

Gin looked at her watch. "Maybe we could go over the highlights, then we'll comb through the electronic file in depth. We have an interview in an hour with Mrs. Stampler."

"And probably the corporate execs from Meridian Pharmaceuticals." Crandon said. "They hover around her like a mama bear protecting a cub."

"Not a problem." Gin thought of the Meridian vice-president with a fentanyl habit, silently wondering if the other company executives, or Mrs. Stampler, knew about his little problem. She put that away for the moment and pointed at the box. "What else is in there?"

Thirty minutes later, Gin, Trey, and Finn walked out of the Miami Police Department and headed toward the parking garage. Americk chose to stay behind and look over what little evidence there was, as well as have a talk with the forensic technicians, so Gin had left her to it. But only after securing a promise from Alvarez to have the doctor delivered back to the hotel when she was finished poking around.

"The meeting with the grieving widow has been set up at her late husband's company. Their offices are in a high rise near Bayfront Park, just a few blocks from here." Finn buckled his seat belt and adjusted the rearview mirror before leaning back with a sideways glance at Gin. "You didn't look too excited about Crandon's plan to retrace Mobley's movements in the days before he disappeared."

Finn was right, but Gin only shrugged. "I doubt if he's going to put much effort into it."

"Why not?" Finn asked. "I'm surprised they haven't already done that since they don't have much else to go on until those DNA results come in." He drummed several fingers against the steering wheel. "I know I don't work homicides very often but it still seems strange to me that Stampler rated the VIP treatment as a missing person, but not in putting those DNA results to the head of the line."

"That's because they've already retraced Mobley's steps and found nothing, which Crandon is playing some other game. Especially about Mobley since in all likelihood, he's as dead as Stampler."

Finn blinked at Gin's bald statement before twisting around to stare at Trey. "Do you think Mobley is dead too?"

"Probably." Trey's flat voice came from the back seat. "If

the killer was the guy in that trail camera, it sure wasn't Mobley."

"So you've figured that out too along with the guy being dead? Care to share with the rest of us?" Finn demanded.

Gin snapped her seatbelt into place and rolled her shoulders back. "Because as our search and rescue expert pointed out when we were on the scene, the guy on the trail cam carefully retreated out of the trees after he threw Stampler's wallet and jewelry away. He didn't walk too far in, choosing to heave that garbage sack rather than take a stroll in the woods. And even then he acted like he was watching his own back." Gin shook her head. "Not a guy who is too comfortable in the forest, which would not describe anyone who grew up in Maine. The whole state is one giant forest."

"That's only an interpretation of the video, so not a sure thing," Finn stated before engaging the engine. He backed out of the parking space, then hesitated a long moment before moving any farther. "But probably a good one." He shrugged as he put the car into gear. "I was leaning in that direction anyway. My gut says Mobley is dead. And they probably know, or at least had a strong suspicion, that the blood they found could be Mobley's, which would have made Stampler the murder suspect. Politically speaking, that wasn't a road they would have rushed to go down."

"He's probably not a serious suspect. Like the captain said, there wasn't any motive," Gin said before stifling a yawn. The night before had been short on sleep, and she was feeling the effects of that now. But there was still an interview to get through, and hopefully a yacht to inspect if they could squeeze that in.

The Meridian offices were on the top floor of a high rise, with jaw-dropping views of the water from the lobby windows. A brunette receptionist with red-rimmed eyes had greeted them in a muted voice, and there was a fresh wreath of flowers beneath the picture of Benjamin Stampler hanging on the far wall.

Gin studied the portrait as Finn talked to the woman behind the desk. It must have been fairly recent, because Stampler looked to be in his mid-fifties. The light-colored hair, high forehead, and blue eyes matched the body she'd seen, but in the portrait his cheeks weren't sunk into the bone and pulled tight into a death mask.

She hoped his wife would accept the official identification and not insist on seeing him after the elements and the natural course of decay had had their way for over a month. Some things were best left alone, but the odds were against that.

Gin walked over to the floor-to-ceiling window, not really seeing the spectacular vista beyond the double panes. She let out a soft sigh. The family almost always wanted a last look, and it inevitably became the one that stayed with them for the rest of their lives.

In that respect, it was probably a good thing she hadn't seen her mother before she was buried in the small graveyard on the outskirts of her hometown. On the other hand, she never had a chance to say goodbye. Or say much of anything, actually, even when her mother had been alive.

She gave a start when Finn's reflection behind her suddenly appeared in the window glass. "Mrs. Stampler and her bodyguards are ready to see us." His low voice didn't carry beyond the two of them. "Are you ready for this?"

Even in the reflection she could see the hesitation in his eyes. She turned and gave him a tight smile. "I'm good. Are you?" When he nodded, she leaned to the side and saw Trey waiting for them next to the reception desk, along with a slender young woman in a dark burgundy pant suit with a black armband circling her upper right arm. It seemed that the whole place was in mourning. Stepping around Finn, she crossed the lobby and smiled at the stylishly dressed woman. "I'm Special Agent Reilly."

"And I'm Ms. Tavish, Mr. Stampler's administrative assistant. Mrs. Stampler is waiting for you in the executive conference room." She blinked to hold back the tears, before taking a step toward the doors behind the receptionist's desk. "If you'll follow me?"

There was a deep hush along the hallways. Even the sound of their footsteps was muted as their shoes sank into a thick carpet. The conference room was at the end of a long hallway. The stoic Ms. Tavish opened the double doors to a room with two walls paneled in a deep brown oak, while the remaining walls were all glass. A woman dressed in a severe black suit with a short-sleeved jacket sat at one end of the table, her back to the windows. She was surrounded by three men in various stages of middle age. One stood behind her, his hand on her shoulders, while the other two had taken up positions on either side.

"Special Agent Reilly?" The man standing behind the widow, clearly the oldest of the three executives, directed the polite inquiry at Gin, who nodded in return.

"Yes, sir. I'm Agent Reilly." She'd already unbuttoned her jacket and made sure the badge hooked to her belt was visible as she took out her credentials case and held it open. One of the widow's side guards stepped forward and examined it before giving a brief nod and returning to his assigned spot.

"I'm Jardin Hunt," the older gentleman said. "Chief Operating Officer and acting CEO for Meridian Pharmaceuticals. These are two of our vice-presidents, Mr. Lamon with the research division, and Mr. Peters, head of our international and domestic operations. And this is Theresa Stampler. Ben's wife."

"You saw him." Theresa stated in a faint but audible voice,

A HARD TRUTH

her unblinking stare glued to Gin. She had blue eyes with an exotic tilt at their corners, underneath a sweep of platinum-blond hair. "You're the one who saw my husband, aren't you?"

"Yes." Gin let the simple word hang between them as she made a slight gesture toward Trey. "We both did. This is Special Agent Robard, with the Critical Crimes Unit, and the gentleman next to him is Special Agent Sullivan, based in the FBI office here in Miami." Which wasn't exactly true since Finn usually worked out of Quantico, but at the moment he was attached to the Miami office so she went with that.

"I was told that Ben was..." Theresa Stampler tapered off before trying again. "That Ben had nothing on and was buried under a pile of garbage beneath an electrical tower. Is that true?"

"Now, Theresa," Jardin Hunt said in a low, soothing voice. "There's no need to go into all that."

The grieving woman straightened her spine and made a subtle move that dislodged Jardin's hands from her shoulders. "I *need* to go into it. I've imagined all kinds of horrors over the last month. Now I want to know what actually did happen." She kept her focus on Gin. "Is all that true?"

Gin quietly drew in a deep breath, then let it out slowly. "Your husband was found at the edge of the woods near a large electricity pylon, but not directly under it. The rest of what you've been told is accurate." She paused for a long moment. "I'm sorry for your loss, Mrs. Stampler, and even sorrier for having to bother you so soon, but I'm hoping you're able to answer a few questions?"

Theresa's eyes closed and a single tear leaked out of one corner. "I don't know what I can tell you that I haven't already told the police."

"I'll try to be brief, Mrs. Stampler," Gin promised.

"Traci," the woman said. "Everyone calls me Traci. And right now, I need as much normal as I can get."

"Traci." Gin smiled. *Named his boat after her*, she thought. That said a lot about their relationship. "Can you tell me why your husband went down to the marina the day he disappeared?"

"Was killed," Traci corrected. "The day he was killed." When all three of the Meridian executives protested, she waved them off. "No more polite words about what happened. My husband was murdered." Hollow blue eyes stared right through Gin. "He didn't deserve to die like that. Alone in some horrible place he'd never been to, and tossed out with the garbage. I want his killer found and punished. I want to think of him rotting in a jail cell for the rest of his life." When the three men subsided into an uneasy silence, Traci Stampler leaned slightly forward in her chair. "Ben went to the marina because he'd received a note from Gerald about the boat."

"What kind of note?" Gin asked.

Traci lifted an agitated hand and smoothed down one side of her hair. "It was an email. He always called them notes."

"Ben sent that email from his work computer," Jardin Hunt interjected. "It was in response to a message he received from Gerald Mobley. We printed off a copy of their entire exchange and handed it over to the Miami police. A Captain Caldron, I believe."

"We'll contact them about getting a copy," Gin said smoothly. "In the meantime, do you know what was in that message? Was it about a potential leak?"

"Yes, it was," Traci responded before Hunt could protest again. "Ben told me about it, and that he was going to meet Gerald at the marina after his work was wrapped up for the day and take a look. He didn't want me to wait on him for dinner because he wasn't sure how long he'd be at the dock."

A HARD TRUTH

"Did he say anything about taking the boat out?" Gin asked.

Traci slowly shook her head. "No. But he usually did. Ben enjoyed cruising. He liked to take the kids with him, and any neighbors or friends who wanted a day on the water."

"Do you like cruising, Traci?"

"When the weather is good and there isn't much chop on the water." Traci's mouth curved into a smile despite her damp eyes. "I wasn't as fond of being out on the ocean as Ben was."

Gin carefully steered the widow through the maze of questions, asking about any stress over neighbors, friends, or any other part of her husband's private life. When she was done, she turned her attention to the three men, zeroing in first on Hugh Lamon. "Mr. Lamon?" She waited until he managed to get his gaze focused on her. "Was there anything going on in the research division that was causing internal issues?"

Hugh Lamon ran the palms of his hands down the sides of his very expensive-looking business suit while he kept his gaze averted from hers. "I'm not sure what you mean?"

"We've been having a few bumps with the trial of a new shot for the common cold," Hunt intervened smoothly. "But nothing we haven't run into and successfully resolved before. I doubt if it had anything to do with Ben's death."

Gin worked up a polite smile. "A cure for the common cold?"

"Not a cure," Jardin corrected while the vice-president of research kept his silence. "But a big step in mitigating the worst of the symptoms." He shifted his weight and stood up straight enough to look down his nose at Gin. "The company is in excellent shape and on a good path, Agent Reilly. We've turned over anything of relevance to the Miami police, including all of Ben's telephone logs and calendars. We've had a banner year,

143

even increasing our donations to several charities that Ben had a particular interest in."

Gin waited politely through Hunt's blatant stumping to be the permanent replacement as the company's top dog. "Some charities, but not all of them?"

"We're a generous company, Agent Reilly, with a generous budget for donating to various charities. But it *is* a budget. Naturally, when Ben wanted to increase our giving to one organization, we had to adjust our commitments to others." Hunt stated. "I can send you a list of charities and highlight the ones that received an extra boost this year, as well as the organizations which received a lesser amount if you want to look into that. But frankly, I doubt if it will get you anywhere. I hope that will be the end of this questioning? We are all going through a very difficult period, especially Traci." His hand snaked forward again to curl around her shoulder. "She needs her rest."

"Just one more thing, Mr. Hunt," Gin said, thinking of Miguel Rivera and his occupation. "And this question is for you. Did the company have any expansions or building projects going on in the last two years?"

"No, I don't believe so." Hunt turned to the thin, balding man who had yet to say a word. "Jim, this would be under your area."

Jim's bony features arranged themselves into a thoughtful look. "No. We haven't had a need to do any domestic expansion for the last five years. I would need to consult the files if you are interested in any such investments overseas."

Gin shook her head. "No. Just the domestic projects. I'd appreciate a list of those going back ten years."

"I'll send it to you as soon as possible, Agent Reilly. Just leave me your email address," the vice-president said.

Gin reached into her jacket pocket and handed him a business card while the acting CEO drew himself up to his full height with an audible sniff.

"Of course some of our charitable donations have gone to building new facilities and such," Jardin said. "But we do not get involved in any of those details aside from the donation itself. Now, I assume that satisfies all of your questions."

Not by a long shot, Gin thought. She exchanged an unblinking stare with the man before reaching into her pocket and laying her card on the conference table. "Thank you. I'd appreciate that list of the charities. And their addresses, if it's not too much trouble."

"Do the police still suspect the deckhand?" Lamon blurted out. When Gin turned a hard stare on him, he dropped his gaze to the top of the table. "The last time they were here, they made it clear that he was a person of interest," he finished on a mumble.

"I can't comment on an ongoing investigation, Mr. Lamon." As a flush crept up the side of the man's face, Gin slowly swung her gaze over to Traci Stampler. "With your permission, we'd like to take a look at the yacht."

The widow pulled her purse closer and flipped open the snap. Reaching inside, she withdrew a set of keys on a chain attached to a rectangular piece of polished metal. "I was told you would want to do that." She held out the keys and Trey discretely stepped forward to take them. "I brought the keys to the cabin. The code to the security gate is engraved on the key chain. Please take all the time you want, Agent Reilly. I have no intention of ever setting foot on that boat again."

Perfectly understanding her position on that point, Gin nodded. "Thank you. If we need anything else, we'll be in touch."

The widow rose in one graceful movement. Gathering up her purse, she shook off Jardin's hand when he tried to slip it underneath her elbow. Without looking at the acting CEO, she stepped away from the table. "Special Agent Reilly?"

Traci's soft voice had Gin freezing in the middle of turning to exit the room. "Yes, Traci?" She ignored Hunt's disapproving frown and kept her attention on the widow. "Is there something else?"

"When can I see my husband?"

Chapter Eleven

Because it was a weekday, the marina was deserted in the early afternoon. Approaching the security gate, Gin didn't see a single person walking along the dock that separated the berths. Large boats, ranging from thirty to sixty feet long floated silently side by side, with even larger ones lined up bow to stern at the outer edges of the docks. It was quiet and peaceful, with only the quiet slap of water against hulls and the occasional screech of a seagull overhead breaking the silence.

"All these docks look like the rows at the grocery store," Finn joked from behind her.

Gin coughed to cover her laugh. "A very expensive grocery store." She looked up at the cameras pointed at the security gate. "Those won't capture much of the marina beyond the gate," she mused out loud, then silently wondered if there were any cameras mounted farther out on the docks.

Since they'd know soon enough, she stared at the key chain in her hand, holding it up until the number etched into the rectangular metal surface was clearly visible. Tapping the six digits into the panel on the security gate, she waited until she heard the distinct click of the lock give way before pushing open the iron gate. Stepping through it, she took the wide gangplank that slanted down onto the dock. Other docks with multiple berths lining each side jutted out into the water from the main pathway.

Gin looked over at Trey. "The *Traci Marie* is moored in berth C-15, which would be where?"

"Go left," he said. "C dock should be the third one from the end, then head down it until you reach berth fifteen. It should be painted on the dock box."

Gin headed in that direction, then stopped when an older man popped out from a row of docks behind them. A full inch shorter than Gin's five feet, six inches, he scurried along the wooden boards, expertly keeping his balance against the slight sway of the dock as he waved his arms in the air.

"Stop, stop," he huffed out, slowing his step when he realized the group of three strangers was waiting for him. "This is a private marina. You can't just walk around. You have to have a vessel here."

Gin flipped her light jacket back so her badge was visible. "I'm Special Agent Reilly with the FBI, and these are two of my colleagues." When the old man skidded to a halt and gaped at her, she smiled. "We have the owner's permission to take a look at the *Traci Marie*."

"The *Traci Marie*?" The man's mouth drooped at the corners and he rubbed a hand along one cheek stubbled with a mixture of gray and white hair. "You're here because they found Mr. Stampler's body up there in New York, aren't you?" He dropped his hand to his side and stuck it into the pocket of his baggy jeans. "I heard about it on the news. It's a shame. A real shame. Mr. Stampler was a nice man. Never forgot to ask how a body was getting on, and always tipped well if he needed something done. Kind of old-fashioned too. He'd sneak in and leave a little something extra during the Christmas holidays as a kind of gift from Santa. I always knew who it was from, but never let on because he got such a charge out of that." The man squinted against the sun as he peered up at her. "The FBI, you said?" When Gin nodded, he blew out a long, quiet breath. "Then I guess you've been to see his wife. How's Mrs. Stampler doing?"

"Holding together," Gin said. She pointed first to Trey and then to Finn. "This is Special Agent Robard, and Special Agent Sullivan. And I take it you work here, mister...?"

"Jake," the man said in a gruff voice. "I'm Jake Bean, and I sure do work here. I've been the daytime security and general handyman going on twenty years now. I was here when Mr. Stampler first brought that boat over from the dry dock. That yacht company he bought it from was piloting it in for him. Kind of showing him the ropes, if you know what I mean." Jake's gaze held a tinge of sadness. "Not that he needed to be shown much of anything. The *Traci Marie* wasn't the first boat he owned. Not by a long shot."

Gin smiled. It seemed Jake was a big fan of Benjamin Stampler's. He certainly had a lot more compliments for the man than the Meridian executive team had. Between the three executives, all clad in their expensive silk suits, they'd hardly mentioned the dead CEO's name. "Maybe you could help us, Jake. Were you here the night Mr. Stampler disappeared?"

Keeping one hand in his pocket, he waved the other one in the air. "Not that night. The *Traci Marie* was still in her berth when I clocked out of my shift. And it was there the next morning. But I was told by the police that it had been seen headed out just after five that afternoon." He paused for a moment, then spoke more slowly, as if it was painful to get the words out. "I saw Mr. Stampler come through the gate that day, though."

He turned and pointed to the opposite end of the dock. "I was working over there, securing a board that felt like it had come loose a bit. It was too far to go shouting a hi or something, and he didn't notice me crouched down low like that, so I just kept an eye as he continued on his way toward C dock." He bowed his head. "That's the last time I saw him. Just walking down that dock like he didn't have a care in the world." He looked at Gin and squared his shoulders. "I told all this to the cops when they came by."

The handyman's interview would hopefully be in the case file, but for the time being, Gin preferred to ask her own questions. "We like to verify everything," she said without missing a beat. "What about Gerald Mobley? He usually served as a crew member on the *Traci Marie*. Did you know him?"

"Sure, sure," Jake confirmed. "Hard not to since he was around here so much. Nice young man. He would crew on quite a few boats moored here. Everyone liked Gerald. Always had a smile, never a mean word to anyone." Jake looked off into the distance. "No one's seen him either. Not since Mr. Stampler disappeared anyway. At least that's what the police told me."

"That's right," Gin said. "Did you see Mr. Mobley that day?"

Jake nodded. "Sure, sure," he said, repeating what was obviously a favorite phrase. "He came through the gate just a few minutes before I was supposed to clock out for the day. I ran into him when I was coming up from C dock, checking on a complaint. Gerald told me he was meeting Mr. Stampler so they could take a look at a reported leak." Now Jake's craggy features pulled down into a frown. "But I don't know who reported that because there was nothing about a leak recorded in my log."

Intrigued, Gin widened her stance and crossed her arms

over her chest. "Really? Would you expect that leak to have been reported to you first?"

"Sure, sure," Jake insisted with some force behind his voice. "That's how it works. If there's a complaint or something wrong with one of the boats, I get the call and record it in my log. Then I call the owner." His chin jutted out. "And I record that in my log too. I thought maybe I just didn't remember getting that report, so I went back and checked my log." He shook his head. "Nothing recorded there. No one ever told me about it."

"Jake." Trey took a half step forward as he spoke up for the first time, drawing the old man's gaze in his direction. "Did the Stamplers ever rent out the *Traci Marie*? Or maybe let a friend use it for the day?"

The handyman coughed out a laugh. "Ha. No. Never. Not even once. That boat was Mr. Stampler's baby. He never let anyone except Gerald walk onto the *Traci Marie* unless he was there to greet them. I don't even think he'd let his wife do that, and he named the boat after her."

"Thank you," Trey said before politely stepping back again.

"Was there anything recorded in your log around the time of Mr. Stampler's disappearance?" Gin asked, taking up the questioning once more.

"Nothing to speak of. Berth B4 let me know someone had left a trash bag on the dock. Turned out it was full of empty liquor bottles. I got rid of those real quick," Jake stated with a hard nod. "I don't need any broken glass on my docks. Then there was a complaint about a dinghy tied up in berth C19. That's the second one from the end. I just left a note on it, warning the owner that he wasn't allowed to use that berth and if he didn't remove his boat, it would be hauled out of the water and disposed of." Jake rocked back on his heels with a sheepish grin. "Not sure I could actually do that, but it must have worked. When I got to the marina the next morning, the dinghy was gone."

"The dinghy wasn't supposed to be in that berth?" Gin asked.

"Nope. The *Deep Fisher* belongs in that berth, but the owners have her out for the entire month. I think they're taking a run up the coast to Tampa, so I know that dinghy didn't belong to them. But it wasn't any big deal. It was filled with fishing rods and a bait box, so I figured some guys had tied up at a convenient spot and went out to have themselves a beer, that's all. We don't get a lot of that going on around here, but it happens every once in a while. Usually I spot them coming or going, but not always. Sometimes one of the owners loan out their code." He pursed his lips and stroked a hand underneath his chin. "You know, I was just coming back from leaving that note when I ran into Gerald. That's when he told me about the leak."

Gin's eyes narrowed slightly. "And you told all this to the Miami PD?"

"About seeing Gerald and the leak? Sure, sure," Jake said. "I don't recall if I told them about the beer bottles, or the dinghy illegally moored in the *Deep Fisher*'s spot." His eyebrows beetled together as he thought it over. "No. I don't think they asked about it. Just about Gerald."

"And that's the last time you saw Gerald?"

"That's right." Jake drew in a slow breath and peered off into the distance. "I started in on a job on the next dock over, but I kept an eye on the *Traci Marie* so I could wave a friendly hello to the boy. He was always on the flybridge, fiddling around with that fancy electronic equipment Mr. Stampler liked so much. But he must have been down below checking out that leak, 'cause I never saw him come onto the deck."

Gin paused and looked around. There still wasn't much

activity in the marina, but they needed to take the opportunity to canvass the area and overturn some rocks. "Jake? Would you mind accompanying Agent Sullivan and introducing him to anyone who's around? Maybe someone saw something that night and hasn't reported it yet to the police."

Jake scratched his head, then slowly nodded, but there was obvious doubt in his eyes. "It was a weekday. Just like this." He lifted an arm and swung it around in a half circle. "You can see, not much going on about now. It will be jumping on the weekend, but in the middle of the week like this?" He dropped his arm and shrugged. "Not so much."

Finn lightly clapped the handyman on the shoulder. "That's okay, Jake. If we don't find anyone to talk to, then we don't. But it's our job to try. Maybe you can show me where the dinghy you scared off was tied up?" He glanced down the dock. "Now, which way is it? Down here?"

"Yep." Jake started off with Finn by his side.

Gin and Trey exchanged an amused glance before falling into step behind them. She listened to the banter of the two men ahead of her as Finn expertly asked questions about the owners of the boats in the berths immediately around the *Traci Marie*.

As the small group walked down the wood planking, it looked like each boat they came to was more spectacular than the last. Sunlight gleamed off pure white hulls and polished hardware, while gulls circled overhead, and the sound of creaking ropes played an odd sounding symphony all the way down the dock.

If I ever imagine a toy box for the rich, this would have to be it, Gin thought. She blinked at glimpses of mahogany decking and sunning areas bigger than her living room. Now granted, her apartment back in Denver didn't boast a lot of floor space so that bar wasn't very high, but still, knowing the amount of money that was sitting on the water around her made her goggle in spite of herself.

When they reached the *Traci Marie,* Finn stood for a moment admiring the sleek lines and heavily tinted windows before lifting a hand in the air and continuing on down the dock with Jake.

Trey walked over to a ladder attached to the side of the boat and looked back at Gin. "There isn't anyone to put out a gangway, so the ladder will have to do." Without waiting for a response, he easily swung himself up the small steps and onto the deck.

Gin barely managed not to applaud at what she considered a superb feat of balance and agility, especially since even the small movement of the boat could make you lose your balance on that narrow stepladder.

With little experience on boats, she warily eyed the ladder and gauged the distance between it and the rolling dock. Reaching across the small gap, she closed one hand around the guardrail of the steps and pulled herself onto them. She didn't even pretend to come close to the graceful boarding demonstrated by the former Navy pilot, but was happy to just keep her feet on the rungs and haul herself onto the deck without taking a header into the water. Which she considered a victory, even if after watching her performance Trey felt it necessary to reach out a hand to steady her.

When she muttered a thanks, he grinned back at her. "All part of the rookie service, ma'am."

Straightening up, she took a careful look around. Once she got moving again and walked toward the back, she stopped and put her hands on her hips, studying the cockpit area at the stern of the boat. Spacious, with a scattering of tables and chairs, it was easy to imagine lounging around in the sun, a drink with a small paper umbrella sticking out of it in one hand and a fan in

A HARD TRUTH

the other. She was sure she remembered a scene or two out of a movie that had looked exactly like that.

Trey came up beside her. "What do you think?"

"I think the Stamplers have a lot of money," she said before glancing at him. "This is more your area of expertise. What do *you* think?"

He'd donned a pair of sunglasses when they'd first walked onto the docks, and now he adjusted them as he took enough steps forward to be standing in the middle of the cockpit that also served as the entertainment deck and sunbathing area. "She's a beauty." The admiration in his voice had a slight twinge of envy in it. "If there is a leak, there's no way Stampler would have taken her out and risked this boat. That would have been criminal."

"And if there isn't any leak?" Gin prompted. "Then maybe that witness Crandon didn't believe was right after all, and Stampler did take it out for a little spin."

"So the call claiming his boat had a leak was a way to lure Stampler out here?"

Gin stared at the water lapping gently against the hull of the boat moored across from the *Traci Marie*. "By someone who didn't know about the usual protocol of calling problems into Jake and letting him contact the owner."

Trey glanced at the keys Gin was still holding in her hand. "Any chance the engine key is on that ring?"

Since she had no idea, Gin lightly tossed the ring over to Trey, who caught it in one hand. "Maybe. You can try them if you want. But is there any reason you want to turn the engine on?"

"Jake mentioned there were a lot of fancy electronics on the flybridge." His teeth flashed white in a wide grin. "I'm hoping he has a chart plotter on board that automatically boots up whenever the engine is turned on."

"Which will then what?" she asked. "Record wherever the boat has been?"

Looking mildly surprised that she knew that, Trey smiled. "That's right. It will show location markers, if Stampler had the plotter as well as the power set on automatic because I doubt that the killer would turn it on." He shrugged. "Which is only worthwhile if the guy the Miami PD had out here knew how to read the plotter and the boat was actually taken out."

"And that seems to ride on whether or not there's a leak." She tapped a slender index finger against her bottom lip. "Which brings up the interesting question you raised about Stampler letting other people use the boat."

"Yeah." Trey held up the keys in his hand and studied them. "Jake was positive that he did not."

"Uh-huh." Gin watched as he carefully picked out a key, then walked over to the cabin door and inserted it. "If he never loaned the *Traci Marie* out, then who reported the leak to him? From what we've been told, neither man knew about any leak until someone contacted them about it. But how did that someone know, and Stampler didn't? I mean, according to Jake, Stampler was here whenever anyone else set foot on the boat, including his own wife."

"Except for Mobley. He was allowed on board without Stampler being present." Trey turned the key in the lock, which gave way with a soft click. He pushed down on the handle, then grinned as the door swung open without so much as a squeak. "So, where do you want to start?"

Gin glanced at the closed door leading into the interior living space and cabins. Where would you start if you wanted to search a boat? She switched her gaze to Trey and gave him a speculative look. Leaning into your strengths sounded good to her. "Why don't you take a quick look around for that leak, then do a check of the electronics on that flybridge. Do you know how to operate a chart plotter?"

Trey's face dropped into a pained look. "I'll manage. And what are you going to do?"

"Take a look around this area for anything wonky, then work my way up front. Maybe the cops missed something."

A moment later, Trey had disappeared down the stairs and she was slowly walking around the entertainment space at the rear of the boat. She lifted cushions and got down on her hands and knees to get a closer look at the deck. Finding nothing, she made her way to the very back of the cockpit and stood in front of a large storage box tucked into one corner. Since there wasn't a lock, she lifted the cover, only to find nothing inside. Frowning, she closed the lid, then moved a few feet to the side and looked down at a wide platform, attached to the hull and floating just above the water. A small ladder led down to it. After debating with herself for a moment, Gin shrugged and started down the ladder.

Gripping the thin rails tightly enough her fingers started to ache, she slowly descended, carefully placing one foot at a time on the rungs until she could step onto the platform. It was wide enough she could easily balance on it, but even the slight movement of the boat made her feel unsteady on her feet. She kept a firm hold on the ladder as she carefully looked around for any evidence of blood or something out of place. Coming up blank, she returned to the deck just as Trey emerged from the inner cabin.

At her questioning look, he shook her head. "No leaks in the bilge. It was dry as a bone. I'm going up top to check the equipment."

"Fine," she said to his back as he sprinted up to the flybridge. She lingered in the cockpit, her gaze returning to the empty box in the corner. Moving back toward it, she reached over and fingered the latch. There were scratches on the outside and the latch was slightly bent, as if it had been tampered with. *Or pried open*, she thought. She stared at it for several long minutes, her mind running through possibilities until she finally rubbed two fingers against her temple.

The start of a headache gave a warning signal. Sometimes they descended on her like a clap of thunder, with no warning at all, so she was grateful to have some advanced notice to take her medication. But it still wasn't a reason to jump up and down with joy. The slam of a migraine could put her down for a day or two, and she didn't have time for that right now. While the attacks were thankfully rare these days, when they came, they still had to be dealt with.

"Oh, shit."

Trey's voice ripped through the air like a bolt of lightning. Startled, Gin looked over her shoulder at the same time that Trey leaped from the flybridge.

"Bomb. Jump! Jump! Jump!"

He landed on the balls of his feet and shot forward, his arm out with the clear intent of shoving her along in front of him. But she'd already turned, and with the years of practice from swimming in the large pond on the farm, stepped up on the gunwale and launched herself into a perfect arc over the stern of the boat.

She was still in the air when the explosion ripped out, knocking her for a loop, and sending her cartwheeling head over heels toward the water. Automatic reflex had her throwing an arm over the back of her head to protect her neck as she sucked in a lungful of air a split second before she plowed full speed into the brackish water of the marina.

It felt like she'd hit a brick wall that then crumbled beneath her weight as she plunged beneath the surface. Stunned by the impact, she fought to keep the black edges of unconsciousness

A HARD TRUTH

threatening to completely engulf her. She waited, eyes squeezed shut against the sting of salt water, and arms moving to keep her down until her lungs burned. With the last of her breath, she kicked upward, and kept kicking, fighting to get to the surface.

As soon as her head broke the surface, she pulled in a breath, and then another, coughing hard between each one. After the third breath the coughing eased off, so she opened her eyes, squinting against the water dripping from her hair down into her face.

She stared at the scene in front of her, barely hearing the jumble of noise rising all around her. Still panting, she blinked in confusion. There were boats, but they didn't make any sense. The rows marched down on either side, and beyond them was a clear path to open water. That wasn't how the dock looked. The boats were all wrong. They weren't in individual berths but lined up in a row. And she couldn't see the *Traci Marie*. Or what was left of the yacht if it had been blown to bits. She bobbed in the water, willing her breathing to slow down so she could think straight.

Past C dock. The random thought popped into her head. She was no longer between docks with individual berths, but in the slightly wider channel that led out to sea. Her nose twitched as she fought off a spurt of panic. She couldn't be far from the explosion because she could smell smoke, and there was debris floating in the water. It took her a long moment before she realized she was floating along with it. Toward that open water.

Tide. Shit, she thought, willing her arms and legs to move faster. Used to swimming in ponds, not oceans, she could slow her drift, but not completely stop it. Before she could muster up enough energy to turn herself in the right direction, something snaked around her neck. She yelped and instantly grabbed at it, intending to pull it away as her feet kicked wildly out to the sides.

"Gin, stop. It's Trey. Stop fighting me."

The sound of Trey's voice next to her ear had her going limp with relief. "Trey?"

"Yeah. I've got you. Let's get both of us out of here."

"Great," she croaked. "Have you got a boat handy?"

"We aren't going to wait for one. Rest your chin on my arm and relax. Can you kick enough to keep your body horizontal?"

Gin dutifully kicked a little harder, floating on her back while Trey steadily pulled them along until they were back inside the waterway for C dock.

"Got an idea how we're going to get out of here?" she asked. The circle of his arm around her neck didn't allow her to turn her head to see where she was going, but now that she was no longer fighting for air, or the current, she became aware of the shouting, sirens, and chaos of activity rising up from the docks.

She made out Finn's voice, yelling Trey's name, getting louder as the rescue pilot headed toward it, pulling her along with him. It was barely a minute before his arm disappeared and she saw Finn reaching over the edge of a swim deck attached to a yacht even bigger than the *Traci Marie*.

She lifted her arms and felt more than saw Finn's hands grab her wrists. He slowly drew her out of the water until Trey's hand on her butt gave her a firm boost that had Finn dragging her onto the swim deck. The big Irishman rolled her onto her back, letting her feet dangle into the water as he turned and offered a hand to Trey. She felt the deck dip slightly under the additional weight and opened her eyes as Trey collapsed next to her, breathing heavily.

"You two stay put. I'm going to get the paramedics over here."

"No problem," Gin said. Once Finn hurried away, her eyes

A HARD TRUTH

narrowed on Trey's face as she struggled to prop herself up on one elbow. There was a wicked bruise, already turning several colors of the rainbow, stretching from his cheekbone all the way down to his neck. "What happened? You look like you got smacked by a two-by-four."

He kept his eyes closed. "I got smacked by a two-by-four," he repeated back to her. "Or something like it. It hit me before I reached the water," he croaked out before cracking open one eye to stare at her. "I saw you do that somersault and then disappear. You were down so long, I thought you'd drowned."

Suddenly becoming acutely aware of the battering her own body had taken, she gingerly lay back down. "There was a pond on the farm in Iowa where I grew up. A pretty big one. Devin and I used to go out there and have contests to see who could hold their breath the longest. I usually made it to about two and a half minutes."

"Who's Devin?" Trey asked. "Your brother?"

"Uh-huh." Gin tried to bend her leg, then winced. She was pretty sure her knee was just as swollen as it felt. "Older brother. He always won those contests."

She could hear a stampede of footsteps running down the dock. She wasn't fond of hospitals, but at the moment, she wouldn't say no to some pain meds. With a sigh, she looked over at Trey, who was still lying on his back with his eyes closed. "It sounds like the cavalry has arrived. And oh yeah, by the way, Agent Robard?" She paused until he let out a deep grunt. "Your break-in period is officially over. Welcome to the team."

Chapter Twelve

A sharp ring jarred her awake. Still fuzzy from the pain meds she'd received at the emergency room the night before, Gin kept her eyes tightly shut as she reached out an arm, scooped up her cell phone from the nightstand, then blindly jabbed at the screen. When the loud noise didn't stop, she painfully cracked open one eye and waited until the phone came into focus.

For some weird reason, the icon for the alarm clock wasn't on her screen. In fact, the damn phone was dark, but the ringing was still going. She dropped the phone onto the mattress and closed her eyes again as her hand crawled across the top of the nightstand, looking for the landline supplied in every room by the hotel.

When she finally found it, she knocked the receiver off the cradle. Swearing under her breath, she groped around before locating it and bringing it over to her ear. "Whatever this is, I don't want to hear it."

"This is your FBI contact in Miami, standing outside your door with a cup of hot coffee."

A HARD TRUTH

She winced at Finn's booming voice. "Why didn't you call me on my cell phone?"

"Because you can decline those calls. This phone keeps ringing until you answer it. Can you make it to the door?"

She tentatively moved a leg. It was sore, but not enough for her to stay in bed all day. But it told a different story when she tried to sit up. The soreness in her leg switched to a sharp pain radiating outward from her ribs. She immediately stopped wiggling and lay still on the bed. "No. As much as I'd like that coffee, I'm not crawling over to the door to get it."

"Okay," Finn said. "I hope you're decent."

Before she could say anything the line went dead, and there was a faint clicking noise. A second later the door opened and Finn strode into view, juggling a paper bag along with a cardboard carrier with two cups of coffee nestled inside it.

"I bring gifts," he said with a grin. "Coffee and bagels. I figured you'd need food before you took any more pain meds." He set both the tray and the bag down on the small desk, then turned to give her a thorough once-over. "You don't look as bad as I thought you would."

Gritting her teeth, Gin squirmed her way into a sitting position against the pillows. "That's funny, because you look very annoying, standing here in my room. Is the front desk handing out keys to just anyone these days?"

He plucked a coffee cup out of the tray and walked over to the bed. Holding it out, he winked at her. "No. I got it from you. Or rather from your jacket. You had two keys, so I took one after I tucked you in last night." He shrugged when her eyes shot wide open. "You didn't object, and I very politely waited until the ER doc told me those pain meds would be wearing off before showing up this morning."

Gin glanced at the clock on the nightstand. It was not exactly the crack of dawn, but it was still several hours away from noon. "Thanks for that, but I could hardly object to anything since I was out cold," she tossed back at him. She lifted the covers and looked down at her body.

Except for her bare feet, she still had on the same clothes she'd worn the day before. Having been soaked in seawater, they weren't very comfortable now that she was awake enough to realize it, but that was a lot better than having to endure the horrifying image of Finn undressing her. She wasn't a prude, but he was like a brother, and a fellow agent to boot, so the whole thought was a little creepy.

Dropping the covers, she reached out and took the coffee he was offering, bringing the cup to her lips and closing her eyes over that first sip of the hot brew. "This is good." She almost hummed the words as the warmth spread through her midsection and helped chase the last of the fog from her brain. "Really good. Thanks."

"No problem." He put his hands on his hips and tilted his head to the side as his gaze slowly roamed over her face. "Think you can keep a bagel down?"

She silently took inventory before nodding. "Yeah. I'm starving. But I don't want any more of those pain meds. They worked great but made me loopy, and I'd rather put up with the aches and pains."

"I know that feeling." Finn reached into his pocket and drew out a small, amber-colored bottle. "So I filled this for you this morning from the prescription the ER doc gave you. Not as powerful, so they're only going to take those aches and pains down to a tolerable level, but they won't make you loopy." He set the bottle on the nightstand, then retreated to the bathroom for a glass of water while Gin continued to sip her coffee. When he returned, he grabbed the brown bag before walking over and putting the glass of water next to the medicine bottle.

A HARD TRUTH

Opening the bag, he held it out to her. "Napkins are on top, and all the bagels are plain. No garlic, cheese, or anything else."

She smiled as she reached in and retrieved a napkin and bagel, taking in a deep, appreciative breath. "Thanks. It smells wonderful." When she lifted the bagel to her mouth, Finn took a giant step backwards. She bit off a piece of the warm roll, chewing slowly as she watched him tense up. "Is something wrong?"

He shook his head, then after a few seconds his shoulders relaxed again. "Nope. Not now that I know you can keep that down. Your new partner took one bite and had to do a quick crawl to the bathroom. I left him there while he was puking his guts out."

Alarmed, Gin lowered the bagel and glared at the big Irishman. "You just left him like that? How badly is Trey hurt?"

"He's still breathing," Finn said with a careless shrug. "What was I supposed to do? I thought while he was busy hugging the toilet bowl, I'd come over and check on you."

"I gather you'd commandeered one of his room keys too?" Gin frowned. Finn was a big, tough guy, and also an old-fashioned one. There is no way he would have checked on Trey before her unless he had a reason. "How bad off is Trey?"

"Worse than you. He's got two cracked ribs and a possible concussion according to the ER doc, but I doubt that. His head is too hard. However, he is showing a lot more bruising than you are. One of his arms is black and purple from the shoulder down to his elbow."

"Then you'd better get back to his room and stay with him. I'll join you as soon as I grab a shower and some clean clothes." She threw the covers back and winced. Annoyed, she grabbed the pain meds and washed two of the pills down with a large gulp from the glass of water before making a shooing motion at

Finn. "You go. I'll give these twenty minutes to kick in while I shower, and then I'll be along."

Instead, Finn walked over to the desk, sat down, and made himself comfortable. "When I first walked in, the guy was on the phone, and judging by the amount of groveling, it sounded like an apology to his girlfriend. At least that's who I assume she was when I picked up the phone to explain to her why he'd made a sudden exit to the bathroom."

Despite her worry for her partner's injuries, Gin couldn't stop the smirk. "Girlfriend? He hasn't mentioned one of those."

Finn met her grin with one of his own. "I gather from what she said that our brave rescue pilot was supposed to fly back to Colorado last night, and somehow neglected to tell her he wasn't going to make it."

"And I'll bet she was fuming," Gin said.

"Makes that fake boyfriend of yours sound a little better," Finn replied, laughing at Gin's glare. "Yeah, I know, I know. He's not fake, he just works in another branch of the Bureau and is undercover a lot, so he can't call or get together very often." He shook his head. "Sounds more like a pal with benefits than a boyfriend."

Not willing to get into a discussion about her personal life, and especially not with so much else to deal with at the moment, Gin took another bite of her bagel as the pain meds started to do their job. "Do we need to take Trey back to the ER? It sounds like he should have stayed overnight."

"I certainly thought so," Finn said. "And so did the doctor. But Trey disagreed. He refused to stay, so I'm thinking we'd have to knock him out to get him back there." A note of admiration crept into his voice. "I tell you, that is one strong sonofabitch. He's hurting like that but still pulled you in before you end up somewhere out in the middle of the Atlantic. It was pretty impressive." He paused to take a sip of his own coffee.

"And by the way, he told me last night when I was getting him settled in that he got a picture of the route before he spotted the bomb."

Gin's mouth dropped open. "A picture of the route? The one the *Traci Marie* took the night Stampler disappeared?" When he nodded, her mind raced over possibilities. "I need to get a look at that route."

"It's from a marine navigation system," Finn pointed out. "Think you can read that?"

"I'll bet Trey can."

Finn lifted a skeptical eyebrow. "Yeah. But even if the equipment had survived that blast, you're talking about our banged-up, barely-can-walk agent who will probably need some more of those serious pain meds to get through the day."

He was interrupted by loud, rapid knocking on the room's door. Over the sharp, staccato sound came Americk's voice.

"Gin? Are you all right? Are you awake? If you don't answer me, I'm going to get housekeeping to open this door."

"Why not?" Gin muttered as she set her steaming cardboard cup aside. "Everyone else just walks in here." She gave Finn an impatient look. "So? Go let her in."

"I hope she brought her own coffee." The FBI agent got to his feet, and still carrying his half-filled cup, went to let the forensic tech in. As soon as the door cracked open, he was forced to step back as it was pushed back hard enough to bounce against the doorstop mounted on the baseboard of the adjacent wall.

Americk rushed by him, her signature hair bun sitting at a precarious angle on the top of her head. She scurried over to the bed and leaned down to engulf Gin in a hard hug that had several new aches throbbing in protest.

"Hey. I'm good, I'm good," Gin said, trying to push back on a surprisingly strong Americk.

The older woman finally let go, then sat down on the edge of the bed, grabbing one of Gin's hands in her own. "How badly are you hurt? I was told by that nice Agent Byers that Trey was in bad shape, but he thought you were all right." She leaned down until she was almost nose-to-nose with Gin and peered anxiously into the younger woman's face. "How are you feeling?"

Gin leaned back as far as the pillows behind her would allow. "I really am good." She pointed to the small amber bottle on the nightstand. "Finn brought me those, and they're taking care of the leftover pain without making me goofy." Not entirely true, but the aches had subsided considerably, and that was all Americk needed to know. When the forensic tech finally moved back, Gin added a smile. "I was about to take a shower and check on Trey. And by the way, who is Byers?"

"He's attached to the Miami office," Finn said. "I've known him for about five years. He's a solid guy."

"Yes, he certainly is," Americk declared. "I was still at the police station when the emergency call came in, so I rode along with Captain Crandon. Agent Byers showed up at the marina just a few minutes later." She wrinkled her nose. "I think the assistant chief contacted the local FBI office and let them know what was going on." She turned her head to look at Finn, who had taken up his seat next to the desk again. "I guess you're the one who called 911?"

He shook his head. "Nope. That was Jake. I was too busy trying to find Gin and Trey."

"Well, you did a good job." Americk beamed at him. "They both made it through that explosion in one piece." She swung her gaze back to Gin. "And Agent Byers made very sure that I was allowed to go over the scene right along with the Miami PD's forensic team. Which, of course, I did. And I met them in their lab first thing this morning. I bullied them into coming in an hour early so we could get a jump on everything."

When she paused, Gin gently retrieved her hand. "Was there anything to get a jump on? The last thing I remember before hitting the water was Trey running across the deck, yelling about a bomb and that I should jump."

"And from what I was told about both of your injuries when I called Finn last night, it's a good thing you did," Americk declared with a frown. "So if Trey shouted out about the bomb, then he must have seen it? I need to talk to him to verify that his visual description matches what we've found."

When she paused, Gin gave her an impatient nudge with her good knee. "Which was what?"

"From fragments we've recovered, I'd say it was a pipe bomb with a cell phone attached to it. But it would be helpful if Agent Robard could verify that for us."

"A cell phone?" Gin snapped. At Americk's startled look, she slowly drew in a breath and held it. She was hardly an expert on bombs, but she knew enough. "That cell phone would have been the trigger?"

The tech nodded. "That's right. At least that's what we are thinking, given the bits and pieces we've gathered from the scene."

Both women looked over at Finn as he slowly rose from his chair. "So if the detonator was a radio signal from the cell phone, doesn't someone have to send that signal?"

"That's right," Americk confirmed. "It's possible that signal could have been sent from quite a distance away. Whatever the range on the cell phone is."

Finn's features had hardened into a mask of anger. "Right. Except how would the bomber have known when to send it unless he had eyes on that boat? I'm not buying that two federal agents just happened to be there when the thing went off.

That's bullshit. Someone had eyes on that boat, and deliberately triggered the bomb."

"I'm not buying it either," Gin added, then gave Americk a direct look. "How big was the bomb? Was the whole boat blown up?"

"Enough that it isn't salvageable, and it might have turned the whole thing into debris if the blast had reached the gas tanks. The damage was significant but confined, with enough strength to take off that top piece." She frowned as she searched for a word. "Flybridge is what Byers called it, I believe. And part of the deck and cabin below it, but not much more." She tapped one finger against her lower lip. "But I see what you mean. While it wasn't powerful enough to completely destroy the ship, it was strong enough to kill anyone standing close to it."

"Trey was on the flybridge when he started yelling, so that's where he saw the bomb." Gin looked to Americk for confirmation, who gave a quick nod. "Then whoever sent that signal must have known he was up there, but didn't blow it right away." Gin's forehead wrinkled as she carefully stepped her way through the events. "Trey was on the flybridge for several minutes, and I was in the cockpit area when the bomb went off. Right after Trey started yelling."

"The bomber might have been waiting to see if he could get you both up on the flybridge," Finn pointed out. "And when that didn't happen, he hit the trigger. He probably knew exactly when Trey spotted the bomb, knew he had been made, and had the number cued up and all ready to go."

"Sounds about right," Gin agreed. "Except. . ."

When she trailed off, Finn frowned. "Except for what?"

She shrugged and gently forced Americk off the bed before swinging her legs over the side. "Except it doesn't make sense.

A HARD TRUTH

He can't have been watching that boat all day, every day since Stampler's disappearance."

"Why not? Maybe we're looking for a local crazy after all," Finn said.

Gin shook her head. "Who also murdered a guy in Northern California, and a couple of other places if Stephen's leads pan out?" She shook her head again before making a successful, if still unsteady, effort to stand on her feet. "This guy isn't local. And he isn't stupid. But he is crazy, and somehow he knew we were going to be on the *Traci Marie* yesterday. Which means someone tipped him off." She frowned. "The number of people who knew they were coming to Miami was pretty small. Or maybe not. Their plans could have been overheard by anyone in the Buffalo forensic lab and innocently passed on to spread through the entire Erie County Sheriff's Department.

Setting that puzzle aside for the moment with a mental sigh, she concentrated on the killer, who very likely was also the bomber. He was following some twisted logic of his own on how he's choosing his victims, and that's where they needed to put their time. They had to figure out the connections between the victims, then follow that back to their killer and put him in a cage where he belonged.

She slowly breathed in and out as she concentrated on keeping her balance. "This guy has a reason for everything he does—from who his victims are to getting rid of the investigators. So he had to have had a reason for making Stampler or maybe Mobley take the *Traci Marie* out that night. I'm thinking he wanted to take care of a couple of bodies."

"A couple?" Americk asked as her gaze bounced from Gin to Finn.

"Yeah," Finn answered, his gaze on Gin. "Stampler, and his crewman, Gerald Mobley."

"Which means," Gin went on for him. "We need to get a look at that navigation chart that Trey took a picture of. If we can figure out where the *Traci Marie* went that night, then we might also find our kill site."

"You take that shower while I go check on Trey," Finn said. "He's in room 402. I'll see you there in. . .?"

"It's still twenty minutes," Gin filled in for him. She glanced over at Americk. "Going or staying?"

"Staying," the older woman declared. "In case you need help getting dressed or walking to Trey's room."

His room was only two doors down, but Gin didn't bother to argue. "Suit yourself," she said before heading to the small ledge where her suitcase was perched. Grabbing some clean clothes, she walked to the bathroom.

Her gait was stiff enough that Americk winced. But the older woman would just have to get used to it because she couldn't do anything more about the pain and stiffness, and right now her whole focus was first checking on Trey, then getting a look at that map.

True to her word, with Americk in tow, Gin knocked on room 402's door exactly twenty minutes later. The wickedly hot shower had helped her aches and pains as much as the medication she'd taken, so between the two things, she now felt almost normal. Or at least a lot closer to it than she had when Finn had knocked on her door. It was only a moment before the door was opened and Finn stepped aside to let Gin and Americk pass by.

"How is he doing?" Gin asked in a low voice.

"Much better than when Finn woke me up this morning." Trey's voice floated down the short hallway leading into the bedroom.

"Which isn't saying much," Finn replied before turning back to shut the door behind Americk.

A HARD TRUTH

Bracing herself, Gin walked into the larger room, and after a look at Trey, couldn't keep the alarm out of her gaze. Half his face, along with his entire upper left arm, was covered in bruises. He looked like he'd been dipped in a can of mixed paints all swirled together. Ugly red with a tinge of yellow around the edges and streaks of purple all intertwined to make a giant, painful-looking splotch across his skin. When his smile quickly dissolved into a grimace, she couldn't hold back the wince.

Not wanting to jostle him, she grabbed the chair tucked beneath the identical desk she had in her own room, and carried it over to the bed. Taking a seat, her gaze slowly roamed over Trey's face. "How the hell did you drag me halfway back up that dock to where Finn was waiting?"

He coughed out a laugh. "I'm an excellent swimmer."

"Now there's an understatement," Finn said from behind Gin. "Have you tried to keep any more of that bagel down?"

Trey's eyes cut over to the nightstand. What was left of his bagel was occupying a paper napkin. "Most of it. Along with the two glasses of water you left me."

Gin reached out and picked up one of the empty glasses, passing it back over her shoulder. "Americk? Would you mind refilling this for our fearless agent here?"

"Not at all." The lead tech grabbed the glass from Gin's hand and did a quick walk to the bathroom.

While the faucet was running, Trey nodded toward the nightstand. "Can you hand me my cell phone? I'm not ready to reach that far yet. Maybe in an hour or so."

Maybe in a week or so, Gin thought but she only smiled. "Not a problem." She picked up the cell and handed it to Trey, who took it with his right hand and did a one-fingered tap on the screen. "I found the last entry on the chart plotter and took a picture before I spotted that bomb tucked behind the Fathometer." He sighed as he kept tapping on the screen. "That was too bad. That equipment was top-of-the-line."

"It's all in pieces now," Americk declared as she leaned over Gin to set the water glass on the nightstand. "And before you dive back into whatever you're doing there, can you tell me what the bomb looked like?"

"Pipe bomb. The favorite IED of terrorists," Trey said in a clipped tone. "I saw several of them when I was deployed to some of our more remote airstrips. This one was a hard cylinder with a cell phone attached to it with duct tape. The cylinder looked like PVC pipe, but I only got a quick look."

Americk nodded. "Which is consistent with what we found. So thank you for that confirmation. I'll let the forensic team know right away." She started to reach into her pocket when her hand suddenly changed directions and she gave herself an open-handed slap on the forehead. "In all this excitement, I almost forgot. Tony called. He said the Buffalo team was still working on their forensic testing, but he wanted me to know they found something odd in some of the body swabs that the ME took from the back of the body."

Three pairs of eyes focused on the older woman hard enough to make her blush. "The swabs of the victim's back, legs, and head hair all showed the peppermint oil solution, but it was mixed with a heavy dose of salt. And from the additional sediment particles found in the hair sample, Tony is sure that it came from seawater."

"Seawater?" Finn ran a hand through his hair. "There sure isn't any seawater in that part of upstate New York."

"That's right," Americk confirmed. "The lakes up there are all freshwater, and in that area, so are Niagara Falls and the Great Lakes. But Tony said the salt content definitely marks it as seawater."

"So he had to have picked it up here, in Miami," Gin said.

"And it was on his back and legs, and in his hair?" Her eyes narrowed in thought.

"Maybe he jumped into the ocean for a swim," Finn suggested, then frowned when Americk shook his head.

"Then it would have been all over him, not just on one side," she said.

A picture formed in Gin's mind. "Like he was lying in seawater?" She didn't wait for Americk's confirmation before looking at Trey. "I didn't spend a lot of time on boats when I was growing up, but I noticed this one had two boxes attached to the back of that cockpit area. Right next to the opening to the swim deck. What are those for?"

"Storage lockers," Trey said without hesitation. "One would have been for a life raft, and on a ship that size, they both probably had life rafts in them."

"The one on the right looked like the lock had been pried open, and it was empty," Gin said. "I checked inside. Nothing was in there."

Trey frowned. "If it wasn't being used for a life raft, it would have had other equipment or gear stowed away in it. But it could be they were in the process of replacing an old one." He pursed his lips at that. "But that doesn't explain the latch being pried open, and there's no reason to remove it until the new life raft was available. And if I were to judge by the way the rest of the ship was maintained, I'd say there should have been an inflatable life raft in there. I didn't spot any down below, and they wouldn't have kept them down there anyway."

"Unless someone took it, used it, and didn't bother to put it back," Gin said.

"And I'll bet I know where it was used." Trey held up his phone, waiting while the other two agents crowded in closer. "I won't explain everything you can see in this photo, but it's this location marker that was interesting." He pointed it out. "I was studying it right after I took the picture because the total time of the trip far exceeded what it would take to cover the distance the boat traveled. For that to make sense, they had to have stopped somewhere, and I'm thinking it would be the last locator point before the Traci Marie turned back. Also, there was no meandering around. She was headed for a certain point, reached it, and turned around. That farthest point is where she spent that extra time. And see here?" He tapped a finger on the photo. "It's also the point closest to land. Too close, if you ask me, but I'm not familiar with that area."

Gin glanced at Finn. "I need to take a trip out there."

Seeing the look the other two exchanged, Trey shifted on the bed. "You mean the three of us. *We* need to take a look out there."

Looking at the bruising on Trey's face, Gin adamantly shook her head. "No. Just Finn and I. Your phone is coming with us, but you are staying here and resting up. We might be doing some flying tomorrow or the next day at the latest. You'll need to heal up some more if you want to tag along on that run." She ignored Trey's protest and focused on Finn. "We'll need a guy who can read this stuff, and who knows the coastline. It's possible the piece of land closest to that location point is our kill site, and we need to know where it is and what's out there."

"Agent Byers is an avid boater and knows every inch of the Miami coastline. I'll have him line some transportation to get us out there, along with some extra guys for backup," Finn said, drawing out his phone while Gin did the same with hers.

"Good," she said. "I'll call Chief Alvarez and see if the Miami PD would like to join us."

Chapter Thirteen

As soon as she'd hung up with Chief Alvarez, Gin turned toward the door and gestured for the others to follow. Once they'd reached the hotel lobby, she headed for a secluded area and gratefully dropped onto one of the couches.

"Agent Byers is on his way," Finn reported. "And he's lined up transportation and some backup for us."

"I hope we're talking cars here. If he can get a boat to that last location point that's great, but I'd rather drive and take a look at it from solid ground," Gin said. "I'm forwarding him the photo Trey took of the route."

"Okay. I'm going to have him meet us here, then I'll call Chief Alvarez back and let him know about the extra FBI agents joining us," Finn replied before stepping away.

Gin quickly scrolled through her emails and pulled up the contact number for Traci Stampler. The widow answered on the first ring.

"Agent Reilly? Are you all right?" When Gin didn't say anything, Traci added, "I got your number from Jardin and entered it into my contacts. I received a call from the police last night, and was told that a bomb had gone off on the *Traci Marie,* and that you and Agent Robard were on it at the time."

"I'm fine."

"Jake also called me," Theresa continued. "He's the handyman out at the marina."

"We've met," Gin said. "He's been very helpful."

"Yes, I'm sure he has. I returned his call to get more information than the police were willing to give, and he said the bomb was planted on the flybridge, and that Agent Robard was up there, and you were close by. He said you both had to be rescued from the harbor and were taken off in ambulances." Traci's voice rose half an octave. "I called the hospital, but they wouldn't tell me anything except that neither of you had been admitted there, which could have meant anything."

"I'm fine," Gin repeated again, interrupting her in order to cut off any impending hysterics. "We're both fine. Trey spotted the bomb before it exploded, so we both got off the yacht." Of course that was due to being thrown through the air by the blast, but that was more information than the widow needed to hear. Although she had no doubt that Jake would fill her in on that little tidbit at some point.

"I'm so glad." The relief in Traci's voice sounded genuine. "I have to confess that the reason I'd asked Jardin for your phone number gave me an excuse to check up on him." When Gin didn't say anything, Traci rushed on. "I wanted to be sure he had sent you the files you asked for, but I also wanted your number for myself. I intended to call you and ask if it would be possible to keep me informed on how the investigation was going."

"We aren't allowed to discuss ongoing investigations, Theresa." Gin delivered the standard line, then smiled to herself.

A HARD TRUTH

She'd bet the widow had enough connections to get around that rule fast enough.

"I wouldn't want to get you into any trouble," Theresa said. "I'll see what I can do to have an exception made. Now, what can I do for you?"

"There are lockers on the *Traci Marie*," Gin said without preamble. "I need to know what's in them?"

A sharp laugh came through the cell phone's speaker. "You mean what's left of them? Really, Agent Reilly, there are several lockers on that yacht, and I absolutely cannot recite a list of their contents to you. But you certainly have my permission to open any of them that haven't been destroyed and do an inventory, if that will help."

"I'm actually only interested in the large ones at the back of the cockpit area. There's one on each side. Next to the stern and close to the opening to that swimming platform." Gin bit her lower lip and held her breath, hoping Theresa knew what those lockers contained.

The widow let out a long sigh. "Oh, those. They hold the inflatable life rafts. There's one in each locker."

The slight hum along Gin's nerves picked up tempo. "Theresa, would you be willing to give permission for us to look into those lockers? We might have to cut the locks open."

Traci's voice lost any nervous edge as she laughed. "At this point, cut open anything you like. According to Jake, the *Traci Marie* is a total loss. And I say good riddance."

"Thank you." Gin hesitated for a moment. "I'm very sorry for your loss, Theresa. I know what it's like to lose someone you love."

"Just catch him, Agent Reilly. Catch whoever did this to my Ben."

When the widow broke the connection, Gin stared at her phone for a long moment. Oh, the grieving widow didn't have to have any doubts on that last point. She was going to catch this guy. He'd tried to kill her, and more importantly, her team. It was also beginning to look like he had murdered more than just the two people she already knew about. One way or the other, his killing spree was coming to an end.

"Okay. Byers will be here in an hour," Finn said, breaking into her internal monologue and pulling her back to the immediate problem. "He's going to take a look at that photo you sent and figure out where that yacht went the night Stampler disappeared." He squinted slightly as he stared at Gin's face. "So? What's up?"

Gin held her phone up with one hand and waved it back and forth. "I just finished talking with Mrs. Stampler. She said that an inflatable life raft was stored in that empty locker. And another one in the locker on the opposite side of the deck as well." She lowered her phone, her forehead wrinkled in thought. "Can we get someone from the local office to go out there and look in that second locker, provided it wasn't blown to pieces? Let's find out if there's still a life raft stored in it."

"Sure. If the thing is still intact. That bomb blew out a piece of the cockpit, along with the flybridge," Finn said as he tapped out a number on his phone. "I'm not sure what all survived since I was busy fishing you and Robard out of the harbor."

"And thank you for that." Gin leaned back against the couch cushion as she waited for Finn to complete his call.

"No problem." Finn reported less than a minute later. "Byers said we still have two guys out there watching the site, and they'll check out the locker. He'll send me a text when he gets an answer. What are you thinking? That the killer transported Stampler over to land in the missing life raft? And then drove his corpse to New York?" He frowned at the thought. "Which might put a bigger spotlight on Gerald Mobley. Who'd know better where that life raft was kept than the guy who regularly worked as crew on the boat?"

"It could be him," Gin allowed. And it might be, but it didn't seem likely. If she had to put money on it, Gerald Mobley was dead. The thought was depressing and added more weight to her already tired body. Between the battering she'd taken the day before and the pain meds, a blanket of fatigue had settled on her shoulders.

"What do you say to thirty minutes down?"

Gin noticed Finn staring back at her, his mouth turned down at the corners and worry in his gaze. "I'm okay."

The big Irishman shook his head. "You aren't okay. You're white as a sheet and looking like you're going to fall flat on your nose at any minute."

"Just stretch out right there," Americk advised. The lead tech had been following them around, not saying a word until now. She walked over to the sofa where Gin was sitting and urged her to lie down.

Gin eyed the throw pillow in a light blue brocade with a touch of envy, but still resisted the older woman's efforts to push her down. "I don't think the hotel would appreciate anyone taking a nap in their lobby."

"Well, isn't that too bad?" Americk responded with a note of amusement in her voice. "If you lie down here, it will save the time and energy it would take to crawl back to your room. We'll keep any hotel staff away while you get a little shut-eye. Even a thirty-minute catnap would help with those dizzies I'm sure you're feeling." Her eyes cut over to the hotel reception desk. "And if anyone comes over here, Finn can flash that very shiny badge of his and give them his most intimidating look."

"Right." Gin rolled her eyes but slid down on the couch until she was lying on one side, her head cradled on the blue brocade pillow. Americk was right. She needed some rest if she wanted to stay upright for the rest of the day. The thought had no sooner materialized when her eyes closed and she dropped into sleep.

Her dream of looking down into the water and seeing Stampler staring back up at her was interrupted when someone shook her shoulder.

"Gin, wake up. We need to get going."

Glad to leave the watery vision of Stampler behind, Gin opened her eyes and almost let out a yelped right into Americk's face, just a few inches away from hers.

"Oh good," the older woman said with a broad smile. "You're awake. How do you feel?"

"Back up a little and I'll let you know." When Americk dutifully straightened up, Gin took in a deep breath. She reached up a hand and rubbed the last remnants of the nap from her eyes while she took a quick, silent inventory. The aches and pains were still there, but doable. And now that her head was clearing up, she felt better. Taking in another breath, she sat up and swung her legs over the side of the sofa. A half dozen pairs of eyes set in solemn-looking faces stared back at her, none of whom she recognized except for Finn and Americk.

Ignoring them for a moment, she took out the band that had all but given up the struggle of keeping her hair from drooping in a sad-looking tail down her back. With a deftness born from years of practice, she pulled the loose strands of copper back into a ponytail, then wrapped the elastic band around them to keep them in place. With that small chore completed, she felt more human and focused on the group standing around her.

A man in jeans and a T-shirt with the FBI logo stamped on the front, stepped forward. He wasn't much taller than her five feet, five inches, with an athletic-looking build and a friendly grin. "Agent Reilly? I'm Special Agent Nathan Byers, assigned to the Miami office. It's a pleasure to meet you."

A HARD TRUTH

Gin pushed up to her feet and took the agent's outstretched hand. "It's good to meet you too, Byers. And you can call me Reilly or Gin, whichever you prefer."

"And I'm Nate." He gave her hand a firm shake, then released it to point at the two men standing behind him. "This is Special Agent Tom Heston and Special Agent Mark Wiles. They're also out of Miami. You can call them Tom and Mark," he added with a chuckle.

Acknowledging the two men with a nod, which they returned, Gin's gaze went from Nate to Finn. "So, where are we going?"

"First things first." Finn stepped forward, dug into a gym bag he was carrying, and withdrew a lethal-looking Glock 19M. Shifting it around so he was gripping it barrel first, he held it out to Gin. "Your boss demanded in no uncertain terms to make sure you and Robard were given a weapon, and he also told me the Bureau's standard issue is your gun of choice. You need to be prepared in case we run into anyone else who wants you dead. I've already been upstairs and left the same gun for Trey," he said before she could ask. He reached into the gym bag again, this time producing a shoulder holster.

Gin carefully set the Glock on the coffee table in front of the couch before shrugging into the holster. After tightening the buckle, she picked up the Glock and slipped it into place. She rolled her shoulders back and forth, a half-smile on her lips at the familiar weight. "Thanks. I appreciate it."

"No problem." It was Nate who spoke up. "If you need to get on a plane, we'll be sure you and your partner have the necessary permits."

"Thanks," Gin repeated before looking over at Finn. "How's Trey doing?"

"Pretty good," Finn said. "He was on the phone with

Stephen and it sounded like they were working on another solid lead somewhere in Nevada."

Gin nodded. "Well, if he's doing that, I guess we'd better do our part here in Miami." Her gaze shifted back to Nate. "Where are we headed?"

Nate set his backpack on the ground and opened up the zippered top. He pulled out a long rolled-up sheet of paper, held together with a rubber band. Working the band off, he unrolled the sheet and spread it out on the coffee table. "Let's take a look." He waited while everyone took up a place around the table. "So the *Traci Marie* made about a twenty-mile run. From here." He put his finger on the marina at Miami Beach. "She went south. Past Key Biscayne and down to a point right here." He moved his finger along the coast, stopping about where Gin had expected. It didn't look like there was anything was out there.

She leaned in and pointed to the closest landing point. "Where is that?"

"Now that is interesting," Nate said. "It's a county preserve, located outside the city limits." He straightened up, but his gaze stayed glued on the map. "The preserve isn't a well-advertised place but it has a hiking trail from the road down to the beach." He looked at Gin and nodded. "In the late afternoon it would be pretty much deserted down there."

"How far is it from here?" Gin asked.

"It's in Coral Gables, about thirty minutes to the south."

Finn gave the Miami agent a quick slap on the back. "Nate here has made all the arrangements. Including calling in a favor and having a Coast Guard boat out of their Miami Beach station meet us there."

"Yeah," Nate confirmed. "They'll head right and sit off the coast right on top of the last location point we have for the yacht." He tapped a finger on the map. "It's not too far offshore.

A HARD TRUTH

Finn told me that you think this guy might have taken one of the boat's inflatable life rafts ashore, and I think that would be doable. We'll see once the Coast Guard is in position, but I don't think I'm wrong about that." He bent down and rolled up the map. "Finn called your contact in the City of Miami Police Department and asked if they'd like to come along, and they are, which is fine. But the preserve is outside the city limits, so I called the Miami-Dade Police Department, and they'll be out there waiting for us too. We sure aren't going to lack any manpower."

Gin nodded. "Okay. Then I guess we should get rolling."

The seventeen-mile drive to the R. Hardy Matheson County Preserve was uneventful, but when the caravan of FBI cars arrived, the only place to park was along the road. Nate directed Finn to pull up behind a line of cruisers, where groups of officers from both the City of Miami Police Department and the Miami-Dade County Sheriff's Office were mingling on the side of the road.

Nate climbed out of the car and grinned at Gin over the roof. "I told you it wasn't a well-advertised place." He pointed to a row of thick hedges. "There's a gate about twenty yards down that's the entrance to the preserve."

Gin rounded the hood and fell into step next to the Miami agent. "Is the gate locked?"

"Nah. It never is. It's just over a mile from the gate down to the beach. Not a bad hike, but it would be a long way to haul a dead body without some motorized help, and it isn't much of a trail. I don't think you could get an ATV back there."

"A small, motorized bike with wide tires would be a better choice," Finn stated. He was walking along with his hands in his pockets, his eyes straight ahead. "Or maybe an electric bicycle in a pinch. There are places to rent those all over Miami. I've chased drug runners using them to get across stretches of trails along the coast or in a desert. Attach a small cart to one and it would be efficient enough to get a body out of here."

Gin could see the logic in that, but it left as many questions as it answered. Putting them aside, she walked with Nate up to a group of officers from the county and shook hands as the Miami agent proceeded with introductions. She patiently waited through them, giving a nod to Captain Crandon when she caught him staring at her. He lifted an eyebrow and jerked his head toward the open gate.

Getting his message, and just as impatient to get started as he was, she smiled at the captain standing next to her. "Captain Juarez? I'm assuming you know Captain Crandon from the Miami PD?"

Juarez turned and trained an eagle eye on Crandon. "I certainly do." He'd also caught the captain's motion to get started. Clearly just as eager to begin the search, Juarez brought his hands together in a single sharp clap. "Let's get walking. It's about a mile down. Uneven ground, so watch your step."

Nate smiled. "I guess you've taken this trail before?"

"Yep, and it's littered with trash, which is a shame. But it's usually quiet down here," the captain said. "It's a nice change from the noise of the city." He nodded at Gin, then headed for the open gate, his officers trailing behind. Crandon joined him, and the two captains started down the narrow, partially overgrown path.

Gin and Americk waited until Finn and Nate had started off before following them. They passed through the metal gate, walking side by side on the narrow track.

"After all this time, I doubt if there's any evidence left for them to be trampling on," Americk remarked.

"If the weather didn't destroy it, the public hikers here would have," Gin replied.

A HARD TRUTH

"Isn't that the truth? Just look at all the trash along here," Americk groused. "If you believe the evidence isn't here to find, or maybe it's lost in all the trash left behind, what *are* you hoping to uncover?"

"Possibilities." Gin grimaced when she stepped on an uneven patch of ground that sent a jarring pain up her bad knee right through her spine. While Americk settled into a one-way conversation on the evidence uncovered so far and what it could mean, Gin concentrated on putting one foot in front of the other and getting to the beach.

Even at her slower pace, it was barely a shade under half an hour when the trees and growth opened up to a narrow swatch of sand. Gin kept walking, right to the water. She stood at the edge and stared at the boat directly in front of her, about sixty yards out. The white vessel with the orange gunwales had "US Coast Guard" painted on the hull. Nate was waving his arms overhead, while Captain Juarez passed a pair of binoculars to Crandon.

Gin took several steps sideways until she was standing next to Nate. "Could one man paddle a life raft from that position to this beach?"

Nate considered it for a moment. "It would depend on how big a life raft, but if he knew what he was doing on open water, and it was relatively calm, I'd say it could be done." He stuck his hands in his pockets and rocked back on his heels. "I know the *Traci Marie* has. . ." He trailed off for a moment. "Well, she had a swim platform. So it wouldn't be difficult to get the life raft in the water, or a body in it, if our guy is strong enough." He shook his head. "Which is all well and good, but then what? Did he drag the body back up the trail for a mile and stuff it in a car he had waiting up there?"

"And hike back to the beach, get into the lifeboat, and sail the *Traci Marie* back to her berth at the marina and somehow find a way back to his car?" Finn asked, having come up behind them, the sand effectively muffling the sound of his footsteps.

Gin let their speculations flow around her as she watched the coast guard vessel floating noiselessly in the water. Not too far, she thought. She lifted a finger and tapped it against her lower lip. That would be close enough to put someone in the boat, and maybe have them lie down while you paddled ashore.

She frowned, her gaze studying the waves gently lapping on the beach. Slowly turning until her back was to the water, she faced the trail leading down from the road. She could picture it. Sticking her hands in the pocket of her jacket she dropped her gaze to the ground and slowly scanned across the sand.

"It would be easy enough," she said under her breath.

Her quiet words still drew Finn's attention. "What would be easy enough? Getting Stampler from the yacht to here unnoticed?"

"I think so." Gin lifted her gaze to his face. "He uses the swim platform to get the life raft in the water and has Stampler lie down in the bottom of it." She nodded as the picture became solid in her mind. "Where maybe there was some water pooled in the bottom from the splash while getting the raft overboard." She switched her gaze to Nate. "Could water get into the life raft like that?"

Nate pursed his lips as he considered it. "Once it's in the water, any kind of splashing would do it, especially if it had a detachable canopy that wasn't, well, attached. Then the raft would be a lot more open."

She frowned. "Canopy? Like a tent cover over the raft?"

"Yeah. That's about it," Nate said. "A tent cover on top of the raft with an opening to crawl through."

Gin turned enough to have the coast guard vessel back in her line of sight. "It sounds like it would be a lot easier to get a man who was probably resisting you into the raft without the canopy over the top."

"Sure," Nate agreed. "Those rafts are built to take a beating. You could toss a dead body into one from the swim platform and it wouldn't damage the raft."

"Or drag a body out of the raft onto the beach," Finn put in, his eyes narrowed as he followed Gin's theory. "If you grabbed the body under the armpits and dragged it ashore, any seawater or sand it encountered would mostly be on its back."

"He probably dragged Stampler ashore and cut his throat here," Gin said quietly. "It would be much easier to cover up blood in the sand than to get it all washed off the boat." She returned her gaze to the vessel riding in the water just offshore. "Inflate the raft, force Stampler into it, get him on the beach, and cut his throat." She sent a sideways glance toward Finn. "Remove his personal items and bag them up, then undress him and toss his clothes away." She looked around at the small beach area which had just as much trash strewn around it as the trail. "Load what's left of Stampler into a wagon or cart attached to an electric bike and have your partner take him back to the road where your car is waiting."

Nate blinked. "Partner? You think we should be looking for two of them?"

"One killer, one helper," Gin stated firmly. "This doesn't work unless there's two of them. One to take care of the body, and the other to motor the yacht back to the marina."

"He could have stashed the body and come back for it later that night," Nate pointed out.

"Too dangerous," Finn said. "You run the risk of teenagers looking for a place to party, or maybe a homeless person needing somewhere to sleep undisturbed. You don't know who might come back here."

"A second person to signal from the beach that it was all clear," Gin

inserted into Finn's story before nodding at the two police captains who'd walked over to stand next to Nate. "It doesn't work without a second person."

Crandon rubbed the side of his face. "Two? Did I hear that right? Now you think there's a pair of them working together? The security cameras at the marina didn't spot even one person we couldn't account for coming or going that night. And now you're saying there were two?"

"Not at the marina. I'm betting only one of them was there. And whoever he was, he was also the guy who showed up in New York," Gin said.

While Crandon made a skeptical noise deep in his throat, Captain Juarez gave her a puzzled look. "How do you know that?"

Her smile was tight as she gave a light shrug. "We have the New York guy on camera. He might be comfortable around boats, but he wasn't when he was surrounded by trees." She turned her head and looked back at the trail. "He wouldn't hike a mile to get here. Not along that remote trail with all those trees around. So he would have stuck with the boat, and whoever else was with him was just a helper."

"Why not two killers?" Finn wondered.

Gin shook her head. She had a handle on this guy now. A strong guy who liked fancy shoes and disliked of being in a place where too many things could remain hidden from view. Like a forest. He knew to keep his back to the wall, and how to get in and out of places without being seen.

"So, how did this go down?" Juarez asked.

Gin's gaze returned to the coast guard ship. "He reported a leak on the boat to Gerald Mobley, who did exactly what you would have expected him to do and informed the owner,

A HARD TRUTH

Benjamin Stampler. Then he simply waited on the yacht. When Gerald arrived to check out the non-existent leak, he was incapacitated by the killer, who then waited again, this time for Stampler. He brought them out here in the *Traci Marie*, got rid of the crewman, and then killed Stampler. With the help of his accomplice, Stampler's body was loaded into a car and driven up to New York, where it was left by that pylon with a message, to hopefully be found at some later date."

"What message?" Juarez demanded.

Gin stared at him for a long moment. "Stampler did something that not only made him trash in the eyes of the killer, but also required revenge."

"That flower found with the body." Crandon's forehead wrinkled into deep lines over a fierce frown. "It was in the case file. Birdsfoot trefoil. It means revenge." He blew out a heavy breath. "Which says that Stampler wasn't a random victim, or a ransom attempt gone wrong. He was targeted."

"And his murder was carefully planned out," Juarez added. "But if he was waiting for Stampler and Mobley, how did he get onto the dock without being picked up by the security cameras?"

Gin looked at Finn and wiggled her eyebrows. "Jake Bean had the answer to that in his complaint log."

Finn frowned, and then his eyes shot wide open. "Shit. That dinghy. He rowed over in that stupid dinghy, out of sight of the cameras." He rolled his eyes at Crandon's puzzled look. "Jake keeps a log of every complaint. He didn't have one about the leak, which makes sense if our killer manufactured it to draw Stampler out to the marina, but Jake did record a complaint about a dinghy being illegally tied up in an empty berth a little farther down the dock from the *Traci Marie*."

"Shit is right," Crandon huffed. "You're talking about the old guy who's a security guard at the marina, right? We asked him if he'd seen any strangers around the docks."

"He didn't see him," Finn pointed out. "He just got a complaint about a dinghy on the same day that Stampler disappeared. Jake left a note on it just before he went off shift, and the next morning it was gone, so he figured the problem was all taken care of."

"Fine." Juarez said. "But if this killer also took care of the other guy, that crewman? Where do you figure he is? Do we need to be searching for another body out here?"

Gin once again looked back over the water. "There's no reason to bring a second body to the beach."

Crandon followed her gaze with his own. "We didn't find any blood, and we went over every inch of the *Traci Marie* with cotton swabs. If Mobley was killed and not doing the killing himself, then it wasn't on that boat."

"Cutting a throat isn't the only way to kill," Gin said in a calm, even voice. "Drowning will work too." She caught Juarez's gaze with her own. "How deep is that water where the Coast Guard ship is sitting?"

Juarez looked blank for a moment, then his eyes widened and his gaze shot out over the water. "Oh, crap." He quickly scanned the beach, his hard gaze landing on one of the officers standing near a large rock jutting out of the sand. He waved a hand over his head until he caught the man's attention. "Tom? We need some divers out here. Right now."

Chapter Fourteen

It was almost five in the afternoon when the exhausted group returned to the hotel. Tired, hungry, and discouraged, Gin sat silently in the front seat of Agent Byer's car, grateful that the Miami agent didn't feel the need for polite conversation.

The waters between the offshore island of Key Biscayne and the preserve were deep enough for most pleasure crafts to pass through freely, but not so deep that it had been hard to find Gerald

Mobley's body. Rope had tightly bound both his feet to a fifty-pound ballast bag, which had most likely been stored on the yacht.

Convenient. Easy, she thought as she stared out the side window. Tie the body to something to make it stay down in the water and toss it overboard. Then inflate the raft and take Stampler to shore.

But it was the fact that Mobley's hands were bound behind his back that haunted her. Maybe he'd been tied up before he was killed. Killed and then tossed into the ocean to float unseen beneath the boats passing by overhead.

But maybe not.

She closed her eyes as her face scrunched up at the thought. This killer was cold and calculating. Lying in wait for his victims. Sticking to a strict killing process along with how and where to dump the bodies. It was more than possible that he'd tied Mobley's hands and feet, then simply shoved the bag overboard, pushing the crewman over with it while he was still alive.

The image wouldn't leave her mind. A barely thirty-year-old Mobley, fighting to get free as he sank into the water, knowing he wasn't going to win that fight. Those vivid images didn't stop with the crewman either. She could feel Stampler's fear at seeing Mobley die and knowing he'd be next. Even her closed cases still haunted her, and when this one was closed, it wouldn't be any different

But it wasn't the victims she'd stood over during her FBI career that had brought on the crippling migraines she'd suffered with for years. But the one living breathing thing that would not go away was her father. Everything always came back to him, and his helpless victims. And how long it had taken her to stop him.

It wasn't until he'd been caught that law enforcement came out with how many possible and even unidentified victims were yet to be found. That was when the headaches had started. Not when she was actually living with a monster, but when she realized that if she had only moved sooner or faster, who knows how many lives would have been spared?

It haunted her to this day, but at least the headaches had become less frequent. The more killers she tracked down and stopped, the longer the periods between the migraine attacks. A *penance rewarded*, she thought sourly. Move sooner, move faster. Stop them. It had become her mantra. A barrier of words against her memories and her guilt at not saving more of them. Of not saving Kayla, her father's last victim.

When the car stopped, she blinked. AS she stared out the window, the view on the other side of the windshield came into focus. The hotel. They were at the hotel. At the same moment she stepped back into the present, her nose twitched at the smell of cooked beef. She looked over her shoulder in time to see Finn exiting the car, holding several large paper bags. She didn't remember them stopping for food, but the loud growl from her stomach made her glad they had.

"That smells great." She glanced over at Byers, who was sitting behind the wheel, watching her.

He studied her for a moment longer before reaching down and unhooking his seat belt. "Welcome back from wherever you went." He gave her a puzzled look. "Do you do that trick often?"

Gin unhooked her own seat belt and reached for the door handle, pausing before pulling it open. "Only when we find dead bodies." She looked him directly in the eye. "It takes me back."

Much to his credit, Byers didn't ask "back where?", but simply nodded. "Those burgers are from the best fast-food dive in Miami." He broke the tension with an easy grin as he patted the slight paunch around by belly. "And I should know because I've tried them all."

"Good choice, then. Did Finn remember to get enough for Trey? When I called him from the scene to catch him up, he hadn't left the room all day." She conjured up a weak grin. "And I doubt even being bedridden with pain would keep him from being hungry."

Byers shrugged. "Then he probably got some room service for lunch." He dropped his gaze to her hands. "Are you ready to get out of the car?"

Gin answered by pushing the door open. She stepped out and hurried over to the sidewalk where Finn and Americk were waiting. The older woman took her by surprise when she stepped forward and engulfed her in a long hug.

"You be sure to take care of yourself," she whispered into Gin's ear before taking a step back. "I wish I could stay and see this through, but I have to get back to Quantico. There's a lot of work I need to put a final bow on before I can move my little family out to Denver." She leaned over and gave Gin another quick hug. "That one is for Trey. Please tell him I said goodbye." Her eyes were sparkling when she winked. "And that I hope to see him in his uniform someday, even if he isn't in the Navy anymore."

Byers smiled and handed a tray with three drinks in it to Gin. "I'm her ride, so you'll need to take these up. I hope you enjoy the burgers."

"We will, and thanks for all your help. And for the gun," Gin said before turning to Americk. "And for your help too. I'm really glad we'll be working together." She was surprised to realize that she meant every word.

Americk fairly beamed at her. "I am too. Now remember what I said. You take care." With a last pat on Gin's shoulder, Americk turned and rounded the hood of the car. She climbed into the passenger seat and waved at the two agents still standing on the sidewalk as Byers drove off toward the street.

"So, it's just the three of us again," Finn joked. "What's next?"

The smell of hamburgers tickled Gin's nose. "Food," she said without hesitation. "We can check on what Trey's been doing while we eat."

A HARD TRUTH

Since they weren't sure what condition the former rescue pilot was in, Finn dug out the spare key to their fellow agent's room that he'd commandeered the night before, and simply let them in. He led the way down the short hallway to be sure the agent was fit for company, which was more for Trey's dignity than Gin's. She was too hungry to care what state of dress or undress the guy was in.

"Hey, is that food?" Trey called out as soon as they stepped into the large room. "Great. I could eat a bear."

Gin set the tray of drinks on the desk and left it to Finn to deal with the food as she walked over to the bed and peered down at Trey. He was fully dressed, stretched out on the neatly made bed, balancing his laptop on his jean-clad thighs. The bruising still made a violent display on his face, but it had faded quite a bit since that morning, leaning more toward a sickly yellow than a deep purple. "You look a lot better. Is there some kind of magic cure you'd like to share with the rest of us?"

He laughed. "Good genes. I heal fast. So does my dad." The smile faded as his expression turned sober. "How did it go? When you called, you said that the divers were down looking for Gerald Mobley."

"They found him. He was about twenty feet down, almost directly under the last locator point for the *Traci Marie*." Gin tilted her head to the side. "If you hadn't taken that photo of the chart plotter, we might never have found him. Or the kill site for Benjamin Stampler."

"So Stampler was killed on that beach?" Trey asked.

"The cops and our guys did a pretty thorough search," Finn said, handing Trey a thick burger, a paper wrapping wound around half of it. "They found a boat shoe with what looks like bloodstains on it. Americk is taking it back to Quantico to test."

Trey took the burger with a grateful nod. "Yeah. She sent me a text to let me know she was headed back and that she'd see me again in Denver. Along with several variations of 'be careful'. She sounded a little concerned." He took a big bite of his burger, closing his eyes in blissful appreciation.

"Well, not to put too fine a point on it, but someone did try to blow you up, along with Reilly," Finn said. He walked back to the desk and picked up another burger, hardly slowing down before returning to the bedside and handing it to Gin. He thumped Trey on the knee. "Make some room so she can sit down."

When Trey scooted his body to the side, Gin sat on the edge of the bed and enjoyed her first bite of hot, juicy meat. It tasted like heaven. "So, you said on the phone that you were working on something we needed to follow up on?"

"Sure did." Trey sat up straighter and used the hand not holding his burger to tap on the laptop's keyboard. "Remember those two cases that Stephen said might be similar kills?"

"Uh-huh," Gin said between bites. "The guy who was buried under some leaves."

"Yeah. In his partner's backyard. It turns out that the partner actually did kill him. The cops found the body when the guy's dog uncovered it. The idiot let his pet out when the cops showed up at the door, and the dog went right for the body, putting up such a ruckus they all went to check it out. And ta-da. Dead guy."

Gin rolled her eyes in disbelief while behind her, Finn chuckled. "So we have a candidate for the world's dumbest criminal?"

"No doubt about that," Trey agreed. "No. What we need to be checking into is that second case Stephen found. In Nevada. A guy identified as Bruce Dredecker was found eight months ago, with time of death put at approximately two months before that."

A HARD TRUTH

"So two to three months before the time of death for the murder in Northern California?" Gin asked.

Trey nodded. "Sounds right. Anyway, it was the same deal. The body was stripped, nothing on it to identify him. Covered in trash. I saw a flower encased in resin listed as part of the trash pile, but there wasn't a picture of it anywhere in the file Stephen sent. There was also one difference with this body." Trey looked up from his laptop. "The mouth had duct tape over it."

"Duct tape?" Gin repeated. "Now, that is different. But there was a flower in resin?"

"Yeah. It was mentioned in the forensic team report, but there wasn't a picture. So I emailed the sheriff's department in Lyon County, Nevada. The body was found in their jurisdiction. Near the border of the Walker River Reservation."

Gin's head turned to stare at Trey. "Reservation?"

"Interesting, isn't it?" Trey's gaze returned to his laptop. "This one belongs to the Paiute Nation, and the body was discovered off a county road just a couple of miles from the northwestern border of their land."

"Okay, okay." Gin's eyes narrowed in thought. "It's a link. But why?"

"Why?" Finn carried the desk chair over next to the bed, then sat down. "What do you mean, why?"

"Is being next to a reservation part of the process, or is there a Native American connection?" Gin sighed and took another bite of her burger. "But the Northern California victim wasn't near a reservation, so that's another piece in the puzzle." She gestured to Trey. "Sorry. Go on."

"Like I said, I emailed the Lyon County Sheriffs, asking if they had an image of that flower encased in resin. And I heard back from them." He turned his laptop around so Gin could see the screen. "Here it is. I called Americk about it, and she identified the flower as a purple hydrangea. Not heat or drought resistant, apparently, so not native to Nevada. And in the world of flower whisperers, it means arrogance."

Gin's mouth twitched upward. "Flower whisperers?"

"Sounds better than flower woo-woo," Trey said, shifting his laptop back around and tapping on keys. "Anyway, the deputy I talked to at the Lyon County Sheriff's Office said that their case had gone cold. But he did give me the name and contact number of the victim's employer." He kept his eyes on his screen when he smiled. "Turns out it's T.L. Construction, and his boss's name is Aldo Twiner. When I called him, he called me right back and said that Mr. Dredecker was one of his crew chiefs, then asked for a phone conversation with me and my boss because he had plenty to tell us. I let him know you're the lead agent on the case and you were out in the field, but you'd be available later today, and he was fine with that. So we're going to talk to him in." Trey paused to glance at his watch. "About ten minutes, actually. I thought you'd be back sooner."

Gin's expression turned grim. "Well, we had another body to find."

Trey ran an agitated hand across the back of his neck. "Yeah." He let his hand drop back to the side of the bed. "Let's hope we can find something solid to follow between these cases."

Amen to that, Gin thought then felt that familiar hum along her nerves. "A construction company, huh? This Twiner owns a construction company?" It was another link, this time between Bruce Dredecker, the crew chief, and Miguel Rivera, the master electrician. But not the pharmacy executive, whose company didn't have any building projects going on. Still, links were coming to light, and she'd find the one that bound them all together. It was just a matter of digging deep enough. She looked down at her half-eaten burger. "Ten minutes, huh? Then I guess we'd better eat fast."

She'd barely taken the last bite of her small meal when Trey picked up his phone. "Ready?" he asked, waiting for her nod before tapping on the screen and switching the talk mode over to the speakers. The three agents listened as somewhere out in Nevada, a phone rang once, and then twice before it was picked up.

A voice, tinged with gravel and impatience, boomed into the room. "Al Twiner. And if this is you again, Gekko, I don't want to hear about that leaking pipe. It's your job to make sure those joints are put together right, so get it done. I can't talk to you right now, I'm waiting on another call."

"Mr. Twiner? This is Special Agent Robard with the FBI," Trey said quickly before the man hung up on him. "We spoke earlier about the murder of one of your employees, Bruce Dredecker?"

"Yeah, yeah, Decker. That's right. He worked for me. Was one of the best crew chiefs I've ever had. Been with us for almost twenty years. Is that boss of yours on this call too? I don't want to have to tell you what I know twice."

Gin immediately spoke up. "Mr. Twiner, I'm Special Agent Reilly. I'm the lead agent on a case the Bureau is working on that we believe ties in with the murder of your employee."

"That's what the other guy said." There was a slight hesitation. "Reilly, is it? Are you Irish?"

When Finn had to cover up a laugh, Gin glared at him. "Probably, sir. But quite a way back, and I've never verified that one way or the other."

"I hear that," Twiner snorted. "Mom was in love with some old-time actor named Aldo Rey. You ever heard of him?"

Since Stephen was the movie buff, not her, Gin shook her head. "No, sir. I haven't."

"Not surprised. Anyway, Mom named me after him and everyone thinks I'm Italian. Not a drop of that in the family, as far as I know. And yeah, I own T.L. Construction. The 'L' is the first letter in my mom's name, and the 'T' is for Thomas. He's my dad and has been retired for fifteen years. That's when I took it over from him. So Decker actually worked for both of us. Him getting killed that way really hit my dad hard. It hit all of us hard. So I got to ask you something first."

"All right, Mr. Twiner. Go ahead," Gin replied.

"Am I a suspect in this case you're working on? Or is Melony? She's Decker's wife."

Gin's eyebrows winged upward as she exchanged a startled look with Trey. "I don't know one way or the other, Mr. Twiner. Should you be?"

"The cops out in Lyon County sure thought so, and from the way the Reno PD grilled me about everything under the sun, I'm pretty sure they thought so too."

Momentarily at a loss, Gin thought it over while the silence drew out. Deciding to trust her instincts, she went with her gut. "Mr. Twiner, I don't believe the trail we're following is going to lead to you. But it does look like your employee is part of it. What can you tell me about him?"

The sound of a long breath being let out in one whoosh came through the phone. "Okay. I'll take that, and you can call me Big Al. Everyone does."

"Thank you. Now about Mr. Dredecker?" Gin prompted.

"Decker was a great guy. The best," Big Al stated emphatically. "He and Melony lived all their lives in Reno. They raised their kids here. He coached Little League when his boys were

A HARD TRUTH

young, and never missed any of their high school games. Decker was a good dad, a good husband, and a good friend. He didn't deserve to die like that, with his throat slit and then tossed away with the garbage in a place so remote, even the cops had to look it up on a map." There was the sound of a hand slapping down hard on metal. "I'll tell you the same thing I told the Reno police and the Lyon County cops. Decker didn't have an enemy in the company, or in this city, and probably not even in this state. Whoever killed him was an outsider, and that's that."

Gin considered it for a moment. "All right. Do you remember the night he disappeared?" She glanced over at Trey, who quickly and efficiently filled in the details from the case file.

"We've been told he was on his way to a casino to meet some friends. They all played the tables together every Thursday, but that night, Dredecker never showed up. He sent his best friend, a man named Darby, a text saying he wasn't feeling well and was going to hang out at home. But his wife gave a statement that he did, in fact, leave home about seven, so she was the last one who saw him alive."

"Besides the guy who killed him," Big Al said. "Because if you're thinking Melony had anything to do with Decker's murder, you're way off base. She wouldn't hurt a fly. Doesn't even have a driver's license. And she adored Decker. There is no way this side of hell she would have hurt her husband."

"Okay," Gin said once Big Al's tirade had run down. "If Mr. Dredecker played every week, did he have a gambling problem? Maybe he owed a lot of money to one of his buddies, or to the casinos?"

Big Al grunted at that. "Casinos don't give out markers to guys like Decker. That only happens in the movies. It's cash or you don't play. And he never gambled more than a hundred dollars. You can ask any of his buddies and they'll tell you the same thing." He let out a harsh laugh. "This wasn't any kind of a hit-for-money deal. Thursday nights were just a guy thing to get out of the house and blow off a little steam with some language the wife wouldn't approve of. That's all it was."

"What about work?" Gin asked, changing direction.

"I already told you," Al snapped. "He had no enemies in the company. Everyone liked and respected him because he earned it."

"I'm sorry," Gin said calmly. "I meant where did he work? Only jobs in the Reno area?" Her voice trailed off, leaving it an open question.

"Nah. We do jobs all over the state, and Decker was a crew chief. He went wherever the job was."

"All over the state," Gin repeated slowly. "Then your company works solely in Nevada?"

"Nah," Big Al said for the second time. "We're licensed to work in California and Oregon. There's a lot of work out there. More than we can pick up in just Nevada. Decker didn't like the travel much, but he knew we had to make a living, so he went where the jobs were. We all do."

"You take jobs in California?"

"Yeah," the construction company owner confirmed. "Why? Is there some federal law against that?"

"No," Gin said. "But we'd like a list of the jobs that Mr. Dredecker worked on for the last three years he was employed. How long would it take to get that to us?"

"I can get it to you tomorrow, but it will have to be a favor for a favor," Big Al stated flatly. "I want to know what's going on."

"In what way?" Gin hedged.

"I'm not stupid, Agent Reilly." Big Al's voice had dropped to a lower, softer tone. "And even out here in Reno we get the news. I saw the report on that pharmacy big shot who was murdered. The news said he was found out in some remote area in New York. And that his throat was cut and his body left under a pile of garbage, just like Decker's was. The next thing I know, I'm getting a call from the FBI." He sucked in a deep breath. "Two and two still make four as far as I'm concerned. They were killed by the same guy, weren't they? That's why Decker was left behind some bushes, way out in the middle of nowhere, wasn't it? Because that's what this psycho does."

Gin didn't say anything for a long moment, letting the silence speak for itself. "We're looking into every possibility," she finally said. "Now, I'd appreciate a list of those jobs."

"Yeah, I heard you loud and clear," Big Al stated flatly. "And for what it's worth, it's good to know you're not looking in our direction. Any answer, even if it turns out to be a psycho, is better than nothing at all, I guess. Text me your email to this number you called, and I'll send you that list. And Agent Reilly?"

"Yes, sir?" Gin responded.

"I'll be waiting to hear the news report about how you caught this guy."

He disconnected the call before Gin could say anything else. She picked up Trey's cell phone, intending to hand it to him, but he was busy tapping away on his laptop's keyboard.

Her brows knit together in curiosity. "What are you doing?"

"Sending a quick email to Stephen, asking him to get hold of that construction company that Miguel Rivera worked for, and get hold of a list of jobs he worked on."

"Good thinking." Gin set the phone down next to him, then took a quick turn around the room, finally stopping when she was back at the foot of the bed. She tapped one finger against her lower lip.

"What's bothering you?" Finn asked.

"He said that the place Dredecker's body was dumped was so remote, even the cops had to look it up on a map."

Finn shrugged. "Yeah, so? Nevada is one of those places where a big piece of it is a whole lot of nothing but miles of high desert."

"Then who found his body? A coyote?" Gin asked.

Trey looked up from his laptop, a startled expression in his eyes. "The county deputies found it. According to the case file, someone called in an anonymous tip."

"Anonymous?" Gin frowned. "Did the file mention anything about the caller?"

Trey went silent for a few moments as he scrolled through documents on his screen. "Not much. Male. The voice was muffled, and didn't sound too excited. The desk sergeant who took the call made a note that the caller had some kind of accent and might have been from Mexico. At first they thought it was a prank call because the guy seemed so calm, and it was almost a fifty-mile drive out there. But they sent a couple of deputies, who found the body right where the caller said it would be."

"Okay." Gin took another turn around the room, silently dissecting the discovery of Dredecker's body. When she came back to the foot of the bed, she stopped again. "A mistake." She nodded, a ghost of a smile playing around her mouth. "He made a mistake." When both Finn and Trey gave her a blank look, she crossed her arms over her chest and stared back at them. "He wanted the body to be found, but the place he'd dumped it was too remote. Not even the cops wanted to go all the way out there. So he had to tip them off."

"The next time, he left the body near a popular hunting trail," Trey put in. "And Stampler was left by a pylon that was regularly visited by utility workers."

"I'll give you the hunting trail, but there's no reason to think the utility workers were going to find a body behind those bushes," Finn pointed out.

"Since they had to do regular weed and growth abatement, the odds were good the whole area would be checked out and someone would find Stampler," Gin countered. "But where he left Dredecker was a mistake. One that he corrected with his later kills." She looked from Finn to Trey. "Dredecker might be his first kill."

Into the silence, Trey's laptop pinged, indicating an incoming email. He read it, then looked over at Gin. "Miguel Rivera worked for a company called Ralfin Construction. Stephen says they got right back to him, and said they'd be happy to give us a list of the jobs Mr. Rivera worked on, but only if we talk to them in person." He looked up with a frown. "It's either that, or get a warrant."

Gin took out her phone and pulled up her text messages. "I'm asking Stephen to get us on the early plane to California tomorrow." When she was finished, she caught Finn's sigh. "What's the matter? I don't think we have enough to get a federal warrant, and showing up there will be faster."

"Oh, I agree," Finn said. He reached into his pocket and held out a set of car keys. "These are for the rental car. I wish I could go with you, but I have work here. Not to mention a potentially hot case of my own that I've put on hold and need to get back to." He walked over to the bed and held out his hand to Trey. "It was a pleasure working with you. I hope we get an opportunity to do it again."

Trey took his hand in a firm grasp. "Thanks. Me too."

Finn dropped his hand with a huge grin. "And I wish I had a picture of you taking that dive over the back of the *Traci Marie*." His face sobered again. "That was good work, man." As Trey nodded his thanks, Finn turned and took a big step forward to give Gin a hug. "Not professional, I know, and probably crossing all kinds of sexual harassment lines." He stepped back and tapped a friendly fist bump against her shoulder. "Until next time, Reilly. Make sure you get this guy."

She grinned back at him. "You can count on it."

Chapter Fifteen

With Finn headed to his apartment on the south side of town, and Trey settled in for the night, Gin slowly walked back to her own room. A symphony of aches and pains was making itself known again. Bypassing the amber container of pain meds, she reached straight for the bottle of aspirin sitting beside it on her nightstand. She washed three down with a glass of water, then dragged herself to the bathroom, intending to change into a pair of lightweight sweats and going to bed, even if it was still light outside.

After scrubbing her face and brushing her teeth, she pulled back the covers on the queen-sized bed and gingerly slipped underneath them. While she waited for the aspirin to kick in, she laid still and stared at the ceiling, letting her mind wander. Which was a mistake.

Finally having her first minutes not consumed by the case, her thoughts glided effortlessly to the journals tucked away in her backpack. Determined to get some sleep, she closed her eyes, and twenty minutes later she was still trying to banish the journals from her mind.

Finally giving up, she wriggled out from beneath the covers and crossed over to the built-in shelf. Grabbing her backpack, she stopped by her suitcase and scooped up her laptop. She carried both things over to the bed and made herself comfortable under the sheet and comforter once more. Leaning into the pillows propped up against the headboard, she unzipped her backpack, then hesitated and reached for her laptop instead. If she wasn't going to sleep, then she'd review the case files. Whatever was in those journals would have to wait until the case was wrapped up and she was back home in Denver.

Booting up the computer, she went right to her email and opened the message from Stephen labeled "like crimes." Clicking on the attachment for the Nevada murder, she went to the first document and began to read.

She went over the reports and studied the crime scene photos, lingering over the one showing Bruce Dredecker's face with the duct tape over his mouth. Frowning, it hit her that this body looked different. Despite the fact it had been found within a month of Dredecker's disappearance, it looked worse. There was extensive insect and animal damage, and his hands and legs were bound with the same duct tape that was over his mouth.

Keeping the file open, she switched to the one from the Siskiyou County Sheriff's. Flipping through the reports, she went directly to the crime scene photos. As Trey had noted about Stampler, there was no duct tape across Miguel Rivera's mouth, and no restraint of any kind on his hands and feet. His death was put at two months prior to the discovery of his body, and yet, there was considerably less damage to his remains. Either the bugs in New York and California weren't nearly as attracted to human remains as the bugs in Nevada, or the killer had made another alteration to his death ritual. Returning to Dredecker's file, Gin read through all the deputies' reports, and the one from the ME, as well as the forensic lab results, and nowhere was there any mention of peppermint oil. It was possible they'd all overlooked it. But not likely.

She leaned back against the pillows and stared out the window, not really seeing anything as she turned over the reports in her mind. Why would he change his routine? What was so important about the bodies being better preserved? It would make the identification easier, or at least more immediate.

Her eyes narrowed at the thought. He wanted the bodies found, and once they were, he wanted them identified right away. And the sooner they were found and identified, the quicker the world would know about their transgressions. A purple hydrangea, a red petunia, and a California lilac.

"Arrogance, resentment, and revenge," she said under her breath. Not exactly the seven deadly sins, so for the moment, she'd rule out some type of spiritual connection, but something else ran through how he was choosing his victims. *Like a personal insult,* she thought. She didn't have any hard evidence to back that up, but it felt right.

Her cell phone broke the silence in the room. Annoyed, she glanced at the screen. The number had no caller ID next to it, but the area code was in Miami. Resigned to dealing with whomever was on the other end, Gin picked up the phone and gave the connect icon an impatient swipe. "This is Special Agent Reilly."

"Agent Reilly? It's Hugh Lamon. We met this afternoon at Meridian."

The voice brought an image of a face with it. "Of course, Mr. Lamon. You run the company's research division."

"That's right."

Lamon's voice was strained, making her wonder if he'd been indulging in his fentanyl habit. "What can I do for you?"

"I'm calling on Mrs. Stampler's behalf. She was hoping for an update on the investigation into her husband's murder."

Since Lamon wasn't in the room with her, Gin drummed her finger against the mattress to help her hold onto her patience. "We just spoke this afternoon, Mr. Lamon. There isn't anything to add at this time."

"Then you and your team will be staying on in Miami?"

Wondering where the Meridian executive was going with this conversation, Gin allowed the shrug to come through in her voice. "We'll be pursuing all leads, Mr. Lamon, both inside and outside of Miami."

"And where would that be, Agent Reilly?" Lamon asked. "I was under the impression that Ben was killed here and transported to New York, but that you'd already recovered the body from up north and processed that crime scene, so we assumed you'd be doing a dogged pursuit of his killer right here in Miami."

Hugh Lamon might not be dialed into the FBI, but he certainly had some good contacts inside the Miami P.D. "Who is making that assumption, Mr. Lamo?" Gin asked.

"What?"

"You said 'we assumed'," she repeated, letting a slight edge creep into her voice. "I was wondering who was included in that 'we' you mentioned?"

A sputtering noise came through the other end of the phone. "I, well, that is, I was referring to the other company executives, of course."

"Yes, of course." Gin paused just long enough to give the clear impression that she didn't believe him. Which she didn't. "I'm sorry, Mr. Lamon. But I can't comment about an ongoing investigation."

"I see. But you'll let me, or rather the company, know of any developments in the case?" Now Lamon sounded almost desperate.

"Sure," Gin said smoothly. "Is this a good number to reach you?"

"Yes. This number will be fine." The sound of a ragged breath came through the speaker. "Call anytime."

"I'll do that," Gin said evenly, her eyebrows knitting together in thought. A moment later she blinked when the line abruptly went dead.

Wondering what that was all about, Gin returned to the bed and spent another hour going over the two case files before updating her report on the investigation. An update she would never share, not even with her most trusted friends or family. And certainly not with Hugh Lamon. She did, however, shoot a copy off to her boss, as well as Trey and Stephen, then closed her laptop with a final snap. She needed to step back for a few hours at least. Let it all simmer overnight, and maybe something would boil to the top by morning.

Still feeling restless, she scooped up the Television remote and clicked through the available channels. She'd never watched much TV — mostly because she was either on a plane or working. When she was young, her parents only allowed their two children an hour of television time on weekends, and made a point of closely monitoring what their two kids watched.

She settled on the local news, listening to a reporter with a grave expression and a dramatic voice relate all the latest details on the murder of Benjamin Stampler, a prominent resident of the city. Jardin Hunt appeared on the screen, dressed in a severe black suit with a dark blue shirt and a tie with stripes in the same blue. He read the usual corporate press release, expressing shock and deep sadness before he disappeared and a picture of Theresa Stampler with her husband took his place. At the very end of the story, the reporter made a brief mention of Gerald Mobley, and that his body had been found off Key Biscayne.

"I'm sure that outpouring of sympathy will be a big comfort to Gerald's family," Gin said in a disgusted voice before turning the TV off. Leaning farther back into the pillows with one hand behind her head, she lets her gaze idly roam about the room.

She considered getting up and closing the curtains, but decided against it — too much work. A second later, her gaze crossed over her backpack lying on the far side of the bed, and stayed there. She considered it for a long moment until she finally gave in. She'd have to read the damn things eventually, so why not get a jump on it now?

Reaching out, she slowly, almost reluctantly pulled the backpack closer. Opening the large, center compartment, she slowly pulled out the first of the three journals and carefully laid it on her lap. Lifting the backpack, she set it on the floor, keeping a hand on the journal so it wouldn't slide off her lap. Not giving herself any chance to change her mind, she carefully opened the fragile cover, took a deep breath, and then looked down at the letter written by her father.

She read the first sentence, then frowned and slowly read it again. It was definitely Byron Reilly's handwriting, but the words were stilted, as if they'd come from an old-time script. "Let my legatee learn from these teachings," she said out loud. "What the hell is that supposed to mean?" She picked up her phone and quickly pulled up a dictionary, just to be sure what legatee meant. "Like an heir," she said to herself as she nodded. "Yeah. That's what I thought." Her gaze returned to the letter, and the next sentence had her blood running cold.

A HARD TRUTH

Hear me. Learn from my journey.

Underneath was a name and a date. Kayla Downey May, 2007. She stared, wide-eyed, at a piece of paper written seventeen years ago.

Kayla Downey had been the last victim of the Black Cross Killer. He'd strangled her to death with a thin wire for no other reason than the fact that he could. Then he'd taken a gold ring from her finger. It had had her initials, KD, on the front, delicately fashioned in a graceful script. She knew that because she'd stolen it from him and turned it into Captain Frank Wilkins of the Story County Sheriff's Office in Iowa. That was in 2007. The year she'd celebrated her fourteenth birthday.

Gin looked away from the letter and drew in a shaky breath, then another, wanting to steady herself. When her heart was no longer trying to pound its way out of her chest, she looked down again, forcing her gaze across the page as she read every detail of what had happened to twenty-three-year-old Kayla Downey. Including where he'd buried her. A detail he'd shared with the police as part of a plea bargain to avoid the death penalty. In the end he'd given them sixteen names, and sixteen locations, and in every one of them the police had found a grave. Right where he'd said it would be.

At the bottom of the page was her father's signature. Gin stared at it, her eyes hot as her hand slowly clenched into a fist. Not able to stand the sight of it for another second, she flipped over the page. Her eyes grew wide and her mouth dropped open. It was a column of names, dates, and places. There had to be over twenty names on the list, with the first one followed by a date of August 17, 1983. She did a quick, silent calculation, then shook her head in disbelief. August 17th was Byron Reilly's birthday. He would have turned twenty in 1983.

Trying to wrap her mind around exactly what that meant,

she turned over the sheet, only to find another, similar one behind it. Only the names were different, and the dates were more recent. Her gaze dropped to the bottom of the page. The second-to-last name listed was Kayla Downey, followed by the month and year she'd been murdered. When her eyes slid to the last name, her breath caught in her throat and she could feel the blood draining from her face until she was sure there wasn't a drop left in it.

Gillian Reilly February, 2008

Her mind recoiled and her stomach clenched so hard she bent over double until her head touched her knees. He'd planned to kill her. His daughter. His own flesh and blood. The Black Cross Killer, was going to kill her nine months after he'd strangled Kayla Downey.

Even knowing what he was, the shock paralyzed her. She grimaced against the pain, even as she wondered what he'd planned to do. A convenient accident on the farm? Or maybe she would have simply disappeared and been labeled a runaway, never to be seen or heard from again. Not that either parent would have bothered looking for her.

But Devin would have. Using that thought as a shield, the pain in her stomach eased, and the cold in her blood was swamped by a searing heat.

That bastard. Five months. That was the difference between her living and dying. She'd left that envelope for Captain Wilkins five months before her own father had planned her death. She'd always wondered if he'd suspected her of sneaking around in that basement, and now she knew. The proof was staring her right in the face. He'd known, and had considered her expendable.

"Got you first," she muttered. "I got you first." She picked

A HARD TRUTH

up both pages with their lists of names and dates and held them in one hand. "And there are a lot more names on here than just the twenty you gave up." Her jaw set into a hard line and her green eyes glittered with satisfaction. It was very bad news for Byron Reilly, because this time there would be no plea bargaining. They would try him, and the Black Cross Killer would know what it was like to face death, the way all his victims had.

She picked up her phone, intending to call the unit's senior agent and tell him what she'd found, but then she hesitated, her hand hovering over the screen. There was no way to turn the list over without revealing the existence of the journals. And she sure as hell wasn't going to open that Pandora's box until she knew exactly what was in them, and what they meant. She'd have to find another way to get that list into the proper hands.

"Hear me and learn from my journey," she repeated out loud. It sounded like he was talking to someone. But who?

Chapter Sixteen

It was barely past dawn when Gin stepped into the lobby, her backpack slung over one shoulder and pulling her suitcase behind her. Her eyes were heavy from lack of sleep and her shoulders drooped with fatigue. Finding out your father had planned to kill you didn't make for a good night's rest.

Trey was already waiting for her, leaning against a wall, holding a cup of the hotel's complimentary coffee in one hand. She crossed over the tiled floor and, without a word, dropped her backpack at his feet before turning and heading straight for the steaming pot set up on a side table. Pouring out a cup, she took several quick sips before rejoining her partner, who was watching her with a steady gaze.

"Are you okay with this trip?"

She looked up and quirked an eyebrow. "Why wouldn't I be?"

"Stephen called last night. He tried your cell first, but you didn't pick up."

"I was probably asleep," Gin lied, even though she knew

the dark circles under her eyes, especially against her pale complexion that was prone to freckles, looked like she hadn't shut her eyes in a week. But the obvious lie was easier than going into any explanations about her restless night.

Trey looked skeptical, but thankfully didn't question her about it. "Well, when he couldn't get hold of you, he called me. He wanted to let us know that he'll do what he can to back the investigation up but won't be joining us right away. His wife had to make an emergency trip to help a friend, and he needed to stay home with the kids."

She wasn't surprised. Her cousin was always running off somewhere to help someone. It was just who she was.

Trey smiled. "How many does he have? Kids, I mean. I didn't get a chance to ask before it sounded like all hell was breaking loose and he had to hang up."

"Two boys, and beating on each other, or their surroundings, seems to be their favorite pastime." Gin's mood lightened at the mention of those two small whirlpools of energy. Since she considered Callie more of a sister than a cousin, she thought of those little hellions as her nephews. She loved them to pieces, but they were a handful.

"You're all related, aren't you?" Trey asked as Gin bent over to pick up her backpack.

She straightened up and shouldered it, then grabbed the handle of her suitcase. "Yeah. Callie's mom is my aunt." She hesitated since she had made a vow last night to never refer to that man as her father again. "Paternal aunt," she finally settled for. She hesitated again, then gave a mental shrug. Trey was part of the unit, so he might as well hear the whole story. Or at least the part she shared. "After the Black Cross Killer was arrested, my family broke apart. Mom followed him, and Dev and I were sent off to live with relatives. Dev went to one of Mom's bachelor cousins in Colorado, and I went with Aunt

Sue. Her husband had died a few years before, and she and Callie lived just a couple of towns over from our farm." She pursed her lips. "Aunt Sue was never close to her brother."

"That must have been tough," Trey said as they made their way through the lobby doors.

"Yeah. It was another small town, and everyone knew who I was." Her shoulders lifted in a dismissive shrug as she crossed the driveway toward the rental Finn had parked at the far end of the lot. "I knew I wouldn't be staying one day past my high school graduation, so it never bothered me much." She'd also known something none of her classmates, or even her aunt and cousin, had — that she was the reason the Black Cross Killer was finally behind bars. She had held that knowledge tightly around her, like a protective cloak, against the odd looks and occasional taunt.

"How did your brother do in Colorado? Isn't that where your father ended up in prison?"

Gin's back stiffened at the word, but she bought herself a few moments to get her knee-jerk reaction under control by opening the car and settling into the driver's seat. "At the Supermax in Florence," she said as she fastened her seatbelt. "But Dev only had a year of high school left, and the trial lasted a lot longer than that. He was long gone before the prison got its newest, lifetime resident." She put the car into gear and slowly backed out of the parking space. Once they were on the road and headed for the airport, she sent him a sideways glance. "So, that's my sordid past. What about yours?"

"What makes you think I have a sordid past?"

The fact that Trey didn't look startled or flustered by the question, said loud and clear that he was as used to fending off unwanted questions about himself as she was. "Hotshot rescue pilot makes a sudden retirement from flying, which in itself is unheard of, and then effortlessly gets himself assigned first to

NCIS and then to the FBI. You either have really juicy blackmail evidence on a General somewhere, or have a sordid past. You choose."

He shot her an annoyed look. "I still fly."

"Okay," Gin said cheerfully. "Then is it blackmail on a general, or a dicey past?"

"In the Navy it would be an admiral, and no, I don't have any blackmail on anyone." He turned his head to look out the side window. "And not a dicey past. Just a classified one."

"And I don't have clearance?"

"No one has clearance that high," Trey said in a barely audible murmur.

Well, she might not have that high of a clearance, but Americk did, because the lead tech had known all about whatever it was that drove Trey out of the Navy. When a deep silence filled the car, Gin let the subject drop. Whatever had happened, it had been bad enough to cost Trey his career and give him a free pass to whatever assignment he wanted next. She had no idea what could do that, but whatever it was, the former rescue pilot had made it crystal clear that he was not going to talk about it.

The fifteen-minute drive to the airport seemed to take forever, and she pulled into the rental car lot with a sigh of relief. The trip through airport security was done in a separate area from the passengers because of the weapons they were carrying. It went smoothly, and before long, they were settling into their seats on the plane. To their surprise, they were given two seats in first class, right at the very front of the plane.

Gin wasn't about to look a gift horse in the mouth but got a good idea of why they'd gotten so lucky when the pilot came out of the cockpit before takeoff and deliberately made eye contact with each of them before getting a cup of coffee from the front galley kitchen. Gin leaned over and said in a low whisper just for Trey's ears, "I guess the Captain felt better if the two armed FBI agents were closer to the cockpit."

Trey smiled his agreement. "Let's hope he doesn't have a reason to feel that way on this particular flight. Shooting off a gun in an airplane is not a good idea."

Got that right, Gin settled the complimentary headsets over her ears. Once the plane was airborne and on its way to San Francisco, she declined the offer of a drink and searched out some easy-listening music on the monitor built into the bulkhead in front of her seat. Thanks to her abbreviated sleep the night before, she was out like a light in five minutes, not waking again until Trey nudged her in the arm as they were making their descent into the Bay Area.

After they'd picked up yet another rental car, Gin rolled her shoulders and settled into the driver's seat. "So where does Stephen have us staying?"

"Out near the headquarters of Ralfin Construction." Trey pulled out his phone and accessed its GPS app. "They're in Santa Clara, which is about forty minutes from here."

"Fine," Gin said. "Let's head there first."

"That would put us there at eleven, and our appointment with the two owners isn't until one this afternoon," Trey pointed out.

Not worried about that, Gin smiled. "I'm guessing they'll be happy to take a meeting a little early rather than have two armed FBI agents sitting in their lobby."

"Good point," Trey said. "Follow those signs to the 101 freeway. It's a straight shot from there."

Since she'd been to San Francisco several times over the previous ten years, Gin knew the way, but she didn't bother to tell her partner that, content to let the GPS chirp out directions as they entered the battle with the Bay Area traffic. "Tell me about these partners we flew across the country to meet."

"Two brothers, both in their late forties," Trey said without hesitation. "From their background sheets it sounds as if they're some kind of prodigies in the world of construction. Built the company from the ground up, starting out as subcontractors on small jobs, and now their company is worth three hundred million. Their personal net worths top twenty-five million each."

Gin let out a low whistle. "That's a lot of millions. Do these wonder boys have names?"

"Peter and Raymond Ralfin. Both married with two kids apiece." Trey's mouth curved up into a smile. "All girls."

"Cosmic justice," Gin said. "Anything hinky in their background? Closet ties to criminals? Under investigation by the IRS? Jay walking tickets?"

"Not a thing. Peter tends to drive too fast. He gets a speeding ticket about three times a year. Raymond came up a big blank on a criminal search."

"Okay. So I guess we'll pick up the jobs list, ask a few polite questions, then head for the hotel." She took a quick peek at her watch. "Which I hope has an option for early check-in. If not, we can camp out in their business center and start comparing lists."

"Yeah. I saw the email with the list attached from T.L. Construction when we landed," Trey said.

"Me too." Gin added as she eased the car over to the right-hand lane when the GPS and the signs overhead announced their exit was a mile ahead. "Now all we need is that second list to compare it to, and hopefully, we'll find somewhere our victims' paths have crossed.

The corporate offices for Ralfin Construction were in a very long and wide, rectangular two-story building set in an office district close to the freeway. The building had a modern look about it, boasting a lot of concrete and dark glass, surrounded by minimal landscaping.

Gin found a parking spot and the two of them walked into the open lobby with high ceilings and wooden, wide-plank floors. No one sat behind the reception counter, but there was a large display in front of it, listing the location of all the building's occupants. Raflin Construction was on the second floor, which seemed like a waste of time for an elevator. But not seeing any stairs, they settled for riding up the one floor. Turning right, they went down a carpeted hallway, stopping at the halfway point in front of an enormous set of double doors.

Raflin's suite of offices was decorated in muted colors, with several chairs and a small sofa occupying the front area. Pictures of buildings in various stages of construction lined the walls. A middle-aged woman with brown hair and a pleasant smile looked up from her computer when Gin and Trey opened the door and stepped inside.

"Can I help you?"

Gin took out her credential case and held it open in front of the receptionist. "I'm FBI Special Agent Reilly, and this is my partner, Special Agent Robard. We have an appointment with Peter and Raymond Ralfin."

"Yes, you do," the woman said without missing a beat. "But I understood it was for one o'clock." Before Gin could say anything, she picked up the receiver of her desk phone. "Let me see if they're available now."

Gin politely took a step back while the woman murmured into her phone. A few seconds later, the receptionist set the receiver back into its cradle and nodded. "They'd be happy to see you now. Pete's admin will be out shortly to escort you to his office. You're welcome to take a seat while you wait."

"Thank you." Gin turned and walked to the far side of the room, but having sat on a plane for six hours, she chose to stand. As she walked the loop around the reception area, she studied the pictures on the wall, stopping to stare at one that caught her eye. She was still staring at it when a woman dressed in casual navy-blue slacks and a contrasting blouse in pale pink opened the door behind the desk. "Agent Reilly and Agent Robard? If you'll follow me, Mr. Raflin is waiting for you."

Gin nodded her thanks to the receptionist before following Raflin's admin down a wide hallway leading to the back of the suite. They walked past a dozen cubicles, all occupied by people talking on the phone or working on their computers before stopping in front of a door that was wide open, with an expansive office on the other side. The admin leaned against the doorframe and stuck her head through the opening. "Here they are, Pete. Should I get Ray?"

"Yes, please, and thank you, Donna."

The voice floated past Gin as the admin stepped to the side. "Go right in."

Gin walked through the open doorway with Trey right behind her. The office had a thick, dark brown carpet and three walls painted in soft beige. The fourth wall was all windows, reaching from the floor to the ceiling. A large ornate mahogany desk was placed in front of the windows, and a man with light brown hair and blue eyes rose from the leather-cushioned executive chair.

He smiled at Gin, then did a double take when he got a look at Trey's face. Clearing his throat, he came around the desk, his hand outstretched in greeting. "I'm Pete Raflin. Which one of you is Reilly, and which one is Robard?"

Gin took the outstretched hand and gave it a firm shake. "I'm Special Agent Reilly, and this is my partner, Special Agent Robard. Thank you for seeing us, Mr. Ralfin."

Pete Ralfin's smile lit up his entire face. "Not a problem. Please, call me Pete." He gave a brief shake of his head. "And no, I don't expect the same informality from you." Pete looked up at the man who strolled through the open office door. Except for the clothes he was wearing, he was Pete Raflin's exact double. "This is Ray, my brother and partner in the firm." He gestured toward Gin. "Agent Reilly." Pete waited for his brother's nod before switching his finger to Trey. "And that one is Agent Robard."

"Glad to meet you both," Ray said with the same wide smile as Pete's. "Ouch," he said as he studied Trey's bruised face. "I'd hate to see the other guy." When Trey only smiled, Ray let out a deep chuckle. "Sorry to drag you here, but we wanted to talk in person. I hope it hasn't caused too much trouble for you."

They'd spent six hours on a plane, but since it was in a first-class seat, Gin wasn't inclined to hold any grudges. "We're here, Mr. Raflin."

"Ray," the second brother interrupted. "And I appreciate that. Agent Reilly, is it?"

"Yes it is," Pete told him. "They're FBI. They don't give out their first names."

Gin moved to a chair placed in front of the large desk and took a seat. Leaning back, she looked up at Pete. "What is it you wanted to tell us, Pete?" As his eyes opened wider, she smiled. "I assume that you insisted we show up in person for a reason?"

"It seems we're going to get right to it." Pete walked around the desk and sat in the imposing executive chair.

His brother followed and took up a standing position next to him while Tray mimicked him by shifting over to stand next to Gin.

Pete leaned back in his chair and steepled his fingers together in front of his chest. "We want to know if you are working on the Stampler investigation, and that's why you called us after all this time?"

Gin kept a polite smile. "Why would you think that?"

For the second time she heard the same explanation. "News reports. It would be impossible to miss the details of what they're saying about the way Stampler was murdered and what happened to Miguel Rivera."

Gin suppressed a sigh. There were times, like right now, when she wished the press wasn't quite so zealous in pursuing its First Amendment rights. "There are similarities," she conceded.

"And then you called and asked for a list of the job sites Miguel worked on," Pete continued. "So we had to ask and didn't think we'd get a straight answer unless we were face-to-face. Are you looking for some crazy out there, or was one of our job sites targeted?"

"Why would you think that?" Gin asked. "Have you received a threat?"

"No," Pete stated flatly. "But a big corporate executive is murdered in the same way as the worker of a company that is involved in big corporate projects? There has to be a link between them."

"Are we going to find Meridian Pharmaceuticals on the list you'll be giving us?" Gin asked. Which would be odd since a vice-president of Meridian had stated the company hadn't engaged in any building projects in the last five years.

"No, you won't," Pete said.

"But you knew Benjamin Stampler, didn't you, Pete?" Gin persisted. "I saw a picture on the wall of your lobby of you standing together in front of one of your projects."

"Met," Pete corrected, then gestured toward his brother. "And only briefly." He inclined his head to include his brother. "We both have. At a few charity functions, and then once when a mobile health van was delivered to a free clinic. I went to the shindig to commemorate it, and Stampler was there with his wife."

"But they're a big corporate conglomerate," Ray interjected. "We do projects for big corporate conglomerates, and a lot of people have a grudge against those types of companies. So it isn't a giant leap to think other projects for big corporations might also be a target."

Thinking it was actually a leap as wide as the Grand Canyon, Gin shifted slightly in her chair. "We'll look into it. Is there anything else?"

Ray Raflin who braced his hands against the highly polished top of his brother's desk and leaned forward. "What else could it be?" he demanded. "Miguel Rivera was with us when we were just small potatoes, scratching up whatever jobs we could to keep afloat. He was a good man and just as good an electrician. Even more importantly, he didn't have an enemy in this world. And he was a lifelong bachelor, so it isn't as if he had a pissed-off ex-wife somewhere in the background."

"It's hard to deal with it when something like this happens." Gin said, then paused. Hearing the description of Miguel Rivera reminded her of what another construction owner had said about his employee. "Do you know an Aldo Twiner?"

Pete shook his head while Ray nodded. "Runs an outfit out of Nevada," the second Ralfin brother said. At Pete's questioning look, Ray shrugged. "I deal with the subcontractors more than you do. He's also been at a few conferences that I've attended."

"Have you ever hired his company?" Gin asked.

"Not that I recall," Ray replied. "But I'll have our admin look through our records."

"What about that threat possibility?" Pete demanded.

"We'll check with the Bureau's domestic terrorism department, see if they've heard any chatter about a threat against construction companies." Gin's gaze shifted from Pete back to Ray. "I have a few questions for you. Have you had any other employees disappear?"

"Shit. Do you think we wouldn't have called the cops in two seconds flat if that had happened?" Ray retorted. He jabbed a stiff index finger against the desk when Gin only silently stared back at him. "The answer to your question is no. A flat-out no."

"How about not showing up for work, and then sending a text message that they quit, or anything along those lines?"

Ray's eyes narrowed suspiciously on Gin's face. "I haven't heard anything like that, but I'm not sure I would have. Do you have a specific reason for asking us that?"

Smart guy, Gin thought. Both of them. They'd known something was up as soon as they got Stephen's call about a list of their past jobs. So they'd lured the FBI out here as their best play to find out what was going on. Too bad she couldn't accommodate them.

"Just covering bases," she said. "Now, about that list?"

The brothers exchanged a look before Pete opened his desk drawer and drew out an envelope. He placed it on the desk, then used two fingers to slide it toward Gin. "There it is. All our jobs for the last five years."

She stood, then leaned over and picked up the envelope. "Thank you for this, and for your cooperation. If anything comes up about Miguel Rivera, we'll be in touch."

Pete Raflin also got to his feet and drew up to his full height next to his brother. "I hope so, Agent Reilly. I hope so."

Trey nodded at the pair before following Gin out the door. They didn't say a word until they were back in the car and the GPS had them heading for the hotel.

"What do you think?" he asked.

"I think that's the second time someone has connected Stampler's murder to another one, and if anybody talks about it with friends, then the press will catch wind of it and we'll have a mess on our hands." She reached into her jacket pocket and handed the envelope that Pete Raflin had given her to Trey. "I think there's a thumb drive in there."

Trey opened up the envelope and looked inside. "Yep. A thumb drive." He tucked it safely away into his own jacket pocket. "As soon as we get to the hotel, I'll run the comparison between Raflin's list and the one Twiner sent us." He shot her a sideways look. "Do you want me to throw that list from Meridian into the mix?"

"Yeah," Gin decided. "Those jobs are old, but why not? We might get lucky."

"Lucky enough to scare up some lunch?" Trey asked, his eyes narrowing when Gin made a show of consulting her watch.

"It's almost past three in the afternoon back in Florida. It's a wonder you haven't keeled over dead from starvation," she said, then laughed when he made a face.

Used to Stephen's constant demands for food whenever the job had required them to travel, Gin simply shrugged. "Fine. It's a big city. I'm sure we can scare up something to tide you over for a couple of hours until dinner."

It turned out the hotel had a small café next door that not only served lunch but featured an all-day breakfast. Gin sat in a booth across from Trey and watched him devour a pound or two of food while she nibbled on some toast washed down with a cup of coffee. The amount of food the man could put away was astonishing, but she appreciated his efficiency at it since they were soon headed back to the hotel desk to check-in.

At first the fussy receptionist declared it was too early and that housekeeping hadn't finished their rooms yet. But once

A HARD TRUTH

Gin casually brushed her jacket aside, giving the clerk a clear look at the shiny gold badge attached to her belt, and, more effectively, her gun, two rooms were magically ready and they were able to dump their gear and set up Trey's laptop.

Surprisingly enough, the desk in his room was large enough to accommodate both of them sitting at it, so Gin kept her eyes on the screen as Trey brought up the list from Big Al that he'd already imported into a spreadsheet. Fortunately, the Ralfin list was in the same format, so it didn't take Trey long to run a comparison between the two. She was expecting the program to take at least a few minutes to find any match, if there was even one to be found. Less than ten seconds later there was a loud beep. Trey leaned closer to the screen, partially blocking her view, as he tapped on the keys.

"It looks like a match," he declared. He scooted back in his chair so she could get a better look, then pointed at the screen. "There. Both companies worked on that project. See the description? They list the same name."

"Terence M. Latcher Clinic," Gin read aloud. She took out her phone and entered the name into the search engine. An entire screen of articles came up, including one on the grand opening with a picture of the ribbon-cutting ceremony. "It's a free clinic in Santa Cruz, funded by private donations." She scrolled through the article. "It opened its doors eighteen months ago."

"Before the first murder," Trey said, then grimaced. "At least the first one we know about."

A tingle slid up the nerves of Gin's arms. *That's two*, she thought. *Let's try for three*. "Can you do a search of the Meridian project list for that name?"

"The one their VP sent you?" When Gin nodded, Trey went to work on the keyboard. "I can, but I already gave that list a quick look, and there wasn't anything less than five years old. That Latcher clinic opened just eighteen months ago." He finished his entry then sat back and watched the computer run through the Meridian list at lightning speed. Unfortunately, the end result was just what he'd predicted. No match found.

"Maybe it isn't a corporate connection," Trey suggested.

Of course some of our charitable donations have gone to new facilities and such. The words popped into Gin's mind. Hunt had said that when she'd asked him about Meridian's building projects. "Run a search for that clinic against the list of charities that Meridian Pharmaceutical donates to."

Trey gave her a skeptical look, but dutifully turned back to the keyboard and pulled up the charity list from Meridian. A few moments later his eyes widened. "I'll be damned. We have a match."

Gin leaned over his shoulder and stared at the screen. "Terence M. Latcher Clinic," she read out loud. Puckering her lips, she let out a soft whistle. "Whoa. That's a lot of donation money." She squinted at the screen. "And look there. It's marked as one of the charitable donations that was increased over the last year."

Trey scrolled through the data supplied by the pharmacy company. "And that's pretty much been the case year over year." He sat back and looked at Gin. "That clinic seems to be a favorite of Meridian's charity committee."

"Or with someone with a lot of pull in the company." Gin straightened up. "Like the CEO who goes to shindigs to celebrate a mobile health van, according to Raflin. I'll bet Mrs. Stampler would know the answer to that. I'll give her a call to verify. In the meantime, we've got a single point where all the victims' paths crossed."

"Yeah," Trey agreed. "They all had something to do with that clinic. One as a major supporter, and the other two as building contractors."

"Uh-huh." Gin pursed her lips as her gaze returned to the laptop's screen. "The Raflins said they've never used T.L. Construction as a subcontractor. But like you said, they both worked this job."

"Hang on. I only did a match search on a few fields. Let me check the rest of the info they sent over." Trey switched to another file, did a quick search, and then pulled up the entire entry for the clinic. "This is Raflin's data. According to their record, they subcontracted on this job." He frowned at the screen. "If Twiner did as well, they weren't working for each other but for the general contractor." His gaze returned to the document displayed on the screen. "Raflin lists the general contractor as Connor Elliot, Inc."

Gin tapped the name into the search engine on her phone. "Out of Salinas." She looked up. "That's south of here, I think."

"Yeah. About an hour." When Gin blinked, he smiled. "I was based at the Lemoore Naval Air Station for six years. There's not much to do out there and it's only three and a half hours from here, so on my days off, I came up to San Francisco pretty regularly. I got to know the area fairly well."

Taking him at his word, Gin pointed at the screen. "Great. Then you won't have any problem getting us to Salinas or Santa Cruz?"

His brows winged upward in surprise. "You want to have a look at that clinic?"

"Maybe. An hour from here?" Gin looked at her watch. "It's just one o'clock. I'll give Connor Elliot a call and see if they can squeeze us in this afternoon." Belatedly remembering that Trey was still pretty bruised, and he'd already spent six hours on a plane, she sent him a guilty look. "Feel like taking a ride?"

He reached over and closed his laptop. "Whenever you're ready."

Chapter Seventeen

Since Trey was more familiar with the area, he drove while Gin made good use of their traveling time doing quick internet searches on the clinic as well as the man it was named after. She read the basic facts out loud to her partner as they made steady progress on the southbound freeway, ahead of the afternoon commuter traffic.

The sleepy town, located eight miles inland from its more pricey neighbors overlooking the Pacific Ocean, was mostly known for its large farms and agricultural community, but it had a small, thriving consulting and service industry as well.

Trey turned into a narrow driveway leading to a small parking lot in back of the building that housed Connor Elliot, Inc. The three-story structure's natural wood siding was complimented by the clean lines of the wide cement steps leading up to sparkling double doors made of glass. The simple, clean look put it somewhere between a budget-friendly establishment and the strikingly modern upper-end building that Raflin Construction occupied. Connor Elliot Inc.'s offices were on the ground floor, and consisted of two rooms — a small outer reception area and a single inner office.

When Gin and Trey stepped inside, an older woman, with steel-gray hair arranged in layers of tightly wound curls, looked up from behind a small desk. A pair of sharp blue eyes studied the two agents over the top edge of gold wire-rimmed glasses. Her gaze zeroed in on the slight bulge beneath Gin's jacket before lifting it up to her face. "You must be the FBI agent who called a little while ago, asking to see Connor?"

Gin smiled under the close scrutiny. "Yes, ma'am. I'm Special Agent Reilly, and this is my partner, Special Agent Robard. Is Mr. Elliot in?"

"He'll be here in a few minutes," the woman said. "He just called and said he's on his way back from his appointment. It was local, so it won't take him long to get back." She lifted one hand and waved a thick finger at Gin. "You got lucky there. If he'd had to go over to the coast, he would have been stuck on that two-lane road through the hills, and it's a crapshoot on how long that takes."

"That is lucky," Gin said, her lips twitching. From the corner of her eye, she saw Trey fighting back a smile. "If it won't disturb you, we'd like to wait in here."

"There isn't anywhere else for you to wait." The older woman waved a hand to the corner where two side chairs were tucked against the wall with a small table separating them. "That's what those chairs are for, so go ahead and have a seat."

"Thank you," Gin said, with Trey politely echoing her before they both moved toward the chairs.

They'd barely sat down before the door to the outside hallway popped open. A man with the size and barrel-chested build of a little person stepped into the reception area. He was dressed in a well-tailored dark blue suit with a shirt and tie in a lighter shade of blue. His dark brown hair, with a liberal sprinkling of gray in it, was a sharp contrast to the smooth skin and youthful look of his face. Eyes as dark brown as his hair immediately went to Gin and Trey.

He sent them a brief nod before his gaze cut back to his receptionist. "Any calls besides our two visitors?"

"Three more," the woman said. "I left the messages on your desk." She jerked her head toward the corner where Gin and Trey sat. "Those two are Reilly and Robard. The young woman is Reilly." Having delivered that information, she reached down and picked up a large purse that had a paperback book sticking out of the top. "And John Mackey still hasn't paid his bill, so you'll need to give him a call." Oblivious to the wince from her boss, the receptionist picked up her purse and scooted around the edge of the desk. "Now I need to get going or I'll miss my afternoon soap opera. We're having roast tonight, Connor, so make sure you get home at a decent hour or it will be all dried out."

"Okay, Mom. I'll be sure to do that." Connor automatically held the door open for his mother, closing it softly behind her before approaching Gin and Trey. He held out his hand as he introduced himself. "I'm Connor Elliot."

"I'm Special Agent Reilly," Gin said as she shook his hand, then stood silently as Connor repeated the ritual with Trevor.

"Let's go into my office, and you can tell me what this is all about." By the time Connor had settled himself behind his desk in a tastefully decorated office with a large window and floor-to-ceiling bookshelves, he'd removed his tie and draped it over the back of his chair. He stacked his hands in front of himself and smiled. "Your message said that you wanted some information about a project I worked on. Now, which project would that be?"

"The Terence M. Latcher Clinic, in Santa Cruz," Gin said.

Connor blinked in surprise. "No kidding? What interest would the FBI have in a free clinic?"

"Were you the general contractor on the building project?" Gin asked.

"That's right," Connor verified. "I assure you that I have a contractor's license, and running building projects is what I do for a living. I also work as a project coordinator, getting the bids and finding an appropriate general contractor if the project is beyond my skill set for the everyday details, or too time consuming for my schedule."

Gin tilted her head to the side and studied him for a long moment. "But that wasn't the case for the Latcher clinic?"

"Well, let's just say it was more prudent if I ran that one myself. I can also guarantee that all the appropriate and required permits were filed, and the construction met every code, both state and county." He pressed his mouth into a thin line as he leaned forward. "None of which do I think the FBI would be interested in. So what's this about?"

"Then I take it you were very involved with all aspects of the project?" At Connor's sharp nod, Gin continued. "And you worked with all the subcontractors, including Raflin and T.L. Construction?"

"They put in competitive bids and they are both excellent companies," Connor snapped out. "Why?"

"Do you remember any arguments or problems between any of the contractors?" Gin asked, ignoring his question.

Connor's eyes narrowed. "The subs usually disagree with whoever designed the building, not with each other. Off the top of my head, I don't recall any problems. That project went off more smoothly than most, probably because everyone wanted to get it done in as little time as possible, since none of us were being paid for our labor."

"Did that cause any resentment on the job?"

The project manager indulged in a short, harsh laugh. "Why? The workers got paid, the owners didn't, and that was the owners' choice in order to stay on Terence Latcher's good side. Overtime was limited, but the job was still finished two weeks ahead of schedule which made everyone happy. The crews went home in time for the holidays, and the owners of all the companies involved stopped bleeding cash." He looked down and pretended to study his fingernails. "Including me."

Surprised, Gin's eyes widened. "You weren't paid?"

"Nope," Connor said. "Just expenses."

She tucked that fact away and pressed on. "What about after work? Did the subcontractors mingle together, maybe go to a favorite bar or some other gathering place to hang out?"

"They were working in Santa Cruz," Connor said patiently. "The boardwalk there was a favorite place to go for all of us, and there are plenty of places to eat or get a drink around there. As for the crews hanging out together?" He gave a quick, indifferent shrug. "Maybe. But on most jobs, crews tend to stick with each other, and I don't recall the clinic job being any different. I mean one crew might be there to do the concrete work, another the plumbing, and a third for the electrical. The work the subs bid for is usually specialized, maybe in more than one area, but generally not for the entire job, so they mostly keep company with who they know, both on the job and after hours."

Feeling she was walking up a dead end, Gin went for a different line of questioning. "And did you attend any of the fund-raising events, Mr. Elliot?"

"Of course I did. Most of us involved with the project did, especially since we all donated our labor. And again, why?"

Again, Gin ignored his question. "Did you meet any of the other major donors who weren't part of the actual construction of the clinic?"

"Yes. Nothing out of the ordinary in that either since we were all rubbing shoulders at the same fundraising events. And you have to hand it to Latcher. He reeled in some pretty impressive donors. One of the largest ones was Meridian Pharmaceuticals. They're a big dog in their industry. Even the CEO came out. . ." Connor's mouth snapped shut as he stared at Gin with the laser-eyed look he'd inherited from his mother. When Gin only stared back, letting the silence draw out, he slowly exhaled. "I was going to say that their CEO, Benjamin Stampler, even attended several of the events. But given the latest headlines, I suspect you already know that, and he's the reason you're here."

"Agent Robard and I are working on the Stampler case," Gin admitted. "And we're interested in learning about that clinic project and the people who were involved with it."

Connor sat back, a frown forming lines across his forehead and down his cheeks. "All right. But first I need some assurances that nothing we discuss will get back to Terence Latcher." When Gin lifted an eyebrow, Connor shrugged. "He's a heavy hitter in my world, Agent Reilly, with his hands on a lot of projects. That's why most of us donated our labor to his pet project out there in Santa Cruz. Latcher can wield a heavy club when he wants to, and if you want to survive in this industry, it's better if you avoid it."

It was a good reason to ask for assurances, and she didn't have any problem with giving them. "We won't be divulging the source of any of our information, Mr. Elliot, and would ask that you not discuss any of our conversation outside of this room. Especially not to the press."

The smile was back on Connor's face. "That's a fair trade. Now, what would you like to know?"

Gin settled more comfortably in her chair. "Why did you call the clinic Latcher's pet project?"

"Because he built it for his daughter. It was Dr. Justine Latcher's dream, and she runs the place. I think she's the only thing Terence has ever really cared about in this world more than his own self-interest, so he made sure her dream came true." Connor's mouth twisted into a wry grin. "And was equally zealous in making sure that the rest of us fell into line to make it happen. Like I said, the man has a heavy step and carries a big stick. And that stick is made entirely of money. He's got it by the truckload. He invested in a lot of real estate in the Bay Area when it was just expensive and not somewhere in the stratosphere like it is today. Then he moved into funding start-ups in Silicon Valley, and he's done extraordinarily well there too. He has a nose for finding those diamonds in the rough that end up being worth millions."

"I imagine you'd make a lot of enemies playing in that sandbox," Gin said.

Connor gave a quick, jerky nod. "And you'd be right about that. But Stampler wasn't one of them. Justine liked him too, and even Evaline, Latcher's wife, seemed to tolerate him, from what I could tell at those fundraiser parties." A sly smile crept across his face when Gin frowned. "Evaline is from an old, well-connected family that outlived their generational money. She attends all of Terence's functions where a wife is required, but she makes it pretty clear she doesn't care for many of his business associates, which includes us lowly contractors. But I think Stampler was an exception. She actually smiled when she was talking to him."

"And the Latchers are still married?" Gin asked.

"Yeah. Second time around for both of them. Not my idea of a good marriage, but he likes her social connections and she likes his money, so it seems to work for them."

"And did his wife support the clinic?"

A HARD TRUTH

Now Connor shifted his position in his chair and his shoulders went visibly stiff. "She attended the fundraisers."

Seeing the uncomfortable look on the project manager's face, Gin pressed a little harder. "Is that it? Did she ever take a tour of the construction site, or maybe head the donation effort?"

Connor relaxed again and laughed. "No. Nothing like that. Not Evaline." He sighed and lowered his voice until it was just above a whisper. "If you ask me, Evaline thought the free clinic was beneath her notice. She owns a small, very upscale art gallery in a prime area of Monterey. And let me tell you, that slice of real estate is not cheap. I know she wants to expand and puts most of her energy into establishing her own donor network along with running the gallery."

And maybe having an affair with Ben Stampler? The only one of her husband's business associates who she liked? Gin speculated silently. But while an affair might push a jealous husband to the point of murder, it didn't explain the similar murders of the two construction workers, and didn't fit with what she knew about Stampler's marriage. Still, she tucked the possibility away in the back of her mind.

"If her husband is so rich, why doesn't he bankroll her expansion?" Trey asked.

The project manager wiggled his eyebrows up and down. "Interesting question, isn't it? And one that's been asked plenty of times. He's listed as a donor, but rumor has it he gives her a pittance. Just enough to show up on her donor's list, for the sake of appearances. Publicly, Evaline has always said she doesn't want him involved with the gallery. But privately?" Connor shook his head. "Rumor has it that she's furious with the whole thing. Especially since her stepdaughter isn't one of her favorite people."

"Why is that?" Gin asked, but only as a matter of form.

Now that he was on a roll, Connor Elliot was clearly in his element as he cheerfully related all the society gossip.

He shrugged. "I don't know. But the consensus among Evaline's acquaintances is that she doesn't like Justine's favored position within the family dynamic. It might cut her out of inheriting anything if Terence dies before her, even if she is his wife. If I had to hazard a guess, I'd say Evaline is right about that point. It wouldn't surprise me, or anyone else, if Terence didn't leave his wife a single penny in his will."

Gin wrinkled her nose as she squinted back at Connor. "You seem to have an unusual amount of knowledge about the Latcher family, Mr. Elliot."

He shrugged. "It's because I do quite a bit of work for Evaline's friends. And their husbands. The group of new and old wealth in Monterey and Carmel Valley is both small and very tight. There's not a lot they don't know about each other, or talk about." He crossed his arms over his large chest. "Now, tell me why you're so interested in this clinic? Knowing Dr. Latcher, I doubt if she's ever broken even a littering ordinance, much less a federal law."

"I'm sorry. We can't discuss any details about an ongoing investigation," Gin said, once again repeating the favorite response of every law enforcement agency. "I would appreciate a contact number for Terence Latcher."

Connor immediately reached for the cell phone he'd set on his desk. "He lives in Pebble Beach." He rolled his eyes as he handed his phone with the contact number displayed on it to Gin. "He's an avid golfer, so where else would he live? But if you're thinking of paying him a visit, it will take you at least ninety minutes to get there at this time of day. And if Latcher knows you're with the FBI, you'll probably be greeted by a wall of attorneys to boot."

"We've dealt with attorneys before, Mr. Elliot," Gin said.

A HARD TRUTH

Once she'd made a note of the phone number, she looked up with a frown. "What about the clinic? How long would it take us to get there?"

"You'd be driving against the traffic, so maybe about an hour or so." Connor set his phone back on the desk. "But you'd better leave now if you hope to catch anyone there." He glanced at a clock on his desk that was encased in wood and gold. "They close at six, as I recall." He slid to the edge of his chair and made a slight hop off it to stand up. "Just jump over to the coast and then head north. If you drive through town, you'll see the signs. Then follow those. The place isn't too hard to find." When Gin and Trey got to their feet, Connor walked around the edge of the desk. "I'll show you out." He reached into a pocket of his vest and pulled out a card. "If you have any more questions, feel free to call me."

Gin took the card and tucked it into her jacket pocket. "Thanks. We'll do that. And we appreciate the help, Mr. Elliot."

It only took a few minutes to reach their car and get back on the highway. Once Trey had made the turn west, toward the coast, Gin propped one knee on the seat and twisted her body sideways to face him. "What do you think?"

"I think he's sitting in his office right now debating with himself on whether to make a couple of calls to find out why we're so hot to know about Latcher, that clinic, and those two subcontractors."

"Agreed," Gin said with a sigh. "I'm hoping he took our bargain seriously enough that he'll decide against making those calls."

"He's a smart guy. I think he'll sit tight," Trey replied as he expertly maneuvered the car through the twists and turns of the two-lane road that led to the ocean.

With the light just beginning to fade, the world was awash

in a golden glow, making the first sighting of the vastness of the Pacific, with its water sparkling under the waning sun, a breathtaking view. Gin sat back and enjoyed the scenery. It was hard to beat the California coastline for sheer beauty, with the largest ocean in the world lapping at its shores.

She missed the rugged mountains in Colorado, and sometimes even the rolling fields of green in the spring in Iowa despite everything that had happened there. But in a pinch, the waves, the stretches of beach, and a body of water that seemed to have no end would do just fine. Gin smiled. At least that was what the millions of people who lived there thought.

Just like Connor had said, the clinic wasn't hard to find. It was housed in a long, flat building with an adobe look on the outside that was a pleasant contrast to the smoked-glass windows set at regular intervals along the walls. It was past five in the afternoon when they pulled into the parking lot.

Judging by the number of cars in the lot, and the steady stream of people entering and exiting the building, the clinic's business day was far from over. Gin stood on the sidewalk that skirted the front of the building, her hands on her hips as she stared at it.

This was the convergence point. The place that all three murder victims had in common.

"Any sudden lightning bolts hitting you now that we've got eyes on the place?" Trey asked. He was standing beside her, arms crossed over his chest. His eyes followed a young mother, carrying an infant in her arms. "Doesn't look like a place that would cost the lives of three men."

Gin's gaze roamed across the front of the building. "No. No, it doesn't."

"Can I help you?"

Since the question came from somewhere behind her, Gin turned and came face-to-face with a tall woman, as thin as a beanpole and sporting a white lab coat, a stethoscope around her neck. Her features were just uneven enough that Gin imagined she'd heard the word "homely" more than once in her life. That image was helped by the fact that she was looking Trey right in the eye. Frizzy brown hair was pulled back into a ponytail, and the name tag on her lab coat identified her as Justine Latcher, M.D.

Well, at least we didn't have to track her down, Gin thought as her mouth turned up into a smile. "Dr. Latcher?" At the woman's brief nod, Gin held out a hand. "I'm Special Agent Reilly with the FBI, and this is my partner, Special Agent Robard."

The doctor looked down at Gin's hand before she finally grasped it in one of her own, gave it a single, shallow shake, then dropped it like a hot potato. "It isn't good for my patients to see anyone with a gun and badge standing outside the clinic's doors. What can I do to hurry you along, Agent Reilly?"

Since the doctor was being direct enough, Gin thought she would do the same. "We wanted to talk to you, Dr. Latcher. Do you have a few minutes right now?"

Annoyance flashed in the doctor's eyes. "Right now? No, I don't. If you'll give me your card, I'll take a look at my schedule and ask Ms. Polen to get back to you."

Gin cocked her head to the side. "Ms. Polen?"

"Linda Polen. She's a personal assistant for my stepmother, and occasionally for me as well."

Gin's smile remained in place as she gazed back at the doctor, who fairly hummed with impatience. "That's handy, because we also want to speak to your father and stepmother."

"About what?" the doctor demanded.

"About one of your major donors, Benjamin Stampler. We're looking into his murder, and that has led us right here to you and your clinic, Dr. Latcher."

The doctor slowly blew out a long breath. Gin could almost hear her counting to ten under her breath. "I can't imagine why. According to the news reports, he was killed on the East Coast." Her eyes narrowed slightly. "In Florida, or New York, as I recall. Neither my father nor I have been to either of those places."

"Never?" Gin questioned pleasantly, holding her smile as a streak of red rolled across the doctor's cheeks.

"Not for a very long time," Justine amended in a clipped voice.

"And your stepmother?" Gin continued. "Has she been to either of those places?"

"I wouldn't know. I don't keep track of Evaline's schedule." The doctor waved a hand impatiently in front of Gin's face before thrusting it into the deep pocket of her lab coat. Drawing out a cell phone, she tapped the screen, then held it up to her ear. "Ms. Polen?" She pursed her lips as her eyes rolled upward. "Yes, I'm fine. I need a time. . ." She cut herself off and held the phone to her chest when Gin lightly tapped her on the arm. "What is it, Agent Reilly?"

"Tomorrow, Dr. Latcher," Gin said politely. "We need a time tomorrow."

Justine glared at her for a moment, then turned her back and lifted the phone to her ear again. "I need a time tomorrow for dad and me to meet with the FBI at our house. It's regarding the murder of Benjamin Stampler." There was a pause while Justine listened to the invisible Ms. Polen. "Yes, I'm not coming into the clinic until late tomorrow, so we can meet at the house. Fine. Thank you." The doctor dropped the phone back into her pocket before turning around to face Gin. "Ten o'clock tomorrow morning. Dad and I can both spare about thirty minutes, so please don't be late. Do you need to take down the address?"

A HARD TRUTH

"Not necessary. We have it." Gin's smile grew at the sour look on the doctor's face.

Deliberately ignoring Gin, Justine adjusted her glasses as she squinted at Trey's face. "I hope you had those bruises looked at and properly treated."

"Yes, ma'am," Trey replied.

"Thank you." Gin interrupted before Justine could dispense any more unsolicited medical advice. "We'll leave you to your work here and see you tomorrow at your house." She stretched her lips into a smile. "Until then, Doctor Latcher."

Chapter Eighteen

The morning dawned with the expected sunshine and warm weather California was famous for. The drive from Santa Clara over to the coast and then down to Pebble Beach was accomplished without any traffic glitches, and given the crowded roads in the area, that was definitely a gift.

The Latcher home was more of an estate than a house. Set back from the road, it had iron gates and a stone wall to keep uninvited guests out. Gin drove up to the gate and pressed the intercom button. She held her badge out the window and within full view of the cameras mounted on both sides of the entrance. Within a minute the gates swung open and she slowly eased the car past them, continuing up the curved drive, and past a wide, neatly manicured lawn bordered by a virtual forest of flowering plants, all showing off blooms in an explosion of vibrant colors.

The house itself was built in a one-story, sprawled out ranch style, with long wings extending out on either side of the main entrance. White rose bushes were planted all along the

A HARD TRUTH

front, and hanging baskets with spidery trailers of ivy hung at regular intervals across the front porch.

The look of the place wasn't as formal as Gin would have expected for a man of Latcher's wealth. While it still oozed out the impression of money, it had a solid, down-to-earth appearance about it that she preferred over the soaring pillars or giant stone edifices of the typical home favored by the extremely wealthy.

Maybe he hasn't reached those lofty heights yet, Gin thought. But Connor Elliot's description of the man having truckloads of money heavily implied that he had. Unless the project manager had been envisioning some very small trucks. Smiling at the thought, Gin exited the car and joined Trey, who was already standing at the bottom of the three shallow steps that led up to the porch and front door.

"Are you ready for this?" Gin asked once she'd stopped beside him.

"He's just a rich guy, and I've met the type before," Trey said. "The politicians liked us to put on our uniforms, making sure all our citations were pinned to the front, of course, and parade us around in front of rich guys just like Latcher. The more citations, the bigger the donations to veteran organizations. Or so I was told."

She shot him a sideways glance. "Doesn't sound like you miss it much."

"No, I don't. At least not that part of it." He swept a hand in front of her. "Should we get this over with?"

She grinned. "By all means." Rearranging her expression into sober lines, Gin looked for a doorbell but didn't see one. She was about to knock when the high, solid oak door opened. The woman standing in the center of the opening was short with a thick waist, choppy brown hair that hung to her shoulders, and large, black-framed glasses over big brown eyes.

"Agent Reilly and Agent Robard?" Her voice was high, bordering on squeaky as she left the question hanging while her eyes darted between them.

Gin lifted a polite hand in acknowledgment. "I'm Special Agent Reilly, and this is my partner, Special Agent Robard. We have an appointment with Dr. Latcher."

"Yes. And with her father as well," the woman responded. "I'm Ms. Polen, Mrs. Latcher's PA. Her Personal Assistant." When Gin raised an eyebrow, the woman blushed before stepping to the side. "And to the rest of the family as well, of course."

"And will Mrs. Latcher be joining us?" Gin asked as she strolled into a decent-sized foyer, featuring a high ceiling and several large vases of flowers hugging walls painted in a light chocolate brown.

"No. Mrs. Latcher had a previous appointment and is not in the residence at the moment." The PA closed the door behind them before turning to the left and starting down a hallway with multiple doors leading off of it.

She stopped in front of the third one and gave the door a soft rap with her knuckles before opening it and once more stepping to the side. The room looked like a cozy second living room, with walls featuring wood paneling halfway up to the ceiling before giving way to a lightly patterned wallpaper, gleaming with silver speckles at random intervals.

Justine Latcher stood in front of a fireplace with an aerial picture of the famous Pebble Beach Golf Course hanging over it. She was dressed in jeans, topped by a brown silk blouse that matched the color of her hair. She turned when Gin walked into the room and glanced toward a high-backed chair facing the large picture-frame window on the opposite side of the room.

A HARD TRUTH

"They're here, Dad." She raised a coffee cup to her lips as a tall, stern-looking man rose from the chair.

He moved to stand next to his daughter, his hands clasped behind his back as his sharp gaze raked over the two visitors. Gin smiled at his blatant intimidation tactic. Too bad it wasn't going to work.

"Agent Reilly and Agent Robard," Ms. Polen stated in her high-pitched voice.

Latcher nodded, his gray hair picking up the light streaming in from the window. Except for the color of his hair, and eyes that were such a dark brown they bordered on black, there was a strong resemblance between father and daughter. When those eyes locked on to Gin, she couldn't help but silently compare Latcher's dark, unblinking stare to a shark, tracking its next meal. That stare would probably unnerve most people, unless you'd lived with someone who had a much more lethal one.

"Agent Reilly. I'm Terence Latcher." His voice was deep and smooth, like a bottomless lake on a calm day. He added a slight incline of his head to his greeting before his gaze shifted to Trey. His eyes immediately narrowed on the former rescue pilot's face. "Agent Robard, is it?" When Trey nodded, Latcher looked like a man flipping through a mental Rolodex file. "Captain Treynor Robard? Of the Wranglers stationed out at Lemoore?"

Trey's shoulders went stiff and his expression blank. "Formerly attached to the Wranglers, Mr. Latcher. I'm no longer on active duty."

Their host's mouth curved into a broad smile, although the intensity of his gaze never wavered. "Well from all accounts, you had a brilliant career." He stepped forward and offered Trey his hand. "And now you're leading investigations for the FBI?"

Trey gave Latcher a brief handshake while tilting his head toward Gin. "I'm with the FBI, but Special Agent Reilly is the lead on this case."

Latcher gave him an amused look before switching his attention to sizing up Gin. "Is that right? Why don't we all have a seat?" He led the way to the small sitting area next to the picture window. He waited until Gin and Trey had settled into overstuffed chairs and Justine onto one end of a two-cushioned sofa before he took a seat next to his daughter. "Justine was a little shy on the details of why you requested this meeting, Agent Reilly."

"I'm sure you're aware that Benjamin Stampler disappeared over a month ago, and that his body was recently found," Gin said.

"It's been all over the news, so yes," Latcher replied with a faint edge of disinterest in his tone. "I'm aware."

"We're looking into the circumstances of his murder and asking questions of anyone who has had close contact with him over the last year." When Latcher's expression didn't change, Gin pursed her lips in exasperation. Either Latcher really was a completely self-centered prick the way Connor Elliot had described him, or he was the best poker player in the world.

"And you came here because. . .?" Latcher said after a prolonged silence.

"I understand he was a major donor to your clinic in Santa Cruz."

Latcher's amused smile was back. "You mean his company. Meridian Pharmaceuticals was a major donor to the clinic. And the clinic isn't mine. It's a corporation, with my daughter as the President and CEO. I have no position in it."

Now it was Gin's turn to smile. "It's your name over the door, Mr. Latcher."

"And my very substantial donation that put it there," he

tossed right back. With an air of absolute authority, he lifted a hand and brushed away an imaginary obstacle. "But for the sake of bringing this all to a conclusion, let's agree that Ben *was* a big donor. What does that have to do with his murder?"

Gin took a split second to consider it, but there was something about this guy, and this whole clinic thing that had her gut churning. She leaped in with both feet. "We have reason to believe it's tied in with your daughter's clinic."

Justine's gasp had her father immediately reaching over and placing a heavy hand on her knee. "In what way?" he snapped.

"I'm not at liberty to divulge details of the investigation at this time." Gin's voice was cool and flat. "But I would like to know when you last saw Benjamin Stampler?"

"Five months ago," Justine spoke up as her father pointed at the waiting PA, who promptly consulted her iPad. "He was at the spring charity event we held for the clinic," the doctor stated. "He flew in with Traci. She's his wife." Justine blinked rapidly for a moment. "But I'm sure you're already aware of that."

Gin only smiled, then looked over at the PA, who had obviously been sent a silent message to "look it up".

"That's correct," Ms. Polen said. "I've checked both of their personal and business calendars, and there were no scheduled individual meetings with Mr. Stampler or Meridian Pharmaceuticals. But Mr. Stampler was invited to the charity ball, and it's marked on the list from that evening that both he and his wife attended."

"Besides the charity ball, did you see them any other time during their trip to the West Coast?" Gin asked.

Latcher shook his head. "No. As I recall, they were going to visit the Tenderloin District in San Francisco, and then head straight back to Miami."

Trey did a double take. "The Tenderloin? Why would Benjamin Stampler visit the Tenderloin district?"

"Because there isn't much there besides homeless people? The frequent byproduct in cities with mild weather." Justine stated in a direct, coldly clinical assessment. Her full lips twisted into a bitter smile. "Ben went there to pay his respects. His younger brother suffered from a severe crack addiction, and he died on those streets, Agent Robard. Something that might not have happened if he could have received the proper medical help."

Wondering why that little gem wasn't anywhere in Benjamin Stampler's background information, Gin silently nodded. "Which is why he was such a generous donor to your clinic."

"That's right," Justine shot back. "No one at the clinic would have any motive to harm Ben. He's one of the reasons we're able to keep the doors open." She brushed her father's hand off her knee, stood up, then walked over to the fireplace and took up a position in front of the mantel, her thin arms crossed over her chest. "In honor of Ben's commitment, I can only hope that Meridian continues to support us in our mission to make healthcare available to everyone, and not just to the people who can afford it."

"Very moving, Justine, but I don't think the agents are here to be lectured on any noble causes." Latcher slowly moved his gaze to Gin. "Now that we've answered your question about our last interaction with Stampler, will that be all? Or perhaps I should contact our attorney?"

"Of course you're free to do so. But I can tell you that right at this moment, neither you nor your daughter is a suspect in Benjamin Stampler's murder." Her very slight emphasis on the words, "right at this moment" had a tic forming along Latcher's jawline.

"How closely were either of you involved in the day-to-day construction details when the clinic was being built?" Gin asked.

"I visited the site every single day," Justine piped up. "It was exciting to see the progress, and Connor always gave me a full tour whenever I requested one."

"And what about you, Mr. Latcher? How involved were you with the build?"

"Mainly writing checks, Agent Reilly. That was my primary involvement," the businessman stated. He sent his daughter an indulgent look. "I didn't spend the time that Justine invested in the project. But beyond ensuring there was a healthy cash flow to keep it afloat, there wasn't any need for my presence on site. I don't know a damn thing about the proper way to pour concrete, or how a building should be wired. That's why I hire professionals. In the case of the clinic, the Connor who my daughter just mentioned, is Connor Elliot. He served as general contractor on the project." Latcher propped an ankle on top of one knee and leaned back into the sofa, looking relaxed. Except for his eyes. His gaze still bored into Gin. "Feel free to discuss the project with him. I'm sure you have the resources to find his contact information."

Gin's smile was tight. "Yes. We do. Have you been involved in any other building projects that required the use of contractors, or with a charitable organization that you helped raise money for?"

Latcher shook his head and let out a low whistle. "Thinking anyone who donates to my causes might be a target is really grasping at straws, Agent Reilly. But to answer your question, no. My daughter's clinic is the only project I gave a substantial boost to for. . . " He paused to smile. "Shall we call it a good cause? And it's the only one that I have been personally involved with. Otherwise, I've simply written checks, or paid for overpriced dinners at an event. The clinic is also the only major building project that I've had a personal hand in for a number of years now. Of course I still hold a great deal of influence in the construction industry across the state, and am not shy in using it, but for the past decade, most of my newer endeavors have been in the field of high-tech."

"But you have used contractors quite a bit in the last few years, Dad," Justine said, contradicting him. When her father frowned at her, she shrugged. "Right here at home, mostly." The doctor put her back squarely to the fireplace and faced Gin. "My stepmother mounted a serious crusade to turn this house into the most prestigious home in Pebble Beach, but Dad wouldn't let her remodel the place."

"I like it the way it is, and she had other outlets for her creative side," Latcher said.

"Oh yes. Her little gallery in Monterey that she constantly insists is more worthy of your donations than the clinic to bring healthcare to hundreds, even thousands of disadvantaged people," Justine sneered. She tossed her head back and stuck her hands on the protruding bones of her hips. "It is unbelievable how much she harps on you about that."

Latcher got up and headed for a sideboard displaying an assortment of liquor bottles. "Which I very politely ignore." When he poured himself a generous drink, Gin knew that the discussion was an old and frequent one. Enough so that the man with the spine of steel needed a drink.

"Uh-huh," Justine plowed on, unmoved by either the tall glass of whiskey in her father's hand or the annoyed set of his mouth. "So then Evaline goes to Andy and tries to get him to use his influence to pry money out of you for a complete remodel and expansion of her gallery. And when that didn't work, she went after everything but the house," Justine said directly to Gin. "We had to have a tennis court because it's her favorite form of exercise. But she's barely stepped onto the thing since it was completed. And then there was the hothouse so we could grow fresh vegetables and she could boast of a farm-to-table experience for all her little dinner parties. And let's not forget the greenhouse so she could have whatever she wanted to decorate the gardens that became her personal kingdom, and of course there was the artist's studio all tucked away in a corner of the property just in case the about-to-be-famous painters she sponsors needed a peaceful spot to indulge in their art. Thank god we haven't been overrun by them, because I really thought that was going to happen." The doctor paused long enough to suck in a breath. "All of those projects required a contractor, Agent Reilly, and I'm sure Ms. Polen will be happy to get you a list of them." She sent the PA a telling look, triggering Polen to rapidly bob her head up and down as she furiously tapped on the screen of her iPad.

"Fine." His patience clearly worn thin, Latcher marched over to the fireplace and stood shoulder-to-shoulder with his daughter. "If you will supply your email to Ms. Polen, she will send you the list of subcontractors who did work on the grounds. Now, since this entire discussion hasn't been very productive, I suggest we call an end to it."

Gin had to admire the man's technique. As dismissals went, that one was brutally direct. She got to her feet while Trey did the same. "Thank you for your time, Mr. Latcher, Dr. Latcher. If we have any other questions, we'll be in touch."

"Of course," Latcher said, his dark eyes boring into hers. "But it will be through our attorney, Agent Reilly. Ms. Polen will send you his contact information. I suggest you make use of it first if you want to call either of us or visit this house again. And that statement includes the clinic. I trust I am making myself clear?"

"Very clear," Gin said. She held his stare for another few

seconds before turning to follow the waiting Ms. Polen. When they reached the front door, Gin dug into her pocket and brought out one of her cards, holding it out to the PA. "My email address for when you get that list together." When she caught the PA staring past her with a frown, Gin turned her head and followed the direction of the woman's gaze.

Another car had joined their rental in the driveway, and a man dressed in black sweatpants and a gray sweatshirt was polishing the hood with an oversized tan-colored cloth. "Who is that?" Gin asked automatically. When she glanced back at Ms. Polen, the PA was glaring at the man.

"That is Mr. Nagy. He's the household driver, and he shouldn't be here."

Gin's eyebrows drew together. "Why not? If he's the household driver, it seems reasonable he'd be here on the grounds."

"Of course," Ms. Polen said quickly. "But not lounging around in the driveway."

Since the man was diligently working on giving the car a glossy shine, it didn't look like he was taking some time off to Gin, but then maybe the PA simply didn't like cars cluttering up the driveway. People who lived in rich houses, even if it wasn't their own house, often had some odd ideas.

Gin started down the steps, then turned, catching Ms. Polen's eye before she could retreat into the house. "How long have you worked for the Latchers, Ms. Polen?"

"Almost ten years, Agent Reilly. Now, is there anything else?"

After Gin barely got a "no" out, the admin walked up the steps and closed the door with a sharp snap. Amused by her behavior, Gin trailed behind Trey as they walked toward the car. Nagy didn't look up, but Gin could sense that he was watching every step they took. Narrowing her eyes on him, she took out a pair of sunglasses and slipped them on.

A HARD TRUTH

Casually walking toward the car, she studied the man and then, out of habit, the vehicle as well. It was a late model Mercedes Benz, four-door sedan, with a maroon carriage and a gold top. The man who was making sure the hood still gleamed in the fading sunlight looked to be a few years older than her, with dark hair and a solid build.

Gin continued to slowly walk around the Mercedez, pretending to admire its sleek lines and gleaming finish. All the while Nagy kept his head down, ignoring her as he went right on silently moving the soft cloth over the car's smooth surface.

When she came up next to the chauffer she stopped, put her hands on her hips, and waited for several, drawn out moments. "That's a beautiful car. How often do you have to polish it?"

Nagy's hand stopped moving and he rested it on the hood as he straightened up. He took his time about it, but Gin waited until he turned and looked her right in the eye. "I polish it when it needs it."

Surprised that his English was clear, without the heavy, more guttural sound of the Eastern European languages, Gin added a smile to her nod. "And how often would that be?" Nagy's dark gaze was flat and lifeless. Deep in their depths she could see that telltale hint of violence. A violence she'd seen before. She didn't back away from it, but kept her hands on her hips and a smile on her face.

"Once a week," he finally said with a barely contained disdain. "More often if it needs it." He picked up the cloth again and pointedly turned his back on her.

Gin took the slow, easy walk back to where Trey was waiting beside the rental. She opened the car door then glanced back over her shoulder. As if sensing her look, Nagy straightened up and rolled his shoulders back before turning his head and looking straight at her, his dark eyes boring into hers.

More like an athlete than a chauffeur, Gin thought. An athlete with dead eyes that sent a slight shiver up her spine. She slid into the passenger seat and snapped on her seatbelt. "Interesting looking guy for a driver," Gin said once Trey had made the turn onto the road.

"Yeah. Really enjoyed him watching us like a hawk. What was that little show you put on for?" Trey asked.

"I wanted to hear him talk. To check if his accent was too heavy to be mistaken for one from Mexico, even if the voice was muffled."

Trey shot a glance toward Nagy. "*Was* it too heavy?"

Gin's smile didn't reach her eyes. "No. Not at all. Do you think he looks strong enough to carry a one-hundred-and-eighty-pound man from that access road near the utility tower in Buffalo over to the bushes where Stampler was found?"

Trey's head whipped back around until he was staring at her. "You're kidding? What motive would he have?"

Gin considered it. "I don't know. At least not yet. Let's get a run on him. The PA said his name was Nagy. Stephen should be able to run him down. And throw in Polen on that request too, while you're at it."

Trey nodded and took out his phone and began tapping on keys. "Good idea." Once he'd sent the text off, he set his phone into the center console. "All right. Where do you want to go next?"

"Why don't we pay his other employer a visit at her gallery in Monterey? I can pull up the address on my GPS." Without waiting for a response, Gin did just that, then set the phone in the console between the seats as Trey put the car into motion. While it called out directions, she leaned back and looked out the windshield, studying the scenery.

The entire area was a canvas of green plant life, blue ocean, and sandy beaches. And it was hard to beat the weather, as it

A HARD TRUTH

held steady at seventy-two degrees with no humidity. It might be worth the million dollar plus price tag to live here, but even so, she knew she would miss her mountains.

"Did you get anything out of that talk with Latcher and his daughter?" Trey asked, breaking into her peaceful thoughts, bringing her back to a world with murder in it.

Gin dutifully held up a hand and counted off fingers. "He definitely has a marriage of convenience, and the doctor isn't too fond of her stepmother. The clinic is the only charity he deals with. Anything else is just a matter of a tax deduction. Likewise, the only building project he's been involved with was also the clinic, but he was mostly the money guy. I doubt if he knew the contractors who worked on the job, even if they all did attend the same charity events. And he still calls that PA Ms. Polen, even though she said she's worked for him for ten years. And the doctor calls her Ms. Polen too."

"Maybe that's what the super rich do, Trey said. "Keep a formal distance from the help. And you forgot that Latcher is a prick," Trey said.

"Why? Because he remembered you from your service days?" She tapped a finger against her lower lip. "And by the way, what is a Wrangler?"

"It's the name of the search and rescue unit stationed at Lemoore Air Base."

When Trey said nothing else, Gin gave a mental shrug. It was his past, so there was no requirement that he had to talk about it. Which was a good thing. Because she'd already told him everything about hers that she was willing to share. "Besides him being a prick, did you get anything else out of that conversation?"

"Yeah. You didn't make any friends back there. The man doesn't like you."

"No, he does not," Gin agreed. "But his daughter is the talkative one. Next time, we'll just go straight to her."

"And beat against a wall of lawyers to do it."

Remembering that Connor Elliot had said much the same thing, Gin smiled. "Well, I've dealt with lawyers before." She leaned her head back and closed her eyes. "Oh. And there's something else we learned when the doctor was going through her tirade about her stepmom."

Trey gave her a quick glance. "What was that?"

"They have a greenhouse. I think what Justine Latcher said is that they can grow whatever they want to decorate the gardens. Which I assume means flowers, since the grounds were covered in them." She was interrupted by the shrill ring of her cell phone. Plucking it out of its slot in the console, she saw Senior Agent Moore's name on the caller ID. "Yeah, boss? We've just come off the interview with the Latchers. He built the clinic, and she runs it."

"Great. Put the details into your daily report and shoot it off to me. We've got another slight glitch. Sounds like you're in a car. Is Robard there with you?"

"Yes."

"Good. Put us on speakerphone so I don't have to go over this twice."

As Gin complied, she mouthed the word "glitch" to Trey. Once the speaker was engaged, she set her phone on the dashboard. "Okay. We're both listening."

"Your interview with the senior Latcher has caused a small tsunami, and he has the juice to turn it into a much bigger one," Moore stated.

"How much bigger?" Gin asked in a flat voice.

"As in big enough that I just got off the phone with Blake, who left strict orders that you aren't to talk to Latcher or his daughter again without their lawyer present. And that doesn't mean receiving the attorney's permission to speak to his clients, it means the guy has to have his boots in the room too."

Trey whistled while Gin rolled her eyes. "Latcher works fast. We just left there fifteen, maybe twenty minutes ago."

"Yeah," Moore's tone was as dry as dust. "Like I said, a lot of juice, and he isn't afraid to use it. Where are you two headed now?"

Trey kept his eyes on the road as he negotiated through the traffic that had grown at a steady pace ever since they'd left the Latcher estate. "We're just coming into Monterey, on our way to stop in at the art gallery that Mrs. Latcher owns and operates."

"Another Latcher?" Moore blew out a breath that came through the speaker sounding like a burst of wind. "Probably not a good idea."

"But not off limits," Gin cut in. "Latcher made that same attorney threat back at his house, and he specifically said it applied to his daughter and himself. And coming onto his property without permission. He didn't say anything about his wife, his employees, or any other piece of real estate. I'm thinking what he told us is the exact same thing he told whoever he had twist Blake's arm, as unbelievable as that is."

"Floored me too," Moore agreed. "Especially because Blake said the man called him directly. And given the speed with which he made that call, I'd say Latcher knew exactly who runs the Critical Crimes Unit. The last time I checked, that was not printed on our cards."

"Or tattooed on our foreheads," Gin said with more than a small touch of sarcasm. There was juice, and then there was the supercharged kind that Latcher clearly possessed. And Mr. Shark Eyes had made damn good and sure that she'd be gifted with a full demonstration of his influence.

"Hold off on that visit to Mrs. Latcher," Moore said. "Let

me check with Blake. He wasn't too thrilled with that call himself, so he might see his way clear to going with the technicality and explaining himself to Latcher *after* your visit with his wife."

"Will do." When Moore disconnected the call, Gin looked over at Trey. "Do your know your way back to the hotel from here?"

"Sure," he said. "I'm thinking we need to do a strategy session on next steps from here."

Gin turned off the GPS. "Yeah. That sounds good."

Chapter Nineteen

It was late afternoon when they reached their hotel in Santa Clara. By silent consent, they headed straight for the spacious lobby bar, snagging a high table with a couple of stools tucked into a corner. Trey flagged down the waitress and once she'd left with their order for one beer and one glass of wine, Gin tapped a steady finger against the wooden tabletop as she silently sorted through their options.

When the drinks arrived, Trey lifted his frosted beer mug in a small salute. "I think we're onto something with the Latchers."

Lifting her own glass to her lips, Gin peered at him over the rim. "Why do you think so?"

He slowly lowered his mug as he stared back at her. "You don't think so?"

She took a sip of the wine, enjoying the crisp taste of it before setting her glass on the table. "As a matter of fact I do, but I'd like to hear why you think that."

"Latcher senior clearly didn't like your line of questioning, and he's hiding something," Trey stated.

"Agreed." Gin's fingers played around the stem of her glass. "But I would guess that any man as powerful as Latcher would have a lot he'd rather not be questioned about." When Trey frowned, she shrugged. "Like a wife who clearly married him for his money. Usually in those kinds of arrangements, they'd prefer that little fact not to be so obvious."

"Money is a good reason to take a closer look at him," Trey maintained. "He could have hired anyone he wanted to get rid of Stampler."

"But why would he?" Gin's simple question had Trey scowling into his beer mug. "And what reason would he have to kill a couple of contractors?"

Trey's mouth flattened into a thin line. "A diversion, maybe? To throw us off the actual target, which was Stampler."

Possible, Gin thought. But the dots weren't connecting for her. "Again, why? The chances of it being a business rivalry aren't great, simply because they aren't in the same business." She stared out the window closest to their table, not really seeing the view. "Maybe Latcher holds a large block of Meridian stock and it took a dive. If he lost a lot of money that way, he might have held Stampler responsible."

Her partner nodded. "Yeah. Maybe. I can look into that the profit and loss thing isn't my strong point."

"Stephen can do it," Gin said. "I'd go for a love triangle but frankly, I don't think Latcher would care if his wife had an affair as long as she didn't flaunt it. I doubt it would surprise anyone if he was having an affair, but I can't see Traci Stampler looking for a fling outside her marriage. And why else would Latcher kill her husband if it wasn't because of her?"

Trey didn't look up as he kept tapping on his phone. "Since she lives in Miami, I'll call Finn or Byers and see what they can run down."

"And then there's his daughter. By her own admission, she

was at the construction site every day. Which would have given her a chance to meet anyone on a work crew. And so was Connor Elliot." Gin returned her gaze to the window as she did her thinking out loud. "Of all the players, he's the one with the highest probability of knowing all three victims. He told us himself that he attended the same charity events as Stampler, and since he was the self-appointed babysitter for Justine, then he would have been out on the job site every day. There's also a good chance he ran into Miguel Rivera and Bruce Dredecker. Maybe he struck up a conversation."

"Then decided to kill them?" Trey shook his head. "It's like we're behind a pane of glass, looking in and not able to see all the pieces."

"Or how they fit together," Gin agreed, her mouth turning down at the corners. "And if we are staring at our prime suspect, I still don't know how he or she knew when two federal agents were going to show up on that boat on the other side of the country. Is his helper someone inside the Bureau? Or the execs at Meridian? Or maybe even Mrs. Stampler. I don't know."

"How about simple logic?" Trey suggested. "The press put it out there that Stampler's body had been found, and he disappeared from Miami, so agents were bound to show up there." His shoulders slumped. "But then we're back to him hanging out, waiting for the day we'd show up. And that doesn't seem likely."

"Unless he's from Miami," Gin said. "And had a place with a view of the marina. But if that's true, what are we doing out here?"

Trey gave her a half smile. "Looking for his employer, and that could be Latcher."

"And we're back to where we started." Exasperated, Gin drained her wine before sliding off the high stool. She was tired. And her bruises still hadn't healed, although Trey was worse off than she was. "I think we need to do some legwork to cover a few bases. If you'll make that call to Finn or Byers about Traci Stampler's private life, and then track down someone at Quantico to get a deeper dive into the background and whatever else they can come up with on all three of the Latchers, plus Linda Polen and especially Nagy. We might kick something loose." She thought it over for a moment. "And why don't you include anyone who works full or part-time in the Latcher household with that request?"

"Good idea," Trey said. "That chauffeur gave off an odd vibe."

"Yeah. He seemed out of place," Gin said with a nod. "I'll make some phone calls to the Raflins and Aldo Twiner and check if their respective employees had any beefs with other subcontractors on that clinic job." She let out a resigned sigh. "And then I'll write up the daily report and get it off to Moore so he won't have anything to complain about."

Trey sent her a sympathetic look. "Paperwork's a bitch, isn't it? Hopefully Moore can get us the go-ahead to visit Mrs. Latcher at her gallery tomorrow."

"Hopefully." Gin reached down and grabbed the backpack she'd dropped on the floor next to her chair, slipping an arm through one strap and balancing the pack on her shoulder. "I'll send you a text in the morning when I'm heading to the lobby. And I think we should move to a hotel closer to the coast, since that seems to be where all our potential suspects are." She studied the bruises on Trey's face that had turned all green and yellow. "Oh, and order room service for dinner tonight. I don't think either of us is in the mood to drag our butts out again."

"Sounds good. And I'll find us a place close to Monterey that won't make the accounting department's eyes water," Trey said as he lifted his own backpack and fell into step beside her.

A HARD TRUTH

They parted ways at the elevator, with Gin exiting on the third floor of the hotel and Trey continuing to his room two floors up. When she got to her room, Gin leaned the backpack against a wall and set her cell phone on the nightstand before grabbing one of the complimentary bottles of water from the counter built along the entire length of one wall. She carried it to the bed and sat on the edge, opening the bottle and taking a long drink. Toeing off her sturdy walking boots, she stretched out on top of the covers, with the pillows propped up behind her back. She took another swig of water, then consulted her watch before reaching for her phone.

Scrolling through her notes, she stopped at the entry with Raflin Construction's phone number. It only rang twice before a cool, professional sounding female voice came on, advising the caller that the offices were closed, then reciting the business hours before rattling off a separate number to leave a message. Gin made a note of the number, then dialed it, waiting through several long moments before the call was picked up by the company's answering service.

After identifying herself and leaving a message requesting one of the Raflin brothers return her call, she hung up and tried Big Al Twiner. Since he'd given her his private cell number, she was hopeful they'd be able to connect. Thankfully, she wasn't disappointed.

On the second ring, a loud voice boomed through her cell phone's speaker. "This is Al. Is that you, Agent Reilly?"

"Yep, it is," Gin confirmed. "I've got some follow-up questions to ask you."

"Okay. Shoot."

Despite her aching muscles, Gin still grinned. It was a funny thing to say to someone who was most likely armed. "According to the records you sent us, Mr. Dredecker worked on a job in Santa Cruz, California."

"Yeah, yeah," Big Al said. "Hard to forget that one since our arm was twisted to donate all the labor. It was one of those public health clinics for poor people."

"Who did the arm twisting?" Gin asked.

"Latcher did. But I had the actual discussion with Connor Elliot, who was working as the general contractor on that job. However, the direction came right from Latcher. Elliot told me straight up that he wasn't getting paid for his time either. Didn't sound too happy about it, but Latcher throws a lot of business his way." There was a brief pause, followed by a low grunt. "I've gotten a fair share of referrals to jobs through Latcher too. Mostly in Silicon Valley, so I shouldn't have any complaints. But I met the guy at a couple of the fundraisers we all were expected to attend, and he's an asshole, plain and simple."

Gin gave a silent "amen" to that. "Either during the job, or maybe after it was complete, did Mr. Dredecker ever mention having a fight or disagreement with any of the other contractors?"

"What kind of disagreement?"

"I'm not sure," Gin said. "But anything at all?"

She could hear a quick scratching noise through the phone. "It was close to two years ago, Agent Reilly. I don't recall which complaint went with which job. But I tell you what. Tomorrow I'll have a talk with the guys who worked the job with him. They might remember something since they were all there together. Will that work for you?"

"It'll work fine, Big Al. Thanks. Give me a call if you hear anything."

"Sure will," he said. "Now, you tell me something. What does that clinic job have to do with Decker's murder? And don't tell me you can't comment on an ongoing investigation. I have a stake in this, and I know how to keep my mouth shut."

"I don't know if it does or doesn't," Gin answered honestly.

"But on your word that you'll keep your mouth shut, I will tell you that Mr. Dredecker wasn't the only construction worker murdered. We've identified another one."

There was a sharp intake of breath. "Sonofabitch," Big Al said softly. "And did the other guy also work on that clinic?" He didn't wait for her to say anything before answering his own question. "Of course he did. Why else would you be asking it? I'll make you a promise right now, Agent Reilly. If that asshole Latcher had anything to do with Decker's murder, I'm going to be on his doorstep quick as lightning during a big ass storm and beat him to a bloody pulp. After that, you can lock him up and throw away the key."

"Right now, Big Al, I haven't got anything on Latcher, so you be sure to keep your lightning and that big ass storm in Nevada," Gin warned. "My partner and I are simply trying to eliminate the possibilities."

"Well then, you keep me informed about those possibilities, and I'll let you know if the guys who worked with Decker on that job have anything to say."

"Thanks. I appreciate it," Gin said before hanging up. She hadn't even set her cell phone back on the nightstand when it rang again. She pressed the connect button and lifted it to her ear. "This is Special Agent Reilly."

"Agent Reilly?" A tinny-sounding voice on the other end asked as if he hadn't heard her. "This is Ray Raflin. I got a message from our answering service that you had called."

"Yes, sir. I did." She posed the same question to Raflin as she had to Big Al, and got the same response. Off the top of his head, he had no idea if Miguel Rivera had gotten into an argument with another subcontractor, but he'd ask around and get back to her.

With her calls completed, Gin gave into the rumbling of her stomach and pressed the button on the bedside phone for room service and ordered a salad, figuring she could use a few vegetables to counterbalance all the burgers she'd been eating lately. It arrived fifteen minutes later, just as she was starting her never-ending paperwork.

The sun had gone down by the time she finished her report, checked her emails, and eaten the last bite of her salad. She was debating between going to bed or watching some television, and even picked up the remote and turned the set on. But that was as far as she got.

She had another problem, and she couldn't just leave it hanging over her head.

For the last several nights, before sleep had claimed her, she'd given it some thought, and had come to the conclusion that she didn't have any idea what to do about those journals and the list she had found. Whether she wanted to or not, she was going to have to ask for help. Which left her with two choices: the Iowa captain who had made the arrest while she stood watching from inside the barn, or Ricki James, her friend who was an investigative agent with the National Park Service.

Since Frank Wilkins had retired from the Story County Sheriff's Department eight years earlier, he wasn't tightly dialed into the law enforcement community anymore. Which made Ricki the logical choice. She was not only a trained investigator, but her new husband was a former homicide detective turned police chief. Maybe with their combined experience and contacts, they could find a way to "discover" the list of names written out by the Black Cross Killer, and somehow reveal its existence without naming the source of the information. Gin did not want those journals found until she knew everything that was in them, and what it meant.

She reached for her phone but kept her hand hovering in the air. Ricki had become a good friend since they'd worked on a drug running case together in the North Cascades National

A HARD TRUTH

Park. With that first encounter a bond had been born, and with it had grown a deep well of trust.

Ricki was one of the few people who knew that Gin had been in the barn, watching, when her father was arrested and not away visiting relatives, which was the story that had been given out to the media. The one cop, Frank Wilkins, who had seen her there that night, had made sure that the story of her whereabouts that night had been answered and put to rest. Her mother had been so traumatized that she couldn't remember where Gin was, which had gone a long way to solidifying her story. Only Wilkins and the judge knew about Gin's role in the arrest.

But while she'd told Ricki a lot about that night, including the fact that despite what the papers had said, she had been there when her father was arrested, she still hadn't told her friend everything. Including any mention about her turning her father in to the police. Which is why she still hadn't picked up her cell phone.

She sat with her head bowed and her forehead wrinkled in thought as she tried to silently navigate her way through a minefield. When she finally made her call, she held her phone so tightly that her fingers began to ache as she held her breath and to the hollow ring on the other end.

An annoyed voice growled through the speaker. "Hello? And I hope this is good."

Gin cast a quick glance at her watch and made a face. She'd completely forgotten about the time difference. "Hey, Cap. I'm sorry I woke you up."

"Gin? Is that you?"

"Yeah, yeah," she smiled into the phone, easily imagining the grumpy look on Cap's face. "It's me. How are you?"

"Fine and dandy," the retired captain said. "But I can tell from your voice that you have a problem. What is it?"

Not believing that he could read her so easily, Gin sniffed. "How can you possibly know that? I've said all of one sentence, Captain Wilkins."

"Fine," Wilkins said. "Let me rephrase that. Do you have a problem?"

Annoyed that she actually did, Gin almost denied it just to prove him wrong, but then stopped herself. She needed help with that damn list, and Wilkins, who she'd always called Cap, was her best bet, even if she was as transparent as glass to him. "Both my grandparents died in a car accident," she started out.

"Uh-huh. You told me that a while back, Gin. May they both rest in hell."

She smiled, her heartbeat slowing to a more normal rate as she latched onto a bit of courage. She hated, absolutely hated, talking about that time in her life. But it had a way of popping up at random intervals and slapping her in the face. "I recently got to their home in upstate New York and went through some boxes stored in the basement."

"Go on," Wilkins said, his voice soft and even.

"The boxes belonged to my mother." She could hear the tension in her voice, but didn't possess the skill to control it. "I found some journals in them. Three, to be exact."

When she went silent, Wilkins cleared his throat. "Are they your mother's diaries?"

"No. They belonged to him. And some others."

"Others?" Wilkins' voice went razor sharp. "What others?"

"I don't know," Gin confessed. "I haven't had a chance to read all the entries yet. But I came across a list that he wrote." She paused, trying not to choke on the words. She finally got it all out in one breathless rush. "A list of names. Kayla Downey was on there, with a date. May 2007."

"We figured that was when she was killed. Did you recognize anyone else's name on this list?"

A HARD TRUTH

Gin had to close her eyes in order to get it out. "Yeah. The sixteen that he made a plea bargain for, and one other one. Mine. It was the last one on the list with a date five months after you arrested him."

"Five months aft. . ." Wilkins broke off, then let out a string of vicious swear words. When he wound down, his breathing was harsh. "The bastard. I ought to make a trip out to that Supermax prison and shoot him myself."

"I wouldn't stop you," Gin said, tears stinging her eyes. It was good that there was at least one person on this earth who knew the entire story and still cared about her. Of course there was Dev, but even he hadn't known the sheer terror she'd gone through not only the night the cops had come, but a lot of nights before that.

Her mother had been there too and hadn't cared. Neither had her grandparents. But Cap had. He knew the whole ugly story. Even about her grandmother's hate-filled letter. And he still cared.

The thought had her straightening her shoulders and stiffening her spine. He told her all the time that he was proud of her, and she was not going to let him down. Or herself. She'd been through a lot already and had figured it out. With Cap's help, she'd figure this out too. "I need to get the list to the proper authorities without them knowing where it came from."

"Because of those journals and what's in them," Wilkins stated slowly, drawing the words out.

"Because of those journals and the fact that I don't know exactly what's in them," Gin corrected. "That's a deal breaker, Cap." She paused for a long moment to let that sink in. "So how do I do this?"

"Hang on a moment," he said. She heard the sound of footsteps, and then liquid being poured into a glass. "Okay, Gin.

I've got a whiskey and I'm sitting down. How many names are on that list?"

"About fifty, maybe a few more," Gin said, jerking the phone away from her ear at the sudden explosion of noise.

"That bastard. That fucking bastard. His plea bargain said twenty, but he only gave us sixteen. He gave us sixteen names. He swore that was all he could remember and that there weren't any more. And most of those had already been found. Now you're telling me there's more than fifty?"

"What do I do with this list, Cap?"

"The first thing you do is verify every name on it. Make sure they're real people who have been found murdered or have gone missing and never been found at all. Let's make sure half those names weren't a figment of his sick imagination. Better yet, take a picture of that list, send it to me, and I'll verify them."

"No," she said immediately. "I don't want a copy of this list on your phone or anywhere that it might end up in the cloud, floating around for some ambitious hacker to find. I'll do it."

"Good. Once that's done, then we'll figure the rest out."

Beyond tired, Gin nodded. "I'll get started once I wrap up the case I'm working on."

"Have they got you on that Stampler deal?" Wilkins asked.

"Yeah. And right now I'm in California trying to sort out the list of players with my temporary new partner, Treynor Robard."

A surprised chortle burst out of the speaker. "Robard? As in Captain Treynor Robard? The Naval helicopter pilot who was in the news a few years back? Hey, wait a minute. Do not tell me you and this Robard character were the two agents that almost got themselves blown up on Stampler's yacht in Miami? It was all over the news."

"Yes, that's him, and I plead the fifth on that whole boat-

A HARD TRUTH

blowing-up thing," Gin said. "Right now I need to get some sleep. We've got a load of work ahead of us tomorrow." *Unless we can't talk to Latcher's wife or kick up another lead,* she thought, but kept it to herself.

"Okay. But case or no case, I want an update from you in the next ten days about that list," Wilkins demanded.

"Yeah. I hear you loud and clear. Goodnight, Cap."

Chapter Twenty

The next morning Gin was surprised at how well she had slept. Deciding that doing something to fix a problem, even one as horrific as that list, was better than sitting on your hands and doing nothing. With a last yawn, she finished packing her small suitcase and strapped on her gun harness. After slipping the Glock 19 into place, she adjusted the harness so the bulge barely showed under her lightweight jacket. She checked her email one last time, happy to see the three word missive from her senior agent. All Moore had written was "go for it."

Relieved that they had an agenda to follow, even if the only thing on it at the moment was to corner Evaline Latcher in her own gallery, Gin ran through the rest of her emails. She responded to a few and left the rest to be answered later. Remembering to first send a text to Trey to let him know she was on her way down to the lobby, she grabbed her backpack and headed out the door.

Trey was already waiting for her by the time she walked past the registration desk. He tilted his head in the direction of

A HARD TRUTH

the restaurant. "How about breakfast while I fill you in on what I found out last night?"

"Sure." Gin followed him into the dining area, with long tables holding a breakfast buffet that took up one whole wall. She set her backpack down next to the table Trey had chosen. He was already loading his plate up with food while she looked over the morning's choices and settled for some yogurt and fruit.

When she returned to the table, she eyed the mountain of food on her partner's plate and shook her head. "I thought no one could eat more than Stephen, but I'm going to have to rethink that." She pointed a fork at Trey's loaded plate. "I was hoping we'd be able to get a start sometime before noon."

Trey looked at his plate and then back up at her. "This won't take long. When you grow up with three brothers you learn to eat fast, or you'll go to bed hungry."

Gin skewered a fat strawberry with her fork, then dipped it in the yogurt before popping it into her mouth. "Just brothers, no sisters?"

"One sister," Trey said with a grin. "She was the oldest and kept us boys in line better than any Chief Petty Officer I ever encountered."

"I'll bet," she laughed. "Do you get to see her very often?"

"Not as often as she would like, since she's currently in Denver helping me set up my new apartment." He plucked up a slice of toast and waved it in front of him. "At least that was the plan, except I'm not there. She's giving me hell about it, too."

"Ah." Gin's quick laughter faded into a smug grin. "Was that who you were getting a lecture from over the phone in Miami?"

Trey blinked in surprise. "Probably. How did you know that?"

"Finn overheard you. Even talked to your sister for a couple of moments."

Now Trey nodded. "Yeah. I heard. Barb said he was rude."

Gin lifted an eyebrow. "Oh? And what did you say to that?"

"Nothing," he said with a grin. "Finn *can* be rude." He pointed at the small bowl in front of her. "Are you going to eat the rest of that fruit?"

She rolled her eyes but pushed the bowl toward him. "Help yourself. How much longer is this food demolition project going to take? Maybe you can talk around your eating and bring me up to speed on what you've found. Or should I go first?"

"Go right ahead." Trey dug into the bowl of fruit as he eyed her expectantly.

"I put in a call to both Raflin and Twining, asking them if our two construction workers had gotten into an argument or disagreement with any of the other subcontractors. They couldn't recall anything, but they're both going to check with the rest of the crew who worked on the clinic job and ask if they remember anything. I wrote up the report and sent it in, so we're all caught up on our paperwork. And last but most importantly, I got an email from Moore that said we can interview Evaline Latcher. Now all we have to do is catch her when she's out of the house. But since she doesn't seem to spend a lot of time there, that shouldn't be too hard to do."

"Great." Trey swiped a napkin across his mouth, then picked up his coffee cup. "We can go over to her gallery right after we make a stop at Wei Chang's house. It's on the way into Monterey. And I booked us into a hotel there, so we need to grab our suitcases and take them with us."

"I'm all packed." Gin eyed his nearly empty plate. "Are you ready to go?"

"Yep."

"One question," she said as they walked out of the restaurant and toward the elevators. "Who is Wei Chang?"

"The Latcher's gardener." Trey pressed the up button, then glanced her way. "I called Connor Elliot last night and asked him who all worked at the Latcher residence, and he was a veritable fountain of information."

When the elevator stopped on her floor, Gin latched onto Trey's arm and pulled him out with her. "Okay. Let's hear this bounty of information. What did the talkative Connor have to say?"

Trey moved off toward the window taking up the outside wall near the elevators, with Gin following right behind him. "He had a lot to say about Linda Polen because he spent the most time with her. Apparently she guards the family's time like a dog with a bone, but especially when it comes to Evaline Latcher. According to Connor, Polen worked for Mrs. Latcher but that was only for the last four years. The rest of those ten years of employment the assistant mentioned yesterday, she worked for just Evaline, before she became Mrs. Latcher. The same is true for the family chauffeur, who spends most of his time driving Latcher's wife around, rather than the man himself. And Connor said he made a habit of avoiding the chauffeur. Apparently Nagy, who doesn't appear to have first name he's willing to share with anyone, made Connor nervous. But it was the gardener who caught my attention. Wei Chang has been the full-time gardener there for as long as Elliot could remember. Connor claimed the man was a genius with flowers, which is why Evaline decided to keep him on. He also has a daughter who owns a shop in town that sells jewelry."

"Jewelry?" Gin repeated with a slight frown. "As in smaller, maybe pendant sized versions of flowers preserved in resin?"

"The thought crossed my mind," Trey said. "I still need to

track her down. Connor wasn't sure where her shop was, or its name."

"But he did say that this Mr. Chang lives somewhere near Monterey?"

"Just north of it, in Seaside," Trey confirmed. "The real estate is just slightly less expensive there."

It only took Gin a minute to grab her suitcase and return to the lobby, beating Trey there by thirty seconds since he had to make the trip up to his floor. Even so, first was first, so she flashed a smug smile at him before heading out to the parking lot.

The ride to the turnoff for the coast went smoothly, and the traffic wasn't too bad on the sometimes narrow, two-lane highway that wound through the hills separating the ocean from the inland corridor.

It wasn't long before Trey made the left-hand turn onto the highway running south toward Seaside. While he expertly navigated their Ford SUV through the streets of the small, bedroom community, Gin mentally shook her head at the two- and three-bedroom homes with price tags starting at half a million dollars and rapidly increasing from there.

The weather was wonderful, the scenery spectacular, and all the outdoor activities were great, but that was a lot of money for a small to mid-size tract house. And definitely out of her price range. Which didn't make a difference one way or the other, since she wasn't looking to settle down.

The thought had her frowning and wondering if she would ever be ready to settle in one place. Right now, Denver was good. Actually, it was a lot better than good. But she didn't think of it as "home". That image still belonged to a small farm in Iowa, with a brick house, no garage, a run-down barn, and every inch isolated on a never-ending sea of fear.

When the car stopped, she shook off the thought and

focused on the house set back from the curb. It looked like most of the surrounding houses, with wooden sides painted a stark white, with a front door painted a deep blue. There were two steps leading up to the door, and Gin stood on the bottom one as Trey knocked and waited through the sound of several chains rattling on the other side.

A small Asian woman with dark eyes and a thick waterfall of even darker colored hair stood in the doorway with her hands on her hips. "We aren't buying anything today." Her eyes dropped to the badge clipped to Trey's belt. "But I'm guessing you aren't selling anything." She peeked around Trey toward the waiting Gin, who moved her jacket aside so her badge was also showing. "Are those real? They don't look like the ones the police around here wear."

"No, ma'am. We're with the FBI," Trey said, then stopped at the woman's loud gasp.

"What, what? Has something happened to Papa? Have those bastards arrested him? I told him not to go, that it was too dangerous. But did he listen? Oh no. Not Papa." She suddenly stopped talking and her expression turned sour. "Wait a minute." She looked at her watch, then glared at Trey. "He hasn't even arrived in Beijing yet. So what are you doing here?"

"Your father is Wei Chang?" When the woman nodded, Trey's eyes narrowed. "And you said he's on his way to Beijing?"

The woman took a wider stance and crossed her slender arms over her chest. "That's right. Now, who are you and what do you want?"

Trey took out his credential case, flipped it open, and held it up so it was clearly visible. "I'm Special Agent Robard with the FBI." His body turned slightly as he gestured toward Gin. "And this is my partner, Special Agent Reilly. We were hoping to have a word with Mr. Chang."

"Well, he isn't here."

Chang's daughter took a step back and was about to close the door when Gin moved up beside Trey. "We're sorry to disturb you, and your father isn't in any kind of trouble. We just wanted some background information on his job."

The woman froze, a confused look on her face. "His job? He's a gardener. Why would the FBI be interested in a gardener?"

"Yes," Gin said, adding a smile in the hopes they wouldn't get the door slammed in their faces. "For the Latchers?"

"That's right, and I still don't know what. . ." The woman trailed off as her eyes widened. "You're interested in the Latchers?"

"Background check for a high-tech security project," Gin improvised. "We interview all the direct employees of the household."

A look of relief flooded the daughter's face. "Oh. Of course. But my father isn't here. He had a chance to visit China and he jumped at it. Papa was born there and still has several brothers and sisters who live in Jinan, in the Shandong province." She smiled as she rubbed a finger across the tip of her nose. "I have no idea where that is except by looking at a map." She held out a hand. "I'm Suzanne, by the way. Suzanne Chang. I live here, and so does my older sister, but she's at her shop in Salinas."

Gin shook her hand, then waited for Trey to do the same as her mind zeroed in on Suzanne's statement that her papa had not yet landed in Beijing. "When did your father leave for his trip?"

Looking much more relaxed, Suzanne leaned against the door jamb. "This morning. He got a call last night from Ms. Polen. She's Mrs. Latcher's personal assistant." A smile bloomed across the young woman's face. "You should talk to her. She probably knows a lot about the family."

A HARD TRUTH

"Yes, she's on our list to be interviewed," Gin supplied. "So the Latchers are paying for your father's trip?"

"Absolutely. He could never afford it on his own, and I just graduated from nursing school, so I couldn't help much either. But this was all expenses paid for a month."

"Wow." Gin smiled. "That's very generous. Did Ms. Polen give any reason the Latchers were gifting this trip to your father?"

Suzanne blinked as her smile dimmed at the corners. "For working on their grounds for the last twenty years and never missing a day on the job." She straightened away from the door jamb. "At least that's what we both assumed."

"I'm sure that's right," Gin quickly put in. "I was just curious. And he heard about this trip last night for a departure this morning?"

Wei Chang's daughter still looked concerned, but she dutifully nodded. "That's right. We were up most of the night getting him packed and ready for the trip. The Latcher's chauffeur picked him up early this morning."

"And he's staying a month?"

"Ms. Polen said it was a long way to travel, and he should make sure he spent enough time there to make it worth his while." Suzanne frowned. "Or something like that. Papa asked who would do his work while he was gone, and Ms. Polen said that was all taken care of, and his job would be waiting for him when he got back, along with a raise in his wages." She rubbed her hands together. "I can't tell you anything else." Her gaze darted between the two agents as she took a step back. "I have a job interview to get ready for, so if you'll excuse me?"

"Of course," Trey said, retreating down one step.

The non-threatening move had Suzanne's shoulders relaxing as she smiled at him. "It was nice to meet you. Good luck with your background check." Still smiling, she shut the door.

A bemused Gin turned and gave the stationary Trey a light push. "Let's go."

"Pretty girl," Trey said absently as he turned and shadowed Gin back to the car.

"Full-grown woman, not a girl, and you can get her number later." Gin slid into the passenger seat, frowning out the front window as Trey got them on their way again. "Now isn't that strange? This unplanned trip to get Wei Chang out of the country as quickly as possible."

"Arranged and paid for by the Latchers," Trey added. "Which they must have done the minute we left their house last night."

"Yeah." Gin tapped a finger against her lower lip. "Why don't we go ask Mrs. Latcher about that since it was her assistant who made the arrangements, and her chauffeur who took Mr. Chang to the airport? Let's hope she's hanging out in her gallery this morning."

Trey's grip on the SUV's wheel tightened. "We should know that pretty soon. The gallery is only five miles south of here."

Twenty minutes later, Trey was easing the rental into an empty parking spot about a block away from the gallery. The sidewalks were busy with shoppers already carrying brightly colored bags, while others strolled along at a leisurely pace, simply enjoying the sunshine and atmosphere of the quaint downtown area. Gin secured every button on her jacket to keep it closed and her gun and badge hidden as she and Trey walked toward the gallery, matching the slow pace of the crowd around them. As they passed a side street, Gin abruptly stopped and backed up, staring down the narrow strip of pavement before joining Trey on the sidewalk.

"What is it?" he asked.

"There's a car parked down there," Gin said in a low voice. "Looks like a Mercedes with a maroon bottom and gold top."

"Any signs of the driver?"

Gin shook her head. "Nope. At least not that I spotted. But those windows are pretty heavily tinted, so he might have been sitting in the car."

"I guess we won't know until we get to the gallery. It's just a half block down," Trey said.

Evaline Latcher's gallery was located in the prime real estate that Gin had been told about. Sandwiched between a candle shop and a store featuring local crafts, The Rodinique had a small striped awning extending several feet out over its door, and a large front window with its frame painted in a mint green.

A small bell tinkled softly when Gin opened the door. She'd barely taken two steps inside when a striking middle-aged woman with long black hair and wispy bangs covering her forehead rose from her chair behind a delicately ornate desk situated close to the back wall.

She wore dark red lipstick and a bright smile as she glided across the highly polished wood floor. "Hello. I'm Andrea, and welcome to The Rodinique. Is there anything special you're looking for today?"

"Yes. We'd like to have a word with Mrs. Latcher." Gin said as her gaze lasered in on the necklace around the smiling Andrea's neck. "That's a lovely necklace. What kind of flower is that?"

Andrea automatically lifted a hand and fingered the large pendant dangling from a gold chain she wore around her neck. The centerpiece was made from a clear piece of resin formed into a circle, with a small red flower encased inside it. "The proper name is an anemone, but they're usually referred to as windflowers. Such an ethereal name, don't you think?" She dropped her hand, but her smile remained. "It was a gift from Anne. That would be Anne, Mr. Latcher's first wife."

"You must have known her very well," Gin said.

"Oh, yes." Andrea's smile dimmed and her voice dropped to just above a whisper. "I was her Personnel Assistant. When she passed away, I stayed on with the family, and then when Mr. Latcher remarried, I was offered the position her at The Rodinique."

"Ah," Gin smiled. "Did the first Mrs. Latcher make jewelry?"

Andrea's smile faltered even more and now her friendly expression faded just a bit. "Of course not. Wei Chang's daughter did. He was her gardener for many years, so of course Anne would regularly visit her shop in Salinas as a show of support for her staff. Wei Chang was a favorite of hers. Mr Latcher's current wife is fond of him as well. The man is a genius with flowers."

"Speaking of the current Mrs. Latcher," Gin said then looked around the small gallery floor. "Is she here?"

"As a matter of fact she is, but I'm afraid she isn't available at the moment. I'd be happy to assist you with any of your selections." Andrea swept a hand around to draw attention to the modern pieces of art hanging on every wall. "I'm sure we have several pieces that will interest you."

Gin doubted if her meager bank account would stretch anywhere close enough to being interested in anything in the gallery, so she unbuttoned her jacket and pushed the sides away. "Just Mrs. Latcher, thank you."

The gallery attendant's smile faltered at the sight of the gold badge attached to Gin's belt. "May I tell her what this is about?"

Gin's stoic expression didn't change as she stared back at the woman. "Right now would be convenient."

Andrea's smile disappeared and her mouth dropped to her chest, but she was distracted by the sound of the door tucked behind the desk opening. She let out a sigh of pure relief. "Ah. Ms. Polen. We have some visitors who have requested to see Mrs. Latcher."

The PA scurried across the room, coming to an abrupt halt in front of Gin. "Yes. Of course. Thank you, Andrea." She curled her hand around the attendant's upper arm and urged her toward the front door. "I'm sorry to be tardy at relieving you for your break, but feel free to take it now."

The gentle push earned the PA an annoyed look from Andrea, but she took the not-so-subtle hint and walked over to the desk, retrieved a large handbag, and went out the front door. As soon as it closed behind her, the PA turned to face Gin. "I'd be happy to inform Mrs. Latcher that you're here, but unfortunately I have been instructed that no one in the family was to take part in any more of your interviews unless Mr. Forest was present." She gave Gin an apologetic look. "He's the family's attorney."

"Those instructions only included Mr. Latcher and his daughter, Justine, which I assume you are aware of since you were standing right there when they were given," Gin stated. She kept an unblinking stare on the flustered PA. "I also wanted to talk to you about Mr. Chang?" When the PA looked like a deer caught in bright headlights, Gin smiled. "I understand he was sent on an unexpected trip to Beijing this morning. Who made the decision to gift Mr. Chang with such an expensive trip?"

"Um." Polen's eyes bounced around the gallery, as if she was looking for an escape. "Mr. Latcher. Yes. He told me to arrange it all, but it took some time, so I was only able to let Wei know about it last night."

Boy are you a bad liar, Gin thought, even as she gravely nodded her agreement. "Okay. We'll contact Mr. Forest and talk to him. In the meantime, we have clearance from our office to speak with Mrs. Latcher. Either here, or in less accommodating surroundings."

Clutching her iPad tightly to her chest, Polen took two steps backwards, putting more space between herself and Gin. "I'll let Mrs. Latcher know." Without another word, the PA turned on her heel and fled.

Gin didn't move from her spot, while Trey slowly wandered around the room, carefully studying the paintings. She retrieved her phone when it pinged, signaling a new message. Frowning, she sent back a quick response before tucking her phone away and waiting for Evaline Latcher to make an appearance.

It was several minutes before the rear gallery door opened again and a slim woman, almost Trey's height in her tall shoes with needle-thin heels, stepped through the opening. She was dressed in a silk pantsuit of pure white, accented by a green-and-gold beaded necklace with a matching bracelet circling her wrist. Shoulder length, platinum-blond hair was perfectly styled in soft waves that caught shimmers of light coming in from the front window.

Evaline Latcher was a seriously beautiful woman who knew exactly how to show it off as she paused long enough to draw any admiring stares before stepping forward with the same walk as a high-fashion model on a runway. She stopped a few feet from Gin, then waited silently until Trey joined them.

"You must be Agent Reilly," she stated. A slight inclination of her head took the place of a handshake. "You've caused quite a stir in my household."

"We usually do," Gin replied. "Is there somewhere we can talk privately?"

"If a client comes into the gallery, we can move to the back room. Otherwise, right here will be fine." Evaline glanced at the PA who was hovering a few feet away, still clutching her iPad. "Linda? Will you please bring me a glass of Perrier?" Evaline glanced over at Gin. "Would either of you like something?"

Gin shook her head, slightly amused at the woman's tactics to set herself above everyone else in the room. But two could play at that game. "No, we're both fine. It must be difficult to run a successful gallery, so we won't interrupt your day for long. We just have a few questions about the clinic." She very deliberately did a slow scan of the empty room. "And then you can get back to work."

Evaline's mouth tightened at the corners and her crystal-blue eyes turned to ice. "What clinic is that, Agent Reilly? There are several of them in the area."

"The one located in Santa Cruz that's named after your husband and is run by your daughter," Gin said.

"Stepdaughter," Evaline was quick to point out.

"Yes. Sorry." The slight venom behind the woman's words told Gin that Evaline wasn't any fonder of Justine than the doctor was of her stepmother. "Do you remember when the clinic was built?"

"Of course." Evaline held out a hand and accepted the glass of iced, sparkling water that the PA was patiently holding out to her. "There were several fundraising events I attended in support of my husband."

But not Justine, Gin thought. "And do you recall any of the major donors for the clinic?" Gin asked. "I mean besides your husband, who I understand funded much of the clinic himself."

The gallery owner lowered her eyes, hiding her gaze behind a pair of thick lashes. But not before Gin caught the flash of anger, shooting out at her before Evaline could conceal it. "Yes, he put a great deal of money into it." She drew in a slow breath, then lifted a calm gaze back up to a waiting Gin. "But of course Terence has a great deal of money to spend on such things," she said evenly. "And yes, I recall quite a few of the donors at those events. I think you'll find a number of them also patronize this gallery."

"Is that so?" Gin's smile was polite but didn't reach her eyes. "Any donors in particular?"

Evaline took a single sip of her water, then held the glass out to her PA. "Agent Reilly," she said with an exaggerated patience. "Your reputation for dogged pursuit proceeds you, even when there is little justification for it." She lifted a hand a pretended to study her highly polished fingernails. "I was told you had shown up at the house, making inquiries about Benjamin Stampler, the CEO of Meridian Pharmaceuticals. If it will move things along, I'm happy to admit that I do know both Benjamin and his wife, Theresa. As well as other executives at Meridian. Some of them have even been to my home for drinks and dinner. But aside from that, I can't tell you anything about the donors or the clinic, for that matter. I've never set foot in the place and can't think of any reason why I should."

"All right," Gin said slowly. "Then I guess we're done here." She started to turn away, then faced Evaline again. "I do want to compliment you on your home. The grounds are beautiful. Lots of flowers everywhere. Are they a hobby of yours?"

"Hobby?" The platinum blond looked offended at the word. "The Rodinique requires my undivided attention all day, every day, so no, Agent Reilly, I do not have 'hobbies'. And that includes flowers. They interest Terence more than they do me. I see them as simply being a frame for the house, to put it in simple terms." She gave Gin a bored look. "He even has them preserved in those tacky necklaces he hands out with flowers floating around in some kind of plastic. His first wife used to wear them all the time." Her mouth twisted into a nasty smile. "You know, the one he divorced."

"I noticed that your employee, Andrea, was wearing a necklace like that," Gin said.

"Was she?" Evaline gave a careless shrug. "I hadn't noticed."

Yeah, I'll just bet you didn't, Gin thought. "Well, thank you for your time, Mrs. Latcher." Gin didn't bother to hold out her hand since she knew it would be ignored, but looked over her shoulder at Trey instead. "I guess that about covers it for our report. Are you ready to go?"

"Sure." Trey gave Evaline a steady look before turning his back on her and walking toward the door.

Gin almost smiled at the look his small slight brought to the woman's face. Clearly Evaline was not used to anyone turning their back on her, let alone any man on the planet. With a polite nod of her head, Gin followed her partner, closing the door and cutting off the tinkle of the overhead bell.

"Now there's the walking definition of a bitch," Trey said as they retraced their steps to the SUV.

"Can't argue with that," Gin said. "I wonder how she heard about my dogged reputation? And why she felt it necessary to make a point of informing me that it was her husband, not her, who was interested in flowers when Justine told us exactly the opposite." She shrugged and held up her cell phone. "We'll have to put that whole conversation on the back burner for the moment. I got a text from Connor Elliot while we were waiting for Evaline. He said he needs us to come by as soon as we can, so let's head in that direction."

Chapter Twenty-One

Gin made a point of looking for the maroon and gold car when they passed the small side street. She didn't break her stride when she saw it still parked in the same spot. As soon as they were in the SUV, Trey rested his hands on top of the steering wheel and looked at Gin. "So what's up with Elliot?"

"He said that he got a threatening phone call at his office this morning, and he wants us to stop by and listen to it as soon as possible."

"Threatening phone call?" Trey's face scrunched in surprise. "Did he say anything else about it?"

"He didn't recognize the number that popped up on the caller ID. He thinks it was from one of Latcher's people, but only because the voice sounded familiar and he couldn't come up with anyone else," Gin said. "He sent me the number, so I'll call Stephen and see if he can put in an emergency request to have it traced."

Trey wove his way through Monterey traffic toward the

highway that led directly from the coastal city to a point just south of Salinas. "It won't take us long to get there."

"Good." Gin settled back, then checked her seat belt. "Besides tagging her as a bitch, do you have any other thoughts on Evaline Latcher?"

Trey made a growling sound of disgust. "I think she and her husband deserve each other. He's a greedy corporate bastard, and she could be the poster child for a trophy wife. And I did wonder how she knew about your dogged reputation."

"Not from Blake, that's for sure. According to Moore, he spoke with Latcher, but that's not the kind of thing he would say. Blake can be a royal pain, but he doesn't talk out of school. I doubt if either her husband or stepdaughter mentioned it since Latcher didn't bother to include his wife in his no-contact edict, and the good doctor wouldn't voluntarily talk to her stepmother."

"And I don't think 'dogged' is the word either one of them would have used to describe you," Trey put in, a smile tugging at the corners of his mouth.

"I agree," Gin said dryly. "But wouldn't it be interesting to know if standoffish Evaline keeps in touch with any of the Meridian executives—all of whom knew we were coming into town?" Gin had her own suspicions on that, but chose to keep her focus on Latcher's second wife, who clearly harbored a deep resentment toward her husband and stepdaughter. That thought stuck with her, making her nerves jump in reaction. "Evaline doesn't think much of her husband."

"A husband who's apparently into flowers," Trey stated, his voice flat. "I guess the subject didn't come up when we were interviewing him. But if it had, I think he would have been surprised to hear that."

"I do too," Gin said almost absently. "I can't see him being into arts and crafts, like resin covered flower pendants for necklaces."

Trey grunted his agreement. "Maybe that's the reason Mr. Chang was suddenly gifted with a trip that put him out of the country and out of our reach. A gardener might have a hobby of preserving flowers. Especially if his daughter is into making jewelry."

Gin frowned. She had to admit it was a plausible explanation, but somehow it didn't fit with her image of the small house with Wei Chang's daughter standing in the doorway. On the other hand, it was also possible that the long-time gardener had no idea what his employer was doing with his flower creations.

But she still felt like they were missing something.

She closed her eyes and went over the conversation. After a few minutes, she slowly sat up. "Linda," she said out loud. Her eyes still narrowed in thought, she looked over at Trey. "She called her Linda."

Trey blinked. "Who called who Linda? Are you talking about Ms. Polen, the family's personal assistant?"

"Yeah. But I wonder about that whole family thing." Gin drummed her fingers against the top of her thigh. "Latcher and the doctor called her Ms. Polen. So did Connor Elliot. The only one who called her Linda was Mrs. Latcher. Even with their long-standing employee-employer relationship, that kind of informality with the staff seems out of place for Evaline." Her eyes narrowed to slits. "Which reminds me. Where was the driver? He never did show up anywhere at the gallery."

"Nagy? He was probably told to wait in the car. Or maybe he was walking around town, stretching out his legs."

"All day every day?" Gin shook her head. "Doesn't anyone else in that house ever need a ride somewhere?"

"Okay," Trey said with a questioning glance in her direction. "So where are you going with this?"

A HARD TRUTH

"I'm not sure," she admitted. "But Evaline and her two personal employees strike me as being off somehow." She sighed, falling silent as she stared at the passing scenery.

The two-lane road had narrowed, a steep bank flanking one side as they followed the cars in front of them. The lead vehicle was driving just under the speed limit, and with no extra room on their side, and limited visibility down the road, there was no chance of passing them, so Trey kept his distance as the small parade made its way toward Salinas.

"That kid in front of us is practically sitting on that guy's tail," Trey groused. "He needs to back off."

"Uh-huh," Gin answered in an absent voice. When the scenery failed to distract her from her churning thoughts, Gin was about to pull up the case file stored on her phone to go over the notes when there were a series of loud, sharp reports.

The slower moving lead car suddenly careened out of control, sliding sideways along the highway. Both Trey and the driver of the car that was directly in front of them, slammed on their brakes, adding the sound of screeching tires to the steady thump of bullets hitting metal.

Gin automatically stiffened her legs and reached out an arm to brace herself against the dashboard as Trey fought to keep the SUV under control. They finally came to a shuddering stop, barely managing to avoid rearending the compact car they'd been following. But the smaller vehicle wasn't so lucky. It slammed into the first car, hitting it broadside and caving in its frame. The noise of the impact had barely faded when Gin and Trey threw themselves down as a series of blasts slammed against the back fender of the SUV.

"Shit, he's aiming for the gas tank. Get out," Trey yelled as he made a grab for Gin. But she'd already shoved open her door and was diving through the opening, landing with a hard bounce as one shoulder smacked against the edge of the pavement.

She twisted at the waist and looked over her shoulder to be sure Trey was right behind her as he hauled himself over the console and dove through the door.

"What are you doing?" he yelled when Gin opened the back door and pulled out her backpack.

She held the pack close and scooted on her knees away from their car. When she got close to the edge of the road's dirt shoulder, she rolled into the shallow ditch between the tall embankment and the narrow road, almost landing on top of Trey.

Quickly wiggling to the side she discarded her jacket and drew the Glock out of its holster. Easily gripping it in one hand, she used the other to unzip the side pocket of her pack, reaching in and pulling out the contents. "Extra magazines." She flattened herself on the ground as another volley of fire struck the SUV, keeping her and Trey pinned down, unable to move in either direction.

A continual series of screams came from the compact car that was sitting with its front end crumbled up against what had been the lead car, but now was just a jumble of metal and broken glass. "We can't stay here," Gin said in a voice loud enough to be heard over the wall of noise around them. She pointed to the crumbled compact. "We need to get whoever is screaming out of there and into the trees."

Trey looked over his shoulder. "Yeah, yeah. The shots are coming from behind us. The shooter is in the trees across the road." He looked up at the hill looming over them. "This bank tapers out about twenty yards past up ahead of us. There were two people in that car that was doing the tailgating. If you can get those screamers out and take them down there into the trees, I'll hold this guy off."

A HARD TRUTH

A Glock against a semi-automatic? Gin wasn't thrilled with their odds, but they didn't have much choice. She grabbed two extra magazines and left the remaining five for Trey. "Okay. On my word," she said. Taking a moment to gather herself, she grabbed her backpack with her free hand and said, "Now."

As Trey did a lightning-fast crawl back to the SUV to use it as cover, she slipped her arms through the straps of her backpack and got into a crouched position, balancing on the balls of her feet. The second Trey steadied his gun on top of the hood of the car and opened fire, she sprinted toward the compact.

The screaming and yelling from inside had escalated to a nonstop blast of wails when Gin yanked on the handle, only to find the door of the ancient vehicle locked. Peeking through the passenger side window she saw a female lying half on the seat and half on the floorboards, her hands over her head as she screamed her lungs out. A male was sprawled face down across the console, his arms wrapped around the woman's waist. When Gin pounded on the side of the car, he looked up at her, his face a stark white and his eyes as wide as two dinner plates.

Teenager, ran through her mind as she yanked her badge off her belt and slapped it against the window. "FBI. Open the door. You've got to get out of the car."

Amid another volley of shots, the young man didn't move but yelled at the girl. "The FBI is out there, Randi. It's the FBI." He added a hard shake as he repeated the words, and the screaming came to an abrupt halt. A girl with freckles across her nose and looked too young to be riding around in a car alone with a boy, stared up at Gin.

"FBI," Gin shouted again. "Unlock the door. You have to get out of this car." When both the teenagers just stared back at her, she slapped her hand hard against the passenger side door to get their full attention.

"Unlock the door, damn it, before this car blows up."

"Open the door, open the door," the boy shouted at the girl he'd called Randi.

She gasped out a sob but her hand shot up and lifted the old-fashioned lock. Gin pushed down on the handle and yanked open the door. In one swift movement she reached over and grabbed the back of the girl's T-shirt and dragged the kid out of the car while the teenage boy scrambled after her. "Get in the ditch. Hurry," Gin yelled, pushing the boy who had landed at her feet toward the shallow dip next to the road. She followed them, keeping her body between the two teenagers and the shooter. Once they were in the ditch, she pointed toward the end of the embankment. "Have you got your phones on you?"

"I called 911," the girl said. "Right after we hit that car, I called them, and I told them someone was shooting at us. But I dropped my phone, and I couldn't find it."

Not ideal but at least the kid had called, so that was something in their favor. Hopefully help was already on the way. They just had to hold out until then.

"Okay. See where I'm pointing?" She raised her voice to be heard over the gunfire. When both teenagers nodded, she did too. "See where the hill ends, and the trees are next to the road again? You crawl down there, get your butts into those trees, and stay put until the police come to get you. Do you understand me?"

The boy looked over his shoulder toward Trey, who was keeping up a steady stream of fire. "But what if that guy who's shooting comes after us?"

"He's on the other side of the road, and we're going to keep him there until the police arrive." She jabbed her finger toward the trees again. "Now get going."

The two kids nodded in unison, and much to Gin's relief, started to crawl along the ditch. She turned around and moved toward the front of their car, getting a look over the hood into the shattered window of the lead car. An elderly man, with a head of thinning white hair, was slumped over the steering wheel. His eyes were shut, and Gin couldn't tell if he was still breathing. But she could see the blood streaming out from a gash in his head.

Taking out her phone, she called the emergency number, telling the operator in clipped tones about the shooter, the injured driver, and that two FBI agents were pinned down. Disconnecting, she immediately slid back toward the cab of the compact, she stood up and steadied her gun against the roof, her gaze scanning the area where Trey had said the shots were coming from.

She saw the brief flash as another volley opened up and hit the back end of the SUV with a steady stream of bullets. She rapidly returned fire, opening up as Trey reloaded. For several minutes, the two of them traded the job of peppering the area where the shooter was holed up until Trey shouted into the sudden silence, "Hold fire."

She instantly eased up on the trigger, but didn't take her eyes off the trees lining the opposite side of the road. A second later, as the booming in her ears died down, she heard the faint wail of sirens. A lot of them. For a very long minute, the only noise was the increasing scream of the sirens as they drew closer at a fast clip.

Gin looked over her shoulder, trying to see any signs of life from the body draped over the steering wheel. "Cover me," she yelled, moving as soon as she heard Trey's, "Roger that."

She slowly inched toward the crippled vehicle, reaching through the side window and releasing the door. Pulling it open, she slid across the front seat. The man's white hair was coated with blood, and a heavily veined, wrinkled hand lay lifeless against the seat.

Gin carefully put two fingers against the elderly man's neck. She didn't feel anything, but that wasn't definitive. After all, she wasn't a fully trained medical person. And she preferred to hope for the best. Not wanting to move him and possibly cause more damage, especially not with help so close, she moved back across the seat until her feet touched the ground again.

"Status," she yelled out to Trey as her gaze shifted to the trees at the far end of the embankment.

"Quiet. The cavalry should be here in less than thirty seconds," he called back. "You?"

"I'm good. One badly injured driver and two teenagers hiding out in the trees. They're waiting for some cops to come get them."

"I can keep this covered for another twenty seconds if you want to go get them."

Gin thought that over. "No. They're hiding somewhere and will come out faster if they see the uniforms." When the first police car rounded the corner, she holstered her gun. Trey did the same and they both stood still, with one hand held out to the side, and the other holding their badges high above their heads.

"Shooter was in the trees on the other side of the road, and we've got a couple of kids hiding out in the woods on this side," Trey called out as the first car skidded to a halt. Gin was grateful for the controlled chaos, watching as two officers carefully approached Trey and looked over his credentials. One of the policemen gestured to several more officers, and the group made their way over to where she was waiting.

"Where in the woods did those kids get off to?" the first officer asked even before he checked her credentials.

"They went into the trees right where the embankment

A HARD TRUTH

ends. Call out and let them know you're the police, and that the lady FBI agent sent you."

The cop flashed a grim smile, then gestured to the two younger officers standing by to head in that direction.

"And there's an injured driver in the front car." Gin pointed to the battered vehicle. "Elderly man, pretty bad off. The kids looked okay, but he'll need immediate attention." Gin paused to squint at the nameplate pinned to the cop's shirt pocket. "Officer Varn."

"Ambulance is still another couple of minutes out." Varn glanced over at the car and spoke rapidly into the radio unit attached at his shoulder, then turned to face the two agents. "Want to tell me what went down here?"

"We were following two other cars down the road." Gin was careful not to look at her partner as she walked the fine line between the truth, but not quite all of it. "The injured man in that car over there was in front. He was driving slightly under the speed limit, and the two teenagers were following him."

"Those kids were riding up his ass," Trey put in. "I was about to flash my lights at them to get them to back off a little."

"We were behind the kids," Gin said, taking up the narrative again. "When the shooting started, the first shots hit that front car. It spun across the road and the kids were following too close to stop in time, so they hit that car, but we managed to stop behind the kids. Agent Robard returned fire while I got them out of the car," Gin continued in a calm, even voice, not stopping until she'd described the first police unit coming around the corner, ending with, "and you know what happened from there, Officer Varn."

"I guess I do. I got a look at your car. The whole rear end on the driver's side is shot up pretty bad. You're lucky he didn't aim a bit more to the left and riddle the interior of the car with bullets."

"He was going for the gas tank," Trey stated flatly. "Too bad for him we rented one of the few cars made with its gas tank on the right side instead of the left. So it wasn't facing the road."

"Dumb luck always helps. It would have made quite a fireball if he'd hit it," Varn declared. "I need both of you to hang tight right here while I talk to the lieutenant. He might want a word with you."

As the officer strode off, Gin took a step closer to Trey. "The EMTs are going to want to check us out, and then we'll need a ride out of here before they start asking why were on this road in the first place."

"The EMTs can try, but I'm okay. If you need them to do a look-over, that's fine by me. I can use the time to secure us a ride into Salinas," Trey said, frowning when Gin shook her head.

"I don't need the EMT's, and we're not going to Salinas." She glanced over her shoulder to make sure neither Officer Varn nor his lieutenant was headed their way. "What do you think happened out here?"

"Some nut with a semi-automatic decided to use the cars on this highway for target practice and had the bad luck that one of them had two FBI agents on board." Trey said. "Coincidental as hell, but if someone was waiting for us, how did he know we'd be coming out this way?"

"A threatening phone call and then playing the best odds on the route we'd take to Salinas." Gin rolled her shoulders back and forth to work out the knots that had formed low across her neck. "He knew the one guy to call who would have us come running, right up this two-lane road." Her gaze roamed over the isolated spot that was temporarily overrun with police cars and a couple of ambulances. Not to mention a growing crowd of onlookers, and a few TV camera crews which had gathered at both edges of the scene blocked off by officers and police tape.

Trey followed her gaze with his. "He picked a good place, pinning us up against that embankment." He paused, keeping an eye on Officer Varn and the poker-faced lieutenant he was talking to. "How did the shooter know to make that call to Elliot?"

"Nothing too cloak and dagger," Gin said. "I'd bet our very chatty project manager wasn't as discreet as he should have been."

Trey rolled his eyes. "And word got around."

"To someone who was listening for any word on the two FBI agents out here to investigate Benjamin Stampler's murder." Gin spotted the two teenagers with blankets around their shoulders, huddled together at the rear of an ambulance. "I have to check on those kids, and we need to take a look around Latcher's house. I forwarded you the email from Polen with the contact information for that attorney. Did you get it?"

"Yeah," Trey said as he took out his phone. "I saw it come across last night."

"Great. While I'm checking on the kids, you call him and tell him to get his butt out here so we can go through that house. We'd only get a warrant if we could convince some judge that the shooter was after us, and somehow Latcher is involved. And we need to move faster than that. So we call the attorney." Since the shoulder rolls hadn't worked, Gin rubbed a hand across the back of her neck.

They were close. She knew it. But there was a link missing somewhere, and she was hoping they'd find it in that house.

Chapter Twenty-Two

Gin spent a good half hour talking the kids down from their jitters and making sure their parents had been contacted and knew which hospital Randi and her boyfriend, Tommy, would be transported to. When she spotted Officer Varn headed her way, with his lieutenant in tow, Gin said a quick goodbye to the teenagers and met the two policemen halfway.

She repeated the sequence of events to Varn's lieutenant, then listened, her expression set in stone as she was told that the elderly man in the first car had died on the scene. After thanking the lieutenant for their help, Gin walked slowly over to the bullet-riddled SUV.

Someone else was dead because she hadn't moved fast enough. Making a silent vow that the killings would stop now, she stuffed her hands into the back pockets of her jeans and surveyed the damage to their car, grimacing at the thought of having to explain it to the rental car company.

Since there was no way she'd ever get the hatch open, she walked over to the rear passenger door and yanked on it.

Crawling into the back seat, she managed to lift her suitcase and Trey's duffel bag and his backpack out of what was left of the trunk area. Setting each one on the seat, she exited the car, then dragged their luggage to the ground.

With that chore complete, all she needed was to find Trey. A quick glance at her watch confirmed he'd been gone almost an hour. It was another five minutes before she spotted him, leaving the cover of the trees across the road and coming toward her at a fast clip, his phone held to his ear. He didn't stop but latched onto her arm and kept going.

"What the hell are you doing?" Gin demanded as he dragged her along.

"Looking for a private place to talk." Trey stopped in front of an ambulance whose EMTs were dealing with the elderly man's body at the rear of the rig. "Something big has come up."

Gin lifted a skeptical eyebrow. "From Latcher's attorney?"

"Yes and no," Trey said. He lowered the phone and held it close to his chest. "The lawyer's name is Edward Forest, and as he pointed out to me repeatedly, he's the attorney for Latcher's investment business. He does not do family or personal law, and certainly doesn't want to get caught up in anything that might involve murder, to quote him directly. It seems Latcher has hightailed it out of town, so Forest said he'd contact Justine and arrange for her to meet us at the house after she gets off work at the clinic."

"As long as we get to look around, I don't care who meets us." Gin frowned. "And this is a big deal because. . .?"

"Because Forest is a corporate attorney. I asked him if he knew why the Latchers didn't have a family attorney, and Forest said they used to but he's dead. As in murdered. Six months ago." When Gin's mouth dropped open, Trey nodded to confirm she'd heard him correctly. "His name was Andrew Darquin, and he was on a business trip to Colorado. He was found in an empty field outside the city limits, but the last place he was seen was at the Stanley Marketplace in Aurora. I've heard of it but haven't been out there yet."

"Yeah, I know it," Gin said.

"Anyway, I got curious, so I called Stephen and asked him to check it out. He got in touch with the Aurora PD and talked to the lead detective assigned to the case." Trey straightened his arm and held his phone out to her. "Stephen's on the line. You need to talk to him."

Not having a clue to what was going on, Gin frowned as she took the phone and brought it to her ear. "Hey, Stephen. What have you got for me?"

"Something I wasn't expecting," Stephen said. "I'm sure that Trey told you about the attorney who was murdered?" He waited for Gin's confirmation, then took in a deep breath. "Well according to the lead detective on the case, he wasn't naked, but he was dumped in an empty field outside the city limits, under a pile of trash. The detective traced the guy's movements back to Stanley Marketplace. The waitress at the bar where he was a regular whenever he was in town said Darquin didn't have time for his usual burger that night. He was dressed in a business suit and carrying a briefcase when he left the bar. The cops found a large bloodstain in the parking lot and figured he was murdered there, then taken away and dumped in that field, minus his watch, wedding ring, and briefcase. According to the autopsy report, he bled out when someone slit his throat."

Gin blinked. That was a hell of a lot more than sheer coincidence. "Okay. Why wasn't his murder entered into the database?"

"They've been slammed so haven't gotten around to it yet," Stephen said. "The briefcase and his personal jewelry were gone, but the killer left a little souvenir behind. In the pocket of Darquin's jacket, they found a flower, covered in resin."

She froze. "What did you say the guy's name was? Andrew — as in Andy?"

"Yeah, I guess so. Why?"

Stephen's question faded away. In her mind all she heard was Justine's voice. *So then Evaline goes to Andy and tries to get him to use his influence to pry money out of you for a complete remodel and expansion of her gallery.* Who else would be a better conduit to advise Latcher to donate money, or not, to his wife's gallery than the family attorney, Andrew Darquin? "Andy," she breathed. "You crossed her and now you're dead."

"What?" Stephen responded from the other end of the line. "Gin? Are you hearing me?"

"I heard you," she finally said. "Listen, we've got to get moving. I'll call you later."

"You'd better," she heard Stephen say just before she hung up on him. Handing the phone back to Trey, Gin crossed her arms over her chest. "We need a car. And we need one right now. Got any ideas?"

Trey's mouth curled into a half grin. "I was thinking the same thing. So while I was waiting for Stephen to get back to me about the dead lawyer, I made a call to a buddy of mine. He liked the area enough, that after he retired from the Wranglers he got a place not far from here." Trey glanced at his watch. "He's already on his way with a car he's willing to let us use and should text me any minute that he's here."

Gin took another look at the bullet-ridden SUV. "Did you happen to mention to your good buddy what happened to our last ride?"

Trey looked off into the distance. "I might have been a little vague about that." His gaze returned to Gin. "But I did talk Stephen into dealing with the rental company. He's going to tell them to come tow the car away or call the police and ask them where they want it towed."

Happy to walk away from the mess and let Stephen deal with the red tape, Gin pointed to the duffel bag lying on the ground next to her suitcase. "I got your stuff out and dealt with Varn and his lieutenant, so we're all ready to go."

Right on cue, Trey's phone pinged. He brought it up to eye level, then grinned as he opened the text. "That's Troy. He's at the roadblock on the west side." Trey bent over and hefted his backpack up to his shoulder, then grabbed the handles on his duffel. "Let's move."

Ignoring the stares of the responding officers, Gin fell in line behind Trey as they wove their way through the wreckage and the police cruisers parked at competing angles on the road. Once they'd skirted the barriers set up to keep the curious and the news outlets out of the way, Trey lifted his hand and waved it overhead.

"There's Troy."

A dark-haired man, the same height and build as Trey, raised his hand into the air and waved back. As they drew closer, Gin kept her eyes on his face. Trey's buddy didn't look mad, but that didn't mean he wouldn't withdraw his offer of the use of what looked like a late model Toyota. Especially now that he'd seen what had happened to their last car.

"Hey, man. How have you been?" Troy's mouth formed into a crooked grin as he walked toward them. Trey dropped his duffel bag to the ground and the two men exchanged a brief bear hug, with Trey getting three solid thumps on his back.

When Troy stepped back, Gin was struck by the close resemblance between the two men. They had the same shade of jet-black hair, and both wore it so the tips barely brushed their shirt collars. The only difference she could easily see between the two was that Troy looked older, and his eyes were a deeper shade of brown than her partner's. Aside from those minor quirks, they could have easily passed as brothers. Or a weird set of mismatched twins given how ridiculous their names sounded together.

Trey clapped a hand on his buddy's shoulder and looked over at Gin. "Gin, this is my good friend, Troy Whitman." He gave Troy's shoulder a quick shake. "And this is my partner, Special Agent Gin Reilly."

Troy extended a hand, a wide grin on his face. "Robard always was a lucky bastard. So is it Gin, like the liquor?"

Gin smiled as she returned the handshake. "Exactly like it." Her gaze swung over to the car. "Thank you for this. It's a big help."

"No problem. I just hope you've got good insurance." He took a step back and frowned at Trey, then inclined his head toward the police barrier. "That shit is all over the news, and I should have known your ass would be in the middle of it."

"Not our fault," Trey said. "Some nutcase tried out his semiautomatic on passing cars, and we just happened to be in one of them."

The former Wrangler stuck his hands in his back pockets and rocked back on his heels. "Uh-huh. And there's a bridge in Brooklyn I'd like to sell you. It's only one hundred and fifty years old and there's hardly a scratch on it." His grin widened at his friend's pained look. "I don't suppose you can tell me what's really going on?"

Trey shook his head. "No, and I'd appreciate it if you didn't ask. I'm not sure when we can get the car back to you."

"No problem," Troy said. "I've got three more at home. One for the wife, one for me, and one for the hell of it. But I do need you to drop me off at my place."

Forty minutes later they let Troy off at a tidy-looking house in the community of Del Rey Oaks before they were on their way to their hotel. With the adrenaline high long gone, Gin was feeling fresh aches and pains on top of the renewed protests from her old ones. Especially from her knees. They had taken the brunt of the contact from crawling over sunbaked dirt and gravel, and was transmitting a sharper sting than even her shoulder's steady throbbing. Hoping a hot shower would take care of the problem, she put it aside and turned her thoughts to murder.

"So, what did you think of Troy?"

She shot her partner a quick grin. "I appreciate the use of his car, and I liked him. Which is a good thing, since he's an older version of you. Trey and Troy. The two of you are like those old-time book characters. You know. The Hardy Boys."

Trey laughed. "I think they were Frank and Joe, but yeah. We heard that a lot when we served in the same unit."

"You're good friends," Gin stated. "It shows."

"We flew a lot of missions together," Trey said and left it at that. After a few more minutes of silence, he relaxed one hand on top of the wheel. "Are you ready to talk about it?"

Pulled away from her thoughts, Gin blinked at him. "Talk about what?"

"The lightning bolt that hit you when Stephen was telling you about the murdered attorney, and about whatever it is you're working out in your head, which I assume has something to do with that lightning bolt." He leaned back in his seat. "I'd also be real interested in knowing why you won't let that backpack of yours out of your sight?"

"The backpack is private business and off limits," Gin stated flatly then pursed her lips as she returned to her game of silently moving the bits and pieces into place to make one recognizable picture. "What would you say are the primary motivations to murder someone, Agent Robard?"

"Well, Agent Reilly. Those would be hate, greed, jealousy,

revenge, and the heat of the moment," Trey ticked off. "Why? Do you have another one?"

She shook her head. "No. But I think we've got four of the five going here. Greed to have all the glory, jealousy when someone else gets it and not you, hate that you don't have the same support, and revenge on anyone who won't give it to you," she repeated right back at him. "Those all fit. As for the heat of the moment?" She gave a light shrug. "Not this time. These kills were carefully planned out."

Trey was silent for a moment, and then spoke very slowly. "You're talking about Evaline Latcher."

"Yes."

He wet his lower lip and then added a frown. "How did she manage to kill at least three and maybe four people? Not to mention dragging that dead weight into those isolated areas? Or planting a bomb to blow up the yacht, or even take a shot at us just a couple of hours ago?"

"By doing what she does best," Gin said. "Planning and directing. Someone else did the executing."

"Now you're talking about the thug who's passing himself off as a chauffeur." Trey's frown grew deeper as he took that in. "What about Terence Latcher? He's the shark in that family, and possibly the one who makes flower pendants out of resin, or maybe directed his gardener to make them."

Gin leaned her head back and closed her eyes. "I think we should concentrate on his wife. Evaline had a motive to deflect attention away from her, but Andrea mentioned that her necklace was a gift was specifically from the first Mrs. Latcher, not her husband. And I just can't see the shark coming up with a message like a flower that would take some serious plant knowledge or research in order to interpret the meaning. He's more the direct, fish-wrapped-in-paper type. The use of a flower to send a message seems way to feminine for him. Andrea also said that his first wife gave out pendants like that to support the staff, but Latcher doesn't have a sentimental bone in his body. I'd bet my badge on that."

"No bet," Trey said. "Then you think Polen is her helper? Which means she pulled off all the murders and got out on that road ahead of us and going on a shooting spree?"

"It could have been Polen. I'm sure not buying that story she told about Terence Latcher sending Wei Chang off to Beijing to visit his relatives. I'd bet that was Evaline all the way, and I'd put my money on Nagy being the shooter."

"Nagy?" Trey's voice registered his surprise. "I'll grant you that he looks like a thug, and he was giving us the hard once-over back at Latcher's place, but even though we didn't spot him there, he was probably somewhere around the gallery. The car was there when we arrived and was still there when we left." He paused and drummed a finger against the steering wheel. "But maybe not. He could have heard everything that was said in the gallery." When Gin opened one eye and stared at him, he smiled. "They've got listening devices planted behind some of those paintings. I thought it was funny how Polen showed up just in time to keep the gallery attendant from getting too chatty. So I took a look around. I spotted them when I did that walk about while we were waiting for Evaline to make an appearance."

Gin nodded her approval. "Good work."

"Yeah. And here's another thought. Nagy would have driven Evaline to the gallery, but Polen might have arrived in her own car this morning."

"A car that Nagy could have borrowed," Gin said. "He and Evaline hear what's going on, cook up their little ambush plan. Nagy makes the call to Connor Elliot, then takes off in Polen's car to wait for us."

A HARD TRUTH

"Wouldn't Polen notice that her car was missing?" Trey asked.

"Not if she's the third cog in this little conspiracy wheel and willingly gave him the key." When Trey shook his head, Gin opened her eyes and leaned forward, twisting her body so she was facing him. "I'll make another bet with you." When he gave her a sideways look, she nodded. "Linda Polen was Nagy's accomplice."

"You cannot be serious," Trey protested. "The woman jumps at her own shadow and hardly looks up from that iPad of hers. You're saying that's all an act to hide a murdering psychopath?"

"Not exactly," Gin said. "What I'm saying is her life revolves completely around her employer and has for the last decade, according to what we've been told. She probably got sucked into Evaline's revenge schemes little by little until she couldn't back out. Evaline Latcher is not the type to dirty her hands with messy details, which leaves Polen to be Nagy's assistant, and I'm betting the three of them come as a set." She settled back into her seat. "It all fits but we have no solid proof. Which is why I want to look around the Latcher property. Especially the grounds and that greenhouse. I wonder what kind of flowers they grow out there." She stretched out her arms and legs, wincing at the stab of pain in her knees. "I'm going to give Dr. Latcher a call and ask her to get to her house in two hours, whether her lawyer is there or not. And I want to know where Evaline, Polen, and Nagy are. If they haven't turned up by the time we've searched the property, we'll head back over to the gallery."

The hotel Trey had booked them into wasn't fancy, but it fit within the FBI budget, and it had hot running water in the shower, which was Gin's major requirement. A steaming shower, followed by her knees taking a fifteen minute wrap in

315

warm towels, had her walking almost normally again. A couple of aspirin took care of the rest of the pain, at least temporarily. Hopefully long enough for them to search the Latcher property.

Dressed in clean clothes and wearing a fresh jacket over her holster, Gin felt close to one hundred percent when she met Trey in the hotel lobby. Judging by the easy gait of his step as they headed toward their borrowed car, she was sure Trey felt the same way. Twenty minutes later they turned into the curved drive leading up to the Latcher's house, right behind Justine Latcher.

The doctor exited her car and slammed the door shut before stalking over to meet them. "This is a complete waste of my time. I had patients to see, which is a lot more important than following both of you around while you look for who knows what."

"Sorry for the inconvenience," Gin said calmly. She moved toward the gate leading into the property behind the main house, with Justine dogging her heels. The coded lock on the gate had Gin turning around and staring at the doctor. Justine came close to stamping her foot in a show of anger before she caught herself and, with her chin stuck up in the air, marched over to the gate and entered the code.

Once it swung open on noiseless, well-oiled hinges, Gin nodded her thanks as she walked past the doctor and into an expanse of green lawn with stone paths meandering off in different directions. Gin stopped at the edge of the lawn and pretended to look around before facing Justine. "Where's your gardener?"

Justine's expression went blank as her gaze darted around the backyard. She stretched her neck to try and see the areas beyond the border of the lawn. "Wei should be around here somewhere." She folded her arms over her chest and stared back at Gin. "I'm not sure. Evaline oversees all the household staff, including Wei. You should ask her."

"Okay," Gin said agreeably, not at all surprised that Justine had no idea that the gardener was supposedly winging his way to Beijing. "Where can I find her?"

The doctor's stare turned mutinous. "How would I know? We don't keep track of each other. She's probably at her gallery. That's where she spends most of her time. Either there, or out here in the gardens." She let out a harsh laugh. "She spends so much time out here that you'd think she didn't enjoy the company of the rest of the family."

"Including your father?"

When Justine's mouth clamped shut, Gin shrugged. "I understand he was called away on a sudden business trip."

"Not sudden. I can assure you he didn't slink off anywhere," the doctor snapped out. "It's some kind of high-tech expo thing in Boston. He goes every year." She glanced at her watch. "He's probably having dinner in the city before catching the red-eye flight back East. That's his usual habit."

Okay. Now we know where he is, so we just have to locate the other three, Gin thought. She glanced over at Trey. "Have him picked up and brought here." As Trey stepped away, his phone already to his ear, her gaze slowly quartered the big yard. "You mentioned that Evaline didn't spend much time on the tennis courts." From the corner of her eye, she saw Justine's whole body stiffen to match the outrage on her face.

"That's right. Why this sudden interest in Evaline? I don't care for her much, but it's beyond ludicrous to think she had anything to do with killing Benjamin Stampler. She's been so busy trying to raise money for her gallery that she hasn't left the state in months."

Ignoring her, Gin spotted an angular structure made of a metal frame and glass. "Is that the greenhouse?"

Justine squinted behind the lenses of her oversized glasses as her gaze followed the direction of Gin's pointing finger. "Yes. So?"

"So, let's have a look." Gin nodded at Trey. "How about walking the perimeter while the doctor and I check out the buildings."

He smiled. "The rule of the three-sixty grid search. Yeah. I'm on it."

When he strode off, Gin headed for the greenhouse. It was large enough to hold three rows of raised benches, with a variety of plants on each side of the rows. She slowly walked along, studying the plants. It was hard to spot the red anemone that was displayed in the gallery attendant's pendant, but in the far corner, along the back was a section bursting with the deep purple of a small forest of hydrangeas, and several feet away were red petunias. She'd found the right flowers, but there wasn't any sign of the silicone molds or bottles of resin that were used to preserve the flowers in transparent blocks that could be used for jewelry — or tokens slipped onto the body of a dead man.

When Gin left the greenhouse, Justine was still trailing behind her like a human shadow, and Trey was slowly making his way along the side of a large cement pond. She looked in the opposite direction, skipping over the small hothouse that would have been frequented by the cook, and landing on a fancy, oversized looking shed with windows on all sides and a compact porch. "What's that?" she asked Justine, pointing at the all-white structure.

"The artist's studio that Evaline had built, but no one has ever used. The only person I've ever seen go in there is Wei," the doctor said, then had to scramble to catch up with Gin, who had sprinted off in that direction.

Finding a lock on the door, Gin backed off the small porch

and did a slow turn around the building, testing all the windows. They were all locked and the blinds were tightly drawn. Selecting one built into the side of the tiny house, Gin stood in front of it and gauged the distance. Adjusting her position, she lifted one leg and smashed through a pane with the heel of her walking boot. Standing next to her, Justine let out a startled yelp.

"That was me. Everything is clear," Gin yelled out for Trey's benefit. When she moved closer to the compact studio, glass crunched beneath her feet. She didn't get a chance to use it often in the field, but years of martial arts training did occasionally pay off on her job.

Pulling the sleeve of her jacket down to protect her arm and hand, she reached through the jagged opening that her kick had created and flipped the window latch to the open position. She shoved up the window and boosted herself over the sill while Justine stayed planted where she was. The doctor put some hard effort into craning her neck up as far as she could to see what was going on inside.

It only took a few seconds for Gin to spot the shelf with bottles lined up on it, side by side. And on a table beneath it were stacks of small, square silicone jewelry molds in various sizes, and plastic boxes filled with chains and gold settings. She leaned over the table and stared at the bottles. The resin labels were prominently displayed on every one of them. So there it was. Proof. Circumstantial, maybe, but at last something solid. And she would find more.

A photograph tacked on the wall over the shelf caught her attention. She leaned in closer and peered at the group standing together. In the middle was a short Asian man dressed in a plain blue shirt and jeans, with dirt smeared across both knees. Thinking that he must be Wei Chang, she briefly studied in the woman standing next to him. She was stout with gray hair and a white apron tied around her waist.

Two more people were in the picture. One was Linda Polen, the PA, clutching her ever-present iPad, and the other was Nagy. The driver was wearing a white shirt and neatly tailored black coat over dark trousers. She leaned in and squinted at the unsmiling figure, her gaze focused on his trousers with the bottom hem turned up into a cuff. The nerves along Gin's arms began to hum as she stared at the man staring unsmiling into the camera.

"What do you want to bet you've got fancy loafers with an expensive buckle on under those trouser cuffs? Which is going to show up very clearly once we get an enhanced version of this picture along with the images on the trail cam." Gin nodded in satisfaction. It was circumstantial but could be used as another nail in Nagy's coffin. "Got you, you son of a bitch."

Walking back to the open window, she carefully inched her way over the sill and onto the ground where Justine was waiting, her hands on her hips.

"Well?" the doctor demanded. "What's in there?"

Before Gin could answer, Trey's shout rolled across the large expanse of lawn. "Here. Quick. Man down."

Gin didn't wait to explain anything to Justine but took off in the direction of Trey's shouts as he kept yelling "man down". She raced across the lawn, leaving Justine far behind as she followed Trey's voice.

At first she couldn't see where he was, but then she spotted him crouching, half hidden behind a bush. As she drew closer, the first thing she saw was a pair of sprawled out legs. It wasn't until she slid to a halt and dropped down next to Trey that she got a full view of the blood streaming over the woman's chest and onto the ground beneath her. And under the mixture of blood and dirt, were the frozen features of Linda Polen.

A HARD TRUTH

"Oh my God," she breathed softly, staring in horror at the wide gash across the PA's throat. "He killed her."

"Get out of my way," Justine ordered, pushing Gin aside and taking her place next to Polen's body.

As the doctor went through the motions of checking for any signs of life, Gin automatically reached for her phone when it started ringing. Seeing Big Al's name displayed on the caller ID, she tapped the connect button. "This is Agent Reilly."

"Hey. It's Al Twiner. I wanted to let you know that I talked to the guys who worked that clinic job with Decker," he said, not wasting time on any small talk. "None of them remembered him having any problems with anyone on another crew, but he did get into a beef with Latcher's wife. She wanted him to do some free work out at an art gallery she owned, and when Decker refused, the guys said the lady blew her top." When he was only greeted with silence, Big Al cleared his throat. "Agent Reilly? That's all I got. Does it help?"

"Oh yeah," Gin said, staring over Justine's shoulder at Linda Polen's lifeless body. "That's a big help."

Chapter Twenty-Three

The EMTs arrived and quickly surrounded the body, efficiently following the low, crisp directions from Justine. Gin stepped around them and poked Trey's shoulder. He looked up from his position kneeling next the PA, mingling sparks of anger and shock in his eyes. Wanting to get him away from the dead woman, where they wouldn't be in the way of the emergency workers and or be overheard, she gestured for him to follow her.

He slowly got to his feet and walked away from the scene, leaving the medical personnel to their jobs. She stopped underneath a large tree forty feet from where Linda Polen's still body lay, staring at the sky with sightless eyes.

"Are you all right?" she asked the silent Trey.

"I've seen dead bodies before, but never a woman killed like that." He heaved a sigh and ran a distracted hand over the top of his head.

She looked down at the object he was holding by the corner with two fingers. "What's that?"

Trey glanced down and frowned at his hand, as if he was

surprised to see it clasping anything at all. "Um. That damn iPad she always carried around. It was lying on the ground beside her. I thought I'd better pick it up before the police arrived so we could get a first look at it, but I didn't have an evidence bag."

"Let me see it." Gin held out a hand. Once Trey handed over the iPad, she lifted it and tapped on the front. A screen immediately came up asking for a password. She turned it around so Trey could see it. "We don't have time for this." She handed the device back to him and took out her cell phone, quickly finding the number she needed on her speed dial list. Her boss picked up on the second ring. "We've got a problem here."

"Trey mentioned the shooting incident, which sound a lot more serious than just a problem. I've got guys headed to the restaurant where Latcher's secretary said he was enjoying a meal with some business associates. Hopefully they'll intercept him before he gets on that plane for Boston. I've got some other background info for you, but you go first. What other problem have you got?"

"Another dead body. Linda Polen."

"The personal assistant you asked for background information on?" The surprise came through in the senior agent's voice.

"Yeah. The one and only, courtesy of our shooter, the family chauffeur."

"That would be Nagy, Endre," Moore stated flatly. "His background information just came in along with Polen's. What makes you think he's the one who killed her?"

"Because he owns a pair of pants with cuffs on them and expensive looking loafers. And because Evaline Latcher is connected to at least two of the victims, and he's connected to her."

In the silence that followed, Gin could imagine the stunned

expression on Moore's face. "How is Latcher's wife connected to the victims?" the senior agent finally sputtered out.

"Stampler and Dredecker wouldn't jump when she told them to, and according to Justine Latcher, neither would the family attorney, Andrew Darquin. All three of them refused to support her little art gallery, and all three of them ended up dead. I'm sure we're going to find that Miguel Rivera turned some demand of hers down too." She paused and her gaze met Trey's before she continued in a soft voice. "Now he's cleaning up loose ends, boss. Polen was one, and very likely Wei Chan as well."

"Who is?" Moore asked.

"The gardener with a daughter who sells jewelry. Apparently he liked to help her out by using flowers from the Latchers' garden to preserve in resin."

A soft whistle came through the phone. "A talent Nagy made use of."

"Not Nagy. Wei Chang's employer, Evaline Latcher," Gin's voice grew hard and matter-of-fact. "She's pulling the strings. She wanted her art gallery to be the focus of the family charitable donations, and it wasn't. That honor went to her stepdaughter's free clinic. So she's been doing away with anyone who turned down a chance to contribute to her personal project."

"When was the gardener murdered?"

Gin's teeth briefly sank into her lower lip. "We're not sure, but he disappeared this morning, supposedly on a sudden trip to Beijing. I doubt if he'll ever arrive there."

"And what about the attorney you mentioned. What was his name again?"

"Andrew Darquin. We found out Evaline wanted him to use his influence with her husband to pry more money out of Latcher, and Darquin refused. He was murdered six months ago in Denver. Same flower-in-resin deal found in his coat pocket."

"Wonderful. Where's the deadly lady now?" Moore asked.

"Last sighting was at her gallery. It's not far from here. Trey and I are going to head over there to do a quick check, and then come back here to talk to Latcher and his attorney." She spotted a furious-looking Justine stomping toward her. "I still don't know if the husband was an accomplice or just clueless. I'm betting on the second one, but we'll check it out. And since he also refused to back his wife's gallery, I'm betting the only reason he's still alive is that according to Connor Elliot, Evaline doesn't figure prominently in her husband's will."

"Okay. Pick her up." Moore stated in a hard, flat voice. "But you watch your back. If it is Nagy behind all these murders, he is one nasty character and has some skills. Got the info on him right here." There was the sound of a keyboard clicking before Moore cleared his throat. "Endre Nagy. Forty-one years old. He spent ten years with the Hungarian Defence Forces, including some time in Afghanistan. Saw quite a bit of combat, and received citations for marksmanship and hand-to-hand. He was also given a slap on the wrist for beating a villager to death for taking a pot shot at him, so I wouldn't get too close to the guy. He's been known to dabble in drugs—on the selling end rather than using. He came to the States fourteen years ago through Seattle, working his way over on a freighter. He managed to find employment with the Yoland family. Yoland is Evaline Latcher's maiden name." Moore paused for a brief moment. "I had Agent Jones do a quick search on both Latcher and his wife. Anyway, from the Yoland house he followed Evaline and went to work for her first husband, a guy by the name of Gretner. She married a very wealthy man but had to sign a prenup, and didn't get much, comparatively speaking, when he died. The bulk of his estate went to his children by his first marriage, and to various charities."

"Which put her in the market for another rich husband to support herself, and her little posse made up of her personal assistant and her chauffeur," Gin said.

"Yeah. It looks that way."

"Can you get an all-points bulletin out with the local law enforcement for Nagy and Evaline? Maybe include San Francisco, and up and down the coast. If those two are cleaning up loose ends, then they're going to rabbit on us, if they haven't already. And I doubt they're in that maroon and gold Mercedes Evaline gets chauffeured around in. I'm thinking they might have Polen's car. It's nowhere in sight, and she got to the gallery this morning somehow." Gin motioned to Trey just as the doctor stomped to a halt in front of her. "We'll check out the gallery and then head back here to listen to whatever bullshit story Latcher and his attorney will be trying to sell." She paused. "And one more thing. Hugh Lamon needs to be picked up on conspiracy to murder a federal agent. At least to start with."

Moore sucked in a breath and then let it out in a single huff. "Lamon? The Meridian executive? You're tagging him as the source who tipped Nagy off that you and Robard were heading for Miami?"

"He's the one," Gin confirmed. "Besides the Miami PD and the Traci Stampler, those Meridian executives were the only ones who knew we were coming to Miami. And Evaline Latcher confirmed that they had all been at her house for dinner, so she knew Lamon, and the two of them must have discovered some mutual ground— he had a drug habit, and she wanted information on Stampler and the company's charity contributions along and could bribe Lamon with a drug connection through Nagy." Her eyes narrowed as she remembered what the executive had said. "He also called me dogged. And so did Evaline when she had no reason to say it, unless she'd heard it from someone else."

"Like Lamon. We'll get him in a box and give him a good grilling," Moore ground out. "I'll take care of that and the APB. I'll also throw in that Latcher and Nagy are armed and dangerous. Call me with any more developments. And like I said, Agent Reilly, watch your back. Tell Robard the same."

"What did Latcher and his attorney have to say?" Justine repeated, her face a mask of fury. "Are you talking about *my* father? Because he's on his way to Boston."

After hearing the disconnecting click on Moore's end, Gin put her phone away and faced Justine. "There's been a change of plans. Your father is being escorted here."

"Escorted?" The word came out as a shriek as Justine glared back at her. "You mean arrested? You're arresting my father?"

"No," Gin said with exaggerated patience. "I mean escorted." She lifted one eyebrow at the doctor. "Or haven't you noticed people seem to be dropping dead around you?" She watched Justine's mouth drop open before the woman snapped it shut again. "For your own safety, you need to barricade yourself inside the house, along with your attorney whenever he shows up, and wait for your father to arrive with his FBI escort. Agent Robard and I are headed over to the art gallery to check on your stepmother." *And arrest her if we can find her*, she added silently to herself.

"And that's it?" Justine demanded. "You're going to leave me here to deal with this mess?" She swept a skinny arm around to encompass the emergency workers, along with a growing crowd of police officers waiting to talk to her.

"At least you'll have lots of protection," Gin said with a

shrug. "And we won't be gone long." She walked off, leaving a sputtering Justine behind as she headed for her car.

It took another fifteen minutes to get the responding patrol cars to move, making a hole big enough for the borrowed Toyota to slip back onto the street and head north toward Monterrey and The Rodinique Art Gallery.

Trey drove well over the speed limit, expertly maneuvering past any obstacles, either stationary or moving. His face was grim and his jawline rock hard as he concentrated on the road, not saying a word until they were barely a mile from the gallery. "Do you really think that Nagy killed Wei Chang?"

Gin sighed. "He picked him up this morning, so there's a good chance. A better one, I'd say, then Wei Chang actually being on that plane to Beijing."

"Yeah, I figured," Trey muttered, then frowned as he leaned slightly forward. "Now what's going on?"

Adding her frown to his, Gin stared at the line of police cruisers blocking the street, their light bars flashing as a small army of officers stood as a human barricade in front of them. She undid her seat belt and gestured toward the side of the road. "Pull over. We'll make better time on foot."

As soon as the car stopped, both Gin and Trey were on the sidewalk, striding toward the barricade. Taking out her credentials, she held them up to the closest officer. "I'm Special Agent Reilly with the FBI." She pointed toward the gallery. "Does all this have to do with The Rodinique?"

The officer, who looked to be in his early twenties, nodded solemnly. "Yes. And I'm afraid we can't let anyone past this point, Agent Reilly."

The stubborn look on the young officer's face told Gin she'd be wasting her breath arguing with him, so she glanced around, hoping to find someone more accommodating without having to call the precinct captain when she spotted a familiar face.

A HARD TRUTH

"Officer Varn." She waved when he turned at the sound of his name.

He gave an unmistakable roll of his eyes but walked over, shaking his head once he was standing in front of her. "I might have known it was your all-points that had us checking out the maroon Mercedes parked on the side street in the downtown area." He nodded to the young officer. "It's okay. They're the ones who ID'd the active shooter." He gestured for Gin and Trey to follow him, stopping halfway to the gallery's wide-open door. "I should warn you, this isn't pretty. My lieutenant is inside with a witness, but I'm sure he's going to want to talk to you." He paused to give her a pointed look. "Again." He started toward the door with Gin right on his heels.

"Witness?" Trey said in a low whisper. "To what?"

Instead of the soft, quiet ambiance they had encountered during their last visit, the inside of the gallery was lit up like a Christmas tree, with all the overhead lights on their brightest setting. Uniformed deputies were milling around everywhere as Varn wove his way toward the small desk and the door that opened into the back room. As soon as she walked through it, Gin saw the body, her clothes covered in the blood that also coated the floor around her.

Evaline Latcher was lying on her back, her hands splayed out to the side and her throat slit. Andrea, the gallery's lone employee, was sitting on a folding chair on the other side of the room, her face buried in her hands as her shoulders shook with sobs. Gin took in the scene, while a single phrase ran through her mind. *Too little too late.* Nagy had claimed another victim, and might have gotten clean away to boot.

Resigned to adding another name and face to her long repertoire of unsettling memories, Gin stuck her hands in the pockets of her jacket and walked toward Varne. The officer was

329

talking to his lieutenant, who looked resigned once he spotted Gin coming their way.

Closer to sixty than fifty, Lieutenant Tamber gave her exactly the same annoyed look he had while standing next to the shot-up cars on the road between Monterrey and Salinas.

"Well, Agent Reilly," he began without offering a handshake. "It seems meeting at crime scenes is becoming a habit of ours. I understand there is also a dead body up at the Latcher estate in Pebble Beach."

"Yes." Having verified the identity of the woman lying on the gallery's floor, Gin's main objective now was to find out what the police knew and get back to the Latcher's estate in Pebble Beach. "Mrs. Latcher's personal assistant, Linda Polen, was found on the grounds in back of Latcher's main house. Her throat had been cut."

Tamber's heavy jowls dropped into a frown. "Her personal assistant? We've tentatively identified this victim as Evaline Latcher. Now you're telling me not only has she been murdered, but her personal assistant is dead too?" At Gin's nod, he briefly shut his eyes. "I don't suppose the personal assistant's death was a suicide?" When she shook her head, he blew out a heavy breath. "Then I guess we're looking for the same killer, who I assume is the guy the FBI put out on the ABP? What was his name?"

"Nagy, sir. Endre Nagy. He's worked for Evaline Latcher for a lot of years as her chauffeur. He's a known drug dealer and he has an extensive military background." She looked over at the two bodies. "A lot of it in hand-to-hand combat."

Tamber followed the direction of her gaze, and his voice dropped to a rough, gravelly note. "It would seem so. Does the Bureau have any idea where this Nagy fellow is?"

"No, sir. Not at this time."

"Hmm." Tamber's frown deepened as he turned and

looked her straight in the eye. "Care to tell me why he suddenly turned on his employer and her personal assistant, not to mention the reason he took potshots at you out on the road?" When she didn't immediately say anything, he shrugged. "I assume it was this same guy?"

Gin nodded. "Yes, sir. We believe so. And these three women aren't the only murders he's committed. But that's all I'm at liberty to say. I can give you the name and contact number for my senior agent, if you'd like to talk to him."

"I certainly *would* like to talk to him, Agent Reilly. Send his contact number to Officer Varne. In the meantime, I'm inclined to be more generous in sharing information about this crime." He tilted his head toward the Andrea. "She didn't see this Nagy person kill Evaline Latcher, but she heard him do it, and from her statement, she has identified the killer as Endre Nagy." He clasped his hands behind his back and rocked on his heels. "If you'd like to talk to her, go right ahead. Officer Varne will accompany you and record anything that's relevant to our case."

Surprised, Gin wasn't about to turn down that kind of gift. "Thank you, sir. I appreciate the share." Not wasting any time, she strode across the room with Trey and Officer Vance following in her wake.

Gin squatted down next to Andrea's chair so they would be eye-to-eye, but the woman kept her face buried in her hands. "Andrea?" Gin reached out and lightly touched a shaking shoulder. "I need you to talk to me. It's important. Can you do that?"

Andrea slowly lifted her head, tears streaming down her face as she stared at Gin. "She didn't say anything. I didn't hear her say anything, but I heard sounds like they were fighting." A sob escaped as her whole body began to shake. "But she didn't say anything. He was trying to kill her. Why didn't she scream, or call out?"

"How do you know Evaline didn't say anything?" Gin asked. "Were you hiding somewhere in the gallery?"

The sobbing Andrea shook her head, sending her long dark hair sliding across her back. "No, no. I never saw them in the gallery. I shouldn't have heard them either. It's my day off. I wasn't supposed to be here." She reached a hand out and took a death grip on the front of Gin's jacket. "It was my day off, but Mrs. Latcher called me and asked if I could come in for a few hours. She had some important errands to run and she said both Ms. Polen and Mr. Nagy were busy with other duties. So I came. I came when I shouldn't have been here, and I was in a hurry, so I left my gallery keys at home. But Evanline had said she would be here, waiting for me, so I came to the front door, but it was locked. Then I went around back." She cast a fearful look over Gin's shoulder toward the door leading into the front gallery. "It wasn't locked, but when I stepped into the workroom, I could hear them. The microphones were on, and at first I didn't understand what was going on. It sounded like there was hitting or kicking, and something fell to the floor and shattered. Then I heard his voice. He said she knew too much, and he kept saying it, over and over. He said she'd never be able to outrun those agents and then she'd tell them that he'd gone back, and he couldn't let her do that."

Despite the gallery worker's death grip on her jacket, Gin slowly stood up until she was standing over Andrea. "You're sure that's what he said? That he was going back?"

"Yes. I mean, I think so." Andrea's hands dropped to her side. "When the noise stopped, I couldn't stand the silence. Like something from a tomb. So I ran out the back door, and kept on running until I found a safe place to hide."

"And then you called the police?"

A HARD TRUTH

Andrea nodded and collapsed into her chair, her shoulders hunched inward, and her head bent in defeat. "I'll never forget that silence. Mrs. Latcher never said a word, and then there was simply nothing." Fresh tears leaked out of her eyes as Andrea's sobs rapidly grew into wails.

A female officer stepped forward and put an arm around Andrea's shoulders, murmuring to her softly. Gin slowly retreated, leaving the hysterical woman to the officer as she signaled to Trey before turning to face Varne.

"I appreciate the chance to interview the witness," she said as Trey shifted his position to stand next to her.

"Can you make anything out of what she said?" Vane asked. "Why would the chauffeur state that he was going back? Back where?"

"Beats me." Gin pointedly looked at the hive of activity. "We'll get out of your way, unless you need us to stay?" She gave a mental cross of her fingers and an inward sigh of relief when Varne shook his head.

"Not necessary," the officer said. "The lieutenant already put in a request to expand this APD to the entire State, and I'm think that you might want to do the same beyond that. I hope we can head this Nagy off before he kills anyone else." He gave her another hard stare. "You wouldn't happen to be on your way to the Latcher estate, would you? One of the other officers mentioned he saw Terence Latcher with what looked like a couple of FBI guys in a plain sedan headed in the direction of his home. Is that true?"

"Yes, it is," Gin confirmed, having a pretty good idea of where the Varne was headed. "We're going out that way. Would you like us to notify him of the death of his wife?"

For the first time, Varne's mouth stretched slightly up at the corners and he looked almost pleased. "That would be very helpful. I'll let the lieutenant know."

"Then we'll take care of that," Gin promised before making a beeline for the exit while she could. Once they were in the car again and on their way, she tapped a finger against the dashboard. "They knew where Nagy was going. At least Evaline did, and I'm sure Polen did too, which is probably what got her killed." Her eyes narrowed as she considered the thought. "

"Okay. So what does that mean?" Trey asked as he battled with the in-town traffic.

"It means that Nagy already had a bolt hole, or a plan of escape." Gin stopped her finger-tapping and folded her arms over her chest. "So where would he go? According to what Moore told me about Nagy's background, he's only worked for Evaline. And he didn't strike me as the type to make a lot of friends."

Trey nodded, taking up her train of thought. "So maybe not a place to hole up where he might be dependent on someone else helping him get food and shelter. He must have some other kind of plan."

"Yeah. He'd need to have a place all stocked up," Gin stated. "But eventually he'll have to go out for something, like more food or fuel. And we know he isn't the rustic type, so I can't see him hiding out in the woods somewhere." She nodded as if coming to a conclusion. "An escape plan might work, but to where? Every state cop and the entire Bureau will be out looking for him. Wherever he's going he has to get there quick, and it has to be out of our reach."

Chapter Twenty-Four

She was still thinking about that when the Toyota made its way up the drive to the Latchers' house. The emergency and police vehicles were gone, and only three cars were left parked out front. One she recognized as Justine's, and a black, plain-looking sedan was tailormade for the FBI. She guessed the third, a high-end sporty looking car belonged to the attorney, Edward Forest. When she rang the doorbell. A pleasant-looking middle-aged man in a dark suit who she'd never seen at the house before, answered with a smile.

"Special Agent Reilly?" He held out a hand. "I'm Special Agent JD Torret with the San Francisco office."

"Glad to meet you, Torret," she said as she shook his hand then inclined her head toward Trey. "This is my partner, Special Agent Robard." As the two men exchanged greetings, Gin stepped inside and glanced toward the large open living room. "I take it you were Terence Latcher's escort home?"

Torret made a face. "That's right. A real pleasant guy." He walked across the tiled entryway, stopping at the edge where the floor went from a highly polished tile to a rich, coffee-colored hardwood leading into the larger of the two living areas. "Brody? Agents Reilly and Robard are here." Torret jerked his head toward his partner. "That's Special Agent Brody Camden, also from the San Francisco office. I believe you know everyone else."

"Agent Reilly. What's the meaning of all this?" Terence Latcher demanded.

"I guess that answers my question," Torret said under his breath.

Gin exchanged a grimace with the agent before stepping around him and walking into the living room. Latcher was sitting on the large, curved sofa, with Agent Camden standing behind him while Justine occupying a high-backed chair. A low, metal and wood table separated her from the two men.

"Well?" Latcher stated, his voice and the stiffness in his posture radiating impatience. "I was publicly dragged away from my meal and brought back here against my wishes without any coherent explanation. I trust you can give me one."

"Mr. Latcher, I just came from The Rodinique."

Evaline's husband's eyebrows shot straight up. "My wife's art gallery? What were you doing there?"

"I told you, Dad," Justine broke in. "She went to check up on Evaline since her personal assistant was murdered in our backyard."

Latcher shot his daughter a leveling look. "I heard you. Now I'd like to hear from Agent Reilly. You were here when the body was discovered, Justine, and I assume your stepmother was the last person to see her personal assistant. Either of you can answer any questions and deal with the details of what happened to Ms. Polen." He shifted his gaze back to Gin. "There was no need to involve me, so I hope for the sake of your career that there's some other more compelling reason that I was escorted back here?"

More compelling than murder happening in your own backyard? Gin thought. This guy really was a cold prick. "As I stated, Agent Robard and I were just at The Rodinique, along with a good piece of the local police force. I'm sorry to inform you that your wife was murdered this afternoon at the gallery." She waited for a reaction, but all Latcher did was blink. Justine gasped loudly enough for it to echo around the room, and then choked back a sob, but her father simply stared at Gin as if she'd said nothing more interesting than reporting on the dinner menu.

"Well," he finally said, then paused to shake his head. "That was completely unexpected. Was it a robbery?"

"No. We suspect she was killed by your chauffeur. We have an all-points bulletin out and are actively looking for him now."

"My chauffeur?" Latcher blinked again, and this time his legs moved restlessly, his feet sliding back and forth, making a small scraping noise against the wooden floor. "Nagy. You're saying Nagy killed Evaline?"

"He's our primary suspect at this time," Gin said, never taking her gaze off Latcher. "We also suspect he murdered Linda Polen, so I have to ask you if you have any idea where he might have gone?"

"He lives here. In an apartment over the garage," Latcher said. He looked around. "Where's our housekeeper? She might know where Nagy is."

"It's her day off, Dad." Justine got up from her chair and went to sit next to her father on the couch. "Why don't you let Agent Camden fix you a drink?" She looked over her shoulder and up at the agent standing silently behind the couch. "Scotch, with a splash of water." She pointed to a long, sleek cabinet against the far wall. "In there."

As Camden moved away, Justine picked up her father's

hand and rubbed it between both of hers. "Why don't you just sit here and have a quiet drink while I talk to Agent Reilly?" When Camden returned with the highball glass, partially filled with amber liquid, Justine took it from him and placed it in Latcher's hand. When he automatically lifted it to his lips, she patted his knee and stood up. "Let's talk on the terrace," she said to Gin before turning and heading toward the wide double glass doors. She opened one and stepped outside. When Gin caught up with her, she was standing next to the stone railing, looking out over the back lawn. "He's not a bad person, you know," she said when Gin stopped beside her. "He's just not very good at showing any kind of emotion."

Considering all the man had done was blink when he was told his wife was murdered, Gin couldn't disagree about that. "Is your lawyer here? I saw an extra car outside and thought it might be his."

Justine nodded. "Dad asked him to wait in the den. He doesn't like airing personal family business in front of his corporate lawyer, so he wanted to hear what you had to say before he decided if it would be necessary to call him into the room." She gave Gin a brief glance. "He's not as good as Andy was with things outside the corporate realm." She returned her gaze to the backyard. "Andy was murdered too. Did you know that?"

"Yes," Gin said quietly.

"I got a copy of the autopsy report. The medical examiner had no problem sharing it with another doctor." A slight shudder went down Justine's spine. "His throat was cut, just like Ms. Polen's was." Now she turned and faced Gin. "Was that how Evaline died, too? Someone cut her throat?"

"Yes."

"And you're saying it was Nagy?" She didn't wait for Gin's nod, but slowly turned back around and once again stared at the yard. "I don't think we can help you find him, Agent Reilly.

A HARD TRUTH

He mostly drove Evaline around. Dad had his own company driver, who he preferred to use, and I'd just as soon do my own driving. I'd guess that in the four years since Nagy has worked here, Dad hasn't said more than three words to him."

"And what about you?" Gin asked. "Did you ever talk to him?"

Justine let out a short laugh. "All he ever said to me were driving rules. Things like, don't stop too close to a crosswalk. And one when I had to call the house for directions, Nagy got on the phone. He gave me directions, but not after lecturing me that if I ever got, I should always go back the way I came."

Gin went perfectly still. "He said that to you? Always go back the way you came?"

"Oh yeah. That was a favorite of his." Justine spun around and lowered her voice to a guttural tone. "Retrace your steps. That is always the best way. And the fastest." The doctor shook her head. "Sometimes I thought that must be the way he walked around, too. Always taking exactly the same path and going back over his own footsteps." She stopped to adjust her glasses and squint at Gin. "Are you all right?"

"I'm fine," Gin coughed out. "Look. I'll have Agents Camden and Torret stay here with you and your dad. You might want to call Lieutenant Tamber at the Monterrey PD to get more details about Evaline and to make arrangements for an official identification of the body." She couldn't do anything about the stricken look on Justine's face. "I'll be in touch later, but right now I have to go." When Justine opened her mouth to protest, Gin waved her off. "You'll be fine here. I promise. Sorry, but I have to go."

She raced into the living area and gave the "come on" hand sign to Trey, who instantly broke off his conversation with Torret and followed her out the door.

"What's up?" he asked as they both trotted toward their car.

"I think I know what Nagy is going to do. Let's go."

Trey slid behind the wheel and started the engine. "Where to?"

Gin didn't look up as she tapped on the screen of her cell phone. "The airport."

As he started down the driveway, Trey shot her a sideways glance. "Are we going anywhere in particular?"

Gin held the phone up to her ear and listened to the first ring. "Seattle."

Chapter Twenty-Five

When Moore stayed consistent and picked it up on the second ring, Gin made a note to bring him a good bottle of California wine. "Hey. I need to know something from Nagy's file. You said he came to the U.S. on a freighter through Seattle?"

"That's right. Why?" the senior agent asked.

"I have reason to believe he's going to retrace his exact steps and escape the country the same way," Gin stated. "He told Justine Latcher to always go back the way you came. To retrace your steps. It sounded like it was an unbreakable rule to him."

Through the phone, she heard Moore heave a sigh. "That's a pretty thin thread, Reilly."

"Yeah," she acknowledged. "But it's the right one to tug on, boss. I know it."

"Okay. Okay," Moore said slowly. "Your instincts on these guys are the best I've ever worked with, so we'll run with it. Hang on while I bring Nagy's background file up again. And let me get some help. Hey, Jones," he called out. "Come in here and bring your laptop."

Gin waited as the sound of keys clacking and a body settling into a chair drifted through her cell phone.

"Here we go," Moore said. "He came through Seattle on a freighter called the *Busa Laut*."

"What flag does that fly under?" Gin asked.

"Um, hang on." Several long moments went by before Moore's voice came through the speaker again. "It doesn't say here, but I put Agent Jones to work on it. Why the flag?"

"Because he'll take a ship with the same flag," Gin stated. "It will be part of retracing his footsteps. And I'm betting it's a flag from a country we have no extradition treaty with. All he'd have to do is get out to sea and he's beyond our reach." She heard Stephen's voice in the background but couldn't make out what he was saying.

"The *Busa Laut* is a freighter that flies under the Indonesian flag," Moore said. "Hang on a minute. Stephen's looking up the extradition information. And surprise, surprise. No extradition treaty with Indonesia." He let out a snort. "But it would be beyond a miracle if the *Busa Laut* just happens to be in port at the moment."

"I don't think it has to be that exact ship," Gin replied. "Just a freighter out of Seattle that's registered under the Indonesian flag."

"Which would widen the possibilities some," Moore agreed before relaying the instructions to Stephen. "Where are you now?"

"Heading for the airport."

"All right. Stephen said it's going to take some time to track all the freighters that are currently docked in the Port of Seattle, or are scheduled to come in within a few days. How long until you reach the airport?"

"About an hour and a half," Gin said.

"Fine. We'll get you an answer about the ship and both you and Robard on a plane."

"We'll need some backup in Seattle," Gin said quickly before he hung up on her.

"I know. I'm on it. You just get your butts to the airport."

It took the full hour and a half to get to San Francisco International Airport, where they left the car in the long-term lot. As they rode the transfer bus over to the gates, Gin tapped Trey on the arm. "Are you sure Troy won't mind us abandoning his car in the long-term lot?"

"I'll let him know where it is. He'll be fine with it."

Since Trey didn't seem at all worried about the car they'd borrowed from his friend, Gin let the concern drop away and turned her concentration to willing Moore to call her back with the lowdown on every ship in the Seattle harbor with an Indonesian flag. Hopefully there weren't too many. They were already inside the terminal, sitting in hard plastic chairs when the call came through.

"Agent Jones worked his magic again," Moore declared. "The *Angin Laut* flies the Indonesian flag and is docked at the pier right now. There's another freighter due there in five days. It seems that ships with an Indonesian registry show up fairly regularly in Seattle."

Gin stood and began to pace, her nerves tingling with a familiar hum. "When is the one already there due to leave?"

"Midnight, tomorrow," the senior agent said. "And I have you both on a plane that leaves in an hour, so get yourselves to the check-in counter, and then to the security office. They'll clear your weapons." He rattled off an airline and a flight number. "I have a half dozen agents from the Seattle office headed over to the docks to keep a discreet eye on that ship. I sent the Senior Agent in Charge a copy of Nagy's immigration photo. They'll keep an eye peeled for him and grab him if they see him. But we need another plan. And Reilly? You made a good call. Homeland Security came through on facial recognition and spotted him passing through the security line at SFO about three hours ago. He had a perfectly valid passport in someone else's name. He might already be on that ship."

"He is," Gin stated flatly, not a doubt in her mind.

"Well in that case, work up a plan while you're in the air, and we'll discuss it after you land in Seattle."

"I'll need a schematic of that ship."

"I'll have Stephen send it to you," Moore said before disconnecting the call.

Gin relayed the information to Trey as they headed to the check-in counter, bypassing the long line and flashing their badges at the airline's agent. Within minutes they had their boarding passes and were sprinting toward the security office. It didn't take long to clear that hurdle either which had them heading straight to their gate and searching out a pair of seats away from the rest of the waiting passengers.

"If he is already on that ship, what's the plan?" Trey asked.

"A careful, quiet approach," Gin said with a grimace. "There must be a thousand places to hide on a freighter. And if we go in with guns blazing, then he'll know we're coming and find one of those places. The ship will be out to sea before we can search the whole thing."

"So, just you and me and a few other guys?"

"Just you and me on the ship, and the other guys watching from the docks. If he's up on the bridge or some other high ground, we don't want him to see any FBI agents coming. If he does, he'll rabbit on us for sure. But to trap him, we need to figure out where he actually is holed up on the ship."

"Probably in the passenger quarters, if there are any. If not, then in the crew quarters would be my guess. Depending on the size of the ship, we'll have three, maybe four decks to search."

Gin gave him a skeptical look. "And how do you happen to know that?"

"I was in the Navy," Trey drawled out. "I spent a lot of time on ships."

"You flew helicopters."

"Yeah. Sometimes off of ships. Do you have the name of this ship? Maybe I can locate a schematic somewhere online."

"The *Angin Laut*," Gin said. "And Stephen is getting the plans for us. Or the schematic. Or whatever it's called."

Trey pursed his lips and looked out the window at the plane waiting on the tarmac. "If we don't catch him in his cabin, the best we can do is drive him up onto the deck."

"Where we will trap him, or the agent down on the docks will grab him when he tries to leave the ship."

"Unless he jumps overboard," Trey pointed out.

"Yeah. There is that," Gin said. "And who would be stupid enough to do that?"

"Someone who has nothing to loose," Trey said. "Depending on how high the ship sitting in the water, and if he's a good swimmer, he could survive it."

"Then he might try it," Gins said slowly. "But if we put Coast Guard boats around that ship, someone's bound to notice and raise an alarm. So we'll just have to be sure he doesn't get anywhere near the far rail." Her forehead wrinkled in thought. "Maybe we can risk putting two or three more people on the deck."

"Those ships run to a crew of about twenty-five guys," Trey said. "We might get away with a couple of strangers on the ship, but four or five? Someone will notice, and the word will spread like wildfire."

"Okay. Then we do this quietly. We'll have the port

authority get the captain into their office on some excuse or other, and get him to tell us what cabin Nagy is in."

Trey's mouth flattened into a line. "Think he'll just cough it up like that?"

Gin's answering smile was almost feral. "He will if he doesn't want his ship impounded."

He looked skeptical. "Can we do that without any evidence of drugs or some other contraband on board?"

"Sure." Gin gave an airy wave of her hand. "Anonymous tip. It will be worth a couple of hours, anyway."

"Fine," Trey said and got to his feet. "I need to make a phone call."

Gin watched him with a shrug as he stepped away, then settled back in her seat to wait for the boarding process to begin. Forty minutes later they were taxiing down the runway, about to begin the two-hour flight to Seattle.

Since Trey's assigned seat was several rows behind hers, she opted to skip the free beverage of choice in favor of reclining her seat and taking a catnap. It seemed as if she had barely shut her eyes when the flight attendant was gently patting her arm, letting her know that they were getting ready to land. Rubbing her tired eyes, Gin put her seatback up and yawned her way through their final approach.

Once they were on the ground, an agent from the Seattle office met them at the gate and escorted them directly to a car waiting at the curb. And an hour later Gin was at the Seattle office, briefing her hastily assembled team on the plan she'd just had approved by Moore.

Because the surveillance team reported no sighting of Nagy a few of the agents sitting in the briefing made it known that they didn't think the fugitive was going to surface in Seattle at all, much less already be on the ship. They were sure Nagy was headed straight for the Canadian border. Having dealt with that kind of negative thinking on more than one occasion, Gin politely smiled, but when it came time to select the final team, she made sure those agents were not in any position that required them to guard their backs.

With the plans in place and the dock team selected, Gin stood outside the port authority office, stuffing her mass of copper-colored hair underneath a woolen watch cap. Baggy jeans and an oversized wool shirt, along with a pair of heavy work boots, made up the rest of her outfit, effectively turning her into a man— provided you didn't look too closely. But it would be good enough to let her board the ship without raising any eyebrows, and that was all she needed.

Trey was wearing a similar outfit, although his clothes were a much better fit. She gave him a critical once-over as she stuffed the final, unruly strands of her hair underneath her cap.

"We need to get up to the office and have the director make the call to the captain of the *Angin Laut*." She put her hands on her hips and watched Trey pace back and forth in front of her. "You said we had to wait for someone. So who is it?"

"Our insurance policy," Trey said before his eyes suddenly lit up at the sight of a lone figure walking toward them.

Gin didn't need any introductions to the man. She would recognize him anywhere. There weren't many guys that tall, built like a tree trunk, and with a self-assured stride that fell just short of being cocky. As ridiculous as it sounded, he was the cook in her friend Ricki's diner.

A cook who was also a former Marine sniper.

Norman Beal only went by his service nickname of Anchorman, and woe to the person who called him anything else. Gin gave the long duffle bag he was carrying a suspicious look as he strolled up, thrust the bag at Trey, and reached out to give her a giant bear hug.

"Hey, hey," she protested, but not too strongly. "I'm working here."

Anchorman stepped back with a huge grin stretching across the entire width of his face. "So I was told."

As much as she enjoyed seeing the man, his presence could cause a huge nightmare if he actually shot anyone, so she turned a glare on Trey. "I'm guessing you called him. And why did you do that?"

"Like I said, an insurance policy," Trey stated. "If we drive Nagy up on deck, Anchorman will make sure he doesn't make it to the far rail."

"Or shoot you in the process," the former Marine said, smiling when Gin scowled at him.

"What? You don't think we have any sharpshooters in the FBI?"

Trey shrugged. "Not with his skill, and not at that distance, and none are assigned to the Seattle office so they can't get here in time." He pointed to the roof of the warehouse next to the Port of Seattle's main office. "None of the warehouses get any closer to the docks than that one, and not a lot of guys can make that shot." He switched his hand until it was pointing at Anchorman. "But he can." He added another shrug for good measure. "And like the man said, he can keep you from being shot. At least once we're back on deck. And you not being killed is a requirement to stay in the good graces of Ricki and the rest of the crew living on the Bay. Which I would like to do."

"I've managed to take care of myself for a lot of years," Gin fired back before returning her full attention to Anchorman. "And you cannot shoot anyone. You don't have the authority to shoot anyone. And if you do, I am not bailing you out of jail."

"Fair enough," the big Marine said. "Glad to keep your guy away from the rail, but I'm mostly here to be sure you don't get hurt. If that happens, Ricki will bring the wrath of God down on all of us, and so will Cheron." He smiled at the mention of his girlfriend and the love of his life. "And I make it a practice to never do anything to make that woman unhappy."

Well aware of that, Gin still opened her mouth to argue against him climbing up on that warehouse roof, but Anchorman cut her off with a wave of his hand. "I'll remind you of the same thing I tell Ricki. It's a public place, and I'm a public citizen, not a member of the FBI, so you can't stop me."

Knowing that was true didn't help her temper any. If that man killed someone, justified or not, the explanations, paperwork, and huge snafu would be enough to keep them all tied up for a month or more. And if it did happen, she'd make damn good and sure that every piece of paperwork was done by one Treynor Robard. Still, Anchorman being there did solve one problem for her.

With a "wait right here", she sprinted to the car she'd ridden to the docks in, quickly retrieving the backpack she'd stored there. Unceremoniously hauling it to where Anchorman and Trey were waiting, she tossed it to the Marine, who caught it in midair.

"If something happens to me, I want you to get this to Ricki and she's to hand deliver it to Cap. She knows who he is."

Anchorman gave the pack a curious look. "Okay. What's in it?"

"Nothing illegal, and it's none of your business. I need your word, Anchorman, that you'll get it to Ricki and not look inside it yourself."

Frowning, Anchorman nodded. "Weird request, but okay. If that's what you want. But nothing is going to happen to you." He lifted an eyebrow at Trey. "Is it?"

Her partner shook his head. "Nope." He glanced at her. "We'd better get going."

Since arguing with either of them would be a futile exercise, and one she didn't have time for, Gin simply said, "right," and headed into the office.

They only had to wait twenty minutes after the call was made for the captain of the *Angin Laut* to make an appearance. Captain Timur Santosa was medium height with deeply tanned skin and dark eyes that were shooting out sparks of temper with every step he took. He walked into the office and stood glaring at the port administrator.

"What do you mean a report of drugs? There are no drugs on my ship. Who made this report?" Santosa demanded.

"Maybe we could overlook the report if you're willing to cooperate with these agents," the administrator said. Pushing his chair back from the desk, he stood up and abruptly left the room without another word.

Santosa's confusion quickly turned to a scowl when he looked at Gin. "What do you want?"

"I'm Special Agent Reilly with the FBI, and this is my partner, Special Agent Robard. We're looking for a man we believe is on your ship."

"There are a lot of men on my ship, Agent Reilly."

Gin nodded her understanding. "Endre Nagy. He's Hungarian and would have arrived earlier today." Because she was watching closely, she saw the flash of recognition in the captain's eyes before it quickly disappeared.

"I don't know this Endre Nagy," Santosa declared. "And we are not a passenger ship. There are only crew aboard the *Angin Laut*."

Gin smiled. "Then I guess we'll need to impound your ship while we investigate this report of illegal drug trafficking."

"No, no," the captain protested. "You cannot do that."

She only shrugged. "Yes, I can. And you know I can."

"Wait." The middle-aged captain held up one hand. "Just

wait." He walked over to the window and stood silently looking out, his hands clasped behind his back. After a long, drawn-out minute, he did an about-face and slowly paced back.

"I might recall taking on a crew member who is Hungarian. But his papers don't say his name is Nagy. His name is Stuart Marks."

"Stuart Marks? Uh-huh. And what cabin did you give to this Mr. Marks?"

"It's on D deck. Number 404. But I don't know if he is in there, or maybe has gone ashore. We don't leave until midnight."

"Well, I'm sure you won't mind waiting here while we go take a look." Gin ignored the mutinous expression on Santosa's face as she pointed to the local agent standing quietly in one corner of the office. "This nice agent will be happy to wait right here with you."

As the captain sputtered, Gin and Trey exited the room, heading for the team waiting downstairs. Since Anchorman was nowhere in sight, Gin assumed he'd left to take up his position on top of the warehouse. After a final, low-voiced repeat of their instructions, Gin watched as the team split up. Once everyone reported being in place, she and Trey started a leisurely stroll down the docks toward the pier where the *Angin Laut* was berthed.

The deck was a hive of activity, with men overseeing the loading of the last of the containers that would make the eight thousand mile trip to Indonesia, deep in the South Pacific. Gin was careful to keep her cap low on her forehead and her head bent as she made her way across the deck, following closely in Trey's wake.

Since he knew more about ships, and had thoroughly studied the schematic that Stephen had sent, they'd decided it was logical that he take the lead. With their guns held close against their sides, they carefully negotiated the narrow stairwell leading to the upper tower that was barely visible over the containers stacked on the main deck. Almost fully loaded, the freighter was sitting low in the water.

When they finally reached D deck, Trey stepped into a corridor that wasn't much wider than the stairway. Gin noted the names posted outside the rooms they passed until Trey stopped at room 404. No name was on the outside.

Gin sidled past Trey and gently pressed one ear against the door. Aside from the steady creaking of the ship, she didn't hear any sound coming from the inside of the cabin. She held up her hand and lifted a finger to count to three. On the third count, Trey turned the knob and pushed open the door as Gin went through it, her gun drawn. She quickly searched through the main room while Trey opened the small closets, but no one was there.

"The crew's galley is down the hallway," Trey said, his voice barely above a whisper.

Gin nodded, and once again found herself following him down a narrow corridor. They'd almost reached their goal when she heard a door open and close behind them.

She turned, intending to guard Trey's back, and came face-to-face with Endre Nagy. His stunned expression turned to pure rage in a matter of a second, and he lunged for the stairwell, even as Gin raised her weapon.

"Stop! FBI," she called out, firing just as he disappeared down the stairs. She raced along the corridor, Trey hot on her heels, stopping only to make sure the stairs were clear before taking them at a fast clip. She hit the level of the main deck in time to see Nagy vanish through the doorway.

Gin followed, stopping at the door, then pulling back as a bullet pinged against the metal sides around the opening. "Shit, shit," she said under her breath as a half dozen crewmen stood frozen in place. Hoping that most of the crew understood English, she yelled out "down, down! Everyone hit the deck now!"

Bodies dropped where they were, scattered across the deck as she went down on her knees and risked sticking her nose out into the open again. Another bullet zinged over her head, high enough that she didn't duck but held her position, keeping her eyes trained on the open deck. Without warning, Nagy broke into the open, making a run for the far rail. With Trey behind her, she had no choice but to step away from the safety of the doorway and out on deck. Keeping her weapon raised, she took aim at man sprinting across her line of fire. "Nagy, stop or I'll shoot."

The man kept running, but before Gin could fire, he screamed and jumped backward as a bullet hit the deck barely a foot in front of him. He turned, his head swiveling as he looked for the shooter when another bullet hit him in the arm. Yelling out a string of unintelligible words, he dropped to his knees.

That's when he spotted Gin standing out in the open, her legs braced apart and her weapon trained on him.

Gin saw the cold hate in his eyes as he raised the gun still clutched in his good hand. She didn't give him a chance to fire. Her bullet hit him squarely in the chest. He got another shot off that was wildly off target before he collapsed like a balloon that had suddenly lost its air.

Staying rooted where she was, Gin kept her Glock aimed at the man sprawled on the ground as Trey ran past her. She didn't move a muscle as he kicked Nagy's gun away then knelt beside the chauffer's still form. Trey put two fingers to his neck to check for a pulse.

While Gin looked on, holding her breath, Trey looked back over his shoulder and shook his head. Slowly exhaling, Gin nodded and lifted a hand to tap on her earpiece. "Suspect is down. All clear on deck. I repeat. Suspect is down." She continued standing, not shifting from her position as a numb feeling flowed from her head down her spine. She barely registered the chaos as the rest of the team sprinted up the gangway and swarmed over the deck.

Trey stood and holstered his gun, then walked over to her. "Nice shot, Agent Reilly. You took him down before he started spraying bullets all over the deck. Who knows how many people would have been hurt or killed?"

"Anchorman gets most of the credit," she said, her voice sounding hollow and flat to her ears. "It was his bullet that stopped Nagy in his tracks and gave me a clear shot when he turned away from the rail."

Trey's response was lost in the sudden burst of activity around them as the four agents who had stormed across the deck began ordering the crew to get to their feet and keep their hands high above their heads. While the rest of the team secured the scene, Trey nudged Gin toward the gangplank and then down it, walking past a tight perimeter of agents keeping any unauthorized person away from the ship.

For the next hour Gin stood on the dock, with Trey staying nearby, and answered questions. First from the other agents, then from the Seattle office's Senior Agent in Charge, and finally from a string of officers in the Seattle PD. When one of the agents from the Seattle office asked for her gun, she handed it over, promising to be available for questioning about the shooting.

Just as it felt as if her legs were going to give way, Trey brushed several fellow agents aside and led her away from the center of activity over to a lone, small crate sitting farther down the dock. As soon as she sat on its sturdy, wooden top, Gin felt the adrenalin rush hit her like a ton of bricks. Trey already had a warm, wool blanket ready, and when she began to visibly shake, he wrapped it snugly around her shoulders.

While he stood like a barrier in front of her, warding off anyone who happened to wander their way, Gin closed her eyes and let the worst of the fight-or-flight reaction make its way through her system. As it began to subside to a tolerable level, and her thoughts became more coherent, she blinked and looked around. In all the flurry of activity that always followed in the wake of a shooting, she hadn't seen Anchorman. Leaning to the side so she could peek around Trey, Gin peered down the dock, but didn't see the tall former Marine anywhere.

It was a good ten minutes before she finally spotted him, walking down the pier, his duffle bag in one hand and her backpack slung over his shoulder. Since it was still iffy whether her legs would be able to hold her weight, she watched as he casually covered the distance between them.

A few minutes later, the big Marien strolled up and gave her a grin. "Good shooting, Reilly." He lifted the backpack off his shoulder and held it out to her. "I guess you'll be wanting this back."

"Thanks." She pointed to the ground at her feet. "Set it right there, if you don't mind." Taking a deep calming breath, she looked up at him and forced a weak smile. "Nice shooting, yourself. That shot into the deck scared the piss out of Nagy."

Anchorman gave a mournful shake of his head. "It must have because I could hear him scream from where I was perched." He reached over and curled a bracing hand around one of her shoulders. "You did good. Boa here told me Nagy killed a lot of people. Thanks to you, he won't be doing that anymore."

Despite still feeling shaky and a little foggy, Gin's forehead wrinkled as she frowned. "Boa?"

Anchorman wiggled his eyebrows. "That's the hotshot

pilot's call sign, officially given to him by his squad after a night spent at a strip club. I believe the story involves too much to drink and a particular lady with a long pink boa who took a liking to him."

She turned her first smile ever since they'd boarded the freighter on Trey. "Oh yeah?"

Trey glared at Anchorman. "Thank you for that."

The former Marine shoved his free hand into his jeans pocket and gave Trey a bland look. "No problem. I need to get going. I've got a new relief cook and he might need some help with the dinner shift." He smiled at Gin and gave her a wink. "I'm telling Ricki and Cheron that you'll be stopping by soon. Don't even consider leaving the area without making a trip out to the Bay."

"I won't," Gin promised, thinking once they were finished up here, she'd better give Devin a call too. "Tell Ricki I'll be out to her place soon."

"Will do." Anchorman turned on his heel and waved a hand in the air as he walked off.

Trey watched him leave then turned back to Gin and lifted an eyebrow as he cocked his head to one side. "I think you've answered all the questions you have to for the moment. Are you ready to get off this dock and have a cup of coffee? That stuff on the plane wasn't worth drinking."

She cast one last glance back at the freighter where Nagy lay dead and thought of all the lifeless bodies he'd left behind in his path of destruction. She'd have to go back to counseling for a couple of weeks, but she didn't mind. She'd get the whole shooting properly compartmentalized in her head, and the killing would stop. In the end, that's all that mattered. But she knew there would be others. There always was. In the meantime she had a list of fifty victims to get to Cap, and three journals to read.

A HARD TRUTH

But not right this minute. They'd done their jobs and stopped a killer in his tacks, and echoing what her partner had said— that was enough for one day.

As more agents arrived on the dock she looked at Trey and smiled. "Yeah. A cup of coffee sounds good."

++

Don't miss FBI Agent Gin Reilly's next case as she chases a serial killer hiding inside a self-proclaimed terrorist group calling itself The Final Line. Now available to order on Amazon: A Dark Road available for order here on Amazon

Keeping in Touch

Thank you for buying A Hard Truth! I hope you enjoyed it.
    ~ CR Chandler

If you'd like notifications for new releases, and a free e-book, you can subscribe to the author's newsletter here:
    SUBSCRIBE TO NEWSLETTER HERE

Other ways to contact the author:
    Author Contact Form
    Facebook:
    CR Chandler Facebook Page

Also by C.R. Chandler

GIN REILLY FBI THRILLER
(Mystery/Thriller)

A Hard Truth

A Dark Road

SPECIAL AGENT RICKI JAMES
(Mystery/Thriller)

One Final Breath

One Last Scream

One Life Gone

Waiting In The Dark

Running In The Night

Hiding In The Shadows

Colder Than Ice

Dead Of Winter

The Blind Spot

No Place To Hide

When Night Falls

Chasing Lies

FOOD AND WINE CLUB MYSTERIES
(Cozy Mysteries)

A Special Blend of Murder

Dinner, Drinks, and Murder

A Burger, Fries, and Murder
Champagne, Cupcakes, and Murder
Tea, Dessert, and Murder

Printed in Great Britain
by Amazon